ᔕᑉᑉᑉᑕ ᔭ ᔭᑉᔉᐱ ᔕᑉᑉᑉ

Ohtha e Ālifeith

Let Loose the Fallen

Book Two of Children of the Nexus

by S. Kaeth

This is a work of fiction. Names, characters, places, and incidents either are the product of the author's imagination or are used fictitiously. Any resemblance to actual persons, living or dead, events, or locales is entirely coincidental.

Published by:
Hakea Media
350 W 6th St #932
Dubuque, IA 52004
hakeamedia@gmail.com
www.hakeamedia.com

In association with Teacup Dragon Co-op

Print ISBN: 978-1-955220-03-3
Ebook ISBN: 978-1-7333281-2-8
Library of Congress Control Number: 2021900482
First Edition

Cover by Dave Brasgalla
https://www.davidbrasgalla.art

Author's website: www.skaeth.com

Content Warning:
Includes descriptions of fantasy violence, caregiver fatigue, self-harm, gaslighting, hallucinations, mental manipulations, psychic call of the abyss, fantasy racism, PTSD, panic attacks, torture, instances of vomiting, loss of animal, loss of child guardianship, physical trauma, and injustice.

A Map of the World, Kanamiyih

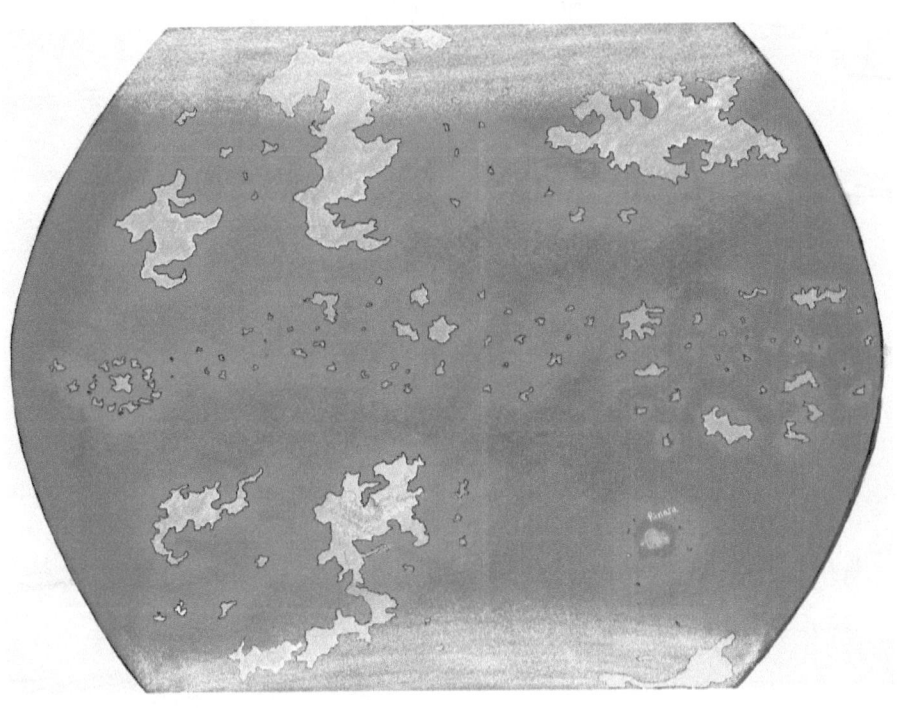

A Map of Rinara

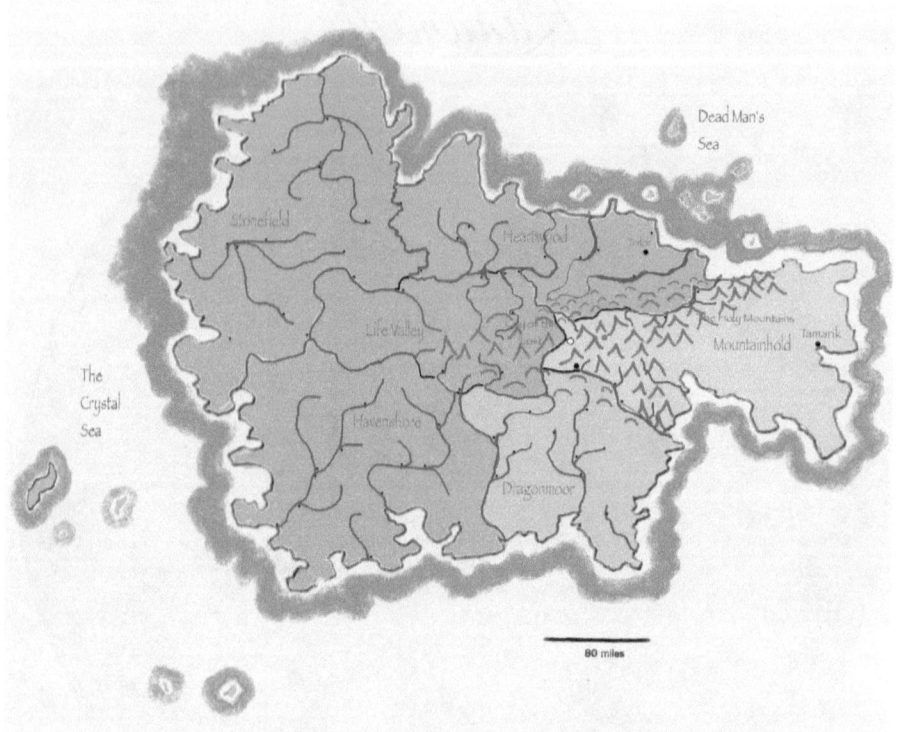

Dead Man's Sea

Stonefield

Heathwood

The Crystal Sea

Life Valley

The Holy Mountains

Mountainhold

Tamark

Havenshore

Dragonmoor

80 miles

Need a Storyteller to remind you of the details?

If it's been too long since reading Between Starfalls and you'd like a refresher on what happened, please visit: https://www.skaeth.com/between-starfalls-synopsis/

Obviously, if you haven't read Between Starfalls, there are spoilers at the link above!

To my family, for igniting my love of speculative fiction.

Chapter One

When the psions broke through the wall of the City of the Lost, they thought it was freedom. How could they predict the terror to come? The Angels came far sooner than they were expected, feasting on those who had only run for freedom. For a chance at life, not mere existence. The Angels gorged themselves for many nights, not even dragging their prey away with them. The survivors made no effort to properly lay the dead to rest, for it was far too dangerous. They huddled in their city, called it the Angels' Feast, and spoke of it only in hushed tones. Even more terrible, with the hole in the wall, the Angels were able to glide through the streets each night, hunting for their prey.

—account of Kaemada Sierso, psion

"Please, little sister, you have to eat." Taunos's strained voice trembled in the close air.

Kaemada stared at the wall, mechanically opening her mouth when he bumped her lips with the spoon. She held the gruel in her mouth without chewing, and the moments stretched long like a thread tugged to breaking. Finally, her throat bobbed as she swallowed. Her eyes never changed their direction, her face wan and expressionless. His sister was dying, little by little, right in front of him, and he could not save her.

Taunos sucked in a harsh breath. His heart was encased in ice, his chest too tight. It took all of his control to help her finish her meal—only half a bowl, even less than last time. Dark smudges had grown beneath her puffy, bloodshot eyes, and she was losing her muscled physique, wasting away.

He paused when she refused to open her mouth. The spoon bumped her lips again as his hand trembled. She didn't respond. He might as well not be there. There was no use forcing her—he had tried that before, and the meal had just run out of her mouth, down her chin, and onto her clothes. He would not damage her dignity further.

He cleared his throat, wiping her mouth gently with a rag. Sitting back, Taunos finished her meal. Just as always, her mind was elsewhere. Hatred for his own Elders burned in him, for they had dealt the final, mortal blow to his sister when they ripped her son from her, after all they had been through to see him safe. She'd been in a daze as they fled: he, his

1

sister, and her two best friends, all four banished from Rinaryn society in an unconscionable act by those who were supposed to be wise. They'd wandered, while the hunting songs of the Angels had driven them ever closer to the City of the Lost. And then, they'd discovered what littered the plain beyond the hole in the wall of the city. Bodies, scattered like so much refuse. How many had joined the escape? How many had survived the Angels' Feast, as it was now known?

Kaemada hadn't spoken a word or moved on her own since, and he knew she blamed herself.

Footsteps scuffed on the dirt outside. Guards? Others who lived in the city, looking for trouble? Taunos leaped to his feet in a ready stance, facing the doorway, bowl in one hand and spoon in the other.

Takiyah and Ra'ael pulled open the poorly-made door and swept aside the tattered rag that hung in the doorway to patch the holes between the shoddily fitting slats.

Takiyah paused for a moment, smirking at Taunos as he relaxed, then limped past him to set down her armful of bread. Ra'ael followed, depositing the food on a blanket stretched on the dirt floor. Both were dealing with their banishment in their own ways—poorly, and with bad tempers. Ignoring them lest politeness spark further trouble, Taunos wiped the bowl and spoon clean and set them to the side then prowled the length of the tiny house. It was too small—this wasn't helping his sister either. This whole city was surely hindering Kaemada's recovery, with all the memories it must bring. It had been a mistake to come here, even though it was the only shelter—so they'd thought—from the Angels' nightly hunting. Even if desperation to survive had driven them to this place of nightmares. He needed freedom. He couldn't stand the quiet, the inactivity.

"How was the market?" Taunos asked, forcing levity into his tone. He'd demanded there be only optimism in the house. Kaemada's song was currently deciding whether or not this world, this story, held too much pain to continue the cycle or not. He meant to weight her on the side of life as much as he possibly could, whatever the cost.

Takiyah dropped her words into the silence. "I'm leaving."

Shock and anger choked him, leaving Taunos to glare at her.

"Me too," Ra'ael said.

How could they even think it? Didn't he know them at all? Taunos stared at them. "You cannot!"

"I'm Fallen, remember? I can do whatever I'd like." Takiyah crossed her arms, her gaze level but unyielding. "I was kind enough to bring food back before leaving."

"Tinker—"

"Takiyah," she corrected him. "We cannot go back to the way it was before."

"What about Kaemada?" He glanced at her. They had to stay together. Everything would fall apart without them. Kaemada was on the edge as it was, and if she died…

Takiyah shook her head. "I cannot help her. All of us have tried. Besides, when I needed to leave, to escape the Kamalti, she stopped to help them. Our enemies, and she needed to risk us to give them aid."

"She was torn between aiding you and aiding the innocent." Taunos's eyes narrowed. How could she not see this? "She wanted a way to do both. And still, she would have chosen you, and you know it."

"That's the point, Taunos. It took her time to decide. I would have chosen her in an instant. There would have been no choice."

"Please." He cast a glance behind him. Eloi's light, hopefully she hadn't heard. How many wounds could a song take before it just stopped?

"This is not a discussion, Taunos." Takiyah's voice was flat, fully without sympathy. "I'm not asking permission. I'm doing you the courtesy of informing you."

"And you?" Taunos asked, looking at Ra'ael. How could they both abandon Kaemada? How was he supposed to help his sister on his own when she needed help with everything, as if she were an infant once again?

"This is not what the spirits intended." Ra'ael's voice was soft, as it always was these days. No more fire, no more passion. She had died inside just as surely as Kaemada had. "I thought this would be the path laid out for us, being Fallen and coming to the city of Fallen. But no—we are still functioning as a miniature kaetal. You, telling stories nightly—"

"I'm not a Storyteller," he cut in.

Ra'ael shook her head. "Even so. We must embrace this new path."

Takiyah snorted. "Embrace being Fallen?"

"This is what the spirits desire."

The heat of her inner fires raged in Takiyah's voice. "And my torture, did they desire this, too? When I was beaten and branded and my leg broken to prevent further escape attempts? I should accept this all as the will of the spirits?"

Ra'ael grimaced, staring at the wall instead of them. "I do not know anymore. We are Fallen. I only know I have to find the spirits' will, to discover the laws that will let me hear the song of the spirits once again.

We cannot combat the Elders. We must find our new path as Fallen."

Taunos pressed his hands to his face, dragging his fingers down his skin. This was foolish. He tried to keep his voice low, and it came out more as a growl than anything else. "What of the plan for the next storm? Even if you make it past the guards, they will increase patrols if they see you. You will destroy the plans—tens and tens of people, Kaemada included, whose bid for freedom will be thwarted due to your selfishness."

Takiyah spun on him, her green eyes ablaze as she stared down at him from her height.

Taunos stood his ground, returning her fire with that of his own.

Her mouth twisted before she spoke, hissing the words sharp as knives. "I will wait until then. But Taunos, do not *ever* call me selfish again."

"With your plan, I'm unlikely to ever see you again," Taunos returned.

She turned away, her shoulders and back stiff. Moments spun past, and then she shook her head, pushing past him to lurch out the door.

Taunos watched her go, clenching his jaw so as not to grind his teeth.

"I'm going scouting. I will stay nearby so you can get some rest," Ra'ael said.

While Kaemada was near motionless during the day, at night fits took her, such that they had to gag her and hold her down. Even so, her fits were violent enough that none of the three had to sing the counter song to the Angels. The Angels could be right outside their door, clawing at the flimsy wood, and still the power of the Angels' song would be disrupted by Kaemada's screaming, babbling nonsense. None of them had even felt the pull since coming here almost a moon ago.

Even so, the missed sleep wore on him. Taunos nodded wearily, hoping his gratitude showed. And then Ra'ael, too, was gone, and Taunos was left alone again with his catatonic sister.

Blowing out a sigh, he moistened a rag from the water jug and washed Kaemada's face, arms, and hands for her and then picked up the comb. Her curls tangled quickly without care, and this was another thing she was not able to do for herself.

"Do not listen to them, little sister," he whispered. "They do love you, just as I do. Their anger and hurt has simply blinded them for a while."

He held a handful of her hair in his fist, working out the tangles from the ends and moving upwards toward the top of her hair. As he worked, he talked, hoping she could hear him, wherever her mind was.

"Remember, life is not only pain, little sister. There is love and beauty, too. Remember listening for the starsong and climbing the great bluffs of

Heartwood? Walks in the forest with the summer sun dappling the ground through the leaves?"

He worked in silence for a while, thinking, and then finally began the story of Kalei and the fae, working his way through the tangles as he spoke, hoping that being reminded of Kalei's trials would help Kaemada come back to them. Once the tangles were free, he braided her dark honey hair to help reduce the knotting. It wasn't as nice a job as Ra'ael or Takiyah would have done, but it would do. But both story and chores had to end eventually, and even extending them didn't bring Kaemada back. She still sat, staring at nothing, heedless of his failure, his ineptitude. He couldn't save her from this.

"Lay down, cha'atanahn," he said, gently guiding her down on her side. He covered her with his old cloak, tucking the top under her chin, and then swept his hand downward over her eyes. "Close your eyes. Rest, little sister. Rest."

Two steps away, he laid down in front of the door and tried to think of a plan before sleep took his exhausted mind.

When he woke, feeling as if there was sand in his eyes, Kaemada's eyes were still open, staring through him. It had been too much to hope. She only shut her eyes during her fits. He rose, groaning and stretching, as Takiyah came in. She limped heavily on the leg that had been broken during their captivity, and Taunos turned his gaze away from her so as not to provoke another outburst.

He paused by the door. "I'm going out for a bit. Are you all right to stay with her?"

"The guards are everywhere out there. Something is wrong."

Taunos clenched his jaw. More problems. "Are you going to watch Kaemada?"

"Yes, Taunos, stop fussing."

"I'm not fussing, I'm—"

"Just go."

Taunos pressed his lips together for a bit, but Takiyah ignored him, taking off her boots and setting them in her corner. He turned, trying to quell his concerns, and cast a last glance at his sister. She stared at the wall, still laying on her side. He hesitated, wondering if he should leave her like that.

"Go!" Takiyah rounded on him, flicking her hands at him as if he were a swarm of spirits'-teeth.

Taunos frowned at her but went.

Outside, clouds had gathered, dark and ominous. The narrow streets were even more gloomy than usual. Even so, a small amount of relief spun through him, loosening his shoulders. It was better than being confined indoors, even if he was trapped under a dome in a ruthless city. Soon, he would feel the wind on his face, and perhaps that would bring Kaemada back. All he had left were fraying hopes for the impossible.

It was too dangerous to bring Kaemada outside—the guards still hunted for her, the psion who had killed their king. The restriction grated on him, for he knew how his sister loved the outdoors. They'd had so few days to spend together in recent summers, but always outside: deep in the forest or climbing the bluffs, racing along the trees or diving into waterfalls. How many storms had they watched together? A slight breeze gusted by, hailing a stronger wind outside the city. Lightning flashed in the boiling clouds, and thunder drummed. Taunos glanced up as rain poured down, spattering off the mysterious dome that covered the city, sliding off its curved surface, except where the rain found the holes in the dome, falling to water the crops planted below.

They'd been waiting for a storm strong enough to keep the Angels from hunting. This one might be exactly what they were waiting for.

A pair of guards jogged past.

Taunos ducked his head and hunched his shoulders. He quickened his pace once they had gone, but even so, he'd barely made progress before another pair came running down the opposite direction. What was going on?

He watched them go, pressing his back against the mud wall of a house to avoid being trampled. They turned a corner, and he crept after them, the hairs on the back of his neck prickling. The guards were always dangerous, always ready to cut you down for the slightest inconvenience, but now, something had changed.

Takiyah was right, as she all too often was.

The dim alleys were littered with filth, and Taunos covered his mouth and nose with his sleeve, trying to avoid breathing the worst of it. Soon, he reminded himself. Soon, he could return to open skies and wide spaces, fresh air and clean water to wash in. It looked like tonight would be the night, given the flashes of lightning.

A clash of metal rang out ahead of him, and he paused. Hardly anyone in the City of the Lost had metal except for the guards—it was one of the many things they hoarded to set themselves apart.

He crept forward then ducked back as a guard tumbled past his tiny alley. The few people who were out scurried away, casting panicked looks over their shoulders as they distanced themselves from the battle. The guard rose to his feet and launched himself at another, and Taunos retreated further into the shadows of the alley.

The guards were fighting each other? Why?

More important, should they take the chance given them by the storm to leave or wait until after the chaos of the guards fighting, lest they be discovered?

Taunos shook his head as a crash of thunder overhead rumbled. Though the guards fighting spoke of danger for any innocents caught in their path, they had to take the chance. Who knew when the next night storm would be? They'd just have to hope that the chaos of the guards fighting would work in their favor.

If they didn't take the chance of the storm, they'd have to sneak out some morning with the other laborers working in the new fields beyond the wall and then make their escape. Even though Kaemada had killed the king, not enough had changed for the City of the Lost. The guards had kept the city a prison, despite the fact that there was a way out now. It allowed them to keep the power, the control over those they considered less-than, especially since they forced the city folk to take shifts working the fields outside the walls. Always under supervision, of course, lest anyone run.

If they tried to escape that way, fewer people would succeed, and at much more risk.

No, tonight it was. It had to be.

The guards were used to spending the nights safe in their houses of stone, away from the threat of the Angels, so if their internal fighting didn't keep them from habit, the night would be clear. And if not, at least they were distracted.

He hurried through the muck toward home, sliding on filth around corners. If they left immediately, they'd be able to get farther before the next threat from the Angels, perhaps even making it out of their range altogether.

"Taunos." Elisabei wandered down the street next to her husband Reinan, who held a pot.

All too aware that unfriendly eyes might be watching, Taunos smiled as if at ease and gestured at the house that confined them. "Elisabei. Reinan. Come in."

Elisabei frowned at their door. "You need a new door, if you can find it. The Angels'll get through soon."

Taunos nodded, keeping up pretenses just as she was. Deep gouges in the wood bore the mark of Angels' fingers, digging at the door to gain access. Their house was near the wall and therefore was targeted more often by Angels, but at least the door faced away from the hole in the wall, sheltering them a little. He opened the battered door and ushered them in, quickly shutting it behind him.

He immediately wanted to escape. The room was far too close with so many people inside. Takiyah was folding their rags, while next to her, Ra'ael chopped vegetables. Kaemada lay in the corner like a child's forgotten doll, while Reinan placed the pot by Takiyah's fire. Ra'ael lifted the lid, and her face lit up with a smile.

"Broth!"

"Do not get too excited. The bones were three days old. It'll be weak," Elisabei warned.

As Ra'ael poured some of the grain and vegetables she and Takiyah had purchased that morning from the market into the broth, Taunos knelt by his sister and gently pulled her arms, sitting her up. He sat next to her, slinging an arm around her shoulders while she stared past Takiyah.

"Any idea why the guards are fighting?" he asked Takiyah.

She raised her eyebrows. "They're fighting?"

Taunos nodded.

Reinan frowned, his heavy eyebrows furrowing. "That's no good."

"I saw it myself," he said then dropped his voice to a murmur. "We need to escape tonight, in the storm."

"The guards never fight among themselves," Elisabei said, then softly, "It'll be dangerous though, with the guards fighting. If they continue, we might be seen."

Taunos smiled. "A necessary risk. Is everything ready?"

"They fight among themselves when there is a dispute over rule," Reinan rumbled, covering Taunos's whisper, though Elisabei nodded to him.

"What does that mean for tonight?" Takiyah asked.

"Not much different," Elisabei whispered. "Stay far away from them. Get to the walls and run."

"When was the last time they fought?" Takiyah's gaze was intense, but Reinan only shook his head. The muscled, barrel-chested Resistance leader who pretended to be a simple cobbler had been born in the city.

Taunos's arm tightened around his sister. Without her, they never would have met, never would have been connected. In fact, Kaemada was the thread tying all of them together—himself to Ra'ael and Takiyah, Takiyah and Ra'ael to each other, the three of them all to Elisabei and Reinan, and then to the Resistance. One thread couldn't hold cloth together though, especially if such cloth wanted to tear.

He dropped a kiss on the top of her head, whispering to her, "Hang on, little sister. Only a little longer, cha'atanahn. Only a little longer."

"Since we're leaving at night, we will have a problem." Takiyah nodded at Kaemada.

"We have to." Taunos tightened his hold further, as if he could guard his unresponsive sister from implications. She was in trouble, not trouble itself.

"I know. But you know as well as I do what happens."

Taunos nodded. His sister's fits took her nearly every night, as soon as her eyes shut. He bent to murmur in her ear, needing to believe some part of her could hear him. "We're leaving soon, under cover of night. Hang on, please, little sister. We will need quiet."

"We might need to tie her up more tightly than normal," Ra'ael said.

Taunos's gaze flicked to Kaemada's raw, bruised wrists, where she had injured herself during past fits.

"And gag her thoroughly," Takiyah said.

"Not too tightly or she'll suffocate," Elisabei cautioned.

"It has to be done." Taunos clenched his jaw. He looked at Elisabei. "When?"

"As soon as it's full dark."

They ate, keeping up a murmur of conversation as if this night was no different than any other. The lie of routine was crucial to their survival, and as such, the four had hosted Elisabei and Reinan often, especially as their house was bigger than the couple's. It had all been planned, ever since their arrival in the city.

And now, escape was finally almost upon them. Taunos felt almost as if he were vibrating with enthusiasm as he helped his sister eat then use the latrine pit. And then, with the sky darkening even further, they laid Kaemada down and began to bind her tightly with ropes and scraps of fabric tied over their blankets. In very little time, she was cocooned in tight strips of cloth, staring sightlessly at the ceiling. Taunos placed the bite stick in her mouth and tied the gags, using a couple extra layers to muffle her as much as possible under Elisabei's wincing guidance.

Kaemada did not resist—she never did. It would have been better if she did.

"Watch her to be sure she continues to draw breath," Elisabei said.

He nodded, pushing his worries away in favor of focusing on the escape at hand. The risk needed to be taken for the chance of success.

Taunos swept his cloak over his shoulders and made sure his daggers were in easy reach. Ra'ael grabbed the bag of their supplies, and just like that, they were ready. He caught Reinan's eye, and the big man glanced at Kaemada and then at Taunos meaningfully. Knowing Reinan, he likely had a contingency plan. Taunos would have to carry Kaemada.

He settled her over his shoulder as gently as he could. Following Reinan, he ducked out of the house, leaving the door open. After all, there was no longer any need to close it.

They ran through the empty streets, Taunos trying to joggle Kaemada as little as possible. In the City of the Lost, no one lingered longer than they needed on the streets at the best of times. With the guards fighting, it was just plain stupid to be where someone could see you. No one would be expecting them.

They cut through an alley and down another street then a quick turn to the right, meeting up with another small group, silent and wide-eyed. Winding their way toward the gaping hole in the wall, more and more groups joined theirs until they were a mass of people, fighters scattered among those who could not fight.

Clashing metal rang out to their left. Elisabei veered away, but their group had grown bulky, and many were too slow in seeking hiding places. Several guards spilled through an alley into the street they'd just turned onto, and more fighting could be heard on the main road behind them.

One of the guards shouted, "Stop!"

The guard fighting him didn't seem to notice them though. "Theron, you maggot, get back here!"

Taunos's blood ran cold. Theron. Was that *the* Theron? He stepped forward, intent on the thoroughfare, where several guards ringed in two combatants, both in the leather armor the guards wore. Both were bleeding from several wounds and panting from exertion.

"Does my life annoy you, *King* Kunos?" taunted one of the guards. "A constant reminder of your failures?"

"My failures?" scoffed the other. "You're the one who let that woman get out of hand. You're the one who failed to control a psion and keep her from killing your king. You're the one who let them escape. I may have failed thus far in escorting you to your death, but that is a far cry from being beaten by a woman!"

Taunos's gaze fixed on the guard who must be Theron. It didn't matter who the other guard was. Theron didn't know it yet, but Taunos's meeting with him had been long overdue, and he intended to repay Theron for all the horrors he'd put Kaemada through the first time she'd been in the city.

"Taunos!" Ra'ael hissed.

Reluctantly, he turned away, shifting Kaemada on his shoulder. First, he needed to get her to safety. His reckoning with Theron could wait a while longer. He fled down the street toward the wall.

A sharp, wild laughter sounded behind him as Taunos hurried to rejoin the end of the group. They were pouring out of the hole in the gates now. Ra'ael and Takiyah were both near the end, and Reinan was running back toward him, his face fierce.

"Down!" Reinan shouted, and Taunos obeyed instantly, flinging himself to the street, his arms stretched forward to cushion his sister's head.

She stiffened and thrashed, catching him in the chin with her knees and knocking his vision white. A terrible keening came from her throat. That was no good. It'd attract the guards. A knife protruded from the wall of the house in front of them—if he hadn't ducked, it would have lodged in his back. He spun around to look for whoever had thrown the blade.

Theron barreled toward him, teeth bared and another dagger glinting in his hand.

Muffled shouting came through Kaemada's gag, and she writhed around Taunos's feet, nearly tripping him. He leaped forward to find clear footing.

Theron drew another dagger in his free hand, his eyes intent on Kaemada. "She never should have come back. Get out of the way."

"She's my sister." After all Theron had put her through, he might as well know who was getting Kaemada's revenge.

Theron paused for a moment and then grinned, the expression full of menace.

And then Reinan darted past Taunos and hit Theron, the bigger man slamming the younger to the ground. Taunos hesitated. The need to join the fight, the thrill of the challenge, thrummed through him. And this was Theron, his sister's tormentor! This altercation had been long in coming.

And yet, Reinan was risking his life to give Taunos a chance to get Kaemada to safety. That was the whole point of tonight, after all.

The conflict within him raged as wildly as Reinan's battle with Theron, but Taunos turned, sheathing his daggers and wrestling Kaemada back over his shoulder. Even bound tightly, she still squirmed with all her might, and it took most of his concentration just to avoid being taken down by his own little sister. He charged down the road to the hole in the wall, darting through a few paces behind Ra'ael and Takiyah, at the rear of the bulk of the Resistance. The glory of rain showered down on him, drenching him with cold and turning the ground sodden under his feet.

Taunos kept watch while the last stragglers streamed by.

Whatever internal power struggle had sparked the guards' fighting kept them distracted. Reinan was charging toward him yet again, and Taunos watched for bows. The guard from before had Theron in a headlock, and they spun wildly as Theron tried to twist free while keeping his head intact. Reinan tugged on Taunos's sleeve just as Theron rammed his dagger into his opponent's chest. Taunos turned, sprinting through the hole in the wall.

Theron's words chased Taunos out of the city. "I am King Theron! Enjoy your freedom for now, cowards, but I'll burn the Resistance like a blight. All who shelter psions will share their death! Especially that psion Kaemada!"

Taunos ran, falling in alongside Reinan once he got up as much speed as he could with his sister thrashing about on his shoulder. Without Reinan, he wouldn't have made it. He needed to do better. With Ra'ael and Takiyah's plans to leave, he'd have to keep his sister safe on his own.

He ran as fast as he could manage until they were past the fields. There was no pursuit right now, but they were far from safe. He settled for a distance-eating lope at a pace he could sustain while carrying his sister, rather than sprinting.

"Stupid, back there," Reinan scolded, steadying Kaemada when she nearly fell off his shoulder. "You could have killed us, your sister included, with that childish stunt. You cannot improvise like that when others are depending on you for sticking for the plan."

Taunos nodded. It had been stupid, and he'd known it. Again, the giant of a man made him feel small, with so much to learn. "My thanks for your help."

He drank in lungfuls of sweet, rain-filled air. The flat landscape was disorienting in the dark between flashes of lightning, and the rain made it even harder to see, but Taunos loved it. His shirt was slicked to him, his cloak drenched and pulling at his shoulders, and his boots squished with every step, but they were free. They were free.

"The Resistance set up near a stand of trees that way." Reinan indicated the direction with his head, and Taunos angled that way. "Most of a day's run."

"I cannot—ow!"

Kaemada jerked, twisted, and kneed him in the head, screeching as she did so. Taunos shifted her again and ran on.

"These fits, they have not gotten better?"

"I'm surprised the fit did not begin sooner, honestly." Taunos panted between phrases. "Normally, she would have been thrashing about the time we left the house. It's fortunate she hung on as long as she did."

"We don't have much for helping."

"I hope, being free and away from that city, with all the memories, she will come back to us."

"You and your sister," snorted Reinan. "All hopes."

Taunos raised his eyebrows at the older man, but the dark likely hid his expression. They ran on, saving strength for the long journey ahead.

They'd left the fields far behind and reached the first hill before Taunos noticed that his sister had gone suddenly, prematurely, calm. He shifted her to his other shoulder, but his senses nagged him. Something was wrong. He glanced back, but no one was pursuing. He stopped, and Reinan paused near him, drawing in deep draughts of air.

Taunos laid Kaemada on the ground, tilting her head to the side to avoid the rain drowning her, and knelt beside her. She lay too still. Fingers clumsy, he removed her gags and the bite stick to listen. She wasn't breathing.

"Eloi's light and spirits around us!" he swore. "Kaemada, you listen to me, little sister. You are not allowed to cross the rim of the sky, do you hear me? You are not allowed to die!" He tilted her head back and breathed for her then slammed his fist onto her chest.

She jerked but then lay still again.

"We're free, little sister. You cannot die now, not when we just got free!" Again he breathed for her and again punched her.

"You will break her bones," Reinan said.

"A healer I knew once taught me this."

"Beating up dead people?"

"She's not dead yet."

But Reinan had a point, and after breathing for her another couple times, Taunos placed his hand on her chest and pressed sharply with his telekinesis, hoping that would accomplish the same thing. Several repetitions later, with Reinan standing sentry, Kaemada jerked halfway upright, drawing in a long, haggard breath. Bound as she was, she soon fell back to the ground and lay there breathing, blinking at the rain falling into her eyes.

Taunos collapsed over her, laughing with relief. "Thank you, little sister. Thank you for listening."

Reinan quirked his eyebrows. "I need for trying beating up dead people more often. Time for going."

Reinan gathered up Kaemada in his arms, for which Taunos was grateful, as he was exhausted. She looked so small, curled up against the big man's chest, her eyes still open. She was calm again, even though she was staring off into the horizon. They ran, then walked, then ran again, gaining ground on Elisabei and the larger group as the second moon crested the horizon, providing only a sliver of a crescent for light.

"I'm not sure why tonight is different, but I'm thankful. Typically, her fits last longer."

"And typically you do not beat her?"

"I really wish you would choose a different word."

Reinan shrugged, trudging along with his long-limbed gait. "It may be my ignorance of psions, having rarely interacted with them before her, but it seems that—well, maybe you know better."

"What, Reinan? I value your input."

"Well, it seems I have seen her thrash like that before."

"In the city."

"No, before. Will you listen? Under the mountain, too, when she was fighting the psions."

It was true. Taunos had seen it, too, and it was so obvious now that it was pointed out. Taunos felt ten times the fool. "How could I not see that?"

Reinan chuckled. "Sometimes it takes someone looking in from the outside for seeing truly. I lived in the city near fifty winters, and yet your sister immediately saw we could do more with the Resistance than just annoy the king. She killed the king and gave us an opportunity. Elisabei and I are grateful for her since. I'm glad for enlightening her foolish older brother in payment."

AHN
Chapter Two

Watch the usage of psionic warfare. The Rinaryns have psionics, and so do the Kamalti. If one were to press too hard, the struggle becomes loud, tumultuous. The rocks of Dead Man's Sea are perilous, yes, but so are the silent, still waters that grab and hold. The art of subtlety creates far superior effects—and has less chance of attracting the attention of dragons.

—*part of a missive from "Mebril" in Stonefield*

Every day Kaemada fought something new. Today, it was thirst.

Thirst drew her out of the minimal shelter the rock walls provided from the wind. Every time she looked at the mountainside, it changed subtly, making her stomach twist with warnings while her mind tried to figure out what had changed and how. Or perhaps it was her memory that had changed, become unreliable. Like her psionics.

We trusted you. You should have fought with us, not against us.

A strong gust snatched away her breath, leaving her gasping. She rubbed her chest—her ribs ached, though she couldn't figure out why. The wind shoved her this way and that as she walked toward a small rivulet, shambling like Angels-food. She arrived to find the water frozen. Shivering, she stared dumbly at it for many breaths before stomping on it with the heel of her boot. The thin ice near the edge shattered but not enough to drink from. She stomped again on the ice, then again. Her feet slipped out from under her.

She landed on her back hard enough to drive the air from her lungs. Pain lanced through her hand, throbbing in time to the beat of her heart. Her solitude was palpable—all alone, deep in the barren mountains, except for the wind that snatched at her, screaming her faults and weaknesses and mistakes.

Betrayed us. You betrayed us! You should have been one of us.

The emotionless rocks rose around her, impassive and indomitable. Not like her. Nothing could affect these ageless mountains. They were always the same, generation after generation. Nothing could hurt them.

And yet... And yet... The mountains did look different, didn't they?

A part of her screamed.

She rolled over, gritting her teeth as she took in her shredded palm.

Another shiver overtook her, and she huddled further into her shawl and cloak. She was just so tired. The effort to get to the water would tire her more. It wasn't worth it. She closed her eyes for a moment, gathering herself, then stood and made her way back along the precariously narrow ridge toward her shallow hollow in the rock—not big enough to be called a cave, really. Back to where she could find some semblance of peace.

Alone. You're always alone. Feel our pain.

Agony lit her on fire from her feet to the top of her head. She screamed, and the screaming caused her ribs to hurt even more. With a gasp, she pushed back. The Collective was attacking her. None of this was real, just a place in her mind for them to punish her. Gritting her teeth, she turned the pain back on them. If they wanted to hurt her, let them feel it too. No pain could be worse than that of losing her son, anyway.

The pressure of the Collective on her mind eased abruptly and melted away into darkness.

Her grief had consumed her at first, making it too difficult to care about... anything. She had accepted the muted, darker world around her at first, just as she accepted snow in winter. This was a cycle, and the thing about cycles was that one part ended so another could begin. Still, a part of herself hoped this portion would continue—the grief, not the attacks of the Collective. It would feel disloyal to stop missing her son and Tannevar, her wolf, to no longer carry their memories in her mind, even for a moment to think of something else, something less painful. Without Tannevar, she had nothing to anchor herself against the tide of emotion and attacks from the Collective. But as her grief went on and on, some small corner of herself grew increasingly agitated. Maybe the cycle was broken and no new season would come, leaving her forever joyless. It was surely no less than she deserved. But if no new season came, the cycle of time would be broken, and that would be the end of the world.

It certainly felt like the end of the world. Yes, she was Fallen, and children could never be Fallen—should never be Fallen. That made sense, why Eian was taken from her. But there was no way back, no way to make amends. The Elders had cut them off from their right of asking for mercy. Why had they done that? Something was wrong.

All psions should join with us. This is where you belong. Why did you fight against us? Why do you resist us now?

Every night, the Kamalti psions found her and washed her away in the ocean of their consciousness. They argued their points, impressing them so deeply on her that there was no difference between her thoughts and theirs. They engulfed her in their rationales and thoughts and emotions and then shoved her back into her body, weak from thirst, hunger, and pain. She hardly ever knew what was going on outside the prison of her mind. Every time she caught a glimpse, they descended on her, the pressure of their minds crushing her.

Other times, they punished her. Her screams echoed over the wilderness, where no one was around to hear her agony. Her tears watered Talahn Valley as she lay gasping for breath in the aftermath, and her nerves were raw with remembered torment for days afterward. The Seeker Tree became her anchor, and she clung to it during the days of suffering and the days of wondering who she was afterward. She clung to the symbol of her faith, spreading her agony like branches in the sky, and her sense of self to ground her like roots deep in the dirt. Not in the hopes of escaping the pain but of enduring it. She was not so naive to think she could escape suffering, not without abandoning Ra'ael, Takiyah, and Taunos to torment, and that was not an option.

She could join the Collective. But she had no intention of joining...

The thought slipped away from her. Her breath caught, her heart pounding, every sense straining. But they were only her imagination's senses, and so not of any real help. Though the Collective infiltrated her consciousness less and less during the day, the moons of torment, of being overtaken by them on a daily basis, had left a mark. Moons of not knowing if what she saw was real or imagined. Not knowing if her thoughts were her own or not. She could hardly keep track of what was important. There was something she had to do...

Did she truly believe that the psions were right to be angry at her? Was she truly a traitor for refusing to fight with her own kind? Sometimes, she believed it. Most of the time, she didn't know. She couldn't help anyone while she was like this, a prisoner of her own mind. But there was no way she could do this while every intention was stolen from her by the Collective. While she couldn't even trust her own thoughts.

She was broken. And therefore, she needed the elves.

The landscape shifted. She was on a ridge, the steep cliff-face below her plummeting through the clouds, toward land too far off to see. Wind buffeted her, toward the drop off on either side. Kaemada braced herself against the wind, but the edge called to her. The view was breathtaking, the craggy peaks around her, the deep chasm of jagged rocks below in shades of grey and brown, all illuminated by the weak winter sunlight.

Why should she continue to fight? What would it hurt to surrender? The pain would end. The spirits would never let her continue across the rim of the sky. They would send her back to learn her lessons, and she'd be able to do it all over again, only better this time.

Except she wouldn't see Eian again.

Kaemada turned, finding the Collective in her mind yet again and seizing them. She pressed on them the way she ached to hold her son again, one last time, to say good-bye. How she missed the faint tread of Ra'ael's feet as she inevitably rose before her in the morning to walk out into the sunrise. She missed Taunos's easy, carefree laugh and Takiyah's verbal sparring with anyone who would take her on. She missed the tickle of Tannevar's fur on her face, the reassuring warmth of the wolf's presence, always in her mind even when he was not nearby. She missed the bustle of kaetal life, the warmth and openness. Now, there was only this desolate waste, just as the gaping hole inside her. The chasm rose up, swallowing her.

She'd betrayed those she should have helped. The Collective. *How could you dare be so angry at your Elders?*

She shook her head. "How could the Elders have ignored us? They didn't act like the wise council I always thought they were."

You broke your own laws.

"It had been meant for the good! Did they deserve punishment? For trying to do good? Maybe I do, but surely not the others. Surely it did not merit stripping my friends and brother of their status or tearing Eian from everyone he knew and loved."

She hadn't even been able to say goodbye. Storyteller Zeroun and Saimahkae Maeren had told her they would not easily let them go, but they'd been cast down from their positions at the same time that she, Taunos, Takiyah, and Ra'ael had been banished.

The wind taunted her, crooning Eian's name and then buffeting her as it swept around the rocky crags surrounding her. She threw a rock, which bounced down the steep slope as she muttered the old saying to herself, "May as well be angry with spirits and shout at the wind."

It was not a rock.

The awareness chilled her. This was yet another hallucination from the Collective. She had to get free of them. She had to gain distance from them, to weaken their hold on her. Which meant she had to wake up.

Her song was a ragged piece of cloth being ripped apart slowly by unseen hands. Each thread breaking lasted an eternity and pierced her with ever more pain. She tried to bear it, to atone for what she had done. But at last, she was driven by a primal need to diminish the pain. That weakness, that need for relief, made her despair even more for the shame of who she was. She couldn't even handle her just punishment.

She had yet to find any form of relief. She was beginning to think none would ever come.

You misled us. You betrayed us.

She could see their point. The guilt stabbed her like a knife, and she bled, bled, bled.

The memories swarmed her yet again. The mistakes she had made. They held her in their grip and made her watch the horrors over and over. When she'd killed the king in the City of the Lost, her mind-explosion had exposed all the psions there. Many had been murdered before the survivors broke through the wall with the Resistance, and people flooded the plains for freedom. How many had the Angels killed, not only during the Angel's Feast but also as they came through the hole in the wall nightly, looking for prey?

More deaths on her conscience to go with those of the Collective.

But she couldn't stop fighting. The Collective wanted her to surrender, so that was something she could never do. If she could keep their attention, Takiyah, Ra'ael, and Taunos would be free of these hallucinations, for surely the Collective bore them a grudge as well.

The Elders said you were dangerous. Taunos said you were drowning in your grief, Takiyah said you were wallowing, and Ra'ael said you were weak.

They didn't understand. Or maybe she didn't. There was no stability, no immovable truth. What was true? What could she safely dismiss as only fickle emotions? What was truly real anymore?

Except her love for Eian was real, right? And her grief.

Truth! That was it.

She held tight to who she was, just as when she'd fought the Collective under the mountain. She was Lína's daughter. She was Afarei's daughter. She was Galod's student. Kaemada grabbed her tormentors and made them watch, turning their tricks back on them as she showed a memory of her own choosing.

She was small, crying because she wasn't able to keep up with her older brothers. Her father had found her and held her, his serenity unaffected by her tears. She clung to the memory of that peace. "You have to dance to your own music. You cannot follow along in another's story."

That had made her mother laugh and say, "Isn't that why you and Storyteller Zeroun have been arguing lately?"

"Harmony is not everything."

"It is important."

"It is, dearest," her father conceded, as he always did. He'd risen and embraced her mother. "Storyteller Zeroun wants me to stop writing."

"Why?"

"He would like me to be his apprentice, and so he tells me I must only tell true stories."

"That is quite an honor."

"Truth is not always true. Sometimes a story can be true but still miss the truth. In making my own stories, I am looking for the truth—the real truth—even knowing some details may not be true."

"So you will not accept?"

And they had argued, lightly and lovingly, as they always did.

Kaemada clung to the tune of her parents' songs, embracing the memories. The part of her song that was Tannevar's rang true, and she collapsed against the whisper breath of his scent, his memory. Her father had rejected honor and harmony for truth, and now she must do the same, for all their sakes.

I will collect you in my own story, Collective, she warned them. *Or you could let me be. Surely I have suffered enough for my mistakes. Harmony is important, but so is truth. And I need to find the truth about the Elders.*

She had to find out what had happened to the Elders before she could possibly reunite with her son. She'd tried and failed to be her mother. She needed to follow her father's advice, too.

The Collective buzzed around her, their smothering pressure easing from her mind. Something jostled her rhythmically, as if she were moving. She froze, but her surroundings stayed the same, though the jostling continued, from far away. And yet, had she moved, somehow? Had she moved, somehow?

"Come back to me, little sister." Her brother's strained whisper surrounded her.

He was still here? She snapped open her eyes, sucked in a deep breath, as if she'd been drowning for real, rather than just by mind. There was her brother, his arms encircling her like safety personified. Beyond him, no icy mountain landscape. Just the wide open sky sprinkled with stars and the wavy tops of the prairie grass. Tears shone in her brother's eyes, and new lines creased his face.

The Collective was coming. She could feel their anger, rumbling toward her like a wave crashing down on a rock. Which was real, her brother holding her or the Collective coming? Desperate, fearful, she took the chance that this was really reality, even if she was only lucid for a moment. If her brother could take her body away, the Collective's attacks would weaken. She would have a chance.

"Farther," she whispered.

And the vengeful currents pulled her under again.

No Fallen shall be welcomed among the kaetalyn, for those who will not respect the laws of the kaetal and their fellow people have no place among others. Cast them to the wilderness, and hunt them as a rabid animal. Weep, for they are lost to us. Those who wish for peace may find it in the City of the Lost.

-scrap from the Monks of Annularei

The sky bled red and purple as the sun died. The brightest of the stars already sparked in the deepening night while Ra'ael the Fallen climbed down from the ridge. Her full water pouch sloshed at her side as she headed back to her cave. Fallen lived in the wasteland between the arms of the Holy Mountains or in the city. She couldn't go back to the city, so for the last half-moon she'd been living in the mountains. Spring may have been waking the green lands below, but winter still lived in her heart. The barren landscape looked like a mangled bedmat, all crumpled and neglected. She longed to smooth it out, as if she could smooth out the wrinkles of the past moons. Nostrils flaring, she breathed deeply to calm her song. Comparing the imagery and her own situation was foolish. Lives weren't so easy that they avoided wrinkles.

Ra'ael checked the snares as she walked, grimly freeing her next meal from the slender rope that had taken its life. She thanked the spirits for her meal as she reset the snare. Though she wasn't sure if Fallen did such a thing, she couldn't abandon that simple act. When she neglected to give thanks, it niggled at the back of her mind like an itch she couldn't scratch. She hadn't followed the law and therefore had Fallen. Perhaps if she could follow the rules of Fallen, her circumstances would change, but the rules were not so clear cut as they had been among her people.

The lack of clarity nagged at her. She missed the starsong and the closeness of the spirits. Ra'ael could no longer feel the song of the spirits. How was she supposed to align herself with it if she no longer knew it?

She ducked under the threshold of her cave, following the dull glow of the embers she'd left near the back. It was low-ceilinged, sloping ever lower toward the back, cinching tight enough in the middle that the Angels couldn't get in if they happened to hunt here, but the opening was large and there was enough space inside that she didn't feel trapped. The

22

smoke from her fires followed the slope of the roof upward as it escaped into the night air. Ra'ael poked up the coals, feeding it more tinder until it crackled merrily.

Grabbing her knife, she quickly skinned and cleaned the carcass of the large rodent. Halfway through, she realized she was humming, and abruptly stopped herself. Fallen did not hum, she was almost certain of that. She needed to walk the path the spirits gave her to the best of her ability if she wanted a more desirable path to become available to her. She would prove herself to Eloí, if this was all a test. It would be so much easier if she could still hear the song of the spirits.

Closing her stinging eyes, she allowed her frustration to wash over her, through her, to leave her behind. She was being too loud, that was all. Her bitterness was natural. After all, her aspirations had been torn from her. She'd worked so hard to be priestess, poured herself into it, following the system set before her so that eventually she could become Great Mother. That path was forever closed to her. Now, she was Fallen, and there was nothing for it but to act Fallen.

The thinking was the problem. It was getting her into trouble, all those melancholy thoughts. She needed to simply act.

Ra'ael grabbed one of her prepared skewer sticks and set her meal to roasting. She chewed on her lip, considering the rodent's skin and entrails. A Rinaryn would use those, wouldn't let them go to waste. She hadn't figured out yet what a Fallen would do. Clearly, she hadn't paid enough attention, hadn't asked the right questions.

With a sigh, she hung the skin to preserve it in the smoke, just as she had done previous times. It wasn't in her to be wasteful, and she would eventually need fur-lined boots and a hat for winter. The entrails she laid on a flat rock to sizzle. No sense letting those go to waste either, whether or not a Fallen would. Didn't that count? Wasn't everything she did something a Fallen would do?

She shook her head, banishing such philosophical nonsense. Why talk herself in circles? Without insight from another mind, worrying over it was foolish. So she cooked her meager meal and ate it by herself and tried not to miss the murmur of other voices around her, laughing and talking and contemplating. The tasteless meat stuck on the lump in her throat, but she forced herself to swallow and dispelled even the thought of tears from her eyes.

Leaving the others was the right thing to do. She'd made it quick, immediately after their escape from the city, at the same time as Takiyah, though they'd veered away from each other in unspoken agreement. They couldn't pretend to be their own kaetal. That hadn't been working. She had to find what did work, what the spirits wanted of her. What laws could she follow that would allow her to gain back the song of the spirits? Without a goal, she was left to think far too much, but what goal could a Fallen have beyond survival? It was all she had. It wasn't enough.

"What am I supposed to do now?" Her voice echoed back to her in the desolation.

With a growl, Ra'ael threw the spit. She ground her teeth as it splintered against the rocks of her cave and then turned her back, seeking the peace that eluded her. What was she doing, making a home, as if anything was permanent anymore? She needed to accept her path, to let go of her frustration.

It was an impossible task.

Banking the fire, Ra'ael curled up to sleep, her only company the hunting song of the Angels going down to the city west of her, as they did every night.

In the morning, she packed her things and spread the coals of her fire to become ash. Slinging her pack on her back, she left without a backward glance, hiking up the traitorous trails that led into the mountains. She almost didn't need to make the decision a conscious one. It was the only option left, ludicrous as it was. She couldn't go home, she couldn't go back to the city, and she couldn't live as a Fallen. The only thing she hadn't tried was going to Dode. Who better than the Kamalti to soothe the discordance of her song with order and permanence and a strict adherence to the right way to do things? She needed rules to follow to set her on the right path, and the Kamalti overflowed with rules.

Her feet were sore and bruised, and night was falling by the time she reached a trail she thought she recognized. The paths in the mountains were known for their false trails and dead ends as much as they were known for their traps and pitfalls. But Ra'ael was searching for a very specific spot, the way into the city of Codr.

She found it after long hunting, or at least, she thought it was the correct place. She and Takiyah and Taunos had all had to work together to get inside, to force the doors open to the Kamalti realm. It was only her this time, and besides, she knew now how the Kamalti felt about that. If she wanted to ask for aid, if she wanted to keep her sanity, she would have to do things the Kamalti way. Perhaps that would be easier than being Fallen, since she could no longer be Rinaryn. Even if she couldn't be Kamalti, their careful control of emotion was something she sorely needed, before the grief and pain inside her tore her apart.

Settling down, Ra'ael waited. After a time, her eyes drooped, and she dozed in the sun with the warm rock at her back.

The stone scraped. Ra'ael leaped to her feet. The cliff face effortlessly glided apart to form a doorway. Her half-formed smile froze as she met the stern gaze of the three Scouts that stepped out, their faces shadowed by their large hats and the goggles they wore, armored against the summer air by their many layers. As they took ready stances, Ra'ael raised her empty hands for peace.

"I am not here to harm you. I wish to ask for entry, to see the Lady Dode."

The Scouts exchanged glances. One of them spoke to her but in Kamalti. "Who are you?"

Clearly, she was not meant to respond. Ra'ael smiled. Her time under the mountain was not for nothing. "I am Ra'ael, who was once ebr to Lady Dode. Perhaps you remember the attack of the Kamalti psions?"

The Scouts didn't flinch—they would be far too well-mannered to show such base things like emotions—but she knew she'd struck a blow, not just insulting their intelligence but bringing up the battle where she'd saved Kamalti lives. Perhaps even their lives. They couldn't really turn her down, could they?

Indeed, one of the Scouts gestured curtly to her and the other two Scouts, and Ra'ael sat back down, smiling at his discomfited expression as he stepped back within the entrance to the Kamalti realm. She largely ignored her Kamalti guards—they would be annoyed if she tried to engage them in small talk, and she had no desire to pretend to be friendly with them. They were a means to an end.

She snorted at that. It was far more a Kamalti notion—albeit a low-regarded one—than a Rinaryn one, and it surprised her that she'd thought of it. Perhaps it was a sign that this was what she was supposed to do. She glanced upward. Were the spirits finally smiling on her path? With a grimace, she looked back down at her hands. She couldn't jump to conclusions or depend on the spirits' favor. Not yet. Not until she'd passed their test.

The two Kamalti shifted, their demeanors oozing unease despite her clearly nonthreatening stance. Unless it was that they recognized her name. She sneered. If that was it, they really needed to gain some courage. She wasn't some out-of-control animal on the verge of randomly murdering people.

After a time, one of the Scouts leaned toward the other, murmured something terse, and then strode off. Ra'ael watched him go. Where did the Scouts go when they walked under the open sky? What did they do? Somehow, she hadn't thought to ask such questions before. She'd been too occupied with other things.

The Scout who had gone ranging returned, carefully avoiding her gaze and her questions. Finally, the first Scout returned, with a hint of surprise around the corner of his eyes and the set of his mouth. She smiled, knowing the answer before he even opened his mouth.

"The Outsider is allowed. She must report to the Hall of Scouts to be cleared, and then the Lady Dode will meet with her."

Ra'ael rose, nodding. She followed him in through the doors in the mountain, and the two other Scouts followed her closely behind. The small room that separated the Outside from the realm of the Kamalti made her shudder as always, though she was far more used to closed spaces by now, and she hurried the few paces to the next door.

When it slid open, she gasped.

The twin cities were wreathed in smoke, and tendrils of it reached for her, pouring down her throat. She coughed, waving her hand before her face, and peered through the smoke. Where was it all coming from? The cities looked much restored from the devastation of the Kamalti psions' attack, though scaffolding still stood and workers busied themselves where reconstruction efforts were still going on.

Squinting, she could barely pick out Dode's home, low on one of the support columns, just Detr-ward of the papermaker and glassblower quadrants. Still, she could see no fires, other than those contained in the lanterns.

"This way," the Scout in front said, gesturing to the steep, narrow stairs lit by glowing lanterns that provided the way down to the cavern's floor far below them.

Coughs wracked her as she descended farther into the haze. "Where is all the smoke coming from? Is everything all right?"

"We do not expect Outsiders to understand," one of the Scouts behind her said.

"It seems the repairs are going well. No buildings seem on fire," Ra'ael mused.

"What do you care, anyway?" the Scout asked.

There was a murmur from the other Scout. "If she really is Ra'ael, she helped to save the city. My grandmother was saved by the Outsiders. And I would not expect other Outsiders to know to use her name, to use her image."

Ra'ael resisted the urge to look behind her.

"It does not matter," the woman said. "The Lady Dode used the Outsiders to shame the whole of the Scouts. We should not have to answer to anyone."

"It is only for a little while," the man said. "We will regain our proper place."

"If Lady Answer had only stood up to her, we would not be groveling now!"

"Scouts do not grovel."

"They certainly should not."

There was a rustle and a hushed murmur, and Ra'ael knew she wouldn't be hearing any more. She was lucky to have heard what she did, that the slights were great enough to override the younger Scouts' senses of decorum. It was plenty to muse on. What had become of the Kamalti psions when they had left? Had Dode continued to leverage her position to shame the Scouts? Was Answer still paying the price for helping them?

Clearly things had been interesting while she'd been gone.

She stared at the back of the Scout in front of her as they continued to descend. Breathing deeply, she suppressed her smile and robed herself in decorum of her own. She stumbled on the next step, caught by the memory of how self-assured she'd been last time, how she'd wrapped herself in pride, in her shroud of priestesshood. She'd worked so hard for that useless piece of fabric. It was folded at the bottom of her pack—she hadn't been able to bear to actually part with it yet.

Her face burned with embarrassment. She had to act like a Kamalti if she were to gain herself a place here, and that meant every movement needed to be sure and precise, every "base" emotion controlled. If she could control her emotions, surely she wouldn't hurt anymore. Though the Scouts were too Kamalti to do something so base as to snicker, she caught their sidelong looks at each other, the slight tension to the corner of their mouths as they held back smiles. She wrinkled her nose and stared ahead.

They walked along the cobbled streets, and a crowd gathered, just as last time. Shoppers paused in their business to gawk. She tried telling herself they didn't often see Outsiders, but it didn't help her keep from tensing. She was not a thing, to be on display. And yet, she had chosen this path.

The Hall of Scouts loomed before them, the sleek, sharp-edged building so at odds with the cube-shaped architecture the Kamalti favored. The metal buildings were invariably important public buildings, such as their primary shrine to their gods and the Hall of Justices. But the Hall of

Scouts, set a little ways apart from the other irregular buildings, had its doors propped permanently open now, and Kamalti in the finery of the noble classes swept in and out of the building. When she'd seen it before, it had been only used for the Scouts, sort of a haven for them, she'd gathered. Her escorts bristled at the intrusion—she could feel it through their placid demeanors.

The Scouts brought her inside, through the close metallic hallways. Her skin itched at the nearness of them, but the reaction was something she was able to mostly ignore now, perhaps because of living in the City of the Lost for a while. Even so, her skin crawled, as if something was watching her, and she fought the urge to shudder.

Dode's voice came through the closed double doors that made up the Scouts' chamber where borrowed Justices ruled on Scouting matters. The Justices that had welcomed them so coldly the first time she'd come under the mountain, with the others, had been borrowed Justices of that sort, a relationship she hadn't been able to understand for some time, until near the time she'd left. But Dode was a Philosopher.

By the shifting posture of the Scouts escorting her, they weren't expecting Dode to be there either. But then, the old woman often did things that seemed surprising to those who didn't know her well.

The metal doors slid open at their approach. There stood Dode, as strong and elegant as ever. A warm feeling bloomed in Ra'ael's chest for the first time in a long time. She felt… right, almost. Almost content.

"Ah, the Outsider."

The Justice, a middle-aged man standing beside Dode, wiped his hands on his linen skirt and cleared his throat. How like Dode to discomfit her rivals so thoroughly.

"Ra'ael, please forgive Lord Jetl. While a citizen of Codr, his poor manners no doubt are a result of his schooling in Detr. One cannot hold such disadvantages against him, can we?" Dode smiled.

Rage passed over Lord Jetl's face in a wave so comic Ra'ael looked down to keep herself from laughing. She didn't want an enemy of him, though sometimes one didn't get what one wanted, of course. For such emotion to be displayed so clearly, Dode must be putting a great deal of pressure on him—far more than was evident at first.

The more senior Scout beside her cleared his throat. "Lord Jetl, here is the Outsider who claims to be Ra'ael of the Outsiders who were here before, during the Night of Fear."

She scowled. "I am Ra'ael, and I saved many of your—" She caught Dode's warning glance and quickly altered her tone and choice of words.

"Erm... people."

The Justice straightened his shoulders and stared down at Ra'ael with narrowed eyes. "This is all very unusual."

Dode snorted. "Not that unusual. Did you not just have a guest with you from Kedr visiting last face?"

The Justice scowled at her. "The City of Kedr is a Kamalti city, and my guest was Kamalti."

"And? My guest is Ra'ael, and need I remind you of her civil service to our city?"

"She is an Outsider!"

"Kedr's citizens are outsiders as far as Codr law goes! Surely, Lord Jetl, you haven't forgotten that."

"That's entirely different, Lady Dode."

"Oh, it is? Please enlighten me."

"Well, I, erm..." Lord Jetl cleared his throat, and Ra'ael bit her lip to avoid grinning.

Dode swept past him. "Take your time compiling your arguments, Lord Jetl. When you have them together, you know where to find me—and my guest."

The elderly woman took Ra'ael's arm and walked to the doors, but the Scouts stepped in front of them, barring their way. Dode paused and stared at the Scouts with a raised browridge. "Does this madness extend to you as well?"

"The Scouts will not submit to your bullying forever, Lady Dode."

Ra'ael scoffed but held her tongue.

Dode gave the Scouts an indignant look. "I should hope not. To be relegated to a lifetime of chivvying you to be decently behaved? What a horror, what an injustice."

Snickers broke free—Ra'ael couldn't help it—as Dode pushed between the two, leading her down the hallway and out of the Hall of Scouts. As she led the way home, Dode smiled warmly at her. "It is good to see you again, my dear. Come, I will serve you tea this time, and you can tell me what brings you here."

"Oh, no, Dode, let me make the tea." Ra'ael smiled at the elderly lady's surprised expression. "It would be my honor."

After all, she was here to embrace being Kamalti, following all their plethora of clearly defined rules. Perhaps then the spirits would speak to her again and she would have the direction of the song of the spirits. She couldn't follow Rinaryn rules anymore, and Fallen had none. Only Kamalti was left to her, so she would throw herself into it wholeheartedly.

Dode's house was just the same as when she'd left, and in no time, she had a kettle going.

"I hope you do not get into trouble on my account, Dode," Ra'ael said, spooning the tea leaves into the teapot.

"Oh, where would be the fun in that?" The woman groaned softly as she sat down at the table. Ra'ael cast a glance backward. There Dode sat, her posture straight as the rays of the sun, her dignity seeping from her being. Ra'ael's heart warmed, the wounds of her song balmed ever so slightly.

As she poured the boiling water into the teapot and reached for the tea cups, a knock sounded at the door. She froze, ready for danger, for the Scouts to retaliate in some way. Dode laughed, waving her off as she opened the door.

"Ah, Tjodlik, I had forgotten you were coming."

"This is the arranged day and time, Aunt Dode," the young Kamalti Philosopher said as he entered. He paused, seeing Ra'ael. "Have all of you returned?"

Ra'ael laughed, and it felt good to do so. It had been a while, she realized. Should she laugh so? She shook her head, banishing such thoughts as useless. "Only me."

"Did you have trouble with the Scouts?"

"Nothing Dode was unable to handle."

He thinned his lips, turning to Dode. "I do wish you would be careful."

"You worry too much, Tjodlik. I merely reminded Lord Jetl that if he could have a guest from outside the city, then so could I."

"Why did that work?" Ra'ael asked, taking down a third teacup and checking the tea's strength. "I'm not Kamalti. He had a point."

"Tjodlik, explain. Ra'ael, pour the tea, please." Dode waved her hand to hurry her up.

He sat next to Dode, tenting his fingers on the tabletop as his gaze unfocused slightly. "Well you see, travel between cities is restricted. Unless one holds a prominent position in a foreign city, one must present oneself to the foreign Scouts to be vetted, unless one is sponsored by a person of authority in the foreign city. These restrictions are more strict between cities who are not so friendly with each other."

Ra'ael set tea cups on the table and filled them. She placed the pot with precision in the middle of the table, amused and somewhat comforted by the speed at which Kamalti habits came back to her. "I have seen no such thing with travel between Codr and Hadr."

Tjodlik nodded. "Yes, I have no need to do such things to visit my aunt, for instance, because our cities are sister-cities. They function, at least as far as travel goes, as one city."

Ra'ael shook her head. "I'm afraid I still do not understand. In Rinara, one can go to any other kaetal if sent by the Elders and given a token to prove we are not Fallen." She winced at that and tried to cover with a big sip of tea. It was hot though, and she coughed as the tea scalded her throat on the way down.

"In Rinara, all of your cities are governed by a central Council of Elders, correct?" Dode asked. Ra'ael nodded, remembering they'd talked about such things. "So every Rinaryn is subject, directly or not, to that Council. For Kamalti, one is only governed by the ruling classes of the city one was born into."

Ra'ael furrowed her brow. "So you Kamalti... It's as if each city were Outsiders to each other city?"

Tjodlik nodded. "Yes, very similar. Cities have their own styles of government, their own laws. Some nobles own property or conduct business in multiple cities, but this comes with a certain level of annoyance for the landowner. They must abide by the laws of each city their property is in, as well as the laws of their home city, and sometimes these laws are in conflict. So such practices are really only in vogue with families of middling nobility wishing to prove themselves."

Ra'ael nodded. "So back there, you basically claimed me as coming from a different city?"

Dode nodded with a smile.

Tjodlik mused, staring into his tea. "It appears the comparison may not be too far off. But Aunt, the Scouts are still angry with you. Must you continue to needle them?"

Dode raised her browridge at her nephew. "I am not an invalid, Tjodlik. I know what I am doing."

"And I know there have been threats on your life."

"None have succeeded," Dode said, waving away his concerns. "Besides, I have taken your advice."

Dode reached for a small bowl of pebbles sitting on the table. There were several of them, all over the house, but Ra'ael had thought they were decoration. As the elderly woman placed her hand over the bowl, Ra'ael's nose stung with a scent sharper than any thunderstorm. It brought back memories of the time she and Takiyah and Taunos had huddled in the chapel, before it fell on their heads, pulled down by Scouts with the Gift of the Gods. She gasped, shoving back from the table, jostling her tea.

31

"Ra'ael, are you all right?" Tjodlik asked.

On her feet, she panted, trying to calm herself under the stares of Dode and Tjodlik. Dode was holding a rock, and no pebbles were in the bowl now.

"I just... That's not going to help if someone wants you dead."

"It is something though." The sharp smell came again, stabbing at her like needles, and the rock Dode held reverted back into the pebbles.

Ra'ael bit her lip. Whatever was going on with her, she had to control it. The Gift was... while not harmless, it was just a tool. Something many of the nobles were given in a special ceremony overseen by their priests. The Gift would "run through their blood and bones," whatever that meant. It gave them sanctioned "magic," as opposed to the "magic of the Outsiders." She closed her eyes for a moment. She had to get control of herself. This was fine. Besides, she had nowhere else to go.

A hand fell on her shoulder, and cold fire stabbed into her. She jumped, but it was only Dode, looking at her with concern. "I said, are you all right?"

"I'm just... a little jumpy, I suppose." Ra'ael squeezed Dode's hand, ignoring the prickles of her skin when she did, and then embraced the woman, just to prove she could, stomping down her unease. She hadn't felt this way before with Dode. Surely it was just bad memories. After all, she'd rarely had a chance to interact with Dode after the chapel was pulled down on their heads.

Dode watched her sharply as she returned to her seat, concern still shimmering in her eyes. "As I was saying, the Scouts must pay for their atrocities while you were here the first time. One of my colleagues among the Philosophers has been pushing to reform our system, to consider your people as coming from a foreign city. One city, Outside, containing all Rinaryn. Such a thing should not be too shocking, I think. But all such changes of thought have their opponents." She smiled. "I fear I stole his idea to use in my argument with the Scouts. I shall have to make recompense."

"Aunt Dode, you know these things worry me."

Ra'ael raised her eyebrows at Tjodlik. "And you have been looking in on her?"

He nodded. "She needs a new bodyguard, but I do what I can."

Fierce love swelled in her, banishing the last of the odd unease, and she dismissed it from her mind as a fluke. Dode was Dode, and just like last time, Ra'ael would protect her, whatever it took. "Well, never fear. No one's getting to Dode while I'm here."

"Yes, my dear. Tell me, why have you come? You seemed so eager to go home."

Her loss crashed down around her, all that had been taken from her, and Ra'ael scowled at the table. She was nothing, had nothing. After all her struggles to prove to Dode how superior Rinaryn culture was, now here she was seeking shelter from the remnants of her faith, her dreams, herself. "The Council of Elders found us guilty of crimes so severe they cast us out. I am Fallen now."

DEITAE
Chapter Four

Here where the Center meets East,
In the golden bowl of the towering ones,
The City of Tamarik shall rest,
Forever bathed in the light of the sun.

—excerpt from the History of Kamalti

The sand went on forever. Takiyah's mouth had dried out long ago, for she had drunk the last of her water the day before. All around her stretched only sand and rocks. The mountains to the north had tried to kill her. The desert was going to kill her. Everything under the sky was out to take her life: wind, sand, and sun.

At the moment, Takiyah wasn't sure she cared. Her head pounded so viciously she could barely see for the pain. Her boot struck a half-buried stone, tipping her headlong into the sand. Bitter laughter bubbled out of her as the sand ground into her cheek; the beating of the sun had turned the non-branded cheek as raw as the branded one. She didn't have the energy to get up. She didn't care.

A glint out of the corner of her eye caught her attention. Boots scraped on the sandy ground. Maybe she did have some energy after all. She wasn't going to be killed lying down. With a grimace, she gathered herself to her feet and gripped her metal staff as tightly as she could with hands that felt too large.

She tried to set her staff ablaze, but she had no more fire left. A bandit stood before her, taller than average for a Rinaryn, though still significantly shorter than she. Black cloth covered his stocky frame except for his blue eyes and the pale skin surrounding. Was this bandit Kamalti?

"Don't test me," she croaked.

The bandit charged. She sidestepped, tripping the man and then clubbing him unconscious with a spin of her staff.

"Should have listened," Takiyah said.

"Maybe," said a voice.

More bandits encircled her.

All together, the bandits leaped forward. Takiyah dodged and parried and struck, her muscles automatically moving in the quick, precise strikes their teacher Galod had taught them. She lashed out against the pain of the memory, at the bandit in front of her. She and Ra'ael and Kaemada were supposed to be a team, supposed to be prize students of the old hermit. It hadn't helped them at all.

She finished her bandits and whirled in a circle, ready to take out her temper on anyone else who came at her.

No one else was standing. No one to challenge, no one to fight, to unleash her anger on. Spirits knew she had plenty of that. What she didn't have was water—and her fumbling fingers found only mostly-empty water pouches. She drained what little water remained. Surely they must be close to water, if they let their pouches run out. If only she knew where it was.

She trudged eastward, following the strange call that tugged at her. It was as good a direction as any. At least it wasn't the City of the Lost.

Takiyah shook her head at herself. The City of the Lost hadn't been so bad, really. It was just the never-ending reminders of their trauma that she couldn't handle. What Fallen they made, allowing the Elders to break them!

How dare the Elders reach so far? And everyone just let them. They stripped away her parents' honor and positions, and no one lifted a finger in protest.

Not even her.

There were too many reminders, everywhere, of faithlessness. She'd been a good daughter, been a good friend, and this was where her story led. Well, in that case, she was done following rules. Kaemada had struggled to be loyal to her, while it never would have been a question for Takiyah. It only meant she didn't belong.

Something drew her on, on, on, tugging at her in the same way the knowledge had unlocked in her mind the last few moons. As if her mind was tethered with a rope, something dragged her forward, without stopping, without mercy, calling her to come, ever onward, ever east. She'd been following it ever since leaving the others behind. Taunos's neediness, Ra'ael's pompous serenity, Kaemada's mind sickness. Her heart twinged a bit, but she squashed it with the fires of her rage. She didn't need them.

And yet, she was too weak to go up against society, to stand up for her parents.

Served her right to get lost in the desert.

Deliriousness had plagued her for the last day. Waterfalls had turned out to be only more rocks. A large pool of water, just sand. Her friends—

no, not her friends. She didn't have friends. Taunos and Ra'ael had been only pillars of rocks in the sand.

She stumbled around a cluster of boulders and stopped, blinking. A hallucination in the shape of a Kamalti man stood before her. Takiyah shook her head. Clearly her mind thought her torment was not enough. She didn't need anyone. She was stronger alone.

She plowed through the hallucination. She didn't need anyone. Certainly not a Kamalti.

But the apparition didn't dissolve when she stepped through him. She rebounded, her legs weak and clumsy, and fell on her butt on the sand. With a groan, she sank all the way back, staring up at the sky. Just a little rest.

"Well, do you give up, then?" the apparition asked her.

Takiyah craned her head to look up. Impossibly pale skin, too-large eyes, almost no nose, and hairless, with two large knobs on top of his skull. The apparition was a Kamalti, clothed in white-and-black flowing robes, hood pulled up against the wind. The boots were sturdy, thick, and black.

Why was she focusing on such trivial things? Boots.

"Have you given up?" the Kamalti asked again. "Are you ready to die?"

"No!" she spat.

"Then get up."

"Too tired. Just going to rest."

"So you have given up."

"Never!"

"Then get up!"

She glared at the delusion, and he glared back. His face was gaunt and weathered, his eyes dark and challenging. Funny how the mind could put so much detail into things that weren't really there.

Of all things, a Kamalti. Abusive, cruel, and filled with more lies than the desert was filled with sand, the lot of them. And he thought he could judge her!

She rolled over and struggled to all fours. Takiyah would prove to this Kamalti that she was strong. Even if he wasn't real. She was strong. She only needed to get stronger. The world would not break her. The desert would not break her.

"You will not beat me!" she screamed as she staggered to her feet.

The Kamalti nodded, his thin lips curving into a smile. "Good. You have fight left in you, after all."

She stood there, wavering, before her legs folded under her and she collapsed in the sand again.

"Come on," the delusion said as he picked her up. "I suppose I cannot let you die after such a spectacle of obstinance."

Vaguely, she wondered how a figment of her imagination could be carrying her, but she couldn't hold on to that thought, just as she couldn't hold on to consciousness. She slid into the welcoming darkness, where there was no relentless sun beating down on her, no scorching wind, and no scouring sand.

The weight of something nearby disturbed the ground she lay on, waking her. Adrenaline flooded her, and she bolted to her feet.

She was captive again. No. Never again.

In the dimness, granite surrounded her—they were in a cave. Lanterns were placed in little alcoves in the stone walls, but there was a tunnel leading away from the space. An exit, perhaps. Her captor sat in a chair between her and the exit. The same Kamalti apparition in the desert. Clearly not an apparition. No one would hold her again. Never again!

With a scream, she punched him, but he blocked with his forearm, casually knocking her blow aside. She'd already let fly with another punch, which he blocked likewise. She kicked at his head and then spun around and struck out with her foot toward his hip. Nothing damaged his calm demeanor—he ducked the high blows and blocked the lower ones, moving with impossible speed. He didn't even bother to stand. Anger and frustration fueled her, and she had plenty of both. Tall as she was, lower strikes were harder, more awkward for her, and him sitting not only made things difficult, it stabbed at her tattered ego. She longed to release her fire, but she was too dehydrated. Her flames wouldn't flow. She struck at him faster and harder, but still each blow was blocked and still the figure remained serene.

Takiyah retreated, but she couldn't go even a pace before her back hit the wall. The figure did not follow, allowing her the minimal space. Eying her captor, she tried to focus on deep, calming breaths. She would escape. She would. She would not give in—not to frustration, not to despair, not to this stranger.

The figure watched her, motionless.

She looked around the cave. How had they gotten here? Slowly, she sat back down on the pallet she'd awoken on, among the blankets scattered by her attacks. "You're real. You're not a hallucination."

The Kamalti laughed. "You have a pretty rough mind to think you dreamed up an ugly face like mine."

Takiyah stared at him, every nerve on alert. What did he want with her?

The Kamalti moved his hand forward a bit, holding a cup. She blinked. Had he been holding that the whole time? He had thwarted her attack while offering her a drink. She felt the blanket beneath where he held the cup. It was much less damp than she expected. The fact filled her with irritation and awe all at once.

The Kamalti laughed again. "Are you going to drink? You must be thirsty."

She sneered. She wanted nothing from anyone, least of all from a Kamalti. Grabbing the cup, she tossed it in his face, shouldering him aside as she scrambled for the entrance. Her body was sluggish though, and she missed the turn, slamming against the wall and crumpling to the floor at the entrance.

Footsteps behind her. She rolled over, her heart in her throat, breath rasping, too dry. Desperately she aimed her hands at him, flexing her wrists.

No flame—she knew there wouldn't be. She was defenseless.

"Really, we're doing this?" he asked. He seemed not to notice the liquid dripping down his shirt and face. Instead, he wandered over to a pot on a barrel, refilling that blasted cup again. Slowly, he drank. Mocking her.

"I will not be your captive, Kamalti," she spat.

He smirked. "I suppose I skipped over the introductions. I was never very good at etiquette. I am Pek."

Glaring at him, she climbed upward, though she could only manage to get to her knees. She slumped sideways, refusing to kneel before a Kamalti.

The man drained his cup, looking down at her. "And if I wanted a captive, would I take some weakling... whatever you are... who cannot even survive in the desert on your own?"

"I was doing just fine."

"You're half a day from dying."

"Don't make assumptions about me."

Pek shrugged. "It'd be foolish to do so, when I don't even know what you are. You're far too tall to be either Rinaryn or Kamalti. Wrong build, too." He turned around. "You can leave whenever you want. I am not sure what compelled me to save you in the first place. Some spirit, I suppose."

Grunting, she dragged herself to her wobbly feet, leaning against the wall. Her head pounded and her vision swam, but anything was better than being around a Kamalti. He would only wait for a moment to betray her, to hurt her. She turned, her knees buckling, but made it a step toward the desert.

"Or you could stay," Pek suggested.

Takiyah paused, holding herself up against the walls, gathering the strength for the next step. "And exactly why would I want to stay with an ugly old man?"

He laughed at her again, heedless of the anger in her glare. "You could stay, if you want to learn how to survive in the desert."

That would be useful.

But Kamalti were false.

And yet, the tugging on her song continued. She had to follow it, or the not knowing would drive her as mind-sick as Kaemada. But continuing on as she was would kill her. Pek was right about that, at least.

Her legs gave out under her, and she slumped to the ground, staring at him.

"What would you get out of this deal? I will not believe it's simple beneficence. I am not some dreamy-eyed idealist." Kaemada would make friends with this man in a heartbeat.

"Of course you are not. What I get is help keeping up the place, someone to talk to, and help carrying supplies when I go to the city. But mostly, I get help guarding against bandits and the dragons."

"City?"

"Yes. When you are well and not weak as a newborn babe. It's not too far. I will take you there."

Takiyah scowled. "I don't need your help."

"Or you can go out there and die. I will not interfere again."

Her scowl deepened, but Pek was unaffected. "You do not even know me."

"And you do not know me. Now, shall I get you a drink, or are you going to waste this one, too?"

There wasn't really a choice, and it grated on her. But she didn't want to die. So she dragged herself back to the pallet and drank the water he gave her, and she tried not to think about how indebted she was to him. Once again, a Kamalti held power over her life and death, and it tasted bitter in her mouth.

Pek sat on his chair again, his cup refilled, sipping calmly from it, a model of serenity. Another conceit of the Kamalti.

"All right, Pek, who are you?" she demanded. "Do you make it a habit of rescuing people from the desert?"

He laughed, and she clenched her fists. How dare he laugh at her!

"Oh, if I did that, I'd be terribly bored. No one comes through the desert, except bandits. Which makes you very interesting."

Her shoulders hunched, and she drew back from him. She didn't want to be interesting. She swallowed hard.

He smiled and sipped his drink. "For a long while, I was the lead sparring trainer of the City of Tamarik. Now, I am retired."

She snorted. The Kamalti had a concept of "retirement", where they sat around and got fat. It was typically a pampered time, not spent in desert caves. "Some retirement."

"Indeed. So, what are you, young wanderer who is neither Rinaryn nor Kamalti?"

Straightening her shoulders, she held out her cup. "Thirsty."

He laughed, taking her cup and walking to the crates in the corner. She'd fought him, and he wasn't so much as limping. She'd been thoroughly beaten, and somehow, even knowing how dehydrated she was didn't spare her ego. Despite his boasting, even Taunos wasn't that good. Galod only ever cheated.

Pek looked over his shoulder at her with a grin. "Do you like honey in your tea? Or do you prefer it bitter?"

"Honey. How'd you beat me so easily?"

He laughed. "Here's your tea. It wasn't hard, with you so out of it."

Takiyah ground her teeth in frustration.

"That," Pek clucked, "is very unladylike."

With a groan, she took the tea and sipped it quietly. What a mess she'd gotten herself in. Again.

All that day, Takiyah gathered her strength, while Pek puttered about the cave doing simple chores and constantly refilling her cup. He tried to engage her now and again, but she embraced silence as both shield and weapon, her shoulders tense and ready for the trap to spring. This was how Kamalti tricked people. They pretended to be normal.

Pek finished his tea, washed the dishes, and hummed horribly off-key to himself as he re-wrapped a knife hilt with oiled leather straps before sharpening the blade on a whetstone.

And then he left.

Takiyah waited, hardly daring to breathe. Her heart pounded in her ears. It was just like Hardy and Mettle had given her—little tests, little "lapses" in their vigilance, so they could pounce on her and punish her. She winced, remembering the agony when they'd broken her leg. Her head ached and her stomach turned, but she would not give in to the panic. She unfolded her legs and tested their strength, stumbling toward the entrance.

She was still unsteady, but she really had to pee.

Her bladder decided her. She wobbled to the curtained-off corner of the cave and pulled back the fabric. A hole in the floor greeted her, and she quickly used it then stumbled back into the main room. Her staff leaned against the wall, and she grabbed it, using it to steady herself as she stumbled over the uneven floor. She made it to the tunnel and traced her way along the wall cautiously. Every step she took, she waited for the trap to spring. Every breath, she was certain a Kamalti face would loom, gleefully informing her of her error. Her fingers gripped her staff till they ached.

The wind hit her like a wall. A hot, dry, dusty wall. She coughed and recoiled, back into the shelter of the tunnel. Where was Pek? Where was the trap? Surely, she wasn't free. Kamalti always lied.

The sun had shifted far to the west, and she poked her head out of the cave. There was no sign of the Kamalti.

Seizing her chance, Takiyah raced out of the tunnel, gritting her teeth as the wind caught her again, pulling at her hair, her clothes, holding her back. No one would hold her back anymore. She was free. She lurched her way to the top of the nearest hill, though her balance was off and she fell several times. Her leg ached, throbbing and fatigued, but she pushed on. All around her, as far as she could see, stretched the desert, with scrubby plants clinging to the dry, cracked dirt.

She picked a direction at random and walked, wishing she'd had time to look for a water pouch. She'd been convinced he could come back— would come back—at any time though. Trying to follow the shade severely limited her path, confining her to the mountains and the enormous boulders that littered the ground. Meanwhile, the ground grew watery before her eyes, and her legs gave out.

A long-suffering sigh sounded above her head. "I suppose you learn things the hard way, do you?"

Takiyah glared up at Pek. A full water pouch landed by her hand, and she snatched it, barely remembering to drink slowly.

"Don't tell anyone I'm doing this," Pek said. "After all, I said I wouldn't save you again."

"There's no one else to tell."

"Then don't tell yourself."

Suspicion filling her, she hunched over the water pouch.

But Pek merely turned and walked away, calling back over his shoulder, "I'm going to cook dinner. There's plenty for you, too, if you decide to join me. I'll leave a fire outside to light your way. If you insist on leaving, there's a stream if you keep going. But you'll have to find somewhere to hide from Angels."

Slack-jawed, Takiyah watched as Pek walked away. No trap. No punishment.

Unless it was coming. She twisted, looking around her quickly. The sun was setting. And if Pek was trying to trick her, why warn her of the Angels? What was his game? The warning was foolish anyway—the Angels were going to the City of the Lost now. They weren't hunting normally anymore.

She snorted. He was probably just trying to scare her to come back with him, to ingratiate himself to her. But she had water now, and she wasn't going back. She turned, walking away from him, water pouch clutched in her hand like the precious thing it was. It didn't take her long to find the stream, and she soaked in the cool water a long while, refilling her water pouch. Dusk was settling over the land, and it would be a good idea to find some shelter for the night. She stumbled over the uneven ground, searching for a cave or any sort of shelter just in case, but her feet kept tripping over rocks and at one point she lost her footing and slid down a hill, bringing a tiny landslide with her and nearly losing her staff. She tried to light fire to see, but she still had no fire. She needed to recover further before she could make fire, apparently, and the loss hit her harder than it should have. She'd always had her fire before. Always had options.

Now, she was lost in the dark with no flame to light her way.

The haunting song of the Angels filled the land, ringing off the hills around her. Takiyah froze. Most of her time in the desert, she hadn't had to worry about Angels, for they had always gone to the City of the Lost. Unless they were too far from the city now. Cursing her foolishness, she searched in earnest for a hiding place, but her breath kept catching in her dry throat, and drinking to clear it was turning her stomach. Too much liquid too fast.

A sour taste filled her mouth, and she swallowed hard, but it wasn't enough. She vomited on the rocks. When she was done, she wiped her mouth with the back of her hand, wrinkling her nose at the mess. All that fluid wasted.

And the Angels' song was getting closer.

Had Pek been serious? She struggled to the top of a hill. There, only a few hills over, a fire blazed merrily. The water pouch at her side accused her, its dampness soaking into her pants. Takiyah craned her neck, scanning the skies for danger. Large wings, coming closer. She squeezed her eyes shut, trembling. She'd been terribly stupid.

Fixing her eyes on the fire, she ran. She ran from the dark, from her fears, from the Angel flying toward her and the song she couldn't blot out but for her heart beating in her ears. She ran, expecting at any moment to be caught, to be torn limb from limb. She ran, wishing she'd taken Pek's offer.

Wingbeats thundered behind her.

The fire filled her gaze. Pek came out of the cave's entrance, holding a polished metal surface before him as he turned to face the entrance, his back to the desert—and her. Keeping his eyes on the metal, he pointed a crossbow over his shoulder. Takiyah dove to the ground with a yelp, her staff clattering away from her, and Pek fired.

The Angel screamed, the sound filled with rage and far too close.

Takiyah scrambled back to her feet, snatched her staff, and dove past Pek into the tunnel entrance. She rebounded off the tunnel walls and careened into the cave, tripping and falling on her rump.

Pek wandered back in, crossbow pointed at the ground, gazing at his reflection in the metal. "I always wondered if that would work."

For several moments, Takiyah could only gape at him. "*I* always wondered if that would work! No one would let me try it out though, always saying it was too risky."

Pek grinned at her. "Tell you what. Next Angel that comes around, you get the metal."

"And the crossbow."

"Only if you don't shoot me."

How was it that she was actually talking as if she would remain with Pek for any length of time? She shrugged past that thought, allowing curiosity to tow her on. "Did you hit it? Where at?"

"I think I hit its arm, but it seemed to glance off it. Very odd. I think I more angered it than hurt it."

"But it did not come in here! It did not attack!"

"It's always good to be prepared. They don't expect people to shoot at them." Pek put the weapon away and then placed the metal on the ground. He picked up a plate near the fire, on which was a roasted fish stuffed with greens. "Hungry?"

Paranoia stabbed through her curiosity, dissipating it like sunlight burning away fog, and she was sad to see it go. "How did you know I would return?"

Another grin stretched the old man's face. "As I said, it's good to be prepared. Are you going to eat or try to stab me with your eyes?"

A laugh broke out of her, and she smothered it, pressing her lips tightly together. Accepting the plate, she paused, looking toward the pallets where she'd awakened and then back to Pek. Gingerly, she sank to the ground across the fire from him.

He raised his browridge at her. "Daring."

With her eyes fixed on her plate, busy shoving the food in her mouth, she didn't have to answer. It hit a little too close to truth. In some ways, Pek reminded her of Galod, always pushing her to be better but letting her make her own mistakes. He'd always point those mistakes out to her, but he also pointed a way forward. Maybe it was a requirement of being a hermit.

"Wading into the thick of battle and waiting for your friends to save you only works if you don't leave them behind. If they're not with you, don't step forward unless you want a knife in your back."

She swallowed the last of the fish and drank the cup of tea Pek had poured for her, ignoring the memory of Galod's voice. She had no friends watching her back now. Just her.

And yet, Galod would shout at her for this mistake, too, or more likely run her to exhaustion. Judging Pek purely by his appearance, rather than by his actions. How could she love Galod and hate Pek, especially when he'd given her no cause to do so?

Takiyah forced herself to meet Pek's eyes. "Thank you."

"Oh good, the stabby eyes are gone. Is all you needed a meal?" Pek filled her cup yet again and took the plate, turning his back to her as he washed it in a bin.

No. She needed a great deal more than that. "I need to learn how to survive in the desert, at least until I can get to this city you spoke of. Would you teach me?"

~

Takiyah grunted as she climbed to the top of a small rise in the sand. She trudged forward, struggling against the wind and sand, one laborious step at a time. Her leg carried her weight better, though Pek suspected it'd still be a while before it fully healed.

"Come on, you're still too slow!" shouted Pek.

She shot him a glare, wiping her face with the cloth that draped her shoulders, but picked up her pace. Unease bit at her with how she rose to each of his challenges so readily. He was too easy to like. She had to remember to keep herself apart, or he'd let her down. Sweat tickled her neck, and she scrubbed the back of her head. The short hair was still something to get used to. It was a lot easier to take care of though, and since her parents would never see her like this, it didn't matter.

Takiyah had learned much from the old man in the near moon she'd stayed with him, but soon it would be time to move on. Pek was too charismatic, too kind, even if he chided her every chance he got. He was too like Galod.

Which was exactly why she needed a fresh start. No one to rely on, to entice her to let down her guard. She would be as aloof and self-sufficient as Galod always was. No Taunos to pester her relentlessly. No Ra'ael to passively follow whatever she thought the spirits wanted. No Kaemada, weak and shattered. They needed a new beginning, or at least Takiyah did. She refused to dwell on the past. She simply couldn't manage another day with any of them without erupting in violence.

No, Takiyah had to do what she had to do. She couldn't let herself continue to lean on Pek. Blind trust hadn't ended well for her friends. No friends behind her, so she had to be ready for the knife in her back.

There was no sign of movement on the sands. Takiyah raised her head a bit, catching Pek's eye, and nodded. He returned the gesture, and she cautiously rose and crossed to him. They were relatively safe for a little while, until they reached the edge of what they'd surveyed, and then it would be time to scan their surroundings again. Their paths intersected, and they joined up, walking in silence for some time.

"Look there." He pointed to a low ridge ahead of them. "Once we cross that ridge, we'll see it."

"See what?"

"The City of Tamarik."

"Where you were a sparring trainer."

"The same."

Once they reached the next small rise, he crouched on the lee side of a cluster of rocks, in the shade.

There before them was a beautiful sight—a masterpiece of stone and metal blended together. She could clearly see the joints where stone met stone, all smooth and even. The city below them had one main wall curving around except where it bordered the ocean, but from their vantage point, she could also see walls within the city, separating agricultural areas from the rest. It was unlike anything she'd ever seen.

The land surrounding it was barren and smooth with sand. No bodies outside these walls, no horrors.

Pek grimaced and pointed two fingers outward. She narrowed her eyes but obeyed, giving the area another inspection. He was always so bossy, so confident. It irked her that he was right. He was even right in his reprimand—she was supposed to be watching for bandits.

The walls drew her gaze though.

The City of the Lost was supposed to be the only city in Rinara, but here was another city, hidden away in the desert. The Rinaryn people had much to learn. The walls before her were clearly not a mirage.

The wind whipped past, stealing the moisture from her cracked lips, while the sand clutched at her boots, unwilling to give her passage. It wanted to control her movements, just like Taunos, just like the Kamalti, just like the Elders.

Just like everyone else, it would find she was not one to be controlled.

The wind drove past her, snatching her breath from her mouth in fierce gusts. She hurried to reconnect her face cloth so she could breathe, and she leaned into the wind. She'd come so far. She would not be beaten by weather. How was it possible for it to be so windy?

A roar behind them made her jump, twisting in the air to look. A young dragon was bearing down on them, bellowing his rage. His wings were half folded as he dove, his scales gleaming in the harsh sun.

Pek leaped one way, and Takiyah leaped the other, rolling as she dove to come up on her feet with her staff at the ready. It was useless against the giant lizard—his entire head wasn't much smaller than her full height, she estimated, and he was well armored with his scales. Still, she set the flames to dancing along the metal as her heart pounded in her chest.

The old man pointed to the city. "Come on, the dragons can't get us in Tamarik!"

"You said the saying could be translated either 'by' or 'from'!" she shouted back at Pek as the dragon dove past. "It's a big difference!"

"What?"

"Protected by dragons versus protected from dragons! Big difference!"

The dragon curved upward, his massive wings straining. The wind from his wingbeats swirled sand everywhere, and she squinted against the gale he created.

"Foolish girl—Tamarik is safe from dragons. I'll argue with you about it there. Run!" Pek shouted.

She ran, arms pumping as she struggled to push off against the yielding, shifting sand. Her leg twinged where it had been broken, protesting the sudden demands. It only ever hurt under extreme conditions now. The dragon's tail led them until he turned sharply toward Pek.

She bolted for the city as the dragon dove for them again, this time from the side, so that Pek and Takiyah were in a line.

A yelp escaped her as a great gout of flame emerged from the dragon's mouth, raining down on them. She lost her footing and fell, tumbling down the slope of the ridge and thereby avoiding the dragon's fire. Takiyah leaped up as he passed overhead again. There was Pek, singed but seeming mostly unharmed. He waved her on ahead of him, and she ran as the dragon banked.

The doors of the gate were closed. Even through her exhaustion and fear, she was struck by the sight: tall, solid pieces of worked metal embossed with an image of a Kamalti on one door and a Rinaryn on the other, their hands reaching for one another. Above them, smiling down, was a strange lizard-like face. Her stomach turned. Kaemada would love this—Kamalti and Rinaryn, together. She'd be insufferably smug.

Pek passed her as she slowed, and she cast a glance behind her at the dragon angling for a third pass at them. She raced after Pek.

A guard frowned down at them from a gap in the wall above the gates —Rinaryn, by his looks, wearing strange clothing. "What are you doing outside the gates? Hurry!"

The guard disappeared into a little tower at the side. A moment later, there was a clanking and a creaking, and the gates slowly opened, just enough for them to pass. Takiyah and Pek quickly slipped through. Peeking upwards into the gatehouse, she spied the guard working a large crank. Her eyes followed the crank to a series of gears and eventually to the gate, and she smiled, marveling at the workmanship and the ingenuity. Why waste two men opening and closing gates when you only needed one? And sitting in the middle of nowhere, how often did this city need to use the gates anyway?

The dragon bore down on them. The walls were no match for a dragon —it would simply raze the whole place from above! It had no dome like the City of the Lost did—not that she could see, anyway.

Just inside the gates, Pek turned and pointed at the dragon. Fists clenched against her fear, Takiyah turned and watched as well. The gates began to close, but Pek glared at the young man operating them. "Keep them cracked! Let her see!"

"Oh! Uh... y-yes, Master Pek." The younger guard turned red-faced as he stammered.

Takiyah raised an eyebrow at Pek, but he only pointed up at the dragon, and she dutifully watched, sucking air in through her face cloth. The dragon dove at them, and Pek chuckled. "Sometimes the young ones like to test it."

Takiyah didn't bother asking what "it" was—she'd get no useful answer from the old man. He'd only pretend senility or something. Instead, she watched in horror as the dragon came closer, breathing fire that scorched the sand in a line straight for the city gates. And then, once the fire got within a pace of them, both flame and dragon abruptly wheeled upward, almost as if something had grabbed its neck with a rope and yanked. Takiyah reeled back from the wave of heat that followed the remnants of the dragon's fire, but awe filled her as the flaming goop curved back and down, hitting the sand well away from the city. No dome here, and yet somehow the city was protected from dragons and their fire. The dragon winged slowly back toward the mountains. She could almost swear the overgrown lizard was sulking.

"The dragons have been upset of late—I'm not sure what's been rankling them, but we'll be safe here." Pek grinned.

The guard descended the stairs, dusting off his hands. He considered her with a vague frown. "Who are you? You are not from the city—not the way you're gaping."

Takiyah frowned, stiffening. Here it would come, the questions, the interrogations, the prying into her life. "Does it matter?"

The guard shrugged and crossed his arms, assuming a lecturing tone and a stern expression. "Not as long as you follow our laws. We care nothing for what happened to you before coming here so long as you are a law-abiding citizen from here on out."

"Welcome to the City of Tamarik," Pek said.

"Pek, would you look at this, please?" the guard asked, waving him inside the guardhouse.

"I'll be just a moment," Pek told her.

As if she needed to wait for him. She shouldn't even be tempted to. Takiyah scowled. The call tugged at her. Toward the sea, toward the sea. Now was the time to separate. "You did not think I'd stay with you forever, did you? I have thanked you for your help. Now we're done."

Pek paused in the doorway of the guardhouse. "Ah, well, then—"

No. No talking. No chains made of words.

Takiyah shouldered her way past him. If she waited, she might never strike out on her own. She shoved the seed of regret and the tightness in her stomach at the look on Pek's face way down deep inside of her, smothering it with a focus on the tugging of her song toward the sea and her purpose. Now she would begin a new story on her own, free of all attachments. Including sparring trainers with sharp wits.

Following the tug on her song, she wound her way through the city, ignoring all but the vaguest impressions of straight streets, hot sun, and canopied buildings. East, always east, the call came, and she was finally free to answer. Takiyah stopped when the sea opened up before her, glittering blue as waves tossed only a few paces below her. She stood on top of a wall, with a ramp switching back and forth down the wall until it submerged beneath the waves. The design, so accommodating for the variable tides, impressed her.

East, east, east, the call continued. She needed a boat so she could sail onward, past the horizon, to find out why whatever was within her drove her so.

Her boots clattered on the ramp as she ran, slipping on a patch of algae and nearly going down. Galod's training and having her staff helped her keep her feet, but the men tying up boats snickered. Face hot, Takiyah kept her focus, dismissing the first few until she found someone who appeared mostly Rinaryn.

"I need a boat," she said.

"We don't sell boats," he said, waving her away.

"Let me work on one them. Please, I need to sail."

"After your slip on the ramps?" He grinned, though the expression faded as she glowered at him. "All right, what experience do you have?"

"None, but I'm a fast learner." A large wave splashed against the rock, spraying them both with seawater before the water retreated.

"None? You want to go out now, and you have no experience?"

"Surely at one time you had no experience either."

"Wait till the sisters separate above," he said, pointing at the sky. "No one learns while the waves are so wild."

"Please, I need—"

A man nearly her height stepped between them, folding his arms. His browridge and knobby head indicated he was Kamalti, but his skin wasn't translucent, a light brown instead. "The man said no."

"I—"

"Will be leaving now and coming back later, as he suggested," he said. More men lined the docks, arms crossed, a wall of obstinance that she would break herself against.

Takiyah gritted her teeth, hands fidgeting at her sides. She nodded once. She'd waited this long; she could wait a little longer. Turning her back, she headed back to the top of the wall and the rest of the city. There was plenty to learn and explore here. She could make this city-that-shouldn't-be her temporary home in the meantime.

Chapter Five

We cannot reach the Tsaeyichape'itsan directly. To win control of our fates, we must move him by moving his surroundings. Any attempt to intervene directly is likely to backfire. Involve yourselves only as a last resort. Instead, secure each protector, before they become even more troublesome. There are too many pieces in play to allow a child's tantrum to topple over the careful aligning of chance.
—part of a missive from "Nitil" in Dragonmoor

The summer sun was warm, with just a hint of breeze to cool their shoulders as Taunos headed with the Resistance back toward camp. They were quiet, but while most of the people seemed tired, Olorah kept giving him scathing looks. Reinan's cousin was one of the leaders of the Resistance—the one Taunos worked with on missions to rescue more people from the city. She was capable, even if she was also single-minded and aloof. The people trailing them, encircled by other members of the team, were the latest batch of refugees.

Almost the moment the team entered the forest, Olorah spun around on him. "You are not going on any more missions."

Taunos blinked at the vehemence in her words.

She continued, her tone still as sharp, though her eyes scanned the trees instead of piercing him. "You cannot seem for managing staying on task, and no one can predict your actions. You are terrible at working as a team."

For a moment, Taunos was transported back to training with Galod. Olorah was perhaps the one person who could compete with Galod in lecturing abilities. Still, to be scolded for doing exactly what he was supposed to do, rescuing a family from the prison of the City of the Lost? That was foolish. He couldn't protect Eian anymore, having no idea where the Elders sent him, what family they placed him with, and he couldn't save his sister from the battle raging within her mind. Saving those he could lessened the sting of powerlessness.

He leaned in, his voice low and fierce. That family had suffered enough. They didn't need to hear this as well. "I saved those people. They were not in the plan because we had no way to know they would be in trouble. What did you want me to do, just leave them?"

Olorah glanced past his shoulder and gestured. Shoulders tense, Taunos turned so he could see her and the rest of the Resistance, but the team just trailed silently past the two of them, heading into the trees. They always angled away from the Resistance camp—Camp Freedom—when they came from the City of the Lost, just in case they were being followed. They wouldn't head toward the camp until they'd reached the rendezvous point first.

One little boy smiled and offered a tiny wave as he passed by, and Taunos returned the gesture. The child was even younger than Eian. And now, he was free.

When Taunos had turned a corner in the city to follow Olorah's instructions to the check in, he'd encountered the boy, racing through the streets, guards on his footsteps. The boy had darted into a house, so of course the guards had knocked the door down, and the screams rang out before Taunos even got there.

No one helped each other in the City of the Lost. It was too dangerous, and aid could single a person out for abuse from the guards. While the power had changed in the City of the Lost with Theron's take over, the rules had not. No one was allowed to leave the city. The people were prisoners—a workforce to sow fields and harvest crops, both inside the walls and outside, now that there was that hole in the wall. And the guards loved to unleash their tempers on the prisoners.

"Resistance-friendly families first," Olorah hissed once they were alone, facing him again. She only came up to his shoulder, but her eyes were sharp, her whole bearing fierce. "We don't need for risking the whole movement by bringing someone in when they might turn around and report for the king."

"Theron's not a real king. He's just another bully, and we should bring him down."

"That is not something we can do right now. And I can't always be watching for making sure you don't head off on your own assassination attempt. You don't follow the plan, Taunos. It's too dangerous for having you along anymore."

As if their conversation was done, Olorah turned and walked away. Taunos shook his head. Olorah had been a captive in the palace along with Kaemada and Eian. Kaemada had risked her life to get them out, and she had succeeded, even though she nearly died herself. Rinaryn people protected their children—it was the hope that Taunos clung to that Eian was safe and well while he tried to look after Kaemada.

"Kaemada did not worry about the mission when she saved your life and the lives of your children. She saw you were in need, and she did something about it."

Olorah stopped, her expression flat. "That's another thing. She can't stay in camp."

"What?" The word exploded from him. After all she'd risked to save them, after all he'd done to help them, and they were being banished—again?

"The psions will leave if she doesn't."

Unease crawled on his skin like spirits'-teeth, and his objection came sharp with defensiveness. "Kaemada has done nothing to the psions to earn their dislike."

In fact, although she had improved some, she hardly did anything at all unless directed to do simple tasks.

"It's those fits of hers. She needs for being mentally quieter."

"They're a lot less severe than they were. She's able to remember who she is for a little bit each day now, and she's been speaking once or twice every day." The farther from the mountains they were, the better Kaemada's condition became.

Olorah's eyes were hard and unyielding. "I gather it's like trying for conversing while a hundred people scream in their ears. At least, for the telepaths, anyway. The telekinetics don't care."

"It's not her fault. Reinan believes those fits are her battling the Kamalti psions. The distance may have helped but not enough." Unless her mind was damaged permanently. Taunos refused to speak of that possibility.

"From what the psions tell me, Reinan could be right. But they also tell me that either she goes or they go, and we can't lose them."

"If she goes, I go too."

"I'm aware."

Taunos shot her a glare, but she seemed unaffected. "Have they thought about helping her fight them off?"

"It's not their fight."

"Not their fight? It's because of Kaemada that they're free at all!"

"And because of her that so many died, unconscious and vulnerable, or were eaten by the Angels."

"The guards are at fault for killing them."

"Then the psions are free because they took the chance and found each other and broke through the wall. You can't have it both ways, Taunos."

His teeth ground at the injustice of it all. Never mind that he'd taught the Resistance to hunt, to fish, to gather the forests' bounty—even to shape their homes! One by one, everyone seemed to be turning their backs on them. And now, the Resistance, the next best thing to a kaetal he had left to offer his sister, had decided it was done with them too. The fabric of Rinaryn society was woven together by the connections the women had to one another. The Elders had snipped them out of that fabric, and Ra'ael and Takiyah had shredded what was left even further. And now the next scrap he'd managed to clutch was shrugging them off as if they were no more than parasites.

His shoulders slumped. "How long before we must leave?"

Finally, her expression softened, touched with sympathy. "You have some time. I'm not asking you for leaving immediately. I just thought you should be aware so you have time for making a plan or finding another path. In a choice between all our psions or one mind-sick one, I have no choice. I'm not heartless, you know."

"I never said you were."

Olorah shook her head again. "We're trying to figure out our new society, our place in it, how we all live together, those who were oppressed and those who appeared for supporting the oppression, though they did so fearing of their lives. We have much for learning."

Taunos pressed his lips together, wondering where she was going with this line of thought.

"If you go prepare a place for helping her, we won't put her out on her own while you're gone, Taunos. She's soft in the head, even more vulnerable than we were. She risked her life and didn't betray me or Masa, whatever else she did. While you're gone doing what you need for doing, trying for finding other options, I'm sure we'll have other matters for keeping our attention."

It was a small thing. Too small, really. He was tired of being taken for granted, tired of people pushing them around and banishing them when they became an inconvenience. This was not the attitude of a kaetal. This was not the people he'd grown up believing in or worked all his life to help.

"My thanks." The words tasted like mud in his mouth.

Olorah inclined her head, and continued on.

Taunos shook his head. The Resistance psions were battle-trained, unequipped or unwilling to help with Kaemada's troubles. There were only two options: the elves, who would require his sister to stay with them the rest of her life, or a psion who would help her. A Rinaryn. And since they were Fallen, every Rinaryn was supposed to stone them on sight.

He trailed after Olorah, paying only the least attention to his surroundings until they got back to the camp. If only Takiyah and Ra'ael had stayed with them! If he was going to leave his sister to find help for her, he'd have to leave her with Masa. Reinan's sister already watched Kaemada whenever he went on Resistance missions—which wouldn't be any longer, apparently. Still, he missed Ra'ael's capable leadership and Takiyah's quiet strength.

All this mess because the Elders wouldn't see reason. And now neither would the Resistance.

Once they got to Camp Freedom, he headed directly for their home at the edge of camp, close to the trees. The sun was nearly down, and he needed to check on his sister. The Resistance leaders had picked a good location for the camp. Outside of the range of the Angels, it bordered a quick flowing stream, and beyond the stream stood dense woods. He took Kaemada for walks in the forest to aid in her recovery whenever he could. And there she was in front of their hut, poking at the dirt by the fire listlessly with a stick.

"Hey little sister," he said, dropping down to sit next to her. She raised her eyes to almost meet his, and he thought perhaps he saw a twitch at the corners of her mouth.

Masa came out of the hut, her baby on her hip, and smiled at him. "She's quiet today, Taunos. Did everything go well?"

Taunos nodded, keeping the bad news to himself. Kaemada didn't need to hear it. "Thank you, Masa."

The baby began to howl, clutching at her shirt, and Masa bounced lightly, calming the cries. "Truth be said, she's easier for watching than the little one and less demanding too."

"My son. Where's my son?" The words were a barely audible murmur from Kaemada, but they broke his heart.

Taunos forced a grin at Masa as she left them, walking past the glow of several campfires. Each family unit had their own fire in front of their hut, creating something of a sea of stars at night. He turned that false cheer on his sister as she fumbled, picking up a new stick.

"Good day, cha'atanahn?"

When she remained silent, he told her about his own, stretching sore, fatigued muscles and trying unsuccessfully to illicit a smile from her. She kept her gaze on the fire, occasionally poking at it so it flared brighter. It was an improvement. He had to remember that. Everyone else might give up on her, but he would not. Staring at the stars overhead, he continued talking, filling the silence between them with the sound of his voice.

Something caught his attention—he wasn't sure what. His sister held the poker stick still, very near the fire, and it had lit. Flames had climbed the stick and were now licking at her hand, while she watched impassively.

"Kaemada!" He knocked the stick away with a telekinetic blow. She blinked as he dragged her farther from the fire and inspected her red and angry fingers. Tears shimmered in her eyes.

"Taunos, are you all right?" someone called from the next fire over.

"She burned herself," he called back. "Cha'atanahn, what were you thinking?"

"Dangerous." The tears spilled down her cheeks.

"Stay there." He dove into the hut, digging through his supplies for soothing salve. He returned quickly, fearing she might have done something else to harm herself, but she was sitting where he'd left her. Gently, he spread the salve on her hand to cool the burn and lessen the pain. "You did that on purpose, little sister. Why?"

"I'm dangerous."

"You're not. You're my sister."

Her eyes darted to his then, held him so that he couldn't move, the salve forgotten in his hand. "I do not have much time, brother. The Council, it's broken. Us being Fallen, it's wrong."

"I know that!"

"There's something wrong with the Council."

"What does that have to do with you hurting yourself?" he demanded.

"Eian. Where's Eian?" Her gaze slid away from his, the intensity fading. "Too tired. Cannot fight them any longer. Save you from danger."

He laid a gentle hand on her shoulder, just as the fit began.

The fit lasted a long, long time, and all throughout it, Taunos was uncomfortably aware of the other telepaths in the camp. Yet what could he do? What could his sister do? She'd as much as admitted to being under attack. Asking the telepaths to help her didn't seem to do much good, and it was all he could do to keep her from hurting herself or anyone else as she raged and fought and screamed. Only for the briefest moments did she sound like herself, and he wondered if those times were getting more fleeting or if that was his worry altering his perception.

If he lost her, he'd have nothing left. No honor, no prestige. No family, no friends, no beloved. He'd sacrificed everything for his missions for the Elders. And now, all alone, he'd continue on. He didn't know what else to do.

He surrounded himself in memories of happier times, and of course Amanah came to mind. Her skill in winning the horse race, and the sweaty, horsey smell of her when he'd embraced her. The fluid way she moved, like a pillar of water through sand, during sparring or battles. The way she whispered his name. The suspicion in her eyes the first time he'd left to report to the Elders and then returned to her. How her eyes lit up with mirth. Her wit and inner strength and the generosity of her heart. The banner-dance she'd performed, how the colors had wreathed her. How they'd fought and the tears in her eyes as she'd pleaded with him to give her some reason to trust him.

He closed his eyes. Caught between the greed of the Elders for knowledge from other lands and the desires of his own heart, he'd put himself last. She'd sent him away, and he'd gone, rather than tell her of this land. He'd followed the precautions the Elders and Galod had charged him with, trained him in. He'd never expected they would throw him away and their access to further knowledge with him. Surely they were missing all those reports he had given them. But still, he had ended up here, while his sister had broken even more than he.

The sun rose, and exhausted, he remained holding Kaemada until finally she grew still again. He fell asleep before really being aware of it.

When he awoke, midday had passed, and he felt as lazy as a tserwora in the winter. He checked on his sister first, but she was awake, accepting water when he handed it to her. She seemed worse than normal today, more like she had been back in the city. She barely moved, and her eyes remained unfocused, staring blankly at nothing.

He rubbed more salve on her hand and then bandaged it, cold fear rising in him. This wasn't working. She was getting worse. She'd intentionally burned herself last night. He had to help her somehow. Even if it meant leaving her for a little while.

Unable to trust her alone, he guided her stumbling steps along with him through the camp. The weight of so many eyes felt oppressive now that he knew of the psions' demands, and he held his sister close. He'd worked for so long, given up so much, to keep her safe. Now was no different.

Once he saw Elisabei and Reinan, he waved them down. Reinan came over immediately, leading them to the edge of camp while Elisabei finished her conversation with one of the new families.

"Look serious," Reinan rumbled.

Taunos nodded. His arm tightened around Kaemada, crushing her to his chest as if that would help guard her mind. Reinan was the heart of the

Resistance, a man born in the City of the Lost. He was so tall and broad, Taunos suspected he'd been born a guard, but Reinan never spoke of his past. And then there was Elisabei, the very song of the Resistance, fierce but brave, who'd risked everything to help Kaemada when she'd needed it. He summoned up a smile for them both as she joined them.

"What's wrong?" Elisabei asked, her gaze darting between him and Kaemada, lingering on her bandaged fingers. Between the burns and the ribs he'd broken trying to revive her during their escape, all his efforts were clearly not enough to keep her safe.

"Olorah told me."

Elisabei nodded. "She said. I didn't think you'd take it well."

"It's not her fault. She cannot help it."

Reinan put a hand on his shoulder, and Taunos turned his gaze on him. The man rumbled, "We'll keep her safe, as long as you need to find her a cure."

Elisabei gestured to the bandages. "But you need to go searching. Because this isn't working."

"I need to be sure she's safe."

"She's not," Elisabei snapped. "She hasn't been safe this whole time, but you're too busy worrying about her body and not her mind."

"I'm trying—"

"I know. But you needed a push."

"This was all a ploy? The psions—"

"Oh, no, the psions came to us with their ultimatum. Olorah didn't make that up."

Taunos swallowed hard, staring at his sister, who gazed blankly into the forest. "She burned herself last night. On purpose."

Worry glimmered in Elisabei's eyes. "She needs help, Taunos. We'll keep her as safe as we can while you find it."

He nodded. "Thank you."

Taunos kissed the top of Kaemada's head, speaking into her wild hair. "Little sister, I have to go for a little while. I'm going to get help. I will be back as soon as I can, but I do not know how long it will take me. I will come back though. Please, do not hurt yourself anymore. I need to see you well when I return. Please, cha'atanahn." He let her go to search her gaze.

She didn't respond, not even a flicker of her eyes, but her fingers tightened on his just a fraction.

He kissed her fingers and then the top of her head again, clearing his throat.

Leaving her with Reinan and Elisabei, he threw his cloak over his shoulders, refilled his water pouch, and tucked strips of jerky into a small bag. And then he left to find the one hope Kaemada had for healing—a Rinaryn psion.

Chapter Six

Elvish healing is paired with elvish pay-tience. Only those in most dire need of healing go to the elves, who ask for only the recovery of expended resources. No honorable Rinaryn would accept help from the elves and then run. Oathbreakers you will know by sight:
Pierces and slashes, pierces and slashes.
White marks mixed with red rashes.
Oathbreakers far, oathbreakers near
Run as you wish; you're marked all your ~~years~~ days.
—fragment from the Monks of Annularei

Kaemada had lost track of time. Again. Time had been leaping along in moments of clarity replaced by waves of disorientation or the never-ending struggling. For a while, her moments of clarity had been more numerous, and longer, so far as she could tell. And then Taunos had left again. It'd only been a matter of time before his wanderlust took him, but still it left her heart raw and empty. He'd left, even knowing she needed him. Or had her need finally driven him away?

And yet, there was a brightness there, even through her pain. Taunos had never deserved this punishment. Neither had Ra'ael and Takiyah, but they at least had the sense to go make something of their lives. Taunos would never let her go, not truly. Not for good. She'd have to leave while he was gone, even though Taunos would be furious, would grieve for her. Guilt crushed her to hurt him so, and she gasped for breath. Perhaps then he would go build a life with his beloved, to be happy as he deserved. Then the Collective couldn't get to him, she hoped.

But go where? Where had she been intending to go?

Despair battered her, and she lost time again. She knew that people she vaguely recognized spoke to her. Occasionally, Olorah's voice or Elisabei's or Reinan's would filter through her consciousness. Usually, it was Masa, crooning to her child. Or crooning to Kaemada as if she were her child.

Grief crashed onto her shoulders, dragging her down, burying her. She missed her son as fervently as a drowning person longed for air. He was the song to her story, the branches reaching for the sky that she lifted up high. And now he was gone, and all she could hope was that he was well-cared for, happy, and loved. And most of all, safe, far from the destruction she caused.

Kaemada came back to herself, blinking. Her chest hurt, as if her ribs were broken. A bandage wound tightly around her chest. She picked at it and then stared at her hands, which were also bandaged and in pain. Where had these things come from? How long had it been since her thoughts were her own, since time spun on smoothly, instead of jumping and folding along?

Masa crouched by a fire, stirring something in a pot.

"Where's Taunos?"

The smile Masa turned on her was sympathetic. The smile someone turned on a child or someone completely mind-sick. Was she mind-sick?

Yes, she probably was. Still, it rankled.

"Did you forget again?" Masa was saying. "He went to find help for you, several days ago."

Oh yes. She knew that. She blinked, lucidity sharpening the edges of the world. The wool blanket over her shoulders weighed her down, and each individual fiber scratched against her skin, as if it could keep her here by feel alone. Her gaze slid to the mountains. She needed to get farther away, while she could. Get to the elves.

But she had to move quickly, before Taunos got back. She would set him free and then make sure her dangerous powers were not unleashed on an unsuspecting world ever again. The elves could heal her or at least help her keep others safe from herself.

A shout came from outside. Masa stood and looked at Kaemada then the fire. She pursed her lips. "Come on."

Kaemada remained still, pretending she hadn't heard.

But Masa dragged her to her feet. "I'm not leaving you alone to hurt yourself again."

Her heart squeezed, fluttering in her chest like the birds in cages in the City of the Lost. The world spun around her as Masa pulled her out to a growing crowd.

A man lay on the ground, Elisabei crouched beside him. He gasped with pain as she tended a deep slash in his leg, but still, he gave his report. "Theron's pushing out further. Hunting us down. Killing all psions, everyone who speaks against him."

Kaemada shivered, shrinking in on herself. The psions drew away from her, staring at her with the look people get when they aren't sure if your mind-sickness is contagious or not. The fear Theron sparked in her turned her stomach, and she turned to the side, heaving. Masa let her go, and she vomited into the bushes.

Masa had turned back to the man. The world wobbled with tears and nausea, but still, this was her chance. Kaemada stumbled away, farther into the brush. She shrank deep in on herself. She knew forests. Her feet glided to the places where she would leave no trace. The City of the Lost did not know forests.

It was now or never.

She turned and let the forest swallow her. The familiar peace of the trees, like the embrace of all the spirits beyond the rim of the sky, filled her, nearly drowning out her guilt. Nearly.

The elves. To get there, she first had to figure out where she was. No, before even that, she needed to move far enough from camp so that when they inevitably began looking for her, they would not find her. She pulled the shattered remnants of her mind in, tight and small, to huddle behind the shambles of her mental walls.

The forest felt dead without the extra senses from Tannevar. Tears blurred her vision and wet her cheeks as she went, but lucidity came back to her, little by little. She was wearing dirty clothes—she'd need to patch them, as well as wash them. She had no supplies, only the shawl Elisabei had given her, knotted around her shoulders—that was good. The Resistance needed all the supplies they could get. Especially with Theron hunting them. Another stab of guilt took her breath away, but she kept moving.

The mountains had been behind her. Given the abundance of cha'awoods and the lack of stars-of-evening beneath them, she must be near or within the region of Life Valley. Not far, then, from the elves. And that made sense, didn't it? The City of the Lost was in Mountainhold, and the Resistance would have fled north from there. They wouldn't have trusted going into the mountains surrounding them, blocking their way south, would they?

She hurried onward, even when her legs screamed with exhaustion and her breath came ragged. The occasional shouts of searchers rose and fell and eventually died, but she drove herself on. Good for them to stop looking for her. They had enough problems of their own. They needed to move on, and she needed to heal. The Resistance had already come so far, moving west and north to avoid the Angels, fording a small river to put its waters between them and their past. She wished them well.

Evening came, bringing its shadows and warnings that her time of lucidity was surely drawing to a close. She dreamed the pegasus Shareilon bumped her with his muzzle and longed to reach out to him. Was he all right? What had happened to him? But fear kept her from reaching out. The Collective would still be searching for her. No need to make their job easier for them. She dreamed Tannevar was running beside her, glancing at her with a lolling grin. She was not prey, to tremble in a warren, but a creature free from a trap running to heal her wounds and then turn and confront those who hunted her. In the meantime, she would protect her brother and her friends from herself, for the Elders had banished them on her account.

When she could no longer see, she felt her way through the forest, and when she stumbled on legs that were too weary to hold her, she crawled. The ground gave way beneath her, and a scream ripped from her throat as she fell, plummeting a short way into a cold river. Her ribs burned. The current whisked her away, and she fought her way afloat, though she lost track of which bank she'd come from. That was all right. More distance reduced the chances of being found, and the river flowed away from the mountains, away from the Collective and the Resistance. The water was icy, and her shawl dragged her deeper into the water.

Finally, she made it to the side and scrambled up the bank, shivering violently. She couldn't go any farther, not tonight. Her body burned. Her mind would soon, too, though she tucked herself small and quiet to delay the inevitable.

She peeled off her sodden clothing and wrung them out into the river with exhausted fingers. A fire was risky, maybe too risky, but shivering herself to death was as well, so she dug a hole. Sticks littered the ground in abundance, and she piled them in the bottom of the hole. It took her several tries to find a fire maker, for her hands were shaky and her nerves frayed, continually wondering how real this was. But she had to act as if it was. The rocks close by were not those which produced sparks. It was full dark and her movements were slow and clumsy by the time she managed to light a fire, and she tented her clothes around it to dry, huddling herself in the gap to soak up some of the heat.

The Collective hadn't found her yet, or perhaps she was beyond their reach? She hardly dared even think it and kept her mental self small and still. Every moment was another moment she could be taken, could injure herself. By the time her clothes were dry enough to put back on, she was as exhausted mentally from worrying as she was physically from her escape.

Curling up in the crook of a huge tree root, she shivered herself to sleep.

A weight landed on her, knocking the breath from her and blasting stars into her vision. She woke, blurry eyed and gasping, her chest aching, as a man scrambled off of her and away. He fell again a few paces on, into the river that she'd fallen in last night.

Crawling to the edge on limbs that were still weary and aching, Kaemada reached out a hand. "Grab hold!"

He looked up at her. Red and white marked the brown skin all over his face and arms. She gasped. And then the river swallowed him.

Shaking, she scrambled along the bank, but his efforts to get to the surface were weak. So was she.

But she couldn't let him die.

Kaemada dove in. Grabbing him by the hand, the first thing she could reach, she hauled him back toward the near shore. He clutched at her, panicking, his weight dragging her down. She struggled toward the bank, toward the surface. Her lungs burned for air.

Every time she neared the surface, the man dragged her away, thrashing. Finally, she punched him in the gut, broke away, and gasped, choking, sweet air. Coughing and sputtering, she grabbed the back of his shirt and hauled him to shore, too.

She lay there on the bank just trying to breathe for some time. Beside her, the panicked man lay still, teeth chattering and breath wheezing. His black hair was a wild tangle dripping down his back, but his clothes looked well cared for, aside from the rips in the fabric where red and white welts showed through.

Pierces and slashes, pierces and slashes. White marks mixed with red rashes.

"Oathbreaker," she whispered.

His eyes widened, and he heaved himself to his feet. "My name is Cheros."

"I'm sorry." Sorry for so many things. For her reaction. For the marks on his skin. Had she brought him back to the right bank?

"Me too. I tripped over you." He shivered, looking at his arms, and then raised his hands to his face. A shudder wracked him as he closed his eyes. "I had hoped I avoided them."

"Did they help you?" Kaemada asked, wringing out her clothes yet again.

"Help me? Help me! Well, those elves, they will help anyone, you know. Everyone knows that. But the question is, is the price worth it? That's where they get you!"

"Please," she started.

"Never say please. Listen. You will not get any special treatment. No matter who you are or what you have done or what you need, to them you are just another penitent. And they will get their summers from you, you mind my words. They will."

Kaemada shook her head. "What did they ask of you?"

Again he laughed, but it was anger instead of mirth that filled his voice. "Oh, I got a bargain. Twenty summers is all they want of me."

"Twenty summers! What did you ask of them?"

"They let me stay with them for several days and fed me and occasionally talked with me. But otherwise they left me alone. And for this, for days of their time—not even. Not even half a day really—they want twenty summers of me?"

Kaemada frowned.

He spat, grinding the spittle into the dirt with his boot. "That is what I think of the elves and their elvish pay-tience."

No one spoke of the elves with such vitriol. And everyone knew how to identify oathbreakers. Kaemada stammered. "But you have to pay the elves."

"Did you not hear a word I said? You cannot play by their rules and win. 'Beware elves and their gifts. They are never free.' You and I both should have listened to that. There is good reason 'deal with the elves' is never a positive phrase!"

"They're the *elves*!"

"Have you forgotten the story of Kalei and the elves? Kalei and the fae? If you ask me, the elves should have been the foe in those stories, not the fae."

"You cannot change a story handed down over generations because you do not want to pay the elves."

"Because the elves cheat," he corrected her. "Besides, why should we pay them? We do not pay each other."

"The stories lay it down clearly! The elves help us. They deserve our respect. The fae, on the other hand, only toy with us and steal our children."

He snorted. "You should not put so much stock in stories, young one."

"I am not a child," she snapped. "The stories all agree that they are reasonable and respectable—"

"And who made up those stories?" he interrupted.

She'd fallen for that before, with the Kamalti. And yet, the core of the stories had been true, if not the trappings. She scowled. "They have to have some truths to them. The stories carry truths we must know."

Cheros grumbled to himself, his shoulders slumping. His brow furrowed in a scowl. "Well? We're on the edge. Are you jumping?"

She swallowed hard and looked back across the river, to her past. She was really doing it, leaving it behind. It hardly felt real. But the elves would fix her, and here, she couldn't ruin anyone's lives. The danger would be contained. Taunos would have to give her up, to see reason as Ra'ael and Takiyah had. Staring into the distance, she wished them health and happiness, without her to wrinkle their stories further. And Eian, his story should be full of promise and filled with love, safe far from the wildfire consuming all nearby that she was. Her psionics were dangerous, and she had to keep the others safe from her.

Turning back to this side of the river in the sunlight, her breath was stolen away. The forest she loved so much was only a decaying shadow compared to this one. The trees grew tall and dense, vitality flowing through their bark, and every leaf—even of the ferns—glowed with vibrant life. Everything seemed impossibly healthy.

"We're in their territory now. Smell that?" Cheros asked.

She nodded. A smell like that of the air after a thunderstorm filled her nose, making it tingle.

"This is what the borders smell like," Cheros said. "No one can say they crossed unawares. Especially with the sentries—oh, Eloi's light, here they come!"

He ducked and huddled in a ball on the ground while a pair of butterflies fluttered past in a swirl of colors before rising into the fragrant air. A small flock of birds spiraled around them, too. She stared in awe at such a blessing.

"What's wrong?" she cried. All this beauty, and he didn't seem to even see it.

"And one more piece of advice," he said, turning to peer at her face to face. "Whatever you do, do not thank them."

Her brow furrowed. "Why?"

He rolled his eyes with a groan. "They want you to forever remember what they have done for you. They see 'thank you' as being a dismissal of the action, instead of holding it forever dear in gratitude."

It seemed very rude. "Ameyit—"

Cheros's hand pressed against her mouth. "Do not finish that word."

"What, are all gestures of politeness banned?" she asked, exasperated. Nothing like this was in the stories. Only that they could not lie but could mislead.

"Put away that look," he snapped. "Yes, I regard them with strong dislike, but I have my wits about me. I am not exaggerating. They like to keep us off balance, revering them."

So did the Kamalti, but that didn't work out well for them.

"Why are you helping me?" she asked. Because the mind-sick man did appear to be trying.

"I might as well. I cannot go home looking like this, now, can I? So I have to go back."

Her shoulders slumped and sympathy welled in her. "Am—" she paused, remembering his warning.

Shaking a finger at her, he laughed. "Good. Do not apologize to them. It puts you lower than them, in need of their favor. They will wring enough out of you without you helping them by asking their forgiveness. Asking forgiveness is asking for something, too, you know. It's accepting anything from them that's dangerous, including their forgiveness."

"Would you desire our forgiveness, oathbreaker?"

The voice was melodious, at the same time lightly teasing and accusatory, projecting but intimate. An elf stepped out from behind a tree a few paces away. His hair was long and sleek, the color of the prairie grasses in fall, his eyes mirthful yet wise, set in a somewhat narrow face that was utterly handsome. His smooth skin was various shades of brown, so that he blended right in among the tree trunks. A thick band of leather, stamped with various designs, encircled his head. Every movement was full of grace and beauty as he walked toward them, his robes shimmering as they moved lightly in the breeze as he glided forward. It was more like Kamalti cloth than Rinaryn, but still very different; even Kaemada could see that. She longed to run her fingertips across it but at the same time feared to tear such a wonder. He smiled at them.

Cheros sneered at him. "No better than the fae, you are."

The elf frowned, his beauty becoming horrible for a moment with the force of his wrath. But in the next breath, he composed himself, and the smile returned, though it was tight and no longer met his eyes.

Kaemada suppressed a shudder.

"I am Fearil. It pleases me to welcome you to our homeland. May I make your acquaintance?"

Kaemada watched him sharply, but his forest craft was so far beyond hers as to be invisible. Her balance in the world, everything she had held true, felt shaken. Unease grew in her. If asking something of an elf was so dangerous, why did they begin by giving something? Cheros folded his arms and fixed the elf with a belligerent expression, leaving Kaemada to fend for herself.

"I am Kaemada, and this is Cheros."

"It is good to know you, Kaemada. Cheros, it is good to know you have chosen to return."

"Do you know each other?" Kaemada asked Cheros, who shook his head.

Fearil smiled. "We have not met, but we know all oathbreakers, in hopes they will someday return to their oaths. Your days are short and your time limited. Not all of you are able to return."

"Are you threatening me?" Cheros's hands clenched into fists.

Fearil's smile remained. "Not at all. I was merely noting how quickly your lives flit by." He turned his gaze to Kaemada. "Now then. No elf will forcibly stop you should you wish to leave our lands. However, we tend many tender young plants of great value. For this reason, no visitor is allowed to venture out without a guide, to protect the plants from your ignorance."

She glanced between Cheros and Fearil, but her decision had already been made. She needed to disappear among the elves. Her summers of service to them, perhaps, would help her to atone for all she'd done wrong, too. If they could fix her, she could do all she needed while her body remained with the elves. Maybe the Elders would let Ra'ael, Takiyah, and Taunos return, if they were without her.

And yet, there was fear beneath the anger in Cheros's eyes, beneath the tension in his marked face, the warnings that stood out on his skin. She'd ignored such warnings in the City of the Lost, and among the Kamalti. She would go then, but carefully.

"Do not hurt him," she said to Fearil, biting back the words of politeness even as her heart turned and soured for her lack of courtesy.

"Come now, must we fear? The day is beautiful, and we are simply happy to have our oathbreaker back," the elf said.

Kaemada flushed, feeling rather like a scolded child.

The elf smiled again and gestured. "Will you honor me by following me to the First Stand?"

Cheros glowered at the elf. "We will follow you, but we mean no honor by it."

"Light illuminate you." Another smile curved Fearil's mouth around his honey voice.

Kaemada's nerves prickled as she followed the elf and the glowering Rinaryn, trying to capture all the details. Her weary feet stumbled and tripped several times. She was pretty sure she'd feel slow and clumsy next to an elf even if she hadn't been exhausted from her run here and both swims, even if her body was healthy and fit again instead of wasted from the ravages of the Collective's attacks. Fearil spoke of "Light" the way Rinaryn spoke of Eloí—or Eloí's light. Was that an innocent similarity or evidence of nefarious meddling? Another flock of small birds fluttered by and then a flock of butterflies, spiraling past before rising into the trees. They were so beautiful, but Cheros ducked and covered his head as they went by. A sense of wrong screamed at her, but she couldn't tell from what.

The land of the elves was even more magnificent than the stories spoke of. Flowers of every color and size bloomed, while the air hummed with flocks of birds and groups of butterflies. It was familiar, for they were still in Rinara, in Life Valley, but somehow everything seemed so much more real, more alive. The ground felt somehow more springy and more solid at the same time beneath her boots. It was as if all the summers she had lived, she had lived senseless—blind, deaf, and unable to feel the caress of the wind. It was like an incredibly disconcerting yet wonderful dream, and a fearful love rose in her.

Fear seized her in its talons. It was too much like the dreams the Collective had sent her. Was Cheros right? Was this all designed to create such a feeling in her? It wouldn't take much for them to get her to do almost anything because of the terrible glory she felt being in the elvish lands. Her heart pounded, and she couldn't catch her breath.

By the time they reached the First Stand, her knees were weak and wobbly. Her exhaustion seeped to her very bones. Sweat glistened on her brow, and her limbs felt thick and clumsy. And then her gaze lit on the First Stand, and she sagged helplessly to the ground. Cheros fell to his knees as well, gaping at the elvish home just as foolishly as she knew she looked, but she couldn't help it.

Before her was a clearing, if a clearing could be made of trees. The trunks had been sculpted to grow in ladder and stair shapes, and the tree branches bent gracefully, twining around each other to form house after house, all made entirely of living tree. Vines decorated some of the houses, while at others the branches around windows had somehow been coaxed to grow in a bowl shape, which the elves had filled with dirt so that flowers could grow from a living bowl beneath a living window. House after house grew, the leafy canopy letting the sun stream through in rods of light while hammocks within dappled patches of shadows danced, echoing the leaves dancing in the breeze. The fragrance of flowers and good, rich dirt, and the fullness of life filled her nostrils. The vitality of it all engulfed her and drained her at the same time, as she lost all sense of time and how long she had been sitting there gaping at the First Stand.

Two elves were coming to greet them with movements so graceful tears pricked her eyes and a lump rose in her throat. Both wore shimmering robes and leather circlets with drops of amber and various wooden trinkets attached by threads of various lengths, nestled among the locks of their hair.

Licking dry lips and feeling entirely too clumsy, Kaemada clambered to her feet, tugging her damp, dirty shawl further around her shoulders. Cheros, too, was staggering to his feet and stood there swaying vaguely, his eyes going back to the Stand from time to time. He was obviously trying to collect himself and breathed in raggedly. She blinked away tears and patted his shoulder awkwardly.

Cheros gave himself a great shake and leaned close to her, whispering, "That is how they get you."

She nodded, filled with the sympathy she had no words for, and patted his shoulder again. He covered her hand with his, and she drew in a deep breath, steeling herself to confront these elves.

Fearil gave the other elves a slight bow, hands clasped in front of his chest, and gestured to Cheros and Kaemada with one hand. "These ones are Kaemada and the oathbreaker, Cheros."

"Welcome, Kaemada," the woman said, stepping forward. "I am Ennwhyn. I will be your guide. May I show you the Stand?"

The other stepped forward at the same time, speaking to Cheros. "We welcome your return, oathbreaker. Are you in need of refreshment?"

Ennwhyn drew Kaemada away, though Kaemada kept turning to look at Cheros. He, too, was being led away, in a different direction than her. Fearil followed Ennwhyn and Kaemada, occasionally breaking her line of sight to Cheros, entirely by accident, it seemed. She was going to lose sight of him. Fear gripped her, that she was going to misstep again and cause suffering. How could she trust herself? It felt like a scab being torn too soon from her skin, and she would bleed her brokenness all over, yet again.

"Wait, stop. Stop!" she cried, resisting Ennwhyn's gentle pull on her arm. "What will happen to him?"

Ennwhyn smiled at her but spoke to Fearil. "They are so ruled by their passions, are they not?"

"Light shine on them, it can be quite lovable."

"I am right here!" Kaemada frowned. They hadn't answered her question.

Ennwhyn gave her another smile. "Yes, young one. Light lead you, I can see you."

Kaemada watched with her brow furrowed. She had a vague notion that she had been somehow insulted, but the words all sounded friendly and Ennwhyn's smile appeared nice enough.

She tried to gain control of herself and act like the adult she was instead of a foolish child. Of course, to these elves even the Elders were little more than children.

"Please," she said, making a painstaking effort to seem logical and reasonable. "We travelled here together. You call him oathbreaker. Will he be… punished? For breaking his oath? For running away?"

Ennwhyn laughed, and the sound was the most melodious, most beautiful sound Kaemada had ever heard. "Oh, Light guide you, child, what a notion!"

"That is hardly an answer." Kaemada gritted her teeth.

Ennwhyn laughed again. "You are quite right, quite right, my dear. To answer your very reasonable inquiry, no, he will not come to any harm at the hands of the elves."

Kaemada nodded, sighing with relief. Then her brow furrowed and she frowned. "At the hands of the elves… But will he be harmed by someone else?"

Ennwhyn and Fearil's musical laughter lit up the area. Kaemada tangled her fingers in her shawl, shifting uncomfortably for several long-stretched moments while their laughter subsided.

"May as well ask if lightning will strike that tree," Fearil said at last, pointing to a particularly large rowood formed into an elaborate dwelling.

"Or if the waters will rise to flood tomorrow," Ennwhyn agreed. She smiled broadly at Kaemada, but again directed her words to Fearil. "She is so very amusing."

Kaemada scowled.

"Come now, do not pout," Ennwhyn coaxed. "You have a funny way of saying your mind. But be at peace. We will neither intentionally harm him nor intentionally allow him to be harmed while he remains here. That is as much as I can say."

"Is it true you cannot lie?" Kaemada asked.

Her spirits sank as that question again sent Ennwhyn and Fearil into peals of laughter, and her cheeks burned like fire. She trailed along with them but very alone at the same time as Ennwhyn took her around the Stand. It seemed similar to a kaetal, except they obviously didn't move.

They walked past several houses for the ill and houses of rest for those whose ailment was spiritual or mental rather than physical. Then, through gardens of stone or flowers or shrubs, which Ennwhyn explained were meant to aid in meditation and healing, and to a pool named the Mirror of Tranquility, where she saw some Rinaryn sitting on the banks staring into the water, or dipping their toes along its edge. Orbs hung from trees in clusters, and Kaemada indicated them. "What wonders do those provide?"

Ennwhyn laughed. "Those spiders spin our clothes!"

Something about her response sparked heat in Kaemada's face, as if she'd been very foolish, and she drew her shawl tighter over her shoulders, keeping silent for the rest of the tour.

"Now, what can we do for you?" Ennwhyn asked finally.

Kaemada's gaze lingered on the grounds instead of the two expectant elves. Cheros was convinced of wrong here in this place of beauty. It niggled at her, as well, though perhaps her recent troubles had made her overly sensitive. But she couldn't ignore it like she had before. And yet, this was her plan. This was what she'd intended, to take herself out of the others' stories so they could prosper, and what better place than here? Especially if they could keep her from sending others to sleep again.

The words came out hesitantly and then in a rush. "Something inside of me is broken. I can no longer speak the Traveller's Tongue, so I am grateful you speak Rinaryn." Even though that would make things difficult to hide should there be a need to.

Ennwhyn laughed. "All those who work on the borders speak Rinaryn, the better to deal with your kind. When Fearil noted that you not once spoke in Traveller's, he made sure to get me, as I am one of those fluent in Rinaryn."

"Oh," Kaemada said, nodding. It made sense. She should have seen it before.

Then she frowned. "How did he get you? He was with us."

Ennwhyn and Fearil laughed again instead of answering her, and Kaemada wished she could stop flushing with humiliation. It only seemed to lend credence to the validity of their laughter.

"Go on, young one," Ennwhyn coaxed.

"I… I have hurt others with my psionics. I have invaded their minds, sent them to sleep." Tears pricked her eyes, and the words flowed of their own accord. "I have ruined the lives of those I love best, and I come hoping you can help me, or at least let me stay to keep from harming them further."

Sympathy shone in Ennwhyn's deep green eyes, so like Takiyah's that Kaemada's heart ached. Ennwhyn nodded. "I thought I sensed psionics in you. This is something we may be able to help you with. Do you also want help with your injuries?"

Kaemada rubbed her bandages on her chest, gazing at her hands. "Maybe. I'm not sure what happened to me."

"Come along with me."

Kaemada followed Ennwhyn down a perfectly groomed path to a large tree near the edge of the Stand overlooking the pond. Ennwhyn climbed the stairs spiraling around the outside of the trunk, and Kaemada hesitated, for the side was open to the drop off. Memories of falling into the chasm, of clinging to the walls of stone while hallucinations attacked her, filled her mind, freezing her with fear.

With yet another smile and without a word exchanged, Ennwhyn returned, placing herself on the outside of the curve and laying a hand on Kaemada's arm as she walked her up the stairs. Dimly, Kaemada wondered how Ennwhyn knew what had troubled her, but the thought flittered away from her. They ascended to where a large, vaulted room was formed out of the tree, from which she could see several other rooms and more stairs leading farther up. Other Rinaryn moved about in the other rooms, their motions stately and calm. The serenity and beauty of the place infused Kaemada, and her shoulders slowly released their tension.

They crossed to yet more stairs. As they climbed, the fear returned, but with Ennwhyn's hand on her arm, somehow the fear was more manageable. They climbed past several more rooms until they reached an open space near the top of the tree, gently swaying in the breeze. Ennwhyn gestured inside.

The room was only a couple paces from wall to wall, but no claustrophobia awakened in her, perhaps due to the large windows letting in fresh air. The height should have been a problem, but somehow Kaemada didn't mind, the way she wouldn't have minded before her fall into the chasm. A hammock filled with wool blankets and covered by a shimmering veil hung from a branch just outside the window, while inside, a chest in the room seemed grown from the smooth floor, and wooden hooks for hanging clothes formed smoothly from the wall.

In the doorway hung a cloth, held back by another wooden hook to let in more light and air. It reminded Kaemada of the rainshields of home. How she missed her home, with the circle of huts and the range of the forest she should have been living off of, together with her community. Out of one of the windows, she could see the tossing tops of the rest of the trees of the Stand, and out of another, she could overlook the beautiful pond and the forest beyond.

"Is this to your liking?" Ennwhyn asked, and Kaemada jumped, for she had forgotten the elf was there. She flushed immediately and nodded, trying to bury her embarrassment by looking out the window over the pond.

"This is beautiful. How do you get the wood to grow like this?" she asked, running a finger lightly over the windowsill.

"We tend the trees all our lives. For us, the trees are life. So we carefully shape them, grafting and pruning and nurturing them, coaxing them into the desired shape. We have the time to learn such skills. You are from Heartwood, by your accent? I think, were your people to live longer, you too might learn such things."

Kaemada frowned suspiciously at her. Cheros's words came back to her in a flood, and she could hardly believe she had gone along with them so far, so quickly. And yet, they spoke to her of things she knew, the give and take of life. How could that be wrong?

Ennwhyn bobbed slightly forward. "Will you stay for healing, Kaemada?"

This was it. There would be no turning back once she did this thing, no returning to her old story. Could she really tear herself away from the others, forever?

She had to.

Kaemada swallowed hard, as if she could be rid of her anxieties so easily. "What will it cost?"

CHA'A
Chapter Seven

We must prevent the protectors from fulfilling their purpose. Alone, they are no match for us. Together, however, they could be a storm. Watch and wait, guiding events from the safety of shadows. Take advantage of every opportunity to scatter them, pressing on their fears and hidden desires as they sleep.
—part of a missive from "Sapol" in Life Valley

Taunos peered through the thick summer leaf cover, past the underbrush to the kaetal of Siursiyan several paces in front of him. This was the only way, the only possible hope, and yet, his steps dragged. While he worried and delayed, nothing had actually happened yet. The question of whether they would actually stone him or not remained only a possibility. Once he showed his face, reality would set in, one way or another.

A stick snapped in his hand. He stared down at it before dropping the pieces. He hadn't even realized he'd grabbed it, nor how hard his fist had clenched. His gaze went back to the people moving about their various tasks a shout away from him. He had to stop dawdling and do this. It was for Kaemada, after all.

He'd thought of going home, of beseeching Galod for help for the first time in summers. But there was no guarantee the hermit could help such a condition, despite his vast power. Siursiyan was much closer, and they had powerful telepaths, last he'd known. He hoped that was still true.

But more than that, there lay a pool of terror deep inside him. He didn't think Torkae would really turn against him, but there was a chance. And if they did reject him, then what was he? What value did he give his people when he was kaetal-less, adrift with no people to call his own? His only connection to Torkae had been through his sister, but even the women, the fabric of Rinaryn society, had been cast out with him. He couldn't chance it, and even now found his blood rushing in his ears, his palms slick with sweat.

But he had to try. Kaemada had waited long enough, suffered long enough.

Taunos stepped from the bushes, hands spread in plain sight. He'd only gone a few paces when shouts of alarm rose from the kaetalyn.

Several warriors rushed toward him in a crouch, hands going to weapons.

The first ones faltered as they approached, their eyes going wide. "That's Taunos! It's Taunos!"

Another hushed the first. "Their names are not to be spoken!"

Taunos scowled. Another injustice of the Elders, that. No one had ever had their names erased before. It made it impossible to apply for a reconvening of the Council or for anyone to speak on their behalf.

"But it's… It's *him*!"

"And he's *Fallen*."

"I come only to ask for help." Taunos halted, keeping his stance at ease, his hands empty of weapons. But he'd built his fame in part on not needing weapons. Much good that did him now.

"The law is clear. He is Fallen!" someone shouted.

Just to the left of the group, two eyes peered from behind a prickleberry bush. A face, with features far too beautiful to be real. The smell of the depths of the forest, and rich soil filled his mind for a breath, and then, in the next blink, it and the face were gone. He blinked, unsteadied as surely as if the land had slid out from beneath his feet.

Taunos dragged his mind back to the kaetalyn. Arrows glared at him, stone tips thirsty, while others hefted stone knives. The disappearing watcher in the forest wasn't important right now—they were. They had to listen. He wouldn't let them ignore him, not again. He'd had enough of being ignored by the people he'd bled to protect, over and over again. "I only seek the help of psions, and then I will go, I promise! Please, just your telepaths, just—"

Something hard smashed into his cheek. Like water breaking through a dam, the first stone thrown gave way to arrows leaping through the air. They snagged his shirt as he turned, lashing out wildly with his telekinesis. But telekinesis against so many arrows from so short a distance was no real match, and several stone tips buried themselves in his flesh, with more to come.

There was only one escape. Taunos focused his will, wrapped round in pain like bark around a tree, like leather around a hilt. Ever since the very first time he'd realmwalked, Taunos found it easier when he was in pain, up to a point, at least. For a breath, he held on to every agonized part of himself in his mind. The next wave of arrows arced down at him from the sky. Ripping into the fabric of reality, he realmwalked.

The Everything between realms dragged at him. Blinding white and roaring noise surrounded him with crushing pressure. The limitless potential tore him apart like claws, unwilling to let him leave. If he stayed, he would die. He should go back to his sister. The moments were spinning past—moments when he might survive. It was dangerous beyond imagining to realmwalk without a destination in mind, and yet, he had. He'd jumped without preparation, and he floundered to focus on the normal waypoint, an awful, desolate place where the sun was a black disk in the sky and grey sand floated in the air, clinging like dust to exposed skin while avoiding cloth. His mind was growing fuzzy, losing the details of himself he needed to keep clear in his mind. Instead of the complete, whole idea of his self, down to the dirt on his boots and his destination, his mind went instead to a face beyond beautiful to him.

The flowers she loved filled him with their fragrance, and the silky black waves of her hair brushed across his memory. The way her lips curved in a smile, knowing and teasing. Her laughter in the night. The tree he loved to sit under with her—white bark, silver leaves, a match for his own people's Seeker Tree.

Why had he given up a story with his beloved when the Elders simply threw away all his work, all his strength? Why had he worked so hard to benefit those who would turn on him so completely? It wasn't worth it.

An arid wind assaulted him, occasional particles of sand grinding into his cheek. His legs gave out, and coarse grass prickled his face. Great marble walls rose to touch the blue sky in all directions—four buildings enclosing an enormous rectangle of flowers, shrubs, and trees, all immaculately tended. The guardhouse wing, attached to the palace, then the bamimri, where the Dahuti brought their sick and wounded, and the library. Atop each wing surrounding him, turrets perched like gleaming metal birds clutching pieces of fabric whipped about by the ever-present wind. White flags bearing nine prisms—the emblem of Far Dahutad. The Blessed Land of Nine Illusions.

Taunos was inside the solid walls of Arruk, indomitable against sand and sun.

Even further, he was in the Royal Gardens, beneath a slender white tree shading him with silver leaves, the very tree he'd remembered.

How had he managed such precision? Never before had he been so fortunate. And had he missed the waypoint somehow? Surely, he must have stopped in that horrible wasteland, if only for a moment.

Pain flared in his stomach, sides, arms, and leg. Blood poured from the holes where arrows had struck true as well as from the gashes of the near-misses. He'd forgotten to bring the arrows with him, and the wounds gaped open from the Everything between realms. Realmwalking like that had been foolish at best, but he'd been lucky. He had managed to escape from the Everything. Now he needed to get to the bamimri.

He tried to crawl his way forward, but his muscles refused to obey him. Too much blood flowed into the ground beneath him, soaking his clothes, staining the sharp grass. Blackness crept along the sides of his vision, and weariness dragged at him.

Foolish. He should have known better.

Taunos gritted his teeth against the pain and struggled to focus enough to bring to bear his telekinesis again. His attention kept swimming in and out, until he collapsed face down in the grass.

He needed to rest.

He needed to move, to get back to Kaemada, not lie here in the Royal Gardens. He'd come here to meet Amanah under their "Gods' Tree" some nights.

Memory carried him away. The soft touch of her lips. The teasing gleam in her eyes.

How had he lost so much? Would the guards or the Dahuti soldiers that shared the guardhouse welcome him back? Or would his disappearance be looked on with suspicion? And when he left again, as he'd have to do sooner rather than later, what would they think of him then?

He dreamed of Amanah holding his hand, whispering to him. He drowned, he burned, and she smoothed back his hair, unnecessarily since it was now so short, but he took strength from the gesture. His fingers curled around her hand, fighting to hold on without crushing her. A breeze whisked past him, and then nothing.

~

The first sensation that penetrated Taunos's fuzzy mind upon awakening was pain. The second was softness. He opened his eyes.

Light poured in through large windows, open to let the warm breeze through, sending the white curtains rippling. The walls were stone, the floor a mosaic of grey stone and marble, and great stone pillars supported the roof overheard. Small wooden tables waited underneath the windows, laden with gold-rimmed bowls and trays of painted ceramic pitchers and cups. Bed after bed lined the open space, most occupied.

He was lying on one of the plush feather mattresses, atop a blanket of soft grey wool. Another woolen blanket covered him, and a feather pillow cushioned his head.

How had he come to be here? Gingerly, he sat up, only to fall back again in agony and a cold sweat. Bandages wrapped his torso, arms, and left leg.

A middle-aged bimna paused beside him, her hair tied neatly in a bundle of braids at the back of her head. Her white smock bore the emblem of the bamimri, tied atop a starched white linen dress, tight across her stocky frame, and she exuded an air of authority. "Calm down. You're in the bamimri. You're lucky Nasri found you in the Garden and brought you here in time."

"Thank you."

The bimna nodded and left his side, checking the supplies on the table under the nearest window. Pain snatched for his attention. Taunos reached for his belt pouch, for the bitterroot he kept hidden there.

He stopped, skin prickling. His belt was gone. His clothes were gone, too, for only a soft cloth wrap clad his hips, but the belt was the important part.

The lesson had been drilled into him over and over by Galod, even before Taunos began to work for the Heartwood Elders. Never leave anything behind that might be traced back to Rinara. Never draw attention to himself as different, certainly not by leaving behind foreign plants. Always assume someone could trace it back to his people, and always assume their intentions would be aggressive. It was the best way to be safe.

And now he'd lost a pouchful of Rinaryn herbs.

Struggling to appear casual, hoping his grimace would only look like pain and not fear, he waved down the bimna. "Where's my belt?"

Her black eyes sparked with stern warning. "You just stay in bed. Your things will be returned to you once you are healed enough to leave."

"No, I just need—"

Deaf to his protests, she grabbed a jug from the table, poured a cup, and brought it to him. "Here, drink."

He didn't need a drink. He needed the belt pouch, needed to preserve the secrecy of his people. Taunos shook his head, shoving away the blankets, swinging his feet onto the floor. Black covered his vision for an instant again as his wounds screamed in protest, but he pushed himself upright.

The bimna frowned at him. "It's only medicine, to help you rest. You need to lie down. You'll undo all our hard work."

No. The chance of leading someone back to Rinara was small, but he still couldn't risk it. Secrecy was all the protection his people had.

"I have to find it. I need to—" Taunos staggered forward, nearly careening into her. He crashed into a cart of herbs when his knees gave out, and the clatter of the metal tray against the stone floor filled his ears.

The bimna crouched next to him, scooping a handful of something from the pouch at her side. Raising her hand, she blew pale blue powder into his face. He blinked, coughed, and fell, retching on the stone floor as the powder clogged in his nose and throat.

"Come on," she said, grabbing him by the shoulders.

Pain became a memory, consigned to the darkness with his worries.

~

The shadow of his nightmares chased him to consciousness, and Taunos awoke with his heart racing. He tried to sit up, but agony burned throughout his body. The room spun, and he had to lay there for some moments, just breathing until the lightheadedness passed. His nose itched. He reached to scratch it, but his hand wouldn't move.

He was strapped to the bed, hands and feet shackled. His heart hammered against his ribs. Cold sweat prickled all over his skin. His mind raced backwards, to when the restraints were metal instead of leather, and the mind-fogging drugs flooded his system, preventing him from focusing, preventing him from rescuing them. The whip cracked in the air, against his back, and the crowd roared in his ears with his blood.

Not again. Not again, no, not again!

He slammed against the restraints, which rattled but held.

Taunos gulped air, forcing himself to breathe, to think. He had to get free. He couldn't do anything tied down like this.

Counting between breaths to push back the panic, he closed his eyes, focused. The green of home, the mists that blanketed the land every morning, the deep of the forests near where he'd left Kaemada with the Resistance.

Taunos opened his eyes. The clean stone walls, wide windows, and flowing curtains of the airy bamimri greeted him, just the same as before. He shook his head, but the room spun wildly around him and he had to close his eyes again just to get his bearings. Scowling, he focused again but still could not gain the focus necessary to realmwalk. He was trapped.

He pulled on the restraints again, straining against them, but they didn't loosen.

"Show off." Emin lounged in a chair beside his bed, dressed in the simple white of a bamimri patient. The tall man's face was drawn in lines of fatigue, his tone the casual voice he used when he was more worried about something than he wanted to let on. His black hair was tied back neatly, and his black eyes sparkled with mischief. "You know, sometimes I really hate you. Look at you, lying there, muscles tensing, showing off—"

Taunos scrambled to keep up with the friend he'd fought alongside in battle after battle. The friend he'd left behind—he'd thought for good—seven moons ago. "I was shot."

Emin jabbed a finger at him, straightening a little in the chair. "Exactly what I mean! Pity, renown, and a reason to stay here for an extended length."

Ignoring Amanah's brother, Taunos focused his telekinesis on his restraints. Risks or no risks, he needed to be free, not chained again.

But his vision swam, and his stomach turned. He swallowed back the nausea. Panicking would do him no good. At least Emin was a good distraction. Taking a few deep breaths, Taunos recomposed himself. "If only I had known getting shot would bring your ire, I would have avoided it. Why am I bound?"

Emin smoothed his mustaches. "You aren't very good at that, I'd say."

Taunos's brow furrowed, and the panic subsided for a moment to the background. "At what?"

"Avoiding ire. Dulara hates troublesome patients, you know. That's why you're bound."

"It's not for lack of trying."

Emin snorted and stabbed a finger at him again then slouched back. "I told Amanah I'd punch you next time I saw you, for making her feel worthless, but I think I'll have to wait. Tell me when you're feeling up to it."

"Of course," Taunos said. Emin wouldn't follow through. Probably. And even then, Taunos had bested him in wrestling matches before. Then the words sank in, and Taunos narrowed his eyes, latching onto that instead of the churning in his stomach. "How did I make Amanah feel worthless?"

"You left!"

"She asked me to!"

"You think it still didn't hurt? After two and a half years, you have a fight and you just leave?" Emin shook his head. "Haari Taunos, how you bungle things!"

His nose wrinkled. Was he missing something, some set of cultural expectations unique to the Dahuti? No, he didn't think so. Besides, Emin was prone to far worse relationship blunders. Taunos stifled a snort. "Oh, and you say this with all your vast experience?"

Emin scowled. "No need to be nasty. Once I can get Father to give me some goats, I'll have some status. Maybe no one wants to marry a nomad with no herd, but they will an accomplished soldier."

Pain filled strong undercurrents in Emin's voice. Taunos studied his friend, his own troubles forgotten for the moment. Emin in the bamimri was an odd sight, and wearing the smock of a patient?

"Why are you here anyway?" Taunos asked.

"Why am I not on the border, where the action is? You *have* gotten nasty." Emin's scowl deepened, and he drew back from Taunos as if actually hurt this time. He stared at the far wall, smoothing his mustaches. "My band and I caught an illness and were sent back to recover. Gurseh blames me, of course. He wishes he was back out fighting the Hinanuri already."

Taunos frowned. What was that Emin had grumbled something about no one wanting to marry him? "What happened with Gurseh?"

He was immediately sorry he'd asked.

Pain shadowed Emin's face, and his voice became brittle. "He ended things."

Taunos winced. Gurseh and Emin had been a couple for as long as Taunos had known them, nearly four summers, through rocky times and good times. What a blow to Emin's heart that must have been. But Emin's expression was too brittle for questions, and the man hated sympathy.

"His loss, goats or no goats," Taunos said. "You're already accomplished, Emin, whether or not Gurseh can see that."

Emin snorted, folding his arms and looking out over the bamimri, almost as if he were on guard.

Without conversation to distract Taunos, the panic clawed its way back up his chest. Trapped. He was trapped again. Bound, helpless, and drugged. Some fine hero he made, again so easily made vulnerable. He had to find his herb pouch, to make sure no one could use it as a potential clue to find his homeland. Secrecy was vital, especially in a land full of scholars and traders.

But first, escaping these bonds.

Why had the bamimri strapped him down? Being troublesome? He clenched his fists, resisting the urge to pull at the restraints yet again, battling the clawing panic so it wouldn't show.

For summers upon summers, ever since he left Rinara to search for the identity of the Darks or find anything that might help his people, he'd learned to hide how badly he was injured. Early on, he'd been cornered by suspicions when people he was travelling with had realized he healed more slowly than they did, and after that, hiding his injuries had become a paranoid sort of habit. It didn't dissipate easily. He'd even downplayed injuries at home, to avoid worrying Kaemada, to avoid the kaetalyn thinking less of their hero. He rarely asked for help, and he found the asking a challenge in and of itself.

And if he let onto the panic growing in him, Emin would only have questions, and he didn't have it in him right now to either answer or deflect. Answering would hurt too much, as would deflection, for Emin deserved better.

The large man coughed then shifted, smoothing his mustaches. Emin's pride was worth as much to him as those mustaches. He'd nearly burned them off in a training exercise because he refused to trim them and the oil had ignited. Even that hadn't stopped him.

Taunos appealed to that pride now. Cheering up Emin was worthy in and of itself, with the distraction it provided only an added bonus. "Well, I guess it will give the other soldiers a chance to fight before you win the war for them, right?"

Emin slapped his leg, leaning forward with a grin. "Right. And if you come with us, the war would be over in a blink!"

A smile curved Taunos's lips at Emin's earnestness, even as he shook his head. "I need out of these restraints first."

"I'll ask Dulara when she comes by. Otherwise she'll ban me from keeping you company." Emin leaned forward, black eyes glittering. "What were the names you kept muttering while you were out? Kaemanah and... something very, very strange."

Taunos went still, hiding the wince he felt deep inside. He stared at the ceiling, resting his neck from the strain of turning to see Emin. What had happened to him? He was usually far more careful than this. Losing the herbs, talking in his sleep... It seemed he had no business being here, where he could betray his whole people with a minor slip. What if he'd said more? Something that could endanger his people? And with the wide open room filled with rows of beds, many occupied by patients, anyone could have heard him. If he'd shouted, everyone in the large hall would have heard.

"Who is she?" Emin asked.

"My sister." Taunos gritted his teeth.

"Mmm." Emin smoothed his moustaches again. "Interesting. Information from Haari Taunos?"

Taunos bit back the groan that wanted to escape him as much as he wanted to escape the bonds—and this conversation. He pushed down on the panic filling him, fighting to control his hammering heart.

Across the wide expanse of the open room, Amanah glided among the beds, and Taunos's breath caught just looking at her. Her apron was spattered with blood, and a broad, colorful scarf tied back her array of braids. She set her foot on a wounded man's shoulder and yanked his arm, popping the joint back into place. She bent over her patient, murmuring with soothing gestures as she handed him a drink. Taunos closed his eyes. There she was, as gorgeous as ever, apparently completely untouched by their moons apart.

Coming here had been a mistake. Seeing Amanah and then leaving her again would surely only hurt her further. The memory of the pain in her eyes—the last time he'd seen her—still tore at his heart. He'd failed, both his mission and their relationship. She'd uncovered his secrets and sent him away in a fury.

He'd lost her, all because he'd wanted to keep his people safe. Had it been worth it?

His voice was thick as he spoke. "Is she not the most beautiful woman in all the worlds?"

Emin's smirk infused his voice. "Amanah? Unlikely. But all the worlds, you say? Do tell me more."

Desperation rose in him like the tide with the moons crossing overhead, choking out rational thought. With a grimace, he channeled it, telekinetically pushing on the restraints with everything he had. He was supposed to be better than this. A dull headache was building, warning him of overuse of his telekinesis. Even so, it was getting harder and harder to fend off the claustrophobia, and his injuries screamed protests as he squirmed and shifted, trying to find a more comfortable position.

He'd rather stand-off with a dragon than expose his vulnerabilities, his weaknesses. And at home, he'd been a hero, thought of as invincible. But when he'd needed help, when he'd been vulnerable, they had cast him out. But he couldn't handle it anymore. Couldn't do this himself, couldn't fight off the terror any longer.

Still, he found himself making such an effort to keep his tone light that his voice squeaked. "Emin, be a friend and stop laughing and undo my restraints, will you?"

Emin wheezed, his laughter only increasing as he rocked back and forth on his chair and wiped tears from his eyes.

Gritting his teeth, Taunos tried to focus on his breathing, rather than the throb of his angry wounds. He turned his telekinesis back on his bonds until his stomach roiled. He was pushing too hard. And yet, he couldn't stop, willing his restraints to break, to loosen, even as his head pounded and his vision became fuzzy.

A warm hand patted his shoulder. Concern had replaced the laughter in Emin's voice. "All right, all right. I can't release you, but I'll ask for you. In the meantime, tell me why you think Amanah's the most beautiful in all the worlds. What, are you giving credence to the rumors of you being a sea-wizard?"

Taunos glared at him, pushing one last time, though it did no good. "You aren't going to let me live down that slip, are you?"

"Can you blame me, after so many months of you being a closed book? Now you're practically leaking like a sieve. Or you could tell me why you're so careless all of the sudden."

The room swam before him, and his stomach turned dangerously. To speak of other worlds, or of Amanah. There was no choice, really. "There is no other woman I have ever met that is comparable to her. She outshines them all, and I would give her everything I am. But she told me quite clearly that I am not enough. I cannot give her enough. That is why I left."

"What do you mean?"

"I would fly to the sky to fetch her the sun if I could, should she desire it. For her I would wade across your rivers full of monsters—"

"They are only crocodiles."

"—but I cannot set her before the safety of my people. I could not promise her that."

"No one should ask another that." Anger filled Emin's voice.

Taunos shook his head, sighing. He would have told her, if he could. He would tell them both everything, if only he knew his people would be safe. Panic filled his mind, and no matter what he tried to focus on, he couldn't push it down. He was reduced to writhing on the bed in front of the friend he admired so much. "Emin, please, undo the straps. I cannot..."

Coughing erupted from Emin's chair, and the man doubled over. Taunos's hands tightened into fists, but the terror wouldn't stop, wouldn't be reasoned with. Desperation mounted. He was no longer in control.

Who was he if he wasn't in control of himself? Galod's face, his mother's face, his father's face, all of them ordering him to control himself, and he couldn't.

He squeezed his eyes shut and slammed against the restraints in sudden fury. The Elders, relying on that control, setting him increasingly impossible tasks, and then leaving him to be exiled the moment he became inconvenient for them. Who were they to demand such things of him? Who was anyone to demand things of him anymore? He slammed again.

Something in his wrist popped. Fire lanced up his arm. When next he reflexively pulled at the restraints, blackness nearly took him, and cold doused the flames of desperate claustrophobia. His wrist was agony.

Hands clamped down on his arms, and Taunos fought against the added restraining weight. Pain flaring from his wrist consumed him, turning his stomach. Everything was a blur, his sight dim and fuzzy, and his head pounded from overuse of telekinesis.

"Taunos, stop. It's just me. Stop!" Emin's voice was close, just in front of his face, but Taunos's self-control was ragged wisps and snatching for them was all he could do at the moment.

Just as Taunos began to calm his ragged breathing, the air swirled around him—more people were coming. Another spike of fear shot through him.

"More violence? Make sure those restraints are tight," a woman's voice said.

"He's reacting badly to the restraints," Emin said. "He needs to be released."

"Nonsense. Violent patients are always restrained in the bamimri, for the safety of all."

"Dulara, wait!" Amanah's voice cut in. "Perhaps it's a bad reaction to your powder. Giving him more might only worsen the response. Emin, can you move? Taunos, it's all right. You're all right. Calm down."

Taunos's chest tightened at the calm, cool sound of her voice, as if he were just any patient. How he longed to hear the warmth and love in her voice again! "Amanah."

Emin released him, and Taunos gritted his teeth, focused on simply breathing rather than the pain in his wrist or the pain in his heart from the distance of his beloved.

Amanah gasped, her voice closer now. "What have you done to yourself?"

He shivered as her fingers ran down his arm, the coolness of her skin a welcome distraction. Emin's hand held his other shoulder, steadying him as Amanah inspected his arm.

"Careful," Dulara said, tension in her voice. "He's dangerous."

Breathe in, breathe out. Taunos gritted his teeth through the overwhelming agony, trying to regain calm though the tension in him again built, growing unmanageable. He was going to go mad, strapped down like this.

Amanah snorted. "He's not dangerous. Except maybe to himself. Taunos, you broke your wrist."

The straps around his right arm loosened, and he sagged with relief, hot tears pricking at his eyes.

Emin's hand squeezed his shoulder. "He can't be restrained again. He's not the first soldier I've seen to have trouble like this. It seems the world catches up to even Haari Taunos eventually."

"And when did you train in the bamimri?" Dulara's voice was sharp. "I don't care if he's High God Jattanu himself, I'm not going to let a patient rampage through my bamimri."

Amanah's touch paused. "While he was on this rampage, how many did he injure? Gods above, we know how well he can wound when he wishes."

Dulara's voice turned icy, and it became clear where Amanah had gotten her professional bimna voice from. "I only let you tend him so much while he was unconscious because I thought you had the good sense not to become smitten."

"I'm not smitten!"

"She was the one who ended their relationship, after all," Emin supplied.

Taunos grimaced. "Not helping, Emin."

"On your head be it, Amanah," Dulara said. "If he causes any more trouble, though, there will be no further chances, and you will have to answer for it. Are you sure you want to risk your reputation in this way?"

Amanah's tone was firm. "I'm not going to allow a patient to further injure themselves due to precautions meant to keep everyone safe."

Taunos's heart thundered in his ears, and then the vague figure that was Dulara glided away, while Amanah moved around him, undoing strap after strap. He sat up the moment he could, cradling his wrist, teeth clenched against his pain.

"Thank you," he managed, clearing his throat.

"What happened?" Amanah's voice was tense with worry. "Look at you. Your wrist and ankles are all bruised and raw. And then this wrist..."

"What caused this reaction?" Emin leaned in close, ever eager for answers.

Silence draped their corner of the bamimri. All he could see was the memory of the betrayal and hurt in Amanah's expression the last time they'd talked. Shouted, more like. He couldn't do that to her again. Wouldn't. Taunos looked around, but his vision was still blurry. He blew out a frustrated sigh, hanging his head. "Emin, is there anyone else in earshot besides the two of you?"

"No, but speak quietly and hurry up."

"Taunos? You can't see?" Fear infused Amanah's tone.

He shook his head, drew in a deep breath. It was just the two of them, and he trusted them, as much as he trusted anyone. He'd told them stories before. But the panic still thrummed through his veins and in his head, and the words stuck on his tongue. How could he say what he'd been through without putting his sister in danger, his people in danger?

He took another deep breath and plunged ahead. "Seven moons ago, I was captured by a people who kept me drugged, unable to escape for fear of my sister's son's life. My sister's friends were captive with us, and when we did finally try to run, they tortured us. I thought of you, Amanah, during my captivity. The thought of you kept me going."

He shook his head, swallowing hard and keeping his eyes shut. How much more could he say? Even after everything, he couldn't risk his people.

She hovered close, her lightly calloused fingers brushing against his skin as she splinted his wrist. He focused on his breathing, inhaling the scent of her, subduing the edge of the roiling torment of his emotions.

Emin squeezed his shoulder again. "Jattanu's justice, Taunos."

Amanah said nothing, and he could feel her weighing his words as she worked.

"They cast us out for all our trouble. My leaders. They just..." Trembling overtook him now that his panic had been released.

Amanah's hands left his for a moment, and then a soft blanket draped his shoulders. He gripped it with one hand. Gratitude and the weight of his vulnerability lay heavy on him, stealing away his voice.

"Let me see your eyes," Amanah said. He opened them to see her fuzzy form crouching before him. Her voice became even more worried. "Your eyes aren't focusing. When did this begin? This gash on your cheekbone... Were you hit on the head?"

Taunos shook his head, taking a moment to ensure his voice would be steady. "Yes, but that's not... I tried too hard to get free of the restraints."

Amanah's frown was evident in her voice. "But how did that affect your sight?"

He looked at her and then at Emin, standing with his arms crossed as if he could keep at bay anything to threaten their privacy. Their faces swam before him, but they were close by and they were safe. His secret would surely be safe with them. He wasn't even sure how dangerous it would be if it got out. "Emin already figured it out."

Emin barked a laugh and clapped. With a scowl, Taunos shushed him, relieved when Emin's voice was a barely audible murmur. "I knew it! I knew you were a sea-wizard!"

"He can't be a sea-wizard," Amanah said. "Sea-wizards eat babies and throw lightning."

"You want the truth, Amanah?" Taunos moved his good arm outward, his telekinesis translating the push into a brush of her cheek. His vision swam dangerously, and the ground rolled, but her soft gasp as she brought a hand to her cheek made him grin. He snatched at the bed for stability, and her hands caught him, steadying him.

"All right, that's more than enough of that for today, it seems. Rest." Wonder tinged her matter-of-fact words as she guided him onto his less injured side.

He closed his eyes and just breathed with relief.

"Where's my demonstration?" Emin asked as Amanah finished bandaging his wrist.

Despite everything, Emin brought a grin to Taunos's face, and he opened his eyes to see their vague, wavering forms. "I will give it to you when you deliver the punch you're saving for me."

"Don't leave this bed." Just a hint of fondness remained in her tone, even as Amanah switched back into her bimna role. "I'll have Nasri make a note not to restrain you, that you react badly to the sulim, so they shouldn't drug you anymore. But try to stay calm. Don't hurt yourself any further."

"Oh, I'll make sure he stays until you two can talk." Emin's grin filled his voice.

"Amanah, I'm sorry." Taunos reached out, his fingertips just brushing her hand, though he missed actually connecting with her.

"We will have words, you and I, but it'll keep until you feel better."

Time, then, to weigh his secrets versus his love. His stomach twisted with guilt at both prospects, and then a jolt of urgency went through him. "My belt. I need my belt."

"Why?"

Of all people, he could trust Amanah. Even so, Galod's voice screamed disapproval at him in his imagination as he spoke, keeping his voice low. "There are herbs in the pouch on the inside. They need to be secret."

His heart thudded in his ears as the moments stretched out between them. If she didn't believe him, it'd really be no more than he deserved.

"I'll look for it." Tension laced her tone, but Amanah's word was as sturdy as the stone of the bamimri. He loved that about her, though of course it made his secrets even worse in her eyes.

Her footsteps sounded fainter and fainter as she walked away, and with his mind pain-addled and sulim-influenced, he couldn't help but hope it wasn't for good.

Chapter Eight

When the fae come, be sure to claim a spot at their table. For this reason, any crystal found—save those stored in the Hall of Scouts—has great value, for only these will the fae accept in exchange for their counsel. The family who takes the advice of the fae seriously rises, and the city which listens to fae wisdom gains in power. Choose your questions carefully, for the crystals collected are only ever worth a handful. It would not do to waste such a chance at guiding advice from the fae.

—fragment of a letter in the City of Codr

"I need something to do, some goal to strive for. I'm going to wither away or go mind-sick like this," Ra'ael said, pacing the kitchen floor as Dode browsed the notes from the latest Philosopher's meeting. Everything was scrubbed spotless, with bedmats laid by the fire again, regardless of whether or not that was proper. She couldn't sleep unless she was in front of a fire. It just felt too wrong. And being closed up in a room away from everything... she might as well be dead.

The paper rustled as Dode flipped a page over. "What would you like to do? You have already reinstated yourself as my bodyguard. Ra'ael, please sit down."

The door opened, and Ra'ael spun to confront it. Half inside, Tjodlik stopped in his tracks, his eyes flickering from her to Dode. "Is everything all right?"

Dode laughed. "Ra'ael is just a little jumpy."

Face heating, Ra'ael turned her back as Tjodlik shut the door with a careful click. A cloud of smoke had followed him inside, but she could do nothing about it. It seeped in like the growing unease whenever Dode used her gifts. Some days, Ra'ael found herself sore from remaining tense the whole day around Dode, regardless of how she loved the old woman. She had to find a way to deal with it, for she had no other options. It was agony, for all she wanted was to be able to truly relax and enjoy Dode's company again. She was so giving, so good to her, and Ra'ael couldn't even control her traitorous feelings. They were taking Dode away from her, too, and she couldn't let that happen.

Ra'ael's feet carried her again from sink to table and back in a tiny circuit. "I cannot just course through life aimlessly, driftwood on a stream being carried along."

Amusement filled Tjodlik's voice. "Is accosting visitors at the door your new goal in life? I must say you are doing a splendid job, if so."

Dode laughed again, and Ra'ael knew without turning around how her eyes would be crinkled up, one hand hovering in the air above the table. Facing her with a suppressed sigh, Ra'ael nevertheless found her heart lightening with Dode's mirth.

The elderly woman reached over to pat her hand. "Oh, my dear, thank you for brightening my home. It was too quiet without you."

"Are you all right?" Tjodlik asked, walking to his aunt's side.

"You are like clockwork, my boy. Honestly, do you think I am in danger, still?"

"People are uneasy with the changes you advance."

Dode waved a hand. "People are always uneasy with change."

The thick haze from outside burned in Ra'ael's eyes and throat. She coughed, pulling the kitchen curtains more firmly shut, but directed her words to Tjodlik. "Is it still getting worse outside? I do not remember the air being so filthy last time."

"After the psions from the chasm attacked the city, the smoke of the fires and debris filled the air," Tjodlik explained.

Dode scowled out the window. "They have been using those steam-powered machines that are on every corner these days to aid in the clean-up and restoration of the buildings."

Mirth distracting her from her worries, Ra'ael smiled. "Now who's uneasy with change?"

Dode raised her browridge, but her lips quirked upward. "The steam they put out has been condensing on surfaces and making them slick. The smoke has been making it difficult to see."

"If it continues, you will have to go Outside," Ra'ael said, coughing again. "You will not be able to breathe."

"We have a meeting to discuss that later on this evening. We will be speaking with several other noble families and the scientists they support, to see what solutions they have come up with."

Tension crept up on Ra'ael and pounced. She would be in meetings at nights to guide the future of Torkae if the Elders hadn't banished her. All her hard work gone in one declaration because she hadn't followed the rules.

"About that, Aunt Dode," Tjodlik interrupted with a grimace. "I have heard rumors that there is a fae delegation in the city. Please be careful."

"Now Tjodlik, I am not made of glass. I am not so easy to break, and if you persist in hovering, I will have to take offense." Dode's voice was sharp, and Tjodlik bowed his head, abashed. Dode's eyes gleamed as she rubbed her hands together. "Fae, hmm? It has been a long time since I have interacted with the fae."

"Fae are dangerous," Ra'ael said, the skin of her arms and the back of her neck prickling. "We have many stories—"

"I dare say you do, and for good reason. Fae *are* dangerous, but most of all, they are devious." And yet, Dode smiled, as if warming to the challenge.

"I worry that you think this a game, Aunt Dode."

Dode clucked her tongue. "I have reading to do to prepare for tonight. Are you two going over the stories again?"

Ra'ael glanced questioningly at Tjodlik, feeling an odd sort of relief when he nodded. Several days ago, she'd told Dode about the Kyasewithuwun, those Rinaryn who believed the stories literally and tried to find their own place in the cycle of endlessly repeating tales. She had never adhered to that notion, but Tjodlik had suggested that, since she didn't know her own place anymore, she start by looking at the stories. She should have thought of that, but then, she'd been pushing everything Rinaryn away from her.

Tjodlik smiled. "I wanted to compare stories further, if that is acceptable to you, Lady Ra'ael."

She scowled. The last thing she wanted was to be compared to the snooty Kamalti nobility, too caught up in their own status to see how the world worked. "I am no Lady. I told you that already."

She followed him across the small kitchen and through the wide, arching doorway to the adjacent room. His expression remained unfazed as he settled on the low couches of Dode's sitting room. Greenery framed the room, bought for Ra'ael by Dode, and the curtains there, too, were closed against the smoke.

Why was she even here, trying to fit into a society where there were only two people she admired? Still unable to come up with a clear answer, she sank onto a cushion. She should focus on her task. At least it was something, some small goal to shoot for. And there was friendship here under the mountain, even if Dode's eyes twinkled every time she pointed out a prospective companion. When the Kamalti inevitably shunned her, the women tittering and the men ignoring her, there was always tea and a kind ear.

Tjodlik had already pulled out a book of children's tales and was flipping through the pages. Knowing him, he was searching for a particular passage. Ra'ael opened the last book she'd been looking at, scowling as she painstakingly made her way through the Kamalti script. She still was not fluent in Kamalti and sometimes had to interrupt Tjodlik to ask for a translation, which she hated doing. He was always so studious. Already, he was bent over a book, his pale eyes locked on the pages, flickering rapidly back and forth as he devoured the details of the story.

As if asking for help wasn't enough punishment for her bruised pride, her book was a *My First Tales* for Kamalti children. Many of the stories were familiar to her, but she was growing used to that. Kaemada had started an exchange of stories and songs with the Kamalti, she'd known, but Tjodlik had told her that it'd begun the very night after the Running. Ra'ael wasn't surprised, not truly, even if her stomach twisted at the thought of stories traded while she lay unconscious, beaten nearly to death. If Tjodlik was to be believed, it had encouraged many of his people to think better of the Rinaryn, horrified at what they'd just done. It was difficult to think of someone as an animal when they told the very same stories to their children that you told to yours. No wonder so many Kamalti had come and gone during her recovery, visiting with Kaemada or Dode.

So why wasn't she angry with Dode about all of that?

"Do your people tell the stories of the dwarves, elves, and gnomes?" Tjodlik asked.

"The one you have a statue about, near the Hall of Justice?" Ra'ael shook her head. "No, but Answer mentioned it."

"Ah, interesting. Now I wonder…"

"Not every story has to be true." Even if Kaemada believed them. Yes, Ra'ael had been priestess, but the stories didn't have to be true to teach. And anyway, she wasn't priestess anymore. She could never again be ehreideikae, the one who watches and knows, if she couldn't feel the song of the spirits, even if she wasn't Fallen. Ra'ael turned the page of her book, as if it were so easy to turn her thoughts.

"But what if it is? And we have the statues to remember them." Tjodlik jabbed his finger in the air to accentuate his point.

Ra'ael shrugged. "Artistic fancy."

Tjodlik set down his book with a frown. "It is your people who have the belief that the stories show the way, that they are real."

Avoiding his gaze, Ra'ael fixed her eyes on the page in front of her, filled with clean, blocky Kamalti script. "That's the thing, Tjodlik. I do not know if I believe it. I had never given it much thought."

"What other use is there?"

She'd spent a lot of time with Kaemada and Taunos's family growing up and could still remember the arguments their father Afarei had had with the Storyteller. Ra'ael's own father had scoffed at Afarei's folly for refusing to apprentice to be the next Storyteller. All because he wanted to continue to tell his own stories, stories that were not held as true.

"A story can have worth without being literally true. It can still be a guide for teaching, still have deeper truths." Afarei's words flowed from her lips, though the man was long since gone, over the rim of the sky. Spirits' stories and songs, she couldn't stop being Rinaryn even when she immersed herself in the world of Kamalti, could she!

Tjodlik snorted. "Deeper truths wrapped in untruth?"

Ra'ael raised her eyebrows at him.

"Well, what *do* you believe?" he asked.

Sighing, she set the book back down in the pile. He picked at her like a fingernail digging at a scab still too new to be removed.

"I do not know, Tjodlik. I'm not certain what's real anymore, what's true anymore. Who am I without my people? What's my purpose? I'm trying to be Kamalti, but sometimes I feel I'm just hiding here. Useless."

"You are not useless, Lady Ra'ael."

"I'm *not* a Lady."

"Maybe not by birth." Tjodlik smiled and held up a gold-bound book. "Here, what about Tamarik?"

She shook her head. "You're always carrying that book around, paging through it. What is it?"

"Stories of a fabled city."

"You're a dreamer, Tjodlik." Her heart tightened, pain flooding her song, stealing her voice and pricking at her eyes. She missed a dreamer. She'd loved a dreamer, once.

She gritted her teeth against the guilt. All those summers ago, when Kaemada had brought her home after Ra'ael had lost everything, Ra'ael had dared to hope for more, even knowing that Kaemada wouldn't love her in the way she wanted. She loved her, though, in the way Ra'ael needed.

As if she could clear her head of memories so easily, Ra'ael shook her head. Kaemada didn't need her now. She had Taunos looking after her. Besides, Kaemada wasn't the only one who'd lost Eian.

Tjodlik's laugh jarred her back to the present as he opened the book. "Here, I will read it to you in Traveller's so you do not have to translate it. Then you can tell me if it sounds familiar."

His laughter eased the pain a bit, even more when she mocked him. "You just want an excuse to read the story again."

His pale grey eyes glittered at her from over the top of the book. "So?"

"All right, Tjodlik, read me a story," she said, leaning back against the couch. She couldn't help but smile at the look on his face as he folded himself over the page and began to read.

Ra'ael closed her eyes as Tjodlik spun a tale of a mythological city where the waves of the ocean met the waves of the desert. The very first city of their island, where the gods had touched the land. Who could believe such a place of paradise could exist in the desert, or even more ludicrous, that the ocean with its changeable tides wouldn't destroy it within summers? Everyone knew the ocean around Rinara was impassable, between rocks jutting up, the tossing of unpredictable waves, and the whirlpools that formed randomly. It'd been a miracle that Takiyah as a baby had survived long enough for Galod and the Storyteller to not only find her but climb down and rescue her before the waves took her.

"You do know that only children would actually believe such nonsense, right? Low tide would either strand such a place, or high tide would drown it—or both." The words poured from her, flavored with a bitterness that surprised even her.

Dode peeked in. "What is going on out here?"

"We are investigating—" Tjodlik started, but Ra'ael cut him off.

"Tjodlik is telling me children's tales and not listening to reason."

He stilled next to her, drawing himself up and closing the book precisely.

Each measured movement screamed of his affront. But she couldn't sit and listen to such painful beauty when it did no good. Hope in anything, especially something so ludicrous, was bound to only bring more harm. There was nowhere she, Kaemada, Taunos and Takiyah could live together, not since they were Fallen. They'd lost Eian, lost all chance at a happy story filled with respect and honor. If Tjodlik wanted to be offended by truth, so be it.

She hopped to her feet and turned to Dode instead. "Are you ready?"

"I am not certain I need two bodyguards. It is only a meeting with the fae."

"I'm coming with you, Dode." Ra'ael crossed her arms stubbornly.

"I wish to see the fae for myself," Tjodlik said, packing up his books. "We both know I would make a poor bodyguard, but I make a fine nephew."

Dode smiled, taking his arm as she opened the door. "A reasonable argument."

Ra'ael winced at Dode's obvious choice of words but kept her mouth closed as she shut the door behind them and followed them to the lift. She'd accepted a flowing Kamalti gown as part of life here, partially because it put the other Kamalti more at ease and partly because it was warmer underground and she didn't want to sweat in her alanshorn wool. There was only so much she was willing to cater to Kamalti ways, though, and so she'd left her black hair long. Head high as she joined the others, she turned so her hair and gown swirled behind her—along with tendrils of smoke—as she entered the lift.

Mirth danced in Dode's eyes, but Ra'ael just raised her eyebrows. She may be Fallen, but that didn't mean she couldn't look good.

The lift descended, and she followed Dode and Tjodlik through the familiar streets of Codr. The scars from the fighting were still apparent and dampened her mood more than she'd expected. Ra'ael kept herself busy scanning the streets for trouble until they entered another lift.

"We're not using a public building?" she asked.

Dode shook her head. "Lord Kefl requested the honor of hosting the delegation."

"And the fae accepted?"

"Why would they not? They know they have power, even here in a Kamalti city."

It made sense. It was easier to give the appearance of flexibility and graciousness when one held all the power and prestige. The lift stopped only a level up, and Ra'ael eyed the stairs they could have taken. She should have guessed their lift ride would not be long. In order to host the fae, this Lord Kefl must be of high social standing, which meant a lower house on the columns, away from the smoke, as well as a more central location within the city.

She followed Dode and Tjodlik around the corner to an entrance adorned with engravings on the mantle and sides of the solid wood door, which was embellished with further decorations traced in gold and silver. She shook her head. As if the location itself didn't scream loudly enough of his wealth.

The door opened for them, and a servant ushered Dode and Tjodlik into the house, leaving Ra'ael to shut the door.

"Right in here, Lady Dode. Sir." The servant nodded at Dode and Tjodlik and then faltered when he looked at Ra'ael. Clearing his throat, he brushed past her, hurrying on his way.

The room was ostentatiously large for a Kamalti dwelling. A swarm of people milled around the gaudy furniture, foiling Ra'ael's hasty head counts, though she caught sight of Answer, sparking a flare of rage in her belly. Answer had tried to "civilize" Taunos, and when her drugging of him didn't work and they'd tried to escape, she'd nearly killed them. Yes, she had seemed horrified after the Running, and yes she had spoken on their behalf, arguing that they be freed, but still Ra'ael could only look on her with hands clenched into fists.

Ra'ael settled for sticking close to Dode. Her skin tingled, prickling, until at last their host rose and rang a crystal, and the buzz of conversation quieted while everyone found places to sit. Ra'ael took a position close behind Dode and Tjodlik's seats. Finally, she could see.

There were two fae present, seating themselves with graceful motions on one of Lord Kefl's couches. They needed no introduction, though she'd never seen one before. They never would have blended in, even among Rinaryn. The same height as the average Kamalti, they had a more slender build, with sharp but elegant features and smooth skin lightly patterned with shades of tan and brown, almost like freckles but in lines instead of dots. Their flowing hair, bright eyes, and long, finely woven and embroidered tunics and breeches all combined to create the effect of something beautifully dangerous. When their gazes met hers, their features twisted for a blink into hideous masks, but then the moment was over and they were just there, while her heart pounded.

She chided herself for her reaction. They hadn't done anything, and yet, she'd frozen. If there *had* been danger, a poor bodyguard she would have made. She adjusted her stance, sweat breaking out as she glanced at the others assembled. Bodyguards and servants stood behind their seated masters. The Kamalti nobles were settling themselves, heads held even higher than normal, as if trying to assure themselves or the fae—possibly both—of their own importance.

"Thank you for hosting us," one of the fae began, and Ra'ael stifled a shudder. It was odd, because his voice was musical and pleasing... and yet, the hair of the back of her neck rose.

"Thank you for coming, good sirs," one of the men said. By his too-large smile and the way he hovered about, Ra'ael guessed he was Lord Kefl.

"Have you the tribute?" the first fae asked.

"Yes, yes, right here." Lord Kefl snapped his fingers, and a servant hurried forward with a tray of crystals. The Kamalti mined crystals, digging them right out of the rock, but using them as some sort of currency? That was new.

The fae examined each piece carefully. A smile curved his lips as he picked up one of them, a strange crystal with a slight bend to it. Another shiver crept up Ra'ael's spine, and her spirit shouted at her to flee and not look back. Ra'ael tensed every muscle to fight it back down. Rationally there was nothing threatening about that smile.

"This one was found Outside?" the fae asked.

Lord Kefl stammered, but the fae raised a hand, cutting him off. "It was, I can assure you of that. These pieces are adequate, but this one, this one is worth much guidance."

"How do you know that piece was found Outside?" Tjodlik asked, and Ra'ael strangled the urge to pull him backward. She clenched her fists behind the couch, demanding stillness of herself as the fae's gaze raked over her and then pierced Tjodlik.

"This is a dragon's tooth," the fae said, the musical notes of his voice playing across Ra'ael's nerves with growing alarm. "A piece of one, anyway. They are not commonly found underground."

"I see." Tjodlik nodded pleasantly, apparently unaffected by the fae.

Disdain filled the fae's expression, and he sniffed. "I highly doubt you do." He turned to their host. "Lord Kefl, your question?"

"You will have ten answers of us," the other fae said, speaking up for the first time.

Lord Kefl nodded, licking his lips. "Thank you, my lords."

At once, the gathered nobles competed for the chance to ask wisdom of the fae while maintaining the most impeccable of manners. Questions regarding what to do about this or that, how to solve problems of social strategy, and other inquiries abounded. Ra'ael let her gaze roam the room, less interested in the questions and answers than she was in the dynamic, the very fact that the Kamalti asked counsel of the fae. Even more surprising was the fact that the fae would come to the Kamalti to give it. Rinaryn, those desperate or foolish enough to do so, always went to the fae to get answers. Her gaze went to the crystals, glinting in the lamplight. Why would such things draw the fae to the Kamalti?

She frowned at herself. What did her people really know of the fae? Did they only assume they lived like Rinaryn did? For all they knew, the fae could live underground like the Kamalti.

"You have something to add, Rinaryn?" asked the fae.

Ra'ael jumped, wincing inwardly at her own startle, and shook her head.

One of the nobles seated on the couches leaned forward. "My question is this: What should we do about the Outsiders?"

The fae kept his gaze on Ra'ael, far too many teeth showing. Ra'ael forced her expression to remain calm, meeting his gaze levelly. The fae's smile grew even wider, and then he looked at the nobleman who had spoken.

"Everyone in Kamalti society has his place, is it not so?" the fae asked. The nobleman nodded. The fae gestured with one long-fingered hand. "In all civilizations, each person has their own place, their own function, for society to run smoothly. The artists have their place, the workmen theirs, the nobles theirs… and the Outsiders theirs. Chaos lies in wait when those places are switched."

The fae smiled, and Ra'ael narrowed her eyes. Murmurs grew to fill the room as nobles argued or agreed.

Dode's voice sliced through them. "And, good fae, does this not also mean that the fae have their place?"

The fae's gaze snapped to Dode, and Ra'ael made sure her stance was balanced, just in case.

His smile remained, though it became somewhat brittle. "Indeed, we do."

"And what is that place?" asked Dode.

The smile vanished. "You've already had your question, Lady."

Ra'ael glanced down at Dode, fondness and exasperation warring within her. There she sat, smiling at the fae, who watched her while Answer asked a question about the steam machines. Didn't she see that she was only painting a larger target on herself, that she was inviting more attacks? And yet, Ra'ael loved how the woman stood up to the fae. They had a reputation, among Rinaryn at least, for creating chaos, switching things around—putting things out of place. For them to now proclaim to the Kamalti exactly what they wanted to hear, that the Outsiders should keep their place, which of course was Outside, was chilling. They had some motive behind this, of course. They must, but what did they gain? Or did they merely enjoy the mischief?

Tjodlik's voice snapped her from her thoughts. "Do you know the city of Tamarik? Is it real? Where is it?"

"That is three questions." Though the fae's voice was stern, an eager light gleamed in his eyes. "I will answer you that it is very real indeed."

The other leaned forward. "If you were to find it, the fae would reward you dearly for the location of such a great, holy city."

Great. Now Tjodlik would be insufferable.

The fae smiled at her in passing as he answered another question, and then the two of them, in unison, stood. The nobles fell silent, every eye fixed on them.

"We give you this counsel for free, out of friendship. There is much smoke rising from your mountain these days. You may want to clear it away—you don't want to attract dragons."

Ra'ael avoided wrinkling her nose, though the urge to do so was strong. She wasn't comfortable agreeing so wholeheartedly with the fae, even if they were right. It was stifling in the city, with the smoke from all the steam machines. The poor, who lived higher up in the thick of the smoke, had begun tying cloths over their noses and mouths so they could breathe.

The nobles rose, with Lord Kefl seeing the fae out.

When he returned, the scientists spoke out against the fae's recommendations. "There is no way to keep the machines running without smoke!"

"Closing the vents would only increase our problems."

"The fae never give anything for free. Why would they tell us this?"

Dode interlaced her fingers, sitting tall. "Are the poor, who are even more affected by the smoke, not more important than some machines?"

"That does not mean we stop progress!"

The arguments made between scientists and nobles birthed a headache for Ra'ael, not the least because of the unfriendly looks directed at Dode when she argued for shutting the machines down. Takiyah would have loved this, the discussion of minutiae to find the possibilities. Ra'ael swallowed hard and forced herself to remain alert for danger, letting the words pass by her.

Finally, the meeting proper ended, but the Kamalti would never pass up such an opportunity to fraternize and reinforce social standing. Ra'ael kept close as Dode mingled with the others, nudging thoughts with her questions. It was impressive, how she managed to walk the line of being subtle right up until she drove home her point. The cold stares of the other nobles spoke of their somewhat less admiring thoughts toward Dode, and Ra'ael's hands curled into fists.

"You Outsiders are terrible for maintaining peace." Answer paused next to Ra'ael.

"The peace of ignoring suffering and shattered dreams is a precarious peace indeed," Ra'ael shot back.

"Try to keep Lady Dode from getting killed, will you?"

Ra'ael glowered at Answer. "Is that a threat?"

Answer thinned her lips. "I suppose I deserved that. I was sorry to hear the others did not return as well."

"Is it so hard to do your own work?"

Answer let that go without comment. "Lady Dode has even fewer friends now than she did when you walked in, and her popularity over the faces has been plummeting. While she and I do not always see things in the same light, she is important to our future. As important as progress, though in a different way."

"You disagreed with the fae's suggestion about the smoke."

"They want to keep us dependent on them. I think we will figure things out for ourselves, regardless." Answer inclined her head slightly before striding away to speak to another noble. "Lord Mezguf, about the delegation from Detr..."

What were the fae up to? Ra'ael pushed the question out of her mind. They were mischief, always had been. Trying to figure out reasons for their behavior would only drive her mad. She focused instead on keeping a close eye on Dode and on herself, to ensure both their safeties.

Once the party had ended, they walked toward home with Tjodlik subdued, as evidenced by the lack of conversation.

"Are you trying to gain enemies?" Ra'ael asked Dode, breaking the silence.

Dode smiled. "When one gets to my age, one gets ever so bored."

"You will not be bored when you're dead." Ra'ael shot her a glance.

"Are you so certain of what lies beyond this life?"

Ra'ael sighed. She didn't want to think about things like that. Not when she couldn't hear the song of the spirits anymore. "I just wish you wouldn't barb powerful people every chance you get."

"Oh, I do not. I pass up many opportunities to... 'barb'... them."

"Dode, I worry about you. Tjodlik does, too. We just wish you would be more careful."

Tjodlik's gait was tense as he walked, his fists clenching and unclenching. "I will check the house when we arrive, to be sure you have no... unwanted visitors."

Ra'ael scoffed. Tjodlik had the fighting ability of a newborn baby. But at least he showed an awareness of the danger, even stupid as it was.

"There is a time to be careful and a time to be bold. It does not do to mix the two up." Dode paused a moment and changed directions. Exasperation rode the lines of Tjodlik's shoulders as he followed her, and Ra'ael quickened her pace to keep up.

"Where are we going?" Ra'ael resisted the urge to snap at her.

"I feel the need to cleanse myself after that meeting," Dode said. "Ra'ael, you found comfort in the shrines, did you not? Perhaps this will soothe you, as well."

Ra'ael's heart lifted at the prospect, and she found her steps hurried of their own accord. It'd been so long since she'd found any peace in the spirits, leaving her lost and aimless. Her very self was stolen from her when the Elders banished them. The only solace she knew was in Dode's home and only when Tjodlik wasn't irritating her. Or her own thoughts troubling her.

But as she stepped through the doors of the sharp-edged metal building, her feet halted. Every sense screamed danger. Her spine tingled, and she held herself stiffly, refusing to give in to the urge to flee. But the shrine was safe; it only held memories of the Kamalti gods, and if she were to be Kamalti, she should embrace them. She forced her way farther in, but the sensation only grew, far worse than the unease when Dode used her Gift. The whole building loomed at her, judging her. She should stay, to protect Dode and Tjodlik from the danger her nerves protested, but it was a struggle simply to keep from bolting, shrieking, from the shrine.

"Dode," she croaked, but her voice didn't make it past her suddenly dry lips. She reached a trembling hand out, but like a dream, Dode and Tjodlik drifted away, completely at ease while her own feet were stuck in the mud. She had to get out.

Gasping, she fought her way back to the door. Even that wasn't enough. Her whole body shuddered, and her legs wobbled. She panted in the smoke-filled air half a block away until some of the sense of doom had eased. Wrapping her arms around herself, she paced, unable to force herself any closer. It was worse than claustrophobia, this aversion. It was a barrier, and she was not strong enough to break through.

What did it mean, when even the Kamalti shrines cast her out? What did that mean for her song when no music would accept her?

"Ra'ael, are you all right?" Tjodlik's worry saturated his words as he and Dode approached.

She swallowed hard, straightening. Dode watched her with concern from behind Tjodlik, but the building drew Ra'ael's eye. Her stomach turned. There would be no solace for her anymore from the sacred, even for she who was once priestess.

Chapter Nine

We have known his current form for some years, but now he is wakening. The lower peoples have already moved the Tsaeyichape'itsan. It will be harder to collect him now.

"We are patient," you have said. "They will make mistakes."

Ah, but in the meantime, the Tsaeyichape'itsan ripens. We do not want to wait hundreds more years for such an opportunity to bring the gods back. The situation must be handled and the Tsaeyichape'itsan secured, Mebril. We can discuss this no longer. We must put Sapol's plan into action.

—part of a missive from "Nitil" in Dragonmoor

Kaemada rested her chin on her folded arms atop the massive branch that held her hammock. The wind whistled through the wooden wind flutes and wind chimes the elves had placed around the Stand, creating a haunting tune with the rustle of the leaves. Perhaps somehow she could soak up the vitality and serenity of this place from the very trees themselves.

She felt more herself here, in the trees, rather than interacting with others. Below, a Rinaryn woman and two elves walked the gardens, while farther on, others gathered food near the forest's edge and to the east, more were working in a field. She'd tried to help, but it was as if being Fallen was scrawled across her forehead. It was no better with the elves, for her tongue felt too big around them, and everything about her seemed clumsy and plain.

An older elf, his grey hair tied back with a thick braid of vines, ascended the stairs and stopped at her doorway, turning to her where she lay on her branch. He bowed formally to her, hands clasped at his chest. Swinging to sit upright, Kaemada did her best to copy him, but his expression gave no sign of how well she did at mimicking the unfamiliar greeting with her injured ribs.

"I am Umril, a master psion here," he said, coming to sit beside her. "I have heard you come seeking help with a certain mind sickness that affects your psionic powers?"

Kaemada hesitated. "I... Please forgive me," she said, her brow furrowing in consternation as she glanced again at the figures moving below. Rinaryn. Like she had been. "I did not mean to mislead you or leave this out. But... I am Fallen."

Speaking the word out loud was loaded with power, weighting her again with her exile, and she winced under the load. She drew a shaky breath, trying to calm herself, but her song twisted like falling leaves in a breeze. Who knew where they would land: on nurturing ground or the devastating churn of a waterfall?

A hand fell on her shoulder, and much of the worry and pain eased. It was still there, but as an undercurrent, manageable now. She looked up, meeting Umril's sympathetic eyes.

"Be at peace," he said. "No one may harm you here. We do not recognize this rank of Fallen."

"It means I was exiled, banished from my people and home, for—" Kaemada cut off as Umril smiled.

"I know the word." His voice was low, his words coming slow and stately. "But to us, one Rinaryn is much the same as another. No one will be allowed to harm you within our boundaries. We are a haven for all who need us."

Slowly, Kaemada nodded, resisting the urge to ask him if she could trust him on that. She had no wish to cause him to laugh at her as Ennwhyn had.

"Be at peace," he repeated. Something about his tone was so soothing, reminding her of her father, and of Galod, somehow. "Tell me. Are you telepathic or telekinetic?"

That was not a question she had expected. "Both."

"Finally!" His eyes, his face, his whole bearing lit up. "A whole one."

She started at the sudden excitement in his voice, and his eyes crinkled with mirth.

"Please excuse me. I work often with your psions, and they are always broken, never reaching more than half what they should."

Kaemada frowned. "The Kamalti psions—the Collective—said much the same thing. If we should all be both telepathic and telekinetic, why are we not?"

"I think the answer has to do with events from long ago. Are you searching for answers?" Umril's tone was light, casual.

She winced, her shoulders hunching. She was supposedly being careful, and she had already apologized and asked for knowledge from an elf. Cheros was right. Any efforts beyond setting her friends free of herself were going to be laughable. Besides, she had come here for healing.

The elf's expression remained serene, but he leaned forward, as if sensing her inner turmoil. "How can I know if I can help you if I do not know what is wrong?"

"I cannot speak the Traveller's Tongue, even when I think I am." Kaemada stared at her hands, twisting her fingers together.

Umril waved away her words. "Unnecessary. If you are indeed exiled, who would you be speaking to? This has nothing to do with your psionics."

There was no running from it, no delaying it. She braced herself, wincing preemptively at her admission. "Twice now, I have... I have invaded the minds of others. I did not mean to!" His gaze on her remained steady and calm, and she gingerly continued. "I know not how I did it. I caused others, my own people, my own friends and family, to sleep for a whole day. Anything could have happened in that time. I have done this twice, somehow, and I am afraid to use my powers for fear that I might do it again."

"What makes you think you did it?"

"Who else could it have been? It happened twice when I was using my abilities."

"I assume you have used your abilities more than twice in your life."

"Of course I have." Kaemada tugged her shawl tightly around her shoulders, trying to calm herself. Umril's impassive watchfulness only increased her self-consciousness. She shook her head. "Both times I was doing something very hard, nearly beyond my abilities. What if I broke something?"

"Have you tried reaching beyond your capabilities, or near, since the last time?"

She shivered. "Only the strain of defending myself from the Collective's mind attacks." Oh, but he wouldn't know about them, would he? They couldn't reach so far. "The Kamalti psions, they all work together, sharing one another's minds, and therefore, strength."

Amusement danced in his eyes, at odds with her words. "Calm yourself. You are like a young rodent just come out of its warren, nose all a-twitch for danger and jumping out of your skin at every second sound. You will never get anything to eat that way, little rodent, and will starve yourself to death."

Kaemada fixed her eyes on her worn, dirty boots, her face heating. She couldn't remember ever feeling embarrassed more than she had since meeting the elves. "Can you help me?"

Umril nodded. "Yes. I know what is wrong, and it is treatable."

"Are both problems connected?"

"Possibly. Not that you are looking for answers."

Kaemada glanced up to see Umril smiling gently at her, and she couldn't help but smile back.

"What is the price?" Her voice wavered at the beginning of her question, and Kaemada winced that she was even asking. Cheros would surely scoff at her.

"We would only ask your help to maintain the forest, if you were amenable."

"How long?"

"Of course, the answer to that depends on the healing you ask for."

Kaemada nodded. It made sense, of course. Closing her eyes, she breathed deeply. It was so peaceful here. It was so nice of them to allow her to stay and think for a while.

She straightened. Was this a service? Allowing her to stay? Was she already indebted to them? With a groan, she held her head in her hands. She was only supposed to be here so she couldn't do more damage.

"You must care for yourself, young one."

Her brow knit, and she turned to glare at Umril. "Were you listening to my thoughts?"

A smile was her answer. Oh yes. Master psion.

Kaemada sighed, her shoulders slumping. "I'm a monster though. I miss my friends and my brother. I miss my son so desperately my heart aches! But they're better off away from me. Perhaps this way they can find the happiness they so deserve."

"Where there is no love for yourself, how can you love others?"

"Because…" She trailed off miserably, thoughts vanishing from her weary mind. "What if I'm not strong enough? What if the Elders were right? What if I am Dark-touched?" She shivered, horror gripping her as she strangled her shawl. Could it be that she was working with the Darks, even unwillingly and unknowingly? "Then I have brought trouble here, too. I should never have come."

"Stop being silly." Umril's words cut sharply through her rising panic and guilt. "You already know the lesson you need to learn. All you need do now is discover it."

Kaemada stared at him, but he simply waited for her to catch up to him. To catch up to herself, apparently. She licked her dry lips nervously, turning toward him. "Help me please, Umril. I do not want to endanger others again. The Collective is right about me. They haunted my dreams and colored my every thought until I could not tell mine from theirs, from the spirits. I misled them and betrayed them, and they are right to hate me, but I am so very weary of the struggle."

"It's less wearying when you're not fighting yourself as well as the world. Your mind is like the raging sea, full of emotion," Umril said. "It pains some of the others, less used to blocking out other minds."

Kaemada winced. "Ameyitum."

He inclined his head in a gesture she took for acceptance, and she winced again. Cheros had told her not to ask for anything, including forgiveness, but she'd barely lasted a day. They sat for a moment in silence, until she broke it again. Now that she'd begun speaking of it, the words simply wouldn't stay inside. "Umril, I'm afraid."

"What of?" The elf's voice was soothing and steady, like the ancient trees Kaemada loved of Heartwood. They weren't so perfect, so full of vitality, as these woods, but they were home.

"I fear myself. My choices. My psionics. Am I broken?"

"What makes you ask that?"

She shook her head. "People are meant to grow and to change. That's the way of life, at least Rinaryn life. Change and growth, growth and change. But after all the changes I have seen, all the changes my friends have been through, I do not feel grown. I feel broken. And I worry for them. I worry for their wounds, that they will not heal. How deep can the wounds be to a song before the damage is permanent? How much can a song take before it simply… stops?"

Umril nodded. "It is no wonder your mind is so troubled. Come. I must show you something."

Curiosity dragged her along behind him, off the branch and down the stairs, away from the tree and to the edge of the Stand. A young tree grew there, taller than Kaemada's head but dwarfed by the great trees surrounding it. It bore the wounds of pruning, sap slowly leaking from the holes where branches were cut.

Umril gestured to it. "Sometimes growth requires pruning. It hurts at first, and perhaps the tree feels a step backward has been taken. But the tree will heal and will be better for it. The tree, of course, does not know this, for it cannot see the distance we can."

She reached out, running her hand along the smooth bark. "The stories of my people always end well if the hero is virtuous, if the hero makes the right choices. All I have done is cause harm."

"You assume three things." Umril's voice was stern and vast, and somehow it seemed to echo in her mind. "One, that you are virtuous; two, that you are the hero; and three, that you are anywhere near the end of your story."

A broken laugh burst from her lips. "My pride. So I am a sapling throwing a tantrum because a storm has come and I do not like how it feels?"

Amusement shone in his eyes as he shook his head. "You are not a sapling. But if you were, you would be pretending to be a rock and angry that the storm treats you as a tree."

Between one breath and the next, she went from feeling like she could almost understand to having no more sense of comprehension than a fish could have of flight.

With that ever-present smile, he went on. "When a tree tries to be a rock, it ends up doing a terrible job at being either. And you are a horrible psion."

Everything clicked together for her, and the brightness of understanding released the great storm of anxiety and guilt and fear that she'd been holding back, only this time her emotions bled as laughter instead of tears. It was a nice change, even if it made her bound, still-healing ribs ache.

For so long, she'd resisted embracing her psionics. How many summers had Galod, with increasing frustration, tried to persuade her not to use them only as a last resort? No wonder she was so bad at it, though she had yet to determine if she wanted to be good at it. Did she want to be in control of something so potentially devastating, or merely rid of it?

Finally, she wiped her eyes and smiled at Umril. "Thank you."

He smiled in return. "Thank you for allowing me to help."

She sighed. "I wish I could be certain."

"Certainty is not always a good thing."

Kaemada nodded. She had been certain before. Before the storm. That hadn't worked out very well for her, but it had been more comfortable. But then, maybe comfort wasn't something she should seek. Perhaps she needed to embrace the uncertainty.

She snorted. "You sound like Galod."

For the first time, his serenity broke into an incredulous exclamation. "Galod!"

Snatching for the breath of something familiar, she leaned forward. "Do you know him? He trained me, in fighting and psionics, in defense of my people." Her shoulders drooped. "Before I was Fallen."

"Galod, helping train a psion?" he scoffed. "He's not a psion himself."

Even the elves knew of her teacher. Though, given Umril's frown, it seemed they did not share her respect for him. She tilted her head, her own troubles forgotten in the wave of curiosity. "Has he stayed with you as well?"

"No, no! No elf would allow him to remain near them long!" The elf shook his head. "I find it odd that a technomage would teach a psion or that a psion would learn from a technomage. Does he not make you feel filthy?"

Kaemada frowned. The term "technomage" was unfamiliar to her, but she decided to focus on the other words. *No elf would remain near him long,* and *doesn't he make you feel filthy?* "Are all elves psionic?"

Umril laughed. "Light shine on you, you will be subtle as any soon enough."

She smiled, pressing her question. "Are all elves psionic?"

He raised his eyebrows, his gaze challenging. "Does being around a technomage not make you feel filthy?"

She retreated, playing idly with the fringe of her shawl. He was helping her; she didn't want to offend him. "I do not know what you mean. Galod's a hermit. He has lived outside my kaetal all my life."

His eyebrows shot up. "You do not know?"

"How do you know him?"

He scoffed. "Everyone knows Galod. He travelled long before settling down. He tends to visit the fae more. They do not seem to mind his vile—" His mouth wrinkled as if he tasted something bitter.

Again, Kaemada watched him intently. There must be bad blood between the elves and the fae for some reason.

"Why?" she ventured. Why did the elves have such an aversion to Galod? Well, that wasn't actually so surprising, once she thought more on it. Galod could be impatient and stern and full of pride. She could easily imagine him crossing poorly with elves who expected reverence from everyone. Galod revered no one. He merely respected Storyteller Zeroun and Saimahkae Maeren.

Her heart squeezed. When the Elders had banished them all, they had attacked Galod and pointed at Taunos as possibly Dark-touched. That was ridiculous. There was no way her brother would be working with the Darks. But something must have caused the accusations, sparked the Elders to banish them instead of showing mercy and accounting for the situation. Why fear those who were not Rinaryn?

Why had Saimahkae Maeren and Storyteller Zeroun been stripped of their positions? They had said they would not lightly let them go from Torkae. Kaemada straightened. Was that why? Had her Storyteller and Saimakae traded their positions—in exchange for what? What could possess the Elders to act so against tradition and the Great Mothers to allow it? She was missing something.

Umril snatched her attention again before she could descend completely into pondering the unfathomable. "What would you do if you could do anything? No restrictions."

Kaemada knit her fingers together, straying away from him as they walked. "I would help people. I would help people understand each other and work together instead of being at odds."

"Like a priestess."

"I could not be a priestess. Teros never would have allow—"

"Stop letting others fence you in. What do you want to be? What do you want to accomplish?"

Kaemada frowned, searching her heart, but the answer was right there. It always had been there. Her mother had worked so hard to bring people together, to foster understanding and cooperation, to smooth misunderstandings and fears. Even something as unattainable as trying to make peace with the Darks hadn't daunted her. And her father, never the center of attention like her mother was, wrote his stories to help people grow into the best versions of themselves, to lift up hearts and hopes. To find what was really true. She needed to find the deep truth about the Elders.

"I want to finish what my mother started," she said, "but perhaps in a way more like my father."

"Again, what other people want for you, what other people tell you."

"No," she snapped. "My father turned away from great honor to do a task just as important, even if people did not understand, and my mother's goal was a laudable one. If I can accomplish that, or further it along at least, that will help my people more than anything else I can do."

Umril smiled "Good, then. Finally."

"But it does not matter because I cannot leave. I must stay, and even if I leave here, I cannot rejoin Rinaryn society."

Umril sighed. "When will you realize you're more than arms and legs? I should send all your Elders nightmares for this, that you constantly forget your own abilities."

"I cannot reach my people from here. The range is too great for my psionics."

"How do the Collective reach so far?"

"By working together?" Ahhh, yes, that made sense.

He smiled.

"So you would help me? Why?"

Something shuttered behind Umril's eyes. "It's the way of elves. We serve others, to remind ourselves who we are."

That made sense, and Kaemada nodded. Much like the Rinaryn, in that way. Her boots glided through the grass, and she let herself wonder. What would it be like to glide through her people this way, mind to mind? Except it was forbidden. And she was Fallen. And nothing so far had gone according to plan. If she let go and stepped past her mental walls, she could so easily harm others.

Kaemada sighed, staring at her feet as she walked. "I want healing, but I fear the repercussions."

"Why let fear control your course?"

"Because so much pain has been brought about by my actions—my choices and my psionics. You do not know how much damage I have done to others. I know not how I will ever be able to make it up to them."

They walked in silence for long moments, and then Umril said simply, "You have the pain. Now do you grow or wither?"

"I do not know."

"It's a choice, young one." Umril's tone reminded her of Takiyah's when she was losing patience. "Which do you choose?"

She couldn't wither—that wasn't truly an option. If she withered, there'd be no hope of ever checking in and making sure Eian was all right. But that meant embracing her psionics, once and for all. "I choose growth."

"Let us begin then." Umril turned. His hands sprang forward.

She froze, the elf cupping her face in his hands.

Warmth and tingling spread through her, along with a ripple of awareness. A realization struck her that they were far from others, and that was a good thing, for Umril rapidly broke down her mental walls. Once again, all the effort she'd put into tending those walls and building them strong and thick was torn down in a breath, as if it was nothing. All the emotions that tattered her song to shreds, all of her anger, fear, grief, and pain, were blown away in a gale, until nothing remained but her and the tenderness of a young shoot nurtured by the older trees around it, held upright by a root network far more extensive than its own.

But below that, the core of her remained in turmoil, regardless of the emotions he heaped on her. It was just as the Collective had done. Her stomach knotted. No, no, not again. She'd lose herself again, replaced by someone else. He released her, and she crumpled to the ground.

She was still connected to him, and a psionic link always went both ways. The old elf was impossibly strong. She felt like a child, especially watching the ease with which he worked. A well of fury spiked in him before he abruptly cut the link, leaving her thoroughly disoriented.

"You did not tell me everything. You did not tell me the true problem. This is more than a simple mind injury." His serene face and calm voice were at terrifying odds with the anger she knew he was feeling. She huddled in a little ball, trembling under the force of it.

"Your mind is not broken." A little of the gentleness returned to his voice, but still she sensed the wrath roiling beneath. "You are as a young elf, growing in spurts. Only you had not received the proper training so the growth has been, and will continue to be, rocky. Violent. Disruptive."

"Why can I not speak Traveller's then?" she whispered.

He turned away from her, almost as if dismissing her. His words came sharp as daggers again. "Your troubles come from wounds to the spirit and bad growth in psionics. Probably from the ridiculous notion of a technomage, of all things, training psions."

"My trouble with not being able to speak Traveller's began after I fought some psions to keep the king from killing me and hurting Eian," Kaemada argued. "Before losing Eian."

"The damage taken from the fight must have been too much. You'll never be strong without a bond. You need a new wolf."

"I cannot replace Tannevar!"

"Then you will not be able to speak Traveller's, and you'll continue to put others at risk with your mental spasms."

Kaemada frowned down at the grass. "I have thought about looking for a new animal companion. Maybe a hawk. Something that could fly. That way they would not fall down a chasm again."

"That is a terrible idea."

Startled by his frankness, she looked up.

Umril shook his head at her, as if she had missed something very simple. "What animals have you bonded?"

"Only wolves," she admitted after a while. "But I am friends with a pegasus." Shareilon. She hadn't seen him since before the mountain. Hopefully he was all right, too.

"But you did not bond this pegasus?"

Mute with grief and worry, she shook her head.

"You need to bond another wolf. Since you have been bonded before, you must continue."

"I cannot watch another one die," she whispered.

"That is the pain and fear talking."

She nodded. Knowing that didn't make it any less difficult.

He sighed. "You must bond another companion to heal. There is no other option for you. Then, having already connected with you, I will train you." She drew in a breath, a question on the tip of her tongue, and he cut in. "It will be easier for me to teach you, having already made that connection. Now. Go bond a wolf. Several live within our territory."

Wooziness took her again as she climbed to her feet. The connection with Umril had taken a lot out of her. His psionic power was vast, leaving her helpless in the face of it. No wonder some people feared psions.

Still, how could she bear to lose another companion? She opened her mouth to argue.

But Umril cut her off. "No more arguments. How long did you train with Galod?"

"For twenty summers." Where was this going?

Umril shook his head. "It is unfortunate for Galod he is not here to hear this. I do not intend to say this again and, in fact, never intended to say this in the first place. For putting up with you that long, Galod is a hero."

Kaemada scowled.

"You will go and bond an animal companion—a wolf! I can train you no further until that is done."

"What if I do not bond a wolf?"

"Then your training is over." He threw something at her and stalked away.

Desolation filled her as he left her alone. She turned and looked at the forest, focusing on the trees, not her fear. There was nothing else for it. How could she practice safely without a tether, a hold to reality?

He was right. She needed a companion.

As she climbed to her feet, she picked up the thing he had thrown at her—a thin leather circlet similar to Ennwhyn's, only less ornate. Wooden ornaments hung from strings attached to the leather band, tangling in her curls as she hesitantly tried it on. She should have thanked Umril, she realized. Her spirits sank lower, and she tugged on the corners of her shawl.

Heart heavy, she trudged into the forest. Her feet moved almost of their own accord, for she was far too busy with her thoughts to really watch where she was going. After some time, a cloud of butterflies descended on her, swirling around her in a dizzying array of colors before fluttering off. She watched them go.

What if she bonded and lost this companion as well? Even the very thought made her tremble. She would almost rather think of Eian, though that brought even more fear and pain. Was he all right? What if he wasn't? Had she made a mistake staying away?

Kaemada firmly shut down that line of thinking. She had to simply take this step. She was stalling. Again. If her son—if anyone—was going to be safe from her psionics, she had to do this. And the last thing she wanted to do was hurt anyone else with her out-of-control telepathy, especially Eian.

And yet, her heart thundered against ribs that ached, and her breath hitched. Her psionics were so devastating. Was she really going to take this next step and make them even more powerful? Was the stability that would hopefully come from a bond worth the risk of the strength it would also add, the ability to do even more?

With a heavy sigh, she sat down on a log and stared up at the sky. Such a deep, calming blue. Her chest eased, and breath came easily to her lungs once again as she lost herself in the sky. A flock of birds flew past, so near she could touch one if she reached out. Why was there such a large flock of birds here still? Hadn't they gone north for winter? They whirled about her before breaking apart as they rose into the canopy.

Still stalling. Leaning forward, she scrubbed her face with her hands. The old fear came roaring back, crushing her. She had no safety net. What if she exploded in everyone's heads again? Twice in her story was twice too many as far as she was concerned. And according to Umril, this was a limit she would always have, simply because of how she'd been trained?

She frowned at herself. She needed to focus. Gripping the log with her hands, she reached out uneasily with her mind, searching for animal minds, ignoring everything else. Focus. Control. Focus. The awareness of them flooded to her, along with the old sense of wonder and companionship, only tinged by fear. She floated through them, past them.

Only the right mind would work and only willing. An experienced wolf? No, old age would take them too quickly. A young wolf? She missed Tannevar's youthful enthusiasm, but he had also been overly full of zeal sometimes. Oh, how she missed him!

A mind gently brushed against hers, then shied back. Eyes closed, Kaemada swept out with her mind. A cold nose poked her in the back, and she leaped from the log, twisting about in the air so she came down facing the opposite direction from which she started, eyes wide, breathing hard. There was nothing there, only leaves wafting in the wind.

Something drew her closer. She peered through the thick underbrush, creeping slowly forward, mind stretching out, searching as carefully as her eyes. She felt the mind at the same time as she saw a peek of silvery fur and golden eyes before they vanished.

As gentle as a new vine snaking across the ground, she sent a greeting as she pursued, keeping a distance so the wolf would not feel hunted.

The wolf returned the greeting and bounded ahead, out of sight again. Only flashes of grey and silver and white fur or of golden eyes showed through the dense foliage. In her mind, the wolf did the same thing.

Kaemada stopped her pursuits, both mental and physical. She waited. After several breaths, a silvery muzzle topped with a black nose poked out from under a bush. The wolf lay, head on the ground, watching. Questioning.

The question coalesced, more meaning than words. Who was she?

She sent a mental image of herself, strong and capable, bow in hand, at home in the forest. The wolf changed the image so the mental Kaemada shrank, curled in on herself, and mewled.

Sheepishly, she had to admit the wolf was right. She was afraid. She sent out a tendril of question, changing the image to Kaemada and the wolf, strong once again.

The wolf disappeared from before her and, a moment later, from the image. Black shapes lurked around the lonely image. It seemed a warning, and Kaemada tensed, whirling. She dropped to a crouch and examined the underbrush more carefully.

To her right, the wolf appeared again, giving a huff-huff of breathy laughter.

Brow furrowed, Kaemada continued her inspection. Green and brown faded from view ever so subtly here and there as she watched. She frowned then remembered Ennwhyn telling her that no outsider was left alone for fear of harm to the trees.

She reached mentally for the wolf, sending a question. Was it the elves?

The wolf huff-huffed again, wagging her tail. Again the wolf mind brushed past hers with an impression of searching.

Kaemada's gaze darted to where the elves were lurking in the forest. She had to do this. She glanced back at the wolf and shared her memories of former companions. Sheathe, Híva, and Tannevar, along with what they had meant to her. The whirlwind of emotions and memories whisked her away, and when she came back to reality, she blinked. There, sitting in front of her, was a young wolf with silvery grey and white fur and golden eyes. Her pose was prim, her ears pricked forward but occasionally swiveling to catch some sound Kaemada could not hear.

The images of the other wolves moved, now including this one.

Kaemada smiled slowly, reaching out her hand carefully. She had been looking for a companion, and a companion had found her. The wolf huff-

huffed at her again and stood.

Still gingerly, as if walking across a newly frozen pond, Kaemada quested for the wolf's name. It came to her the same way the wolf herself had. Nimae, the one that ghosts through the forest without leaving a trace.

The wolf padded forward until she was face to face with Kaemada. Gently, reverently, Kaemada wove the psionic cord that would tie them, heart and mind, together. She touched her forehead first, her mental image doing the same, fastening one end of the cord to herself. Then, she reached for Nimae, and the wolf stepped forward so that she could physically lay a hand on the wolf's soft furred forehead at the same time as she mentally fastened the other end of the cord to the image of the wolf's mind.

Awareness bloomed in her. Exhilaration, anticipation, and just a little fear. Kaemada smiled. It was almost a mirror of her own emotions. She bent, forehead to forehead with the wolf, then threw her arms around her. To her surprise, the wolf did the same, strong forelegs gripping her shoulders.

Kaemada smiled. "Are you ready for adventure, Nimae?"

Affirmation and amusement answered her. After all, that was why the wolf had come in the first place.

"Thank you," Kaemada said, burying her face in the wolf's soft fur. For the first time in a very, very long time, she felt whole.

ÍTAL

Chapter Ten

If I could find information on the Darks anywhere on this world, it would be in Far Dahutad. People from all lands flock to the country for trade, for travel, for healing, and for learning. The main city—capital—boasts not only the best house of healing—bamimri—I have ever seen (short of our own healers) but also an enormous library with knowledge gathered from every people known, so they say. Access is restricted only to guards, so I will have to become an Arruk city guard or more. The Elders have charged me to do whatever I need to do to get in. I only hope it will be worth it.

—entry from Taunos's journal

Taunos swam in and out of consciousness, vaguely aware that infection ravaged his body. His arm was on fire, too, with agony. Amanah's voice pierced through the haze surrounding him, murmuring an apology, and then further torment enveloped his arm. Always when he surfaced back to consciousness, Emin was lounging nearby. And even though Taunos was sick to delirium, he was free—no longer bound, no longer drugged.

He could stand pain and illness. It was powerlessness he couldn't handle.

Finally, for the first time in several days, he woke to find his mind clear. His sight had returned, and the headaches had faded—he should be fine so long as he didn't push himself. The fever was gone, and the deeper punctures from the arrows were dressed and bandaged. Hazy memories of stitches came back to him as he passed a hand over the bandages. His muscles trembled with fatigue even from just sitting up—the infection had worn him down.

It was fortunate he'd been able to make it to the bamimri, the best place equipped to deal with those wounds. His people had actually shot him! Anywhere else and he'd never have survived.

He gritted his teeth against the protests of injuries and weakened muscles as he sat up straighter. Emin was gone, but Amanah met Taunos's gaze from across the room and walked toward him, her face lit then shadowed then lit again as she passed through the rectangles of sunlight cast on the stones.

The pain faded to the background as he stared at her, with her intricate braids bound back with a scarf and her brown eyes warm and sparkling, never mind that her bimna smock was stained with the results of her work. How could anyone compare to her? Her brow was too strong, her eyelashes too thick and long, and her mouth too wide for Dahuti images of beauty. The Dahuti were foolish not to see how stunning she was. He relished the memory of her eyelashes fluttering against his cheeks, and her mouth was perfect for laughing—and kissing.

Was loyalty to his people, to the Elders, worth losing her?

She stopped next to him, roses blooming in her cheeks. "You look at me as if I'm from the storybooks."

"You're even more beautiful, being real," Taunos said.

Her gaze went to the window, and her throat bobbed. "I can't, Taunos. I can't just go back to what we were, with all the secrets. I can't pretend..."

"I wish I could fix it."

"I wish you hadn't broken it to begin with."

"You told me to go. I went."

She shook her head, exasperation filling the lines of her body. "Yes, and that's my responsibility. My fault. But we were in trouble before that."

"Amanah—"

It was his fault, but knowing he deserved it didn't lessen the knife in his heart. Amanah kept her eyes on her work as she unwrapped the bandages around his wrist with businesslike movements. The gentleness of her hands belied the clipped tones of her voice, the pain and anger that still lurked there. "I'm going to change your dressings and treat the wounds with salve. The air flow in the bamimri should blow away many of the bad spirits, but the sooner we see infection, the more likely we can stop it."

His forearm was red and raw with a deep gash in it. He stared at it as she rubbed a pungent salve on it with a gentle touch. When had that happened?

Amanah's tone softened a bit. "Your wrist swelled up, and we had to cut deep to relieve the pressure. Are you sure you won't take some sulim for the pain?"

Taunos shook his head once, vehemently. She pressed her lips together and wrapped new bandages around the splint. Her movements were professional, treating him with the same care she showed the other patients in the bamimri, of course, because she'd never take her feelings out on a patient, no matter how he'd hurt her. It made his heart ache with the reminder of all he'd lost with her, and he longed to do something, anything, to cause her to once again look at him with love instead of careful distance.

Pain lanced up his arm as Amanah tightened the wrapping, and he drew in a hiss of breath. She grimaced as she eased the tension, secured the bandage with a knot, and stepped away.

"You're not healing nearly as well as you should be." Worry knit her brows together. "And Dulara said you reacted far more quickly and intensely to her powder than normal."

Taunos caught her hand. "I'm fine. Don't worry about me."

Her dark eyes flashed with anger. He winced inwardly at himself, at the deflection that had become so routine for him but surely only showed her how little he could be trusted. Amanah pressed her thumb to the hand that held her, and his arm went tingly as she stepped out of his gentle grip that could not hold her. He wasn't able to hold her anymore.

"I'm on duty." Her words were clipped, but her tone was soft. "I have to go. Dulara's giving me the evil eye." She made the sign to ward off harm. "We'll talk, but later."

Taunos watched her walk away, wishing she wasn't always leaving him. But what right did he have to stop her? What plan could ever put back together the relationship they'd had, the precious thing he'd shattered? He didn't even have anything to give her, now that he was Fallen. All he had was the longing in his heart, but he was a battered song, unworthy of her.

"You're going to poison yourself with such a dark expression." A hand clapped him on the shoulder, and Emin dropped onto the bed next to him, dressed in Dahuti clothes this time—a long, loose shirt and baggy pants. "Still haven't talked to her?"

Taunos shrugged. "What could I say to her, Emin? Apologies aren't enough."

"Tell her the truth."

"And who will convince her I'm telling the truth?"

Emin grinned. "That's your problem to figure out."

Taunos plucked at the blanket beneath him in silence. Ra'ael had been right all those moons ago. He normally didn't have to worry about the messes he left behind.

The bigger man's shoulder bumped his. "I didn't realize you were actually panicking before. I'm really sorry."

He didn't want to talk about that. He shifted the subject instead. "Thank you. After everything… I don't deserve your friendship."

Emin snorted. "If we all got what we deserved, this world would look very different."

"Why are you still here? You seem better."

"We're talking about you, not me. Get used to it."

Taunos's mind raced. Emin and Gurseh had broken up, but Gurseh had been in his fighting band. "Is the guardhouse siding with Gurseh somehow?"

Emin flung up his hands. "Gods above, Taunos, what about 'we're talking about you' do you not understand? What has you looking all dour?"

Taunos fixed his eyes on the polished slate stones of the floor, his mind racing for a distraction. Emin poked him in the side, and pain flared through his arrow wounds, dousing the flames of his misdirection.

"I've lost Amanah." The words broke from him, unexpected but all too true. Taunos swallowed hard and forced himself to continue. "She deserves someone better, someone who can give her more. But it still hurts."

Emin snorted. "She's incredibly angry with you. And hurt. And still in love. You know her. She doesn't act lightly, not like you."

"So why aren't you angry?" Taunos asked.

"Because for all your many, massive, glaring faults, you're also one of the heroes of Gahimbli. You're the man who risked his life to save me when I was pinned down. You paid my debt when that thief took everything we had. You helped Amanah's plan at Tiam succeed. You helped us both evacuate the people of Nirmawi, and there's no way we would have succeeded without you. Everyone would have been caught by the Hinanuri. You crawled into a collapsed building to rescue a child, even though the Sea Peoples were coming."

"You saw that?"

"Amanah did."

Taunos scrubbed both hands through his hair. Zafril. The guilt of leaving the boy had plagued him ever since that day. "I left that boy there."

"Many others wouldn't have even stopped to try to save him."

"Did..." His voice was a hoarse whisper, and he shook his head, clearing his throat. "Did he make it?"

"Yes, thanks to Amanah."

Breath gusted out of Taunos, his shoulders sagging with relief.

Emin tapped his fingers together. "Why did you leave him? We can't figure that out. And how?"

"I did not want to."

Silence filled the space between them for a bit, and then Emin slapped his knees and stood. "Well, you'll have to do better with Amanah. Like I said, Taunos, we know you. That's why your lies and secrets hurt so much."

"I'm sorry."

"Sorry doesn't make it better." Emin cracked a grin. "I'm just more forgiving than my sister."

That wasn't it. It was easier to be friends with a liar than to love one. And Amanah's pleas for his loyalty, all those moons ago... What must she have thought of his secrets?

Emin mock-punched his shoulder. "I'll provide the opportunity, but you have to do the work."

The afternoon wore on until Dulara proclaimed him fit enough to leave. "Don't tear those stitches, and keep that bandaging clean. And don't get into any more fights. And if you start feeling ill, come back."

Taunos nodded to the barked instructions until Dulara bustled away.

Emin turned to him, rubbing his hands together. "Come on. Let's get you out of here, sea-wizard."

Another bimna swept past, handing Taunos his cleaned, folded clothes. With a smile and a blush, she left.

"I'll show you to the washrooms." Emin grabbed Taunos by the arm and hauled him to his feet. Leaning on Emin, Taunos limped down the airy hallway, turning in at a door made of dark planks of wood, gleaming with polish. "Go on and change. I'll wait here."

"What are you doing?" Taunos asked.

"Trust me." Emin's grin made it clear he knew how difficult that was for Taunos, despite his casual pretending.

But it was really the least he could do. Taunos bit his tongue on his questions and went in. The room was more of a marble hallway, with slats of that same dark wood closing off several closets. He stepped into one and quickly changed, but the string that held the waistband of the baggy pants up defied his broken wrist.

Face hot with embarrassment, he placed the bamimri clothes in a hamper and stepped out to find Emin lounging just outside.

"Must be a sad little sea-wizard who can't even dress himself." A smirk softened Emin's words as he knotted the string. Emin always found action easier than words, and when he was forced to use words, he preferred to use them as clubs. It was a language Taunos was fluent in.

"Must be sadder being jealous," Taunos replied. "Do you have my belt?"

Emin frowned. "No, you should have had everything in that bundle."

Cold fear flashed through him. It wasn't the belt that really mattered so much as the herbs in it. Had Amanah found it? Would Dahuti scholars recognize the herbs? Were they unique to Rinara, or could some scholar use the library to discover where he came from? Galod would be furious with him for losing them, for the risk.

"Don't worry," Emin said. "You can stay in the guardhouse if you need. My war-band's eager to see you again."

"Thank you."

Emin turned, leading him out a door and onto the shaded breezeway that ran along the inside of the rectangle created by the four buildings, separated from the gardens by an intricately worked bronze fence. Around them rose the stone walls of the guardhouse, palace, library, and bamimri. Emin guided him to a table in the corner of the empty breezeway and dropped him in a chair full of cushions.

"Don't mess this up."

Taunos stared as Emin turned and left. What did he have planned?

The late afternoon sun slanted at an angle to stream beneath the canopy shading the breezeway, warming the edge of the metalworked table. Taunos shifted among the cushions. He'd missed the outdoors, the sun on his skin, the brush of the wind flowing past. The gardens drew his gaze, where he and Amanah had spent many long nights with their heads bent together, trading stories. His eyes travelled to the window of the room she'd had in the guardhouse, with ten others. He'd asked her favorite flower, and her eyes had sparked with challenge as she'd responded, "Roses."

But the royal roses were off-limits, so he'd grabbed a potted rose and scaled up to her room. "I cannot let you keep it, but I still wanted to bring it to you, if only for a little while."

The astonishment on her face still brought a smile to his, even at the memory. She'd sworn never to play games with his heart.

And yet, during their last fight, she'd said she thought he'd continued to play games with her. Perhaps while he was healing, he could make it up to her somehow, ease the pain he'd caused her.

Raised voices drifted from the bamimri, and he limped to the window. One of the patients was being released, one of the people he'd watched Amanah tend to. She knelt in front of him, picking up dropped items of clothing while he raged at her.

"Worthless havi." The man snatched the clothes from her hands and charged past her, knocking her to the floor. The sound of her hands hitting the stone floor was loud, as sharp as a slap to his ears.

Taunos lurched to the doorway, but by the time he made it there, the man had gone and Amanah was just disappearing into the washroom. He swallowed his anger, his frustration at his own impotence. He couldn't save her from the prejudice and hatred of others, but he could be there for her.

He sank onto the bench outside the washroom and rested his head in his hands, pain lancing up his arm from his wrist. He loved Amanah, but he'd still left her for his people. The pain in his arm echoed that from the past.

Galod had raged at him that day he'd broken his arm. "Go then, and don't ever return. If you can't realmwalk, you can't be the hero they need. You won't be able to protect them."

They'd fought. It hadn't been a normal training session. Galod had had none of the control he usually held. There had been something raw, something dangerous about the hermit.

The snap as his arm broke. The pain.

The bench moved, and he startled.

Amanah raised her eyebrows at him, settling herself beside him. "You're usually far more aware of your environment."

Taunos gave her a tight smile. Galod would rant at him for such inattention and set him days of challenging tasks focused on perception. Galod wasn't here. "Are you all right?"

Her eyes were red, her face damp as if she'd just washed it, and she still wore a bimna uniform, though this one was clean. She folded her arms around herself, looking into the bamimri. "Emin said you'd be out there. The table by the empty bunkroom."

"I was. I came for you."

She flashed him a quick, tense smile.

"You did not change into your normal clothes," he noted.

"If they see me as a bimna, they see me as worthy of some respect," she said. "Are we talking here?"

"Would you like to talk outside?"

Again, a smile flitted across her face, chased by her pain and sadness. She rose and helped him up, supporting him silently as they walked back to the table. It was more comfortable than Emin's help because she was the same height as him, instead of taller, but her closeness made him ache with the reminder of all he'd lost.

Once he was seated back among the cushions, Amanah set his belt on the table and settled in the chair across from him. "Here."

Taunos snatched it, his fingers shaking as he checked the herb pouch. Empty. Had they been taken?

"I burned the herbs while you lay sweating with fever. They're gone."

Guilt writhed with relief inside him like a monster, and he had no hope of winning that wrestling match. Taunos reached for her hand across the table. "Thank you."

"What were they? Why this reaction? What has you so scared?" She pulled her hand back but leaned forward, her eyes glimmering with wary curiosity.

And there it was.

Galod had always said that a secret only remained safe so long as no one knew it. The moment you shared, it was no longer secret. Anyone could use it against you and those you loved.

For fourteen summers, Taunos had abided by that. Information could lead to more information, could lead to answers to questions. How well he knew that, for that was what he did. So he had tried to give as little away as he could, for fear there was another like him out there, asking questions, listening, looking for answers, except instead of searching for information about the Darks, this shadow-him might be looking for information about his home, to use against him. And if such a person existed, Taunos did not want to be the one to give away those secrets.

But now, he was watching his secrets tear apart the woman he loved. There were a few things in all the worlds he was not willing to sacrifice for his people, for the Elders. Kaemada was one, as with the rest of his people. Amanah was another. He wouldn't sacrifice her again.

The hope was dimming in Amanah's expression. His mouth opened, but no words came.

Bitterness clipped her words as she sat back, folding her arms. "I got those herbs because they seemed so important to you to have them destroyed. Even now, even after everything, I… But you won't tell me the truth, will you."

The last shreds of connection to Amanah, though he'd frayed and burned that, too, until it was hardly more than a thread, were drifting away from him. Still, he couldn't stand to lose her.

"I'm sorry, Amanah." The words broke from him, unplanned, and hung in the air between them.

Her gaze pierced him, full of warning and guarded suspicion and the tiniest flicker of hope.

What were the words he could say to bring her back to him? No, Amanah was never one to be swayed by words or charm. Only action would work, and so much felt far too little, far too late.

He took a breath, despite how his chest felt squeezed tight. "I understand why you distrust me so. I know I've hurt you, though that was never my intention. I just want you to know how much I regret it."

Her gaze flickered between his eyes, searching him. He held himself still beneath it, hoping his sincerity came through, but still the question came. "Is that true?"

Taunos scrubbed a hand over his face. "How can I regain your trust when you're so set on distrusting me?"

"I don't know," Amanah said. "We've already said all we're likely to say because you distrust me."

"I cannot place your curiosity before the safety of my people, no matter how much I want to."

"I'm not asking you to put your people in danger, I'm asking you to trust me. How are you conflating the two?"

"All I want is to keep my people safe. I never intended to hurt you."

"But it did hurt me. And you keep hurting me."

He shoved his good hand through his hair. "Why, because you don't know every detail of my people, my home? I swear I wasn't working against you. I've already told you far more than I should, far more than is safe."

"I thought you were Isemi. That's what you said when you joined the guard, but you're not. And that makes me wonder what else you lied about."

"We've already been over this. Where I really come from doesn't affect you. I needed to gain access to the library, and I did that with as little damage as I could. Only bimnas, guards, scholars, and nobles have access to the library, so I had to become a guard."

"It does though. Your lies do affect me. When you're not where you said you'd be, or when Emin and I cover for your absences. When I try to track you down and the officers think you're with me and the questions start coming. And suspicions come with the questions, of course, and you know what happens to traitors. What could a hero like you see in someone like me? Just a havi to trick, to use and toss away." She lifted her chin, angling away from him.

His stomach turned. "You think I was using you?"

Tears glittered in angry eyes, and she rubbed her face with both hands. "It wouldn't be the first time someone's tried. I left the guard to get away from the suggestions that I'm not entirely to be trusted. I came here and I like it here and I don't want to have to leave here too. But then I saw you…" Her throat bobbed. "Taunos, you scared me. I thought you were going to die. And so yes, it does affect me. In so many ways. I think I'm allowed some questions about why someone tried to kill you, and I know I'm allowed questions when you use me as your alibi."

"We already talked about this. I told Captain Asi I was going to be with you that evening, and I was—after I did what I needed to do first."

"When you came back here for orders to cover for yet another of your mysterious absences, you were seen in the library instead."

"I came to the library to look around while waiting."

Amanah shook her head, her voice filled with pain and betrayal all over again. "And what were you doing in the library, alone, when you should have still be travelling, that you couldn't share with Captain Asi?"

"I'm just trying to keep my home safe. Through all my story, I've worked to keep them safe." The ragged whisper of his voice echoed the strain of his song, torn between two desires. "My people are only safe as long as they are secret. I cannot risk that. I did not mean to cause trouble by holding back information. I tried to lie as little as I possibly could, especially to you. There is a difference between trusting you with my life and trusting you with the lives of all my people."

"Do you really think I would harm your people? I thought you saw me. Despite what other classes say, havi can be trusted perfectly well."

"I do see you, Amanah." He sat back, seeing with new clarity. He'd put her at a disadvantage, shrouded in his secrets so that even the truth tasted of it, while she'd given everything to him, open and whole. Amanah didn't do anything by half. "I've spent so long trying not to give anything away. It's hard to change. But the stories I told you of my home, they were all true."

"Truth sounds so much the same as stories coming from you, it's impossible to tell the difference. I want to believe you, Taunos. I want to believe it wasn't all an elaborate deception. I want to believe I wasn't foolish and naive and that you really are the man I thought I knew."

"I am, the good and the bad of me." What could he give her? All he had was the truth. He took a deep breath. "Ask me some questions. I will try to answer, if I can. If I cannot, I will not deflect. I will just tell you that."

Her gaze weighed him again, and he held his breath. Then, slowly, she nodded. "What were those herbs I destroyed for you?"

"They're from my land. I collect medicinal herbs as I come across them in my travels, if I think they might be useful. But the ones you didn't recognize came from my home. There was a root, called bitterroot. My sister gave me a supply of that, as well as dasavu and spirits' tears, back before... everything."

The familiar light flickered on in her eyes, that eagerness in her bearing he adored. "What are they for?"

"Bitterroot is for pain, and dasavu is for swelling. Spirits' tears are for nightmares."

She raised her eyebrows at him. "Sounds like she sees through you, unless you're more honest with her."

Taunos scrubbed his hand through his hair. She was right. Kaemada had known he could collect all those herbs himself, but she'd done it for him anyway. "She might be one of the few who do."

Amanah reached for him. "More would see you if you let them. What are you so afraid of? When you pull back like that, Haari Taunos, and you throw up those walls thicker than that of Arruk, shields in front of you and in back of you, no one can get to you. You hold everyone at arm's length, pretending with smiles and jokes that's not so. You smile as if nothing affects you, and you change the subject to avoid those that hurt too much, that aim too true to your heart. But it means nothing can get *in* either. I don't want to endanger your people, Taunos. I just want you to let me help you. But you have to let down your defenses to do that. When's the last time you really let someone in?"

Her words rang uncomfortably true. All his secrets welled up within him, and he wanted nothing more than to share them with her. To not be alone anymore.

But still, he hesitated. The breeze gusted past, ticking his hair against his skin. He glanced around for anyone else who might hear. There was no one, and yet, the words stuck in his throat. What if someone overheard?

"Walk with me?" he asked.

Amanah shook her head, sitting back. "You shouldn't be walking far, not with your leg wound."

He shifted in his chair. A hundred ways he could distract her flitted through his mind: non-answers he could give, jokes, deflections.

But this was Amanah.

Amanah, who had seen him vulnerable and saved him, despite her anger with him, while his own people had shot him while he was desperate and friendless.

If he couldn't trust her, who could he trust?

Taunos scrubbed his good hand over his face and dropped his voice to near a whisper, just in case, entwining his fingers with hers. "I have been trying to find a way to help my people. They live on an island, forgotten by the rest of the world, and it needs to stay that way. That secrecy is their best safety, and it's been carefully set up over generations. It must have been, or someone would have discovered them."

Amanah leaned forward, and he tried not to be distracted by the brush of her hair against his cheek, keeping his gaze fixed on the table. He drew idly on the table with his finger, as if drawing the words out of himself, unburdening his cares which he alone had held for so long. The weight lifting felt wrong, his shoulders tensing, waiting for the trap to spring.

"They don't know other lands, they don't sail the seas, they don't have metal, and they don't have massive buildings or cities. They do have an ancient enemy that appears out of nowhere, kills, and disappears into the night. Always, always, at night. I came to try to figure out who this enemy —the Darks—really are, as well as to find any other threats. Even me looking for answers is a risk, because there are those who would take advantage of a lush island filled with such a people. All a people would have to do is find my home, and my people would be destroyed."

"You're so sure of this?"

"No, but it's a danger. Here." Taunos spread his hands. "Here's the world. And the Sea Peoples travel all over the seas, and traders and sailors of all sorts come to Far Dahutad, from all over, right? The seas are busy. What are the odds someone from somewhere wouldn't have found my home?"

"The ocean's big." But she was smiling, her whole bearing attentive and engaged now, with the wariness melted away.

"It is big, but between Ifreesians and Sea Peoples, do you really think they haven't covered most everywhere? If my island was smaller, perhaps, but it's not tiny."

"But how could someone set such secrecy up? Even more, why?"

"I don't know." He frowned, shaking his head.

"These Darks are sea-wizards, like you?"

"Probably. How else can they disappear like that?"

She nodded, her expression thoughtful, while the tension inside him increased.

He rubbed his forehead. "I need to keep them safe. That's been the whole reason behind everything."

"Telling me about you won't be trading secrets from your land." Her intent expression was everything he'd missed throughout the past moons, full of tenderness that masked strength. "It's you I want to know about anyway."

"I've been working with the Elders, who lead our people, since I was seventeen. I gave up everything for them. My friends drifted away. My kaetal—my community—thought I was just struck by wanderlust. All my work was secret—the Elders didn't let me tell anyone what I was really doing."

And Galod didn't come to their aid either when they were banished, though Taunos wouldn't really have expected that. Still, the dismissal stung. It echoed the pain of seeing Takiyah, Ra'ael, and Kaemada fracture and fall apart. Had he not done enough over the summers to prove his worth? Did the Elders and Galod care so little? And Takiyah, Ra'ael, and Kaemada were supposed to be Galod's prize team. Surely he'd heard of their banishment, and yet, nothing.

They were adrift, alone. Only in Taunos's case, it was partially his own doing.

"You couldn't tell *anyone*, even though it was to protect them?" Amanah asked.

He shook his head. *You must be in control of yourself at all times.* With a blink, realization crashed onto him. Over the summers he'd worked for the Elders, he had become increasingly set apart, increasingly like Galod. The crowd of friends he'd had growing up had become frustrated by his long absences and his evasive answers when they asked about his travels.

Only his sister had stayed true, although she'd begun to lighten her own stories for him as well, hiding her troubles as if he wouldn't see. His secrets and the stories he used to hide them were like a contagion, spreading out from him to taint all he touched.

Amanah squeezed his hand. "It's nice to see you... you, again."

He met her eyes. "I'm always me."

"Like this. Alive. Eager to do, to learn, to talk. You've been... almost defeated."

Taunos scratched the back of his neck. "I suppose that's true. There's not been a lot to get excited about." He rubbed his face with both hands. "The Elders would be furious if they knew I told you so much. Even though they banished us—me, my sister, and her two friends."

Amanah entwined her fingers in his. Her dark eyes had drunk in every word as he spoke, and the tension in his shoulders had eased without him realizing.

He smiled. "I've wanted to tell you things like this for so long."

"I've wanted you to, too. Thank you, Haari Taunos." She smiled at him, and for a breath, it was as if the last summer hadn't happened. "What is your real, full name?"

"Adeion Denvin Firerel Taunos Sierso."

"That's a mouthful."

"It's the normal length for my people. Though 'Taunos' is spelled wrong, in Rinaryn, anyway."

Amanah's thumb swept across his knuckles, her hand cool in his. "Well, that wasn't hard, was it? You're getting better at this."

He chuckled, and she grinned at him.

"Let's see," she started. "Do you know much about sea-wizards? If they're real—obviously you are real, though not at all like the stories. I wonder, could any human learn to be a sea-wizard, or is it something else?"

He'd been dreading this one. He stared at the table to avoid seeing the horror or betrayal sure to come. But still he answered. To come so far and still lose Amanah's trust by falling back on his secrets and lies? He couldn't do that. "I'm not human."

"Interesting."

Taunos raised his head. There was no fear in her eyes, just thoughtfulness. "You're not... I mean..."

"You thought after all that, that's what would get rid of me?" Amanah asked.

"I'm Rinaryn," he said, a slow grin spreading across his face. "And I don't know why we look so similar to humans. But I'm tall among my people, and I heal absolutely at normal rates. It's you humans who heal absurdly quickly."

"Could it be all sea-wizards are Rinaryns?" Amanah asked.

Taunos shook his head. "The oceans around Rinara are impassable. Ships that go out never come back, anyway. So no one goes out."

Amanah nodded. "Why do you stay, if you are clearly so attached to your home?"

"I cannot realmwalk right now. It's one of my gifts, what you call me sea-wizard for. It's connected to my telekinesis—the way I can push things with my mind. But with realmwalking, I can walk between the realms. Just not very accurately. But truthfully, selfishly, I don't want to part with you."

Sadness tinged the edges of her smile. "But you'll have to, won't you."

He looked down, the fleeting happiness evaporating like water in the dry, hot air. "I will. For a little while, anyway."

His sister was in need, and alone, and—

The rich scent of mossy bark and rich, loamy soil filled his mind and washed away. He shook himself as if coming out of a reverie. No. He couldn't go back yet. The best way to help his sister was to make the Elders overturn their decision.

A wild, impossible hope floated to the forefront of his mind. If he could finally finish his mission, the one he'd failed last time, perhaps he could force the Elders to take them back. They had constantly pushed him for more knowledge. Perhaps he could buy his sister her community once again with knowledge. Surely, if Kaemada was again surrounded by the community she loved so much, if he could get Eian back to her where he belonged, she would come back to herself.

It was a desperate goal, but if there was a chance it could work, he had to try. And in the meantime, just maybe, he could apologize to the woman he loved.

"I need to bring the Elders something convincing enough to make them let us come back. If there's a chance it could help my sister, I have to take it. And her friends never deserved to be cast out." He rubbed his face with both hands, despite the warning pains of his wrist. "The Elders always greatly valued the knowledge I brought them."

"Is there no way to appeal?" Amanah asked.

"Normally, we could come before the Elders to plead our case in a summer—a year. But the Elders stripped us of our names, so no one will be able to speak for us, to grant us safe passage."

"Sounds like your Elders aren't following the law. Sometimes we have that too, where councilors bend the law to breaking. The only way to hold them accountable is with others in power."

"The Elders prevented that safeguard from happening. Something is terribly wrong with the Council." He tensed to suppress a shudder, his eyes on the table before him.

"So the balance in place for justice is broken, and you've been cut off from the safety net which would allow for appeals, is that right?"

"More or less."

"Why would they want you so isolated? Why would they set you apart?"

"It's not just that. Ra'ael and Takiyah, my sister's best friends for all her life, they both left. They couldn't handle the pain. We're all drifted apart from each other, as well."

"Like a hunter scattering a flock." Amanah tapped her lips, her gaze wandering over the gardens in thought. Her gaze went back to him, and she squeezed his hand. "You're not isolated anymore. I don't know what I can do to help, but I'm willing to try."

He tightened his fingers on hers, gratitude filling his chest and stealing his voice. He'd missed her so much, and to have her here beside him once again, offering her level-headed advice and thoughts to him, it was like a dream, especially now, with the secrecy between them lifted.

~

Emin and his war-band arrived as the sun went down. "Taunos!"

Taunos turned and rose, just in time to nearly be knocked off his feet by the reunion. The next whirlwind involved so much hugging and back-slapping that he grew lightheaded with pain.

"Stop it. He's still healing," Amanah scolded them. "You're going to tear his stitches."

The intensity of the greetings faded but not the sentiment, as every member of the war-band apparently felt the need to show Taunos he'd been missed.

"Hey, did anyone bring wine?" Emin asked, his gaze roaming over his band but skipping over Gurseh.

"No, but I know where we can get some," said another.

"We need food, too. This calls for celebration," said another.

"Taunos is still injured. He needs to be careful," Amanah objected.

"That's all right. We've pulled his weight before, haven't we?" Emin grinned as his band cheered.

"No more than I've pulled yours," Taunos said to hoots and playful jeers from the band.

"This is serious," Amanah said. "If we're going out, Taunos needs a chair."

"We could put Taunos in one of those carrying chairs nobles use," Emin said. "Nobles don't like to move much, so it fits. They're both useless."

"Shut it, Emin." Taunos bristled at the reminder of his current limitations.

But despite his protests, Gurseh disappeared and moments later returned with a small wooden chair painted black and attached to poles. Embarrassment heated Taunos's ears, but he let Amanah chivvy him onto the chair, and two of the war-band hoisted him before he could object.

"Too heavy for you?" Taunos teased to cover as he clutched the arms of the chair for balance.

They tilted the chair at an angle for answer, while he held on tight with his good arm. Laughing, they righted him and took off, the poles resting on their shoulders.

Even though riding at shoulder height through the crowd wasn't what he'd prefer, the beauty of Far Dahutad still warmed his song. He loved the blast of hot wind stinging his face, the spice-laden air, the bold colors of the various styles of clothing, from lands far and near. Men in tall, conical hats brushed past robed scholars and nomads with their heads wrapped in lengths of flowing fabric. Porters ran through the throng, carrying boxes and baskets of goods or chairs with brightly colored cushions upon which perched men or women bedecked in jewels, gold, and silver.

Ignoring the jests of the war-band, he found himself watching Amanah as she walked alongside, smiling at jokes and pointing out the poets dueling for audiences. He didn't want to be set apart anymore. He wanted nothing more than to be walking among them, and his fingers tapped a dance of frustration and worry along the handle. Had he said too much? If his people fell because he shared pieces of his heart with his beloved, could he live with that?

They turned in to the market where wooden stalls covered with striped cloth packed the open space, fed by nine roads which angled off in different directions. The smell of meats sizzling made his stomach growl. Captive birds chirped as they waited to be bought as pets, and around him swarmed a sea of color as people mingled, the hum of voices rising and falling as buyers and sellers haggled and old friends and neighbors called out greetings.

In the center of the market stood an enormous marble book, engraved with what he'd been told were the code of laws for the city. A philosopher stood on a box, proclaiming that the shape of human souls was square and how that should affect their actions. Nearby, another philosopher in ragged clothes mocked him mercilessly, to the enjoyment of the crowd.

With the slower movement in the market, Taunos was finally able to convince the band to let him down. The cobblestones under his feet kept him grounded, and the tension in him melted away, now that he no longer rode above the crowd but became part of it.

"Meet at the fountain," Gurseh said. In moments, the war-band scattered among the stalls, leaving Taunos and Amanah behind among the churn of the marketplace.

"Knowing the band, they'll bring back more food than we can possibly eat," Amanah said.

She took his arm to help him along, pausing as a juggler passed in front of them, tossing colorful balls high into the air. Nearby, a man sat making glass beads, his stall of colored glass samples catching the sun and casting a cloud of colors in dazzling array. It looked difficult but still easier than patching up what he'd broken with Amanah.

"Beautiful, aren't they?" he asked.

She hummed acknowledgement, her pace slow enough that he could keep up. He'd memorized her gait, so he could always pick her out of a crowd even if he couldn't see her face. He knew each of her expressions and had shared more of himself with her than he had anyone else. So he knew something else was bothering her.

"Amanah, are you all right?"

She forced a smile. "I always worry who will see a havi wearing a bimna uniform and who will just see a bimna."

Emin's war-band protected him from the social structure of Dahuti society, which put the nomadic havi at the very bottom. But Amanah had been assigned to a different band, and far too many times, Taunos had seen her let offenses roll past her like water around a stone when she couldn't stand up to them. Even when she could pretend they didn't matter, he knew how deep the insults cut her.

Taunos curled his arm around her shoulder, as if he could shield her from the prejudice of those who chose hate. "You wear it like armor."

She caught his eye and nodded.

He couldn't protect his people, and he couldn't protect his beloved. He couldn't even walk far without her help supporting him. "I wish I could stay with you. I wish I had something to offer you."

Her brow furrowed. "What do you mean?"

"I've lost everything. I'm not exactly a great prospect, even among my people. And among yours? I have no money, no house, no land, no jewels or gold."

She scowled. "I don't want *things*. You never had to offer me *things*. I'm not someone who can be bought, and you should know that by now, after all the years we've known each other."

"I know."

The tension eased from her shoulders some, but her voice was still filled with conviction. "All I wanted was you. As equals, as a partner. Nothing less."

He nodded. "You're everything I've ever wanted. And our talk, sharing with you? Hard as it was, it was also good. I would love to show you my home, if I could."

"And I would love to see it." She smiled. "But even if that's not possible, I want what we had back, the good and the bad to share. The two of us together against any challenge, like we were."

"I want that too." His voice was thick, and he cleared his throat. "Maybe I could travel back and forth. Stay with you, visit my sister occasionally, once she's safe and well. Once I bring back information valuable enough for the Elders to take her back."

As the words were spoken, Taunos was struck with the oddity of it.

He'd always felt a pull back home whenever he was travelling, though with Emin and Amanah, it had lessened. That pull nevertheless increased with time, easing only after he'd been home for a while. It had just been one of those natural cycles, and Taunos had never thought much of it until now.

Where was the drive to do his task and return home now? Could he really be thinking of settling down elsewhere? He'd considered it before but had never brought it up to Amanah. It'd be unfair to her, for them to have to part when the need to go home overtook him.

Right now though, in this moment, it seemed a possibility.

Amanah glanced at him. "What about the knowledge from the library you worked so hard to get into? There's no chance you read every book in there."

He scratched the back of his neck with his free hand. "I finally got a chance to look, only to find I cannot read any of it."

She burst out laughing. "Not even the great Haari Taunos can be good at everything, it seems. Maybe I can help you with that. Nasri will want to meet you anyway. She's been star-struck since she realized she found Haari in the gardens, not just any stranger."

"I doubt I'm still famous."

"You are hard to forget." She smiled at him, and his heart ached at the fondness there. "I'm glad you shared with me."

"Please, do not tell anyone." The words broke from him, exploding in a fit of desperation as they found an empty table by the fountain and settled around it on the low bench seats. Her caution had always balanced his confidence, but for the moment, it seemed they had switched.

"You know I won't."

"I know. I just…"

Amanah patted his shoulder. "Haari Taunos, sometimes you have to stay to face the consequences. I'll help you through the steps."

The war-band arrived, carrying bowls of grains and stews, rounds of bread, and jugs of wine. The mood became boisterous and celebratory as they plunked themselves down at the table by the fountain. The table was burdened under mountains of food, but Taunos's heart felt lighter, less burdened.

"I will pay you back, once I make some money," Taunos said.

Emin snorted. "You're already paying."

Taunos's brow furrowed, and Emin laughed, dropping a bag on the table. Coins spilled out, and Gurseh stared at the bag and then at Emin. Emin avoided his gaze, his smile too broad. But then Taunos's eye caught the insignia on the bag.

He snatched it up. "You were supposed to give this to Amanah when I left!"

Blushing, Amanah stood, stepping away from the table, her arms wrapped around herself. He limped to her, catching her hand in his and gently unwrapping her.

She looked away. "I'm sorry. I... thought you were trying to buy favor. It wouldn't have been the first time someone tried to pay me for secrets or access somewhere or something thinking I'm without honor."

Taunos leaned forward, keeping his voice low and gentle. "I'm not them."

"I know. That's why I'm sorry." She lowered her head, squeezing his hand. "You kept secrets, but I jumped to the worst possible scenario, too."

He bent his head next to hers. "No, I needed to hear it. I hadn't considered how it would feel to you."

"Trust goes both ways."

He nodded. "Trust goes both ways."

Her smile relaxed, becoming real. "Thank you."

"For what?"

"For believing in me. You've always believed in me, even when I doubted you."

Taunos stepped closer, his arms again finding the places they belonged, around her waist. "Only a fool wouldn't see how capable and brilliant and wonderful you are. I will never give you cause to doubt me again."

"We can't turn back the clock, but perhaps we can mend what's been broken, like your wounds."

"Hopefully more quickly." He laughed. She joined him in laughter, and he leaned in, resting his forehead against hers. "I'm a better person when I'm with you."

"I like who I am better when I'm with you, too." Her eyes were so dark they swallowed the night. Their breath mingled as she met him halfway.

He closed the distance, her lips soft on his, his pulse quickening as she kissed him back, pulling him closer as he tightened his arms around her. Their hearts hammered together, as one, as the distance of pain, fear, and time eased in the face of the love they still bore each other.

Emin hooted, the band quickly taking up his call as palms pounded against the table. Amanah broke apart from him breathlessly, and her smile and flushed cheeks only made him want to kiss her again.

"While you're up, get the table more wine," Emin said. "Preferably one of the new varieties the merchants bring from far flung reaches of the world."

"You can stay. I'll get it," Amanah murmured to Taunos.

"If you will help me, I'd rather come with you."

She extended her hand. "Together."

He grinned. "Together."

Dinner was a haze of food and wine and laughter. The market hummed with vibrant life all around them, and Taunos found his gaze continually ensnared by Amanah—the music of her laughter, the sparkle in her eyes, every wave of her hands. The drumming of his fingers on the table caused Amanah to flatly forbade any dancing for him, making him chuckle. She knew sitting made him restless, even injured. But one of the members of the war-band found him a pipe, and he played wild tunes to make them clap in rhythm and stomp their feet, and traded stories as the night deepened.

There was a noticeable tension between Emin and Gurseh, who avoided eye contact, speaking around each other, and Taunos tried to lighten that mood for Emin's sake. Emin turned it around on him though, once they were all heady with the wine that had been brought.

Emin grinned at Amanah. "You made a decision sober. Time to see if it holds up under drink."

The bowls of food lay empty, along with the jugs, now tipped over on their side. Taunos nibbled on the last of the bread as Amanah waved her brother off.

"This is an important decision," he said, and his war-band quieted. "Amanah, do you still think it's a good idea to give Taunos another chance?"

"We've always been better together. It's when we stop sharing that we find trouble."

The cheers that went up filled Taunos's heart with warmth just as the food had filled his stomach. It was nice to have acceptance again, even if only for a little bit. A community. All he needed was to find a way to bring this back home.

ÌTAL-AETHA
Chapter Eleven

The city sits at the edge of land and sea, surrounded by desert, safe from the manipulations of fae and elves. And yet, it is a scar, constantly reminding of our past, when the promise was wrestled from us. We are not even able to exert our own will on the present, for the Printak protected their investment well. Dragons, avoid Tamarik, but feel free to unleash your fury of the bindings on anyone foolish enough to brave that wasteland.

—scrap of notes from the Monks of Annularei

"Takiyah!" Rothan came skidding into the forge. He crashed into the metal ring stands she'd set up, nearly toppling over the vertically stacked iron bars they held, which she'd organized by length.

Takiyah slammed the hammer down again on the glowing rod before her, lengthening the bar and flattening it. It'd better not crack at the edges again, or this time she'd have to cut the end off. Two more strokes of the hammer, and she shoved the billet back into the coals to heat. "Man the bellows, if you're going to stand there."

Squeezing past, Rothan grabbed the bellows handle. As he pumped away with even pulls, she wiped the sweat from her face with a dirty rag and guzzled water from the drinking barrel in the corner. She checked the sun. Nearly midday. Still time yet to finish this last knife before the client came to inspect their order tomorrow.

"Takiyah, I got the contract!" Rothan's hand went to his pocket and then stopped, as if he'd just remembered that waving paper so close to a forge was a bad idea.

She smirked, adjusted her heavy gloves. and fished the heated metal piece out of the coals with long-handled tongs. She took it to the anvil, and Rothan followed her, abandoning the bellows.

"That's good. For you personally?" she asked as she began shaping the knife's edge with a smaller hammer.

"For the forge, of course. I'm not going to leave you out."

Takiyah spared him a glance, raising her eyebrows. "I told you, you need to rely on yourself more. You're going to overreach, Rothan, and get burned."

No matter how many times she told him the dangers of leaning on others, he never seemed to understand. She hadn't either, until… Her leg twinged, and she grimaced, which only pulled at the brand on her cheek. Well, he'd figure it out, and then he wouldn't be able to say she hadn't warned him.

He snorted. "Nah, with you around, we'll have the order fulfilled in plenty of time. I already thought about that. By the Printak, Takiyah, you're a magician with the metals! In only a moon, you've surpassed me."

"If you would work instead of talk, you'd get more practice."

"Seriously, Takiyah, I've been apprenticed to my father since I was ten and forging on my own since sixteen. Then you come along, and it's like the last ten circulations never happened."

Takiyah shook her head, concentrating on shaping the metal edge before her, leaving the ricasso blunt. She'd grind the edge to sharpness later. Straightening, Takiyah replaced the hammer on the bench and heated the blade again. The city hadn't only given her strange memories—all the forge work she'd been able to get had broadened her shoulders and added even more muscle to her arms. Without a doubt, she was now stronger than Ra'ael and Taunos. Not that it mattered. "I worked in a forge some before I came here, and yours isn't the first forge I've worked in Tamarik, you know."

"That doesn't explain the rapid improvement in your skills."

She shook her head again. What could she tell him, that she spent the first moon here dizzy with images and knowledge that flooded her like impossible memories? The first several forges she'd worked at had expelled her for fear she'd get burned due to her inattention. Then whatever was wrong with her had calmed down, and she'd been able to put the fragments of memories to use. It sounded mind-sick, even to her. "Your father must be a good teacher then."

Rothan snorted. "You're never going to tell me, are you? You know, it wouldn't hurt to let someone in now and again."

Statements like that proved he was a child mentally. It did hurt, more than he knew. Memories weren't like blades—you couldn't quench and temper them. They only grew more pointed with time. Taking the glowing blade from the forge, she slid the knife into the quenching barrel. The metal flared, fire licking at her as the oil drowned it. Letting the metal cool, she turned toward Rothan.

"Fine, keep your secrets." Rothan narrowed his eyes at her.

"The contract?"

"Oh, yes!" He bounced on his toes, his natural exuberance hard to keep down for long.

His optimism was so much like Kaemada's had been, and Takiyah firmly steered her mind away from those dangerous thoughts.

"Look, we have three moons to complete three hundred knives. This is for the entire city guard! We'll earn the seventy-five jih easily!"

The city guard. So many of them were Kamalti, including their leaders. Takiyah pulled the blade from the quench and peered down its length. Pride bloomed beneath the resentment that shadowed her. She would not bend on this, no more than her blades warped. Pek may be all right, but the very first Kamalti merchant she'd met had tried to swindle her, and she hadn't forgotten the laughter at the harbor, how they'd turned her away without even giving her a chance.

"You and your father will have to work hard to meet that quota," Takiyah said, turning away and putting her gloves on their shelf. She took the dipper from the water barrel and gulped more water down her parched throat.

"And you," Rothan said.

Takiyah shook her head. "I told you. I will not participate in this contract."

"Why not?" Rothan frowned at her, his free hand clenching into a fist.

"I do not work for Kamalti."

"Takiyah, you have to let go of your grudge. They—"

"Kamalti cannot be trusted. They speak pretty words, and then—" She cut herself short, clenching her jaw. She took a deep breath and repeated herself. "Kamalti cannot be trusted."

"Only one job, Takiyah. Just this one time."

"No." How many times did she have to repeat herself before he'd understand?

"You can make the knives for the Rinaryn guards."

She burst out laughing. "Yes, and then they would all end up in the same bin anyway. Do you think I'm a fool?"

Rothan drew himself up, narrowing his eyes at her. "I do, yes."

Takiyah waved him away, but he scowled.

"Your refusal to work with Kamalti clients has gotten you banned from every forge you'll accept work at. You make it impossible for anyone to help you out."

"I am not a charity case, Rothan. I have done good work for your father, and clearly your business is now booming," Takiyah snapped.

There were thirty smiths in Tamarik, most of them Kamalti-owned or worked, and she had worked in all of the Rinaryn-owned forges. Two moons, seven forges, as well as the masons (also mostly Kamalti-owned, limiting her options there as well) and even carpenters, always keeping her distance from Kamalti-owned or worked businesses. She was running out of options. The moon she'd spent working with Rothan and his father was the longest she'd stayed with any one employer so far.

She narrowed her eyes at her own pain. If it was time for her to part ways, then that was simply what she had to do. Her side jobs would get her by for a little while. Getting attached only got her hurt. She should have known better. At least she'd walk away with her dignity and honor intact.

Rothan gestured around them. "You could do so well for yourself if you would set aside your grudge. Look around you, Takiyah. You live in the City of Tamarik. You'd do well to learn to act like it. Rinaryn and Kamalti live together, work together, raise families together here. Clearly, it's not that way everywhere, from your reactions, but it works."

Takiyah glared at him. "You haven't figured out what they're like yet, Rothan. Trusting them will get you killed."

"Like relying on you will get me burned?"

"Exactly." She turned and grabbed her staff and then her bag, hefting it onto her back with a groan. Rothan was slow, but he'd figure it out.

"Where are you going?"

"Varen's. I have finished my last job for you." She stepped out of the forge, squinting in the bright sunlight, and raised her hood to protect herself from the rays.

"You're really going to leave us?" His voice was stricken, and she armored herself against sympathy.

"You know where to send my pay. Goodbye, Rothan." She headed into the street, joining the flow of the crowd with her long strides eating up the distance. She had time to stop by the market and buy one of those delicious pastries made by a Rinaryn fisher family before Varen was expecting her. The sea would soothe the sting of her heart, even if she couldn't follow the mysterious tug that called her seaward.

Behind her, Rothan's bellow cut the air. "Takiyah!"

She ignored him. She'd warned him and warned him, but some people just wouldn't learn. The only thing to do was to distance herself from them and their imminent disasters.

The bald, knobby heads of Kamalti were everywhere, with their loose, flowing clothes and their love of ornamentation. With Kamalti and Rinaryn being able to breed without issue—though Takiyah couldn't fathom why any Rinaryn would want to marry a Kamalti—Kamalti and Kamalti hybrids made up much of the City of Tamarik, leaving Rinaryn a minority.

And yet, despite the plethora of Kamalti infesting it, Takiyah found she enjoyed the City of Tamarik. She loved the adornment, the carvings and intricate metalwork.

The city was elegant, with immense walls of metal and sandstone instead of plain rock like the City of the Lost. The gates were carved with elaborate designs, and no lethal statues guarded the entrance. In fact, the back of the city butted right up to Dead Man's Sea, and great granite outcroppings were built out onto the angry waters for fishing opportunities during calmer seas. Away from the water, sandstone and metal were married together in dazzling arrays—in balconies and facades, in arches and support columns—often carved into trees with spreading branches. It might be a contribution of the Rinaryn living there, for Tamarik was tree-obsessed. Most of the open courtyards sported at least a few trees, always lovingly watered during the dry seasons, she was told. The main marketplace had a ring of trees along the outer edge, and in the center, a great raised pedestal, always kept immaculate and empty of any burden, while around the entire base of the pedestal were carved a series of trees.

The smooth stone paving the wide road was obscured by the masses, but Takiyah moved through the midday crowds in practiced resignation, occasionally slipping under an awning for shelter from the brutal sun for a few moments. If the pattern of the last two moons held, the rest of the day would be filled with pouring rain—not the gentle rains she was used to, but rain that pelted the skin as if it were rock instead.

Takiyah mostly ignored the other citizens as they did her, all focused on finishing their errands so they could hole up in their houses for the rest of the day.

The city was laid out in strict zones, another mark of the Kamalti influence. The Docks were at the easternmost edge, of course, by the sea. Then there was the Crafting Square that took up a large portion of the northern city, butting up against the Docks. She'd found a small house there. Where better to live than surrounded by working people, people who made things, rather than in the housing section where most people lived? To the south was Ink Square, where the scribes and lawmakers and others who lounged around all day writing worked. The western edge of the city, by the gates, was housing and service-oriented professions, while at the far north and far south were agricultural regions. That left the guardhouse in the middle, which Takiyah avoided. It brought too many memories of her time under the mountain.

At the crossroads marking the border of the Crafting Square and the Docks, her attention was brought back to the present. An itinerant priest stood on a crate, shouting, and a large group of people clogged the intersection, occasionally muttering to each other.

"Listen, listen to me, and I will tell of the Flight of the Faithless!" the priest cried. "For long ago, we lived under the sun in sight of the gods themselves: the Printak, who created us, who protected us from dragons, who built this home for us to thrive. They made the oceans swell and the mountains rise. They make the rains fall and the walls stand firm against the winds. All glory to the Printak!"

He glared at them when only a few responded with the customary, "All glory to the Printak!"

Takiyah put him out of her mind as she worked her way through the crushing masses. All these hangers-on listening to whatever ravings this man told them, and he still wasn't happy. Even if few responded, they were still here, weren't they?

The priest went on about how the Printak retreated to allow free will and almost immediately the Agitator rose up and many listened to him, turning away from the Printak. They stole the Printak's Tree, symbol of the gods' defense of their creations, and left Tamarik, hundreds and hundreds of Rinaryn and Kamalti, never to return.

A young boy reached for her pack, and she spun, catching his hand. The panicked child wiggled out of her grasp and away through the crowd. This was a pickpocket's dream, never mind a prime opportunity for the priests to stir up fear. Some Rinaryn priests had also stirred up fear, especially when the bad dreams had begun, back before Eian had gone missing. Fear was one way to handle a large group of people, but Takiyah preferred her father's gentle guidance.

Grief twisted like a blade in her heart. How she missed her parents! Were they all right?

She cleared her throat and pushed away those thoughts, as she did nearly daily. Why didn't it get any easier?

"The Faithless left Tamarik," the priest growled. "They left the protection of the Printak, and they suffered and died in the desert. Oh, yes, occasionally the Children of the Faithless return to us but only in ones or twos. The masses left, and the masses died by wind and sun and dragonfire."

Takiyah shoved her way clear of the crowd, casting a glance backward at the gathered people. They could believe whatever they wanted. She certainly wasn't going to enlighten them. She had no wish to be pegged as delusional. With the inexplicable knowledge she occasionally gleaned from nowhere, the last thing she needed was her sanity scrutinized. The Rinaryn thought the City of the Lost was the only city left in Rinara—it made sense that the people of Tamarik would be just as mistaken. On she went, following the call of her heart, the tugging that always brought her to the sea.

She grabbed a fish pie from her favorite fisher stall and wordlessly handed the smiling young woman her coins. On a whim, she walked out toward the granite outcroppings as she ate her lunch, ignoring the wary looks the dockworkers cast her. The pie was hot and burned her tongue, but it was worth going out of her way for, even worth braving the crowd listening to the hollering priest. The sea sprayed her face with salt as the huge waves clawed at the rocks, trying to drag them back into the ocean.

To counter the power of the massive tidal swells, enormous wooden posts rose far above the docks, towering above low tide and barely poking above when the tides were highest, when the sisters traded spaces in the sky above. Over the days, the water levels had crept higher and higher, and less than a pace was left of the posts, she estimated. Boats were tied with short ropes to rings that floated up and down the posts according to water level, and the docks were slanted, with switchback stone stairs eventually reaching the sea at whatever level it currently lapped at the rocks.

No boats braved the water today—they'd only be smashed to pieces. The moons would trade places soon, but until they did, the waves would only get wilder. It was amazing any fishing got done at all when the moons were so close together.

Takiyah lifted her face to the wind and breathed in the salt air, leaning against her staff. The familiar niggling tugged at her, as if some long-lost memory was stirring. Nothing came to her, however. It never did, not here. Just a bitter reminder of all that was missing from her life. She finished her pie and turned away.

The press of the crowd held her back, a barrier that she fought her way through, toward the Crafting Square. Varen would have processed the sand she'd harvested for him last night by now, and one of the masons could probably use help. She needed to work, to keep busy. To keep from thinking.

She'd have to avoid Rothan. He would surely try to convince her to come back. She couldn't explain it to him. He hadn't lived through torture at Kamalti hands in the name of some twisted corruption of justice.

Men and women brushed past her, glancing off her as she barreled past the smithies, keeping her speed up so that no one could knock her off course. Then, a careful picking of her way past the weavers, who always insisted on letting their work spill out of their buildings and onto the streets. It was a mess, and her foot caught on a rolled bundle of cloth, sending it careening down the street and setting the merchant, a Kamalti woman, screaming after her.

No. She couldn't stay, couldn't face this woman with her eyes alight with fury.

Her own weakness sickened her as she took off like a thief, like a criminal, shoving her way past the leatherworkers and the tailors and the embroiderers. Tare the jeweler shouted a "Hallo" at her, while Ferl the dyer scowled, but she ignored them both, taking refuge in Varen's shop.

Varen was simply a merchant, and as such, his shop did not exactly belong in the Crafting Square. However, as he chiefly did business with craftsmen, he had thought it prudent to buck tradition and set up shop near his clients' shops. Takiyah could see the logic in that. It made more sense than his insistence that she collect sand from a specific point in the desert and only as much as she could carry in a pack on her back. She'd tried to go out with a sledge once, and the fit he'd thrown had made Varen so breathless she worried his heart would fail.

Apparently, scarcity made for higher prices, and the sand at that spot was somehow special. It didn't actually matter because the work was hard and mindless and brought in enough money for her to survive and buy the odd set of materials to tinker with.

Some of the nearby craftsmen, Ferl included, had raised a fit when she started working for Varen. According to the Kamalti, it was scandalous that he had hired a woman for muscle. Yet another reason to avoid them— the absurd restrictions were clearly their influence. The forges had been difficult enough to convince of her worth, but at least she'd been able to produce quality work as proof of her skill.

That was behind her now, she reminded herself. She'd burned through all of them.

She hadn't expected her stomach to twist so much at the thought.

"Welcome! We have the best sand—extra clean, extra gritty, scouring —Oh." Varen stopped short as he emerged from the curtain that partitioned the private rooms in the back from the shop area up front. "Come to get paid?"

Takiyah fixed him with a sharp look, dropping her bag in front of him. "Generally when I do backbreaking labor, I enjoy being paid for it, yes."

"I won't need you again for a few days." He grinned at her, swishing behind the counter and unlocking the drawers there. "Off to the tea rooms? Nah, not you. Dice, maybe? A lover, perhaps?"

Would he never cease to pry? She didn't need friends, no matter what he thought. "My private life is none of your business."

With a laugh, he straightened, a bag of coin in one hand. "Of course it isn't. I only meant I never see you with anyone in your free time. Perhaps you tend a stone garden?"

Glaring even though it wouldn't stop him, she snatched the coin pouch.

"How's the sand quarry? Are you making sure you hide it?" He leaned forward on his elbows.

She rolled her eyes. She shouldn't push him, but the words fell from her lips anyway. "It's all the same. The same sand is right outside the city walls."

"It is not." Varen sounded affronted. "This sand is special!"

"Of course it is." She spread her hands, trying to placate him.

"I think Saman might need your help to move bricks tomorrow. You may want to check with him. Are you going to count that?" He nodded to the coin pouch still in her hand, a knowing smile on his smug face.

With a scowl, she opened the pouch, quickly making a count. Every coin was there, as always, but she always counted anyway. She wasn't going to be tricked again.

He tapped the counter. "You're going to be quite the rich woman, you know, if you keep at this. All work and no fun."

"All you think of is money, Varen. You need to go somewhere without all these Kamalti and begin thinking straight."

"I do not much care to be a bandit. Running from dragons all my days does not sound to me like a good life."

A snort escaped her as she tucked the coin purse away. "You don't actually think that's all that's out there, do you? Dragons, bandits, and sand?"

He shrugged. "That's what the priests say. Why, do you know something?"

The eager light in his eyes struck her core. For a moment, she saw Ra'ael, smugly explaining something as if everyone should have known it all alone.

Her heart squeezed and her throat clenched on her words. "Trouble and heartbreak."

"But cities? People?"

"One city and too many people." She shifted. It was past time to move on. Where should she go? She needed to get busy again, and of course Varen had no more work for her, nor any more leads for the day. She shouldn't have expected him to. When she started relying on Varen, she'd know her story was as low as it could get.

"A city? You believe the old legend of the Fallen who come here?"

She needed to stay focused on the present. The past was nothing to her. It had no hold on her. And yet, she answered, fists clenching despite herself at the implication she was a fool. "It's real."

"And why would a dragon not destroy this city?" His voice dripped with scorn for the idea.

One of these days she'd have to teach him humility. "It's on the other side of the mountains, Varen. Why don't they destroy this one? They avoid it, like a shield protects it."

"Why, the workmanship, of course. Even an overgrown flying lizard has to respect good workmanship. Or if you're going to be all superstitious and believe in the City of the Lost, then you can believe that this is the Holy City, the Chosen One. Golden Tamarik, untouched forever by the dragons in respect to the Agreement, protected by the sign of the Printak."

"What Agreement?"

Varen snorted. "You do not strike me as the superstitious type."

"Have it your way." Takiyah turned her back.

Varen caught her by the arm. "Really and truly? Another city?"

She glowered at him, considering whether it would be going too far to punch him. "As real as I stand before you. I lived there for a time before I came here."

"If only there was a path to it, we could sell them sand. Or something better than sand! Ah, but the bandits and dragons would never make that possible."

"Why would you want to go there?" Takiyah growled. "You do not listen to me, and you love the Kamalti."

Varen laughed and clapped her on the arm. "Because, you overgrown muscle, I could establish trade routes there—maybe even get myself an exclusive contract. Money, good woman! Fortune!"

Takiyah shook her head. "Money is the only thing you care about."

Varen laughed again. "You could do to think a little about money, too. Why shouldn't you make a fortune for yourself?"

Although Rinaryn physically, Varen had never been part of Rinaryn culture and only knew of it by what he heard, which was largely inaccurate. He'd only ever lived in the City of Tamarik, and the customs and culture here were vastly altered from what Takiyah knew. It was probably the Kamalti influence.

"You'd make more money if you took on Kamalti work," Varen said, a sly tone to his voice.

She glowered at him. "No."

"What do you have against them?"

It wasn't that she didn't like them. She just preferred to avoid them. But Varen's words picked at the truth of it like fingernails at a scab too new. She was trapped, and soon working with Kamalti would be her only choice. The city was going to force her into it, to take choice away from her. She'd be better off out in the desert alone, except her bum leg would kill her.

"Goodbye Varen," she said, stalking out the door and slamming it behind her with her staff.

The clouds matched her mood, stormy and ominous. Wind battered her as soon as she stepped outside. The city walls kept the worst of it out, but its strength was still enough that it roared through the city streets. A few stragglers wrestled down the cloth over their sturdy stalls which lined the streets, tying the cloth up tight and then running for cover themselves.

A powerful gust blew, tossing her into the wall of a building. A cry of frustration welled up within her, and she roared at the empty street. The wind blasted sand into her face.

One of the last few people on the street paused by her, hand extended. She reached to take it but stopped. Pale skin showed under a rough woven sleeve, and too-large eyes watched her from a knobby skull.

In a flash, she was crashing in the balloon again, being pulled from the wreckage by Kamalti hands. Being held down as the hammer was brought down again and again until her leg finally broke. Forced to keep lighting things on fire, forced to walk on her broken leg so it healed crookedly.

Trapped, trapped, trapped.

"I do not need your pity!" Takiyah huddled in a ball as her past came crashing down around her, roaring in her ears. The crack of her leg. The searing pain. The heat of the brand and the stink of her flesh burning. The Elders, casting them out, casting down her parents. All that time depending on Elisabei and Reinan's charity. Ra'ael's cold demeanor, Kaemada's brokenness, Taunos's desperation when she left him behind.

She'd left it all behind. She'd left her whole past behind. Why wouldn't it stay there?

Takiyah despised her short breaths, the pounding of her heart, the tears in her eyes. Once, she'd been whole and strong. And then, betrayal after betrayal. She couldn't handle any more. She should never tie herself to anyone. They'd only betray her.

Chapter Twelve

The library of Far Dahutad is said to hold the collected knowledge of every people, as well as that of several peoples and lands that no longer exist. These scrolls and books are gathered and tended to in an enormous building. Any person above a certain station in Dahuti society can freely come and go through the library, studying as they please, though the books must remain in the building. It would be perfect... if I could decipher Dahuti writing.

—entry from Taunos's journal

Taunos slept in a room at the guardhouse for temporary use that night, and in the morning, Emin and Amanah arrived with clean clothes.

"I brought you some Dahuti clothes in case yours are too warm," Emin said, tossing them at Taunos. "Some boy's from the guards. Probably the only thing that'd fit you."

Amanah shook her head at both of them. "He's not that short."

Taunos chuckled. The siblings stood side by side, Emin in casual Dahuti clothing and Amanah in her bimna uniform. Did they know how much he valued them? "I'm grateful. To both of you."

"If you're going to show your gratitude with a kiss, I'm going to have to decline." Emin's grin was too broad, filled with mischief more than mirth. "I do have standards, after all."

Taunos snorted. "Ah, Emin, ruining the mood as usual."

Amanah smiled. "I thought we might go to the library, since I have the day off. Change, and we'll go. Don't use that leg too much though—Emin and I will help keep your weight off it so you don't pull your stitches."

Dahuti clothes were lighter than Rinaryn, more suited to the arid climate, and the long, loose shirt was easy to slip on over his bandages. Before long, he was ready. He leaned on Emin, who steadied him on the side with his injured leg as they walked toward Amanah. "Don't be such a child, Haari Taunos."

"I will try, if you will try not to be such a cockerel."

"Child."

"Cockerel."

"You're both children and cockerels," Amanah said, slipping under Taunos's arm to steady him on his other side. "In fact, you're little chicks, all fluffy and adorable."

Emin choked. "I'm anything but adorable."

Laughter buoyed Taunos's spirits. This was a nice change from sickness and injury: an outing with the best company he could ask for.

The plain stone hallways of the guardhouse gave way to carpets and large windows when they turned the corner and entered the arched entranceway of the library. Two guards stood on either side of the archway, their gazes flickering quickly over them. One saluted Emin and nodded to Amanah, waving them through, while the other grimaced, murmuring something about havi under her breath.

"He's still a guard, and she's still a bimna," the other hissed as they passed. "They're allowed."

Amanah stared straight ahead, her arm around Taunos tense, but Taunos had no chance to confront the rude guard, for Emin pulled them both forward quickly. And then they were in the library, and Amanah and Emin both relaxed beside him.

Dark wood, polished to a gleam, shone with the lights of lanterns hanging from hooks, and the carpets layered on the floors ate the sounds of their footsteps. Men and women sat scattered at tables in the pools of light from windows and lanterns, books before them. Some whispered together in quiet conversation over their studies, while others read in silence, fingers running over the texts. Still more carried stacks of books through the hallways, weaving past them and each other. Across the library stood wooden banisters and, beyond those, a massive desk and several guards meant to ensure only those deemed "appropriate" came through the enormous doors that led to the city.

All this knowledge surrounding him and still out of reach. Failure crashed on him, the memory of all he'd done to get here, and he hadn't been able to read the information he'd needed. If he had, perhaps the Elders would have seen reason. Perhaps, if they focused on the Sea Peoples, he'd find information valuable enough to get the Elders' attention.

The Sea Peoples were the single biggest threat to his people's existence that he'd ever found. Almost every land he'd visited had spoken of them— fierce fighters who ruled the seas that gave them their name. They raided shores and attacked ships on the open water. And since they, too, inhabited this world, the same as his home, if they discovered his island, they would bring destruction with them far greater than the Darks ever had. He had to know more.

"How do we find the books on the Sea Peoples?" Taunos murmured.

"Why the Sea Peoples?" Emin's eyes widened. "Are they all sea-wizards? Are you a Sea People?"

"No, I am not a Sea People." Taunos scowled. Emin's teasing could let too much slip, but so could Taunos's reaction. No one nearby seemed to be listening, and if they were, hopefully it only looked like he was taking offense to the comparison. Sea Peoples ruled the seas, a culture of pirates. "Sea-wizards" in legends were solitary people who had magic and travelled to various lands. Still, the similarity in wording made him wonder if Sea Peoples were also sea-wizards or if the wording simply reflected the Dahuti admiration for the sea.

"Disappointing," Emin said.

"Well, I have to give you *some* hope of being adequate, don't I?"

Emin clapped him on the back, driving the wind from him and nearly knocking him off his feet.

"Come on. Nasri will know," Amanah said.

They didn't walk far before Amanah waved to a short young woman in a bimna uniform with her hair arranged in the elaborate braids of Dahuti fashion. She was hunched over a text, but on seeing Amanah, her face lit up. "Amanah, are you here for your lesson?"

"Lesson?" Emin asked.

Amanah's cheeks flushed beneath the light brown of her skin. "Nasri offered to teach me to read." She cleared her throat. "Ah, no, Nasri, we're actually looking for information on Sea Peoples. Well, Taunos is."

Nasri's eyes widened, flickering over him. "Taunos? As in…"

Taunos gave a wave and a broad grin as Amanah indicated him.

"Haari Taunos," Amanah said. "And that's my brother Emin."

"But he's the one I—" Nasri flushed, fixing her gaze on Amanah. "I thought he'd be taller, you know. Emin looks more like the famous Haari Taunos than he does."

Taunos snorted at the glee on his friend's face. He was tempted to elbow him, but his ribs screamed at the very thought of Emin's retaliation.

Nasri stared for a few more breaths before giving herself a little shake. She frowned. "Sea Peoples? Are you sure?"

Taunos nodded.

"They're dangerous." Yet she stood to join them. "I'll have to read the plaques."

"Is now all right?" Amanah asked. "We can wait."

"Oh, no, I already memorized that." Nasri indicated the book with a dismissive wave of her hand. "I just wanted to double check that Ilaygna was wrong on the dosage she gave Burlim."

He limped along with Emin and Amanah as Nasri led the way through the stacks of bookcases. She paused now and then at plaques on the side, eyes darting to the scrawled Dahuti letters there. Taunos shook his head at himself, staring at the indecipherable symbols. Somehow, he'd gotten overly used to the fact that Traveller's was found throughout so many other countries. That alone was a miracle. It'd been silly to think that the writing would also be similar enough to figure out.

Dodging a cluster of library pages who scurried past, overwhelmed with books, Nasri led them between two stacks of bookshelves. Emin turned sharply, jostling Taunos from his thoughts. His friend's eyes were alight with mischief, drawing a smile from Taunos regardless of everything. Somehow the man was insufferable and comforting all at the same time. He glanced at Amanah, her thoughts hidden, unguessable, unlike her brother's rough but easygoing ways. All the secrets of the world might be stored in the library, but none was as interesting as her.

"Here," Nasri said, stopping.

"Finally," Emin sighed.

"Out of breath?" Taunos teased.

Emin chuckled. "Nah, you're light as a feather. Like a child."

"You act like a child."

"You're both acting like children," Amanah said.

"What are we looking for, more precisely?" Nasri asked. "Books on the Sea Peoples span from here," she pointed up and to her left, "to here." Her finger swept to the floor a few feet to her right.

That was a lot of books.

"Who are their enemies, besides lands they plunder? Where do they come from? Is there any reference to Darks?" Taunos asked.

"Darks?" Nasri's brow furrowed. "I don't know about that. And not much is known on those things—most of these books are speculation, see the marker?"

A sigil marked the middle of the spine of each book, a squiggle surrounded by a circle. Several more appeared on the rest.

"All right, let's focus on facts," Taunos said. That would narrow it down greatly.

Nasri pulled one book from the shelf. "Here, this one's actually by the Ifreesians. They likely know the most about the Sea Peoples."

"How did you get a book by the Ifreesians here?" Amanah's eyes were aglow with excitement.

Nasri shrugged. "The queen collects books from all over the place. Merchants, traders, shipwrecks, anything." She continued, her index finger trailing across the books, until she grabbed a tattered one. "Oh look, tales of sea-wizards!"

Taunos scowled. Would they never give up on their fascination with so-called sea-wizards? "Fine."

"Here, we'll take these to one of the alcoves," Nasri said.

They trailed after Nasri to a semi-circular notch in the wall, cordoned off from the rest of the library by a thick curtain. Behind the curtain sat a small, round table made of smooth marble, half surrounded by a curved bench covered in colorful pillows. As he sank onto the seat, Taunos stared over the rows and rows of books, beyond counting. All this knowledge, all in one place. Takiyah would love it. His stomach twisted. If only he could have brought her here. Brought them all here.

Nasri and Amanah slid onto the bench opposite him, and Emin buffeted him over to make room for him. Taunos closed his eyes for a moment, recentering himself.

"Thank you." He smiled at Nasri, hoping his gratitude came through.

"What should I read first?" Nasri shuffled the books onto the table.

"The Ifreesians, please." He paused. "Can you read it? Don't they have their own language?"

She grinned. "They don't have a written language—not that I know of. Most books are written in Dahuti because most scribes are Dahuti. We just speak Traveller's because of merchants. The scribes are not so flexible. They'd call out to Jattanu himself for justice before writing in Traveller's."

So the scholars were why he'd been thwarted in his search before.

"Read about sea-wizards first." Emin shoved the book in front of Nasri with a grin at Taunos. "We should know what we're dealing with."

Taunos raised his hands in exasperation, but Emin only laughed at him.

"What are sea-wizards, if they aren't like they are in the stories?" Amanah asked. "Obviously the throwing lightning and eating babies was a fabrication."

"People from the city like the idea of sea-wizards better, so you won't find any throwing lighting or people-eating in these books. It's easier to wonder at power that would be less devastating, I think, than it would be to a nomadic clan." Nasri opened the tome of sea-wizard legends gently, pulling her legs up beneath her on the cushioned seat.

"Oh yes," Emin said, snickering at Taunos. "Extremely dangerous."

The shelves unending that filled the library drew Taunos's gaze again. He'd need to learn to read Dahuti, clearly. Or he just needed to bring Eian here. A laugh nearly broke through the tightness in his chest. An easy solution, if it were possible. He couldn't realmwalk with anyone else, not even the little boy who could translate anything. He could bring books back for the boy though, if he found where the Elders had put him, what family called him their own. He clenched his hands under the table to avoid scrubbing them over his face.

Nasri's voice filled their little alcove as she read, until her words called Taunos back from his regrets. "Young warriors, dressed all in black, carrying iron swords and bows. They were accompanied by an older man. As I watched, the group of young warriors disappeared before my very eyes, leaving only the older man standing in the shade of the tree."

Taunos blinked, sitting up straighter. "Where was this?"

Nasri shook her head. "Somewhere out at sea, north of the moors of Diash. That's west of here."

He struggled to focus. "Is there anything else about that story?"

"No, sorry," Nasri said. "Is that important? Here, there's another, only this time it's an appearance. 'The woman came out of empty air. She stared at us in as much wonder as we must have shown for her. How different her clothes and her appearance were: her hair the color of sunlight and eyes like a summer's day, though her skin was only a little darker than ours. She spoke to us in a tongue like water and—oh, sorry. Never mind. This is from a more modern legend about some sorceress of the Hinanuri, Leen."

Taunos straightened and snatched the book from her hands. His hands trembled as he held it, smoothing down the indecipherable page, his skin prickling as if there were a draft.

No picture adorned the text, but that description! The skin tones of the Dahuti and Hinanuri were often a lighter brown than his, and Palon had inherited their mother's unusual coloring—light hair against dark skin and blue eyes. Such a combination was rare in his travels. A sense of certainty gripped him, that if it had been illustrated, he'd be looking at his mother's face, impossible though that was.

Did that mean the Hinanuri were the Darks? No, likely it was just a coincidence.

Nasri's dark eyes bored into him, the slight girl staring at him as if he might do anything next. He slid the book back to her with care and slumped back against the cushions.

"Need a nap?" Emin prodded him.

"I'm fine," Taunos growled.

He shouldn't have reacted. It could be coincidence—it must be. There was no way it could be his mother. She'd tried to make peace with the Darks, though no one seemed to know how. She'd simply disappeared, and Galod had shut him down every time he'd asked. The Storyteller and

Saimahkae hadn't known, only that she was going to follow the Darks. But he'd never been able to recreate such a thing. And it didn't make sense anyway, as he thought about it, for his mother had been a telepath. She couldn't have realmwalked.

Nasri indicated the book. "Well, there are lots of stories of sea-wizards. Many of the more recent ones come from the Hinanuri though."

Amanah's shoulders drooped, and Taunos forced himself to remain quiet at the loss on her face. She loved learning from all sorts of people— she was the epitome of all the best qualities of Far Dahutad. But almost all communication had stopped between the Dahuti and the Hinanuri when the two countries began battling over territory, the same war he'd joined as a soldier almost four summers ago now, where he'd fought alongside Emin and his war-band. From Amanah's posture, it seemed relations hadn't improved, and Emin had said something about "front lines" and an illness.

It was doubly murky for Amanah and Emin, for their family was nomadic, used to traditional ties with the nomads of the Hinanur Empire. That hadn't made things easy for them in the past summers.

"We could ask our sea-wizard here." Emin grinned.

Taunos ignored him, keeping his loss, raw again, tamped down tightly. Any other response would only encourage the man, but hopefully Nasri would only think Emin was living up to his reputation as an incorrigible joker. Taunos pushed another book toward Nasri. "Here, let's read the Ifreesian one. Any more information on Hinanuri sea-wizards?"

In a smooth motion, Amanah stood, rising up on tiptoes, her attention fixed across the rows of bookshelves. Taunos's attention immediately went to her and then to the larger room.

"What is it?" Emin asked, tensed at his side.

"I thought I heard bells."

Screams shattered the library's quiet. The huge main doors that opened onto the city slammed inward, and a flood of people shoved their way inside. Through the open doors came the sound of city bells ringing the alarm. Every muscle tensed and his blood rushed in his veins. Had someone overheard Emin's jokes? Or was it Taunos's conversation with Amanah—he couldn't be certain no one had overheard. How had he been so stupid?

Taunos's gaze darted to the two other entrances—one to the bamimri and the other to the guardhouse—but both were quiet, though the guards were on alert. There was a small door near them that led to the Royal Gardens, but no one would be coming through there.

The people who had been studying in the library milled about in panic, some knocking each other over in their haste to get to one of the other entrances.

Emin stood, heading toward the main doors, his steps sure and solid, and Taunos slid out after him, keeping low. The ache of his wounds made him limp, but he pushed past it, energy thrumming through him, roaring for the challenge of a fight. The men at the front guarding the library shouted, ordering the people to turn back to the public library, their red vests wine-dark in the muted light. The people swarmed through anyway, stampeding for some sense of safety. Through the rows of books, the people of the city shoved further into the library, past Emin, and the guards let them pass, squaring up instead to face the men with swords chasing the crowd. The guards from the other entrances raced to help shore up the line as swords clashed in the library's main entrance.

"This way!" Beckoning to the panicked crowd nearby, Nasri pushed the door to the Royal Garden open, wide-eyed and pale-faced, ushering them out, away from the screams.

As the first few people got to Nasri, the door was flung open more fully, yanking her outside. Armed men in black clothing prowled in, sending the crowd screaming toward one of the other exits.

Taunos acted from instinct more than thought, stepping toward the black-clad figures by the garden door.

A hand grabbed his arm, pulling him around, and he found himself face to face with Amanah.

"What are you doing?" she asked. "You can't just rush headlong into battle. You're injured!"

"I cannot just stand by."

Beyond Amanah, in the thick of the crowd, Emin waded into line with the red-vested guards. The need to help screamed through Taunos, especially as the black-garbed men who'd trampled past Nasri raced through the stacks, swords in hand, their cloth boots silent on the stone floor.

He held Amanah's gaze, repeating himself. "I cannot just stand by."

Her eyes softened, and she nodded. "Death loves men who race into danger." And yet, she stayed beside him as he made his way forward. He glanced at her, an unasked question, and she bared her teeth. "I can't let death have you."

Joy and hope were near strangers to him by then, but as two black-clad invaders swung to face them, he confronted them with a grin and his beloved by his side. One swung his sword toward them, and Taunos, weaponless and bandaged, laughed at the confidence in his opponent's

157

eyes.

"If you want to read, you don't need swords." Taunos ducked under the slash of the man's sword, slamming with telekinesis against the man's wrist. As his opponent's grip loosened on the sword, Taunos grabbed it with his good hand. He fumbled, his injuries pulling, before he got a good hold on the hilt. Galod would scowl if he saw. The man's eyes widened, and Taunos swept his feet from him with a telekinesis-aided push.

"Ungala!" the man shouted, scrambling back.

Amanah blocked the other's strike, her hands against his wrist, and then spun, kicking the other man's side. On the second kick, he grabbed her leg, and Taunos swept past her with the sword, blocking as another black-clad bandit raced forward to strike at her back. Amanah twisted, sending her opponent to the ground, and Taunos stepped forward to engage with the other. In moments, she was up again, her back against his, and he passed her the sword—she was the faster one right now.

But the strange cry from before was carrying, and the bandits were forming up around them from wherever they had been going. The man in front of Taunos backed away, shouting "Ungala!" and the man from before was still crying out the strange word.

"Come without weapons next time. It's more polite," Taunos said. He peeked to his left, toward the front of the library.

The bandits there were in disarray, while Emin and the guards formed up tightly, pressing forward to evict them from the library. Emin was in the thick of it, as usual. Where Taunos should be—would have been, not so long ago.

Taunos whirled to block another strike toward Amanah, continuing the circle as Amanah cut down another bandit. Three were on the carpet, and the bandits stooped to grab them, wary eyes on Taunos and Amanah as they dragged their wounded away. Taunos paused, catching his ragged breath as the bandits retreated, both through the garden door and through the main entrance, chased by Emin and the other guards.

"Nasri?" Amanah asked, her voice tense with panic.

Taunos shook his head. "What did pirates want with a library?"

"I don't know," Amanah said. "Did you see Nasri?"

In the library, only the wounded remained. No short, dark-haired bimna in sight.

"No. Maybe out the garden door?"

Amanah opened the door to check while Taunos put his hand to his side. He'd torn open some of his stitches, and now that the adrenaline of battle was fading, it hurt. The acrid stench of smoke tickled his nose, and a chill shuddered through him. All these books… smoke was a bad sign.

He limped along, following the smell as questions raced through his mind.

How had the second set of bandits come through the side door? It only led to the Royal Garden, completely encircled by the bamimri, library, guardhouse, and the palace. There was nowhere for the bandits to escape. And why did they leave so quickly? What was the word they kept yelling? And where was poor Nasri?

He stumbled through the stacks following the smell of smoke, holding on to the huge shelves to help himself along. Warmth spread along his back as his wounds pulled and bled, but he kept his attention on his surroundings, looking for the things out of place, the things lying in wait. The danger.

The acrid stench worsened halfway down the stacks, bringing with it memories of homes burning and loved ones screaming. He quickened his pace, stumbling and lurching to the end of the row, but he already knew what he'd find.

"Fire!" he shouted. "Fire!"

Taunos paused beside the basket of oiled rags and the flames licking their way up the nearby bookcase, already smeared with oil. He had nothing to put out the fire with. Grabbing the cushions from the nearest seat, he pressed them against the bookcase to smother the flames. If the fire truly took hold, the library would be destroyed, and the people who had sheltered here could die, lost among the books. Already black smoke was spreading in a haze, filling his lungs. His eyes watered, and he coughed, struggling to continue his work.

"Taunos? Haari Taunos!" Amanah shouted, fear edging her voice.

"Here!" He flinched back from the searing heat at the edges of the cushion. He could only smother the edges and not enough to keep the fire from spreading. He managed to keep the cushion pressed against embers with telekinesis, but his fingers were still getting burned and his broken wrist ached.

Footsteps ran up behind him, and then Amanah touched his shoulder. She pulled him back as she shouted, "Bring it here! Here!"

More footsteps. One of the guards ran to them, carrying a heavy bucket. With a grunt, he poured sand down the bookcase, over the fire.

"Oil. There's oil," Taunos croaked. There was too much smoke, making his voice raw.

Amanah sprang to the bookcase, the sword still in her hand, and used the edge to scrape down the burning oil, while the guard spread the sand around. Taunos grabbed the singed cushion and joined them to finish smothering the fire.

When it was out, Taunos sank to the floor, weary.

Was this what they'd wanted? To destroy the library? Coming in the garden door while the guards were all at the main door had been clever, but how had they managed that in the first place?

They sat, waiting for Emin's return, as the guards swept through to ensure there were no more fires and no more bandits. Amanah checked Taunos's wounds and scolded him for pulling his stitches, but as she helped him to his feet to bring him back to the bamimri, three guards blocked their way.

"There! Those two!" The door guard they'd passed before pointed at them, her finger trembling.

Taunos frowned. "What's going on?"

"You're under arrest on suspicion of aiding the attack on the library."

"That's ridiculous!" Amanah said.

"You, too," said one of the other guards. "Witnesses said a bimna let in the second wave of attackers. You're the only one here."

"Check the gardens. It was Nasri, but they must have taken her. They can't have gotten far," Amanah said.

"No one is in the gardens."

"That's impossible!" Taunos said. "They left through the door to the gardens. Where could they have gone?"

"I knew I knew you from somewhere," the finger-pointer said, her eyes widening. "You're Haari Taunos." Taunos was about to say something charming, but she continued, her tone dark. "You disappeared during the battle of Ihia."

Another guard shook his head, guiding Taunos and Amanah gently but firmly toward the guardhouse. "Come on. If you're innocent as you say, the evidence will show it."

Taunos's gut clenched at the guard's easy words. He knew all too well how easily the law could be twisted, especially by those who formed it to meet their own prejudices.

Chapter Thirteen

We know the pieces in play. We have access to the mother through our brethren. We have sent the hero away. The dwarf has taken herself off the board. There is only one last piece to deal with, one random element to account for.

We take away the berserker.

—*part of a missive from "Sapol" in Life Valley*

Ra'ael scanned the streets, attending vaguely to Tjodlik and Dode's discussion ahead of her. Ash coated the buildings, and smoke filled the space between, shrouding her in wispy constraints. It only added to the feeling the city gave her, like someone was hovering right over her shoulder. Everything was so close down here, there was no room to *be*. And yet, she'd determined she would become Kamalti. She lifted her head, a gesture that in an ordinary world would have upturned her face to the kisses of the sun or the caress of the wind. Here, underground, she only felt foolish.

"Ah, see, my dearest aunt? Even your bodyguard agrees with me," Tjodlik crowed. Or he would have crowed, had he been Rinaryn. Instead, because he was Kamalti, he spoke with a lilt to his voice, a slight grin, and walked a hair taller.

With a flick of his wrist, he gestured for her to catch up and join them more properly. She'd fallen back into the position she'd had to keep when she was a captive. But she was free now, and the rules were different. She quickened her step to walk between Tjodlik and Dode, as if she'd never lagged at all.

"I did not say anything to give you this unfortunate delusion." Ra'ael kept her gaze straight ahead. She scrambled to remember what they'd been discussing. Something about boring Kamalti policy.

"I saw that nod. Surely you agree with me. The next time the fae come, Aunt Dode should ask them about the dreams."

"That's a terrible idea." The words burst from her, laden with an intensity of emotion that was clearly not Kamalti. For all her effort, she was still Rinaryn.

"How eloquent, Ra'ael. And what is your counter-proposal?" Dode's expression was so benign it was easy to overlook the sharp-minded woman of steel underneath the frail, kindly appearance. There was a haggard air to her these days that she couldn't quite mask. Bad dreams plagued the nobles of both cities, much like the Storytellers and the priests had suffered back home when Ra'ael was there.

Just like back then, Ra'ael could do nothing about it. She needed to try harder to be Kamalti if she were to find any solace, any direction.

"You need psions," Ra'ael said. Among Rinaryn, bad dreams were treated with a combination of visits with priests and priestesses, and if that didn't soothe the person's spirit, they'd call on psions to help. Nothing had helped the elders of Rinara though, and doubt crept into her tone.

"Codr and Hadr have no psions," Tjodlik reminded her. "We haven't since the days of subjugation to Detr."

"If there was an option besides the Collective, I would consider it," Dode said. "But we have put ourselves in an awful mess. We do not conduct secret experiments on psions the way Detr does, but our treatment of psions has been an affront to the gods just as much as theirs."

"What then should we do, if we should not go to the fae and cannot go to psions?" Tjodlik asked. "The Collective would not help us, nor would many accept their help if they offered. The wounds of their attack go deep. And their wounds, even deeper, I think."

"Regardless," Dode said, "the Scouts' plan of calling in nobles from Detr to find any remaining Collective surely will only worsen the state of things."

"I wish I could help," Ra'ael said. But she had only telekinesis. If Kaemada was here, she'd be able to do something, but Ra'ael had left her behind. Fallen shouldn't have friends.

She still had no direction, no matter how hard she tried to follow Kamalti rules. The thought scraped across her emotions like a swarm of spirits'-teeth biting at her skin. No song from the spirits, no solace from the shrines. She hadn't even been able to fight any intruders and prove herself, not that she wanted Dode in any danger.

And Dode! Ever since the shrine, she couldn't even be near Dode without feeling anxious. That hurt even more than the shrine rejecting her, the unease that gripped her when Dode, her sole source of comfort here, was nearby.

She could go through the motions and take every prescribed step, but it wasn't working. The spirits refused to sing, and the Kamalti gods shunned her, still repelling her from their very shrines. Ra'ael was still adrift in the rocky seas of rejection, with no path forward.

It left only her and all the places she didn't fit. Somehow, she had to gain back what the Elders had stolen from her, the feeling of purpose and belonging that she missed so much.

"Knowing you are keeping Aunt Dode safe helps," Tjodlik said. "While the fae are dangerous, I think they are the best option."

Ra'ael scowled at him. She was failing again, and his charity only made it worse. She was not just free. Without the Elders, without her community, without her friends, Ra'ael was boundless. It was terrifying to be without bounds.

"Ra'ael?" Dode asked.

"I think Tjodlik pays less attention to the real world than he should, instead, seeing things as he would like them to be." Ra'ael's tone came out sharp with irritation.

Kaemada had been the same way. Her mood only soured further, and she stared straight ahead. No, she wasn't going to think of that. Ra'ael drew in a breath, resolutely pushing her shoulders back, and the grief with them.

Dode raised her browridge. "That selective perception has no merit on the debate at hand."

Tjodlik walked onward, his expression too still. Ra'ael winced. He always became extra proper and extra stoic when her words hurt him.

Her apology died on her lips as running footsteps sounded from a side street. Running, among adult Kamalti, was simply never done except in an emergency, and those footfalls sounded too heavy to belong to a child. Making amends could wait. Ra'ael quickened her pace, positioning herself ahead of Dode and Tjodlik. She'd fulfill her obligations and prove to the spirits that she was faithful, not Fallen.

Kamalti Scouts in their gaudy uniforms and polished boots ran up from a side street and turned toward them, sprinting Detr-ward. Ra'ael grabbed Dode and Tjodlik, pressing them back against the stone of a column, as the Scouts raced by. Shouts came from that direction, a few intersections away, behind the row of sculptors' shops. The hair on the back of her neck stood up. Behind them, the cavern wall curved, like a trap closing around prey.

"Dode, we need to get you home," Ra'ael said, nodding in the opposite direction. "Tjodlik, you too."

Shouting erupted from one of the sculptor's shops. "Send for Scouts! Send for more Scouts!"

"It seems you are correct." Dode stood close behind her without hovering. She always had such poise, always calm in a crisis. It only made Ra'ael love her more. If only her skin didn't crawl whenever Dode was near!

Turning, Ra'ael ushered them away, toward safety. More shouts rang out at her back, closer than they should have been. A scruffy young man in threadbare clothing raced past, a knife in his hand flashing with each stride.

Ra'ael leaped between the stranger and Dode, but he continued on, chased by two Scouts in full regalia. Two more men in fine clothing came around the corner ahead of them, along with five more Scouts in uniform, and the young man skidded to a stop. He looked from one end of the street to the other, and Ra'ael tensed as his gaze paused on them.

Up and down the street, other civilians were scattering for cover, but the pillar behind Dode was devoid of doorways. Ra'ael extended one arm, pressing Dode and Tjodlik backward to where they would be able to dash out of the way.

One of the men in fine clothing frowned, tilted his head, and then locked eyes with her.

Ra'ael gritted her teeth against the hateful crawling unease that grew with his gaze, continuing the retreat toward the corner, toward safety.

"They are going to get you, too." The man with the knife curled his lip at her. "Might as well take them down with us."

"Who are these people?" Ra'ael growled, glancing to be sure the way was still clear as they retreated.

"The two men with the Scouts are a delegation from Detr. I do not know who the ruffian with the knife is." Dode's voice was quiet, containing an undercurrent of fear.

Ra'ael drew her dagger and then, after a moment's consideration, also her short sword. The Scouts hated allowing her weapons, but her instincts were screaming danger, and it wasn't just the odd repulsion from Dode.

"You will not take us!" The man with the knife spun around, wild-eyed, but there was no safety for him either. He glanced again at Ra'ael. Taking a deep breath, he raced toward them, muttering something unintelligible with every pounding barefoot step.

"What is he saying?" Ra'ael asked, taking a step forward and assuming a ready position, her dagger and sword out.

"It sounds like names." Tjodlik's voice was tight with fear.

And then the man was on her. The knife flashed.

Ra'ael was immersed in the familiar dance of dodge, parry, and strike, while keeping him away from Dode and Tjodlik.

Where were the Scouts? They were taking too long, and the man was moving far too quickly to be natural. Ra'ael aided her strikes and dodges with telekinetic boosts just to keep up with him. She'd avoided using her telekinesis all the moons she lived with Dode, for Kamalti did not use telekinesis. But this one had to be using telekinesis, too—he struck too hard and too fast for it to be otherwise. She couldn't let him hit Dode or Tjodlik, even by accident.

"Join with us." The man's knife breezed past her ear. "We can kill them, the harvesters. Protect the rest of us."

"I'm trying not to kill anyone, but you're making it awfully hard." Ra'ael batted his hand away with the flat of her sword.

His other hand extended, and telekinetic force punched her in the ribs. "Let go! They will not blame you if you go into blood rage. You have gotten away with it before!"

"I'm not killing anyone," she growled, kicking him away. She had to get him farther from Dode. Where were the Scouts?

"Then at least avenge us, you who doomed us." He charged at her, and she slapped his knife away, ramming her elbow into his chest as he collided with her. His momentum was too great, however, and they crashed to the ground, limbs entangled.

Her sword was no good in such close quarters, so she slammed the hilt into his face and then tossed it away. He fought in a frenzy, with no regard for his own safety, though she'd prefer not to injure him too much. Was this how it felt for others to fight her in the blood rage? Indeed, he seemed to be trying to trigger it, lashing out hard with his telekinesis.

She had to end this, and soon, because the Scouts sure weren't helping.

He countered each of her telekinesis-aided blows with his own, but there was terror in his eyes. "Help us!"

"I'm not letting you endanger Dode." She grunted as his fist rammed into her ribs again in the same spot, even though it left him open for a punch in the face. She took the opening, letting the pain in her ribs fuel her.

She gasped for breath, her ribs aching. Behind and above her, Dode ranted, far too close to Ra'ael for comfort. What was she doing so near when she should be getting to safety?

"…you are Scouts, and I demand you do your duty!"

"Your bodyguard can surely take care of herself, Lady Dode, can she not? And in any case, we would not wish to accidentally hurt the Outsider."

Ra'ael punched the man several times in the head, breaking open her knuckles as she did so, but at last, he lay still and quiet, no longer lashing out at her. It never should have come to this.

She rounded on the Scouts as she stood. "Fools! What do you think you're doing? Certainly not your jobs!"

"Interesting." One of the men from Detr tilted his head, as if she were a sculpture. His gaze slipped past her to Dode. "What will you accept for her?"

One hand to her bruised ribs, Ra'ael tried to catch her breath. Her stomach turned as Dode reached a hand for her, and she stepped carefully backward. Her skin prickled so intensely it hurt, though the sensation eased some with space from both the men from Detr and from Dode.

That shouldn't be. She was safe with Dode, and Dode was safe with her. And yet, she couldn't force her feet closer to the old woman, not just yet.

"She is her own person, able to go where she wills, without being accosted." Dode's voice was cold with fury. "And you Scouts, to stand by and allow this disgrace! Do you wish to fall further from honor?"

"These nobles from Detr are taking care of the remaining Collective problem," one of the Scouts said, binding the unconscious man in iron cuffs.

Bile rose in her throat, and Ra'ael's eyes flickered to the man from Detr, who was still watching her. She resisted the urge to shudder.

"That is one," one of the Scouts said, glancing at the visitors. "Have you a location of more?"

The man with the knife must be from the Collective. Nothing good would come of this. She should have known. And yet, the implications stunned Ra'ael, along with guilt, for she had helped. "You're hunting them. What are you doing with them?"

The man from Detr with the staring problem smiled. "Come along and find out."

"Stay away from her," Dode said.

"Why?" he asked. "She is free to associate with whom she pleases, is that not so?"

One of the visitors stepped over the stirring man she'd taken down for them, and the intensity of the nervous irritation rose, until it felt like her skin was burning. Flinching despite herself, she retreated, and her nerves calmed with distance. She'd never been a coward, but here she was, forced to flee when once she was first into battle. No wonder the spirits rejected her. She was losing even her bravery.

Chills shot through her. Was this who she was, now that she was nothing?

"Her sensitivity is heightened far beyond what we normally see," one visitor was saying to the other. It made no sense.

"Indeed, and yet, she lives with one who has the Gift. Most peculiar."

She latched onto that hope, that it wasn't a fault with her at all. Did it have something to do with the Gift of the Gods? Dode's Gift made her smell sharp like a thunderstorm afterward, and Ra'ael's skin would prickle in her company for a while. Many of the nobles had the Gift of the Gods, though not all, and they seemed to vary in capability.

Her head was starting to pound. "You use the Gift to hunt the Collective?"

The man answered with a smile. She was starting to hate that expression. "Only certain Gifts. And yet… if all reacted the way you did, it would be easy to find them and root them out."

"They aren't vermin. They're people."

"They are criminals," one of the Scouts from Codr said. "And we need to be taking this one into custody."

"One moment," the smiling man said. "You need to bring this one in too. For assault on my person."

Ra'ael scowled. The brashness of such a lie! "What? I—"

And he *moved*, rushing right for her.

She flinched, her training coming apart in humiliating shambles as her nerves screamed at her. Her skin burned. Her head pounded. As she dropped into a ready crouch, her hands came up, and the back of her right hand smacked his arm.

He spun away from her with a shout, grabbing his arm. Ra'ael glared at him. She should have leveled all her strength into the blow if he was going to pretend to be an actor on a stage.

"You cannot—" Ra'ael started, but the Scouts grabbed her by the arms. The cold weight of iron again burdened her wrists.

Dode shouldered her way forward. "This is an outrage! I demand that she be released at once."

"She is not your ebr any longer, Lady Dode, and therefore your influence does little to protect her."

"She is my guest."

"And she assaulted a guest of the Scouts, one who is working with the Scouts to rebuild the city. And right in front of on-duty Scouts, as a matter of fact."

"This cannot possibly be how Codr does justice. Such a blatant falsehood undermines all authority," Tjodlik cut in.

"He did not touch her. She, an Outsider, dared to strike him, a Philosopher of Detr. We all saw it. And if you would like to see justice, Lord Tjodlik, come to the Scouting Hall."

Ra'ael raised her chin. She had worked with people like this before, small spirits bending the system to breaking just for a chance to get ahead. Was that what had happened with the Elders? No, they weren't meek songs, were they? And yet, they had bent the rules, twisting justice into an abomination.

Her feet stumbled forward as the Scouts led her along, the smiling visitors walking alongside her like predators watching for weakness, until Dode and Tjodlik stepped in, keeping pace on either side of her.

"I will not let this stand," Dode promised.

"Surely you would not endanger the first cooperation between Detr and Codr in seventy circulations?" the hunter asked.

Dode fixed him with a determined look. "Be aware, I would endanger such devious cooperation easily. For Ra'ael, I would endanger my own reputation. Tjodlik, please find a messenger. I think the Philosophers of Codr must have an emergency meeting."

The walk to the Scouting Hall had never seemed so short, nor had the Hall itself ever loomed so threateningly. It didn't make sense. The Scouts were foolish and prideful and altogether loathsome in their arrogance, but she'd been through the Hall before.

Yet this time, every instinct in Ra'ael pleaded for her to flee for her life. She seized up at the entrance, unable to make herself move forward. Her head spun. Danger lurked from every shadow, in every corner, growing and twisting into her certain doom. Her skin felt burned and peeled away. By the time the Scouts tugged her through the doors and into the judgement circle, her muscles trembled uncontrollably and sweat trickled down her back.

The door of the room opened, and Answer paused in the doorway, her gaze flickering over them all, before entering. "What have you done?"

"These *visitors* from Detr and our Scouts have twisted the law so it no longer resembles justice," Dode began.

"If you please, Lady Dode, justice has yet to be dispensed." One of the Scouts sounded bored.

The Scouts unbound Ra'ael and left her and the man from the Collective in the circle. The pressure eased, and Ra'ael could breathe again. Her shoulders sagged—she felt like she'd spent all morning training with Galod. Rubbing the ache in her ribs, her gaze went to the Collective man, who hunched with his arms locked around his folded legs.

"You react worse than most do at first." He spoke to his knees, his voice an eerie drone. "It will be worse for you."

"What's going on? What was that?" Her heart thundered, and she wiped her slick palms on her dress.

"They will take us. They will bring the Gift near, bring it away, bring it near, make it hurt, make us scream. Until the connection with the Collective is broken and we are lost." He blinked. "But you. You have no connection. Already lost. Already reacting to the Gift."

She bit her lip, clenching her arms around herself. It didn't make sense. She hadn't reacted to the Gift before. Not until she lost the spirits' song and was cast out.

"Is that why I cannot go into the shrines anymore?" she whispered. Her voice cracked, as broken as she was.

The man buried his head in his knees. "You should have attacked them. Or at least me. Should have had mercy."

Across the hall, Dode was arguing with the Scouts as vehemently as she'd ever seen her. Answer, against all odds, seemed to be on Dode's side, while Tjodlik, not being a member of Codr and therefore not allowed in the Hall, was gone, probably gathering allies for Dode. Meanwhile, the two men from Detr stood in the room where only Codr citizens and the accused could stand.

Answer glared at them. "What are they doing here? If they are accused, they must stand in the circle. If not, they cannot be in the Hall!"

The hunter scoffed at her, shaking his head. One of the Scouts answered her. "These visitors have a special dispensation. Now, be silent."

"You cannot give her to them!" Answer's voice was shrill.

"This is the agreement. Hear it for yourself, Scout Answer." One of the Scouts handed her a crystal.

Answer snatched it from his hands. She turned her back to the room and held it to her ear. That odd Kamalti preoccupation with listening to rocks, again.

Ra'ael winced. The room closed around her again, smothering her with pressure, beating at her with invisible forces she couldn't feel but could sense nonetheless. She shrank in on herself, covering her head with her hands, embarrassingly like the man from the Collective.

The weight eased, and Ra'ael slowly raised her head.

Dode was arguing again. "I assure you, Scout, if she comes to harm, the Philosophers of Codr and Hadr will be extremely wroth. Under no circumstances is she to be turned over to the tender mercies of the people of Detr."

"You will have to take that up with the Justices. They will decide whether she is worth the risk of war with Detr or not."

"War with Detr?" Answer scoffed. "Let them come. We will beat them back as we did the last time. I told you, Lord Necessity, we do not need this compact. Certainly not enough to send this woman, who helped to beat back the Collective, to Detr, a City that experiments on people with magic. To a City where people with magic disappear, never to be seen again! What are they hiding?"

Ra'ael swallowed hard. She'd never thought she'd consider Codr the more civilized of people toward psions. They had a long way to go toward even approaching reasonable treatment of psions. But compared to the stories from Detr... Secret experiments, Dode had said.

She tried to slow her breathing, tried to ignore the sense of unease coming from the Scouts and Dode, from the very walls and floor themselves. No doubt many of the nobles had the Gift of the Gods, but why should that make her skin crawl so much? Why was it affecting her this way?

Wrapping her arms around herself, Ra'ael stood and paced the circle, not even tempted to cross it. Coming too near the Scouts repulsed her mentally, and the smiling hunter's eyes were always on her, repulsing her further.

"Why is this so important to you?" Answer asked Lord Necessity. "You have been pushing for this since you came up with the idea out of smoke two faces ago."

"The fae advised my father that this cooperation with Detr would be good for Codr, and unlike you, I listen to the advice of the fae," the Scout apparently named Necessity shot back.

"And the fae advised us to shut down our machines, too. Would you send us backward at their whims?" Answer asked.

"We can find all of your magic users and take them off your hands," the smiling hunter said. "Is that not worth much?"

"No," Answer scowled.

"Look, just look at what we can learn," the hunter from Detr said. "No more magic users, lurking dangerously among you. No more wondering if your neighbor might turn out to be a monster. Just the gods speaking their judgement."

"I see two monsters and several slugs." Dode's expression was as flat as her voice, but her eyes burned with anger.

The hunter thinned his lips. "Fine, I will show you. Magic users look just like us, do they not? But once they are properly primed, they react to the Gift and to the Crystals of the Gods. It was a gift for a reason, was it not? Here, hand me that crystal."

Answer folded her arms, but one of the other Scouts grabbed the crystal she'd held and gave it to the hunter. He held it up. "Here it is, off. Watch the Outsider. Watch her as I activate it."

Pressure mounted, unease crawling on her spine, and Ra'ael tried to stamp it down. She bit her lip, trying to avoid squirming, but the victory in the hunter's eyes showed her she was failing.

"Do you see?" he asked. "She felt it when I turned it on, from across the room. Even with it off, watch."

He crossed the room toward her, and Ra'ael gritted her teeth, refusing to cower backwards. Instead, she dropped into a fighting crouch. But the crawling unease grew as he advanced, and her hands began to tremble, so she folded them into fists and imagined using them.

"Now, of course I am Gifted myself, so the demonstration is not scientific, but a heightened emotional state increases the sensitivity. This one is quite sensitive."

"She is not laboratory equipment," Dode snapped. "And you will refrain from approaching her again."

Ra'ael avoided Dode's gaze. She must have seen her shrink back. Given her shrewd eye, she doubtless had realized what Ra'ael had been trying to hide: the unease that made her seize up when Dode got too close. It just showed that she didn't belong here either. She'd never be Kamalti, for their Gifts would drive her out as sure as the spirits were silent. She was losing Dode, losing her last haven. And apparently this somehow stemmed from her own psionics.

Where else was she to go, when all doors were closed to her? She clenched her fists. She had no wish to be anywhere other than here with Dode. Everything else was closed to her. Everything she was had been torn away. What was the use in holding on to this last scrap of who she was if it would give her options once again?

"Is there a way to stop it?" Ra'ael asked.

She didn't quite fit, like a gear too large for one of the steam machines. But perhaps if she cut off a piece of herself, she could fit with Dode again. If it would stop this reaction to the Gift, it would be worth it.

The room silenced, and she straightened her back under the weight of all those eyes.

She clarified. "Is there a way to remove my telekinesis or stop it from interacting with the Gift of the Gods?"

"Absolutely not!" Dode said.

Ra'ael kept her gaze on the hunter. She couldn't bear to continue becoming increasingly uneasy in the presence of her only friend, to be eventually forced out of the only place that gave her solace. She was out of places to go and people to be.

"I do not know," the hunter said. "But I would love to find out."

"Lying, he's lying." The man from the Collective rocked beside her. "Going to tear us apart, going to make us die screaming like all the others."

He was probably right. But she couldn't let Dode sacrifice her prestige for her when she'd only pay her back by becoming increasingly sensitive to her presence. She wouldn't let her last words be weapons. She'd done that already, and Takiyah's and Taunos's expressions still pricked at her memory with thorns of guilt.

Dode stepped toward her, and pain stabbed Ra'ael's heart at the expression on the old woman's face. She must have flinched, though she had tried not to. Dode stopped, her conflict clear in her eyes.

"Dode, what am I?" The words broke from Ra'ael, song to song.

"You are Ra'ael, my bodyguard and my friend." Dode's tone brooked no argument.

"Friends can stand being in the same room as each other."

"We will figure it out."

Ra'ael shook her head. They were scattered to the winds, and there was no home for her anymore. Fallen had no friends. No song to guide her way. Just the looming of the Kamalti gods as they repelled her from their shrines, reminding her always that she didn't belong. Everything had rejected her. She had nothing and was nothing. No rituals, laws, or specific timing was fixing this—it was only getting worse.

Perhaps it was time to let go of the last pieces of herself and embrace the emptiness.

She stepped forward, gritting her teeth at the abrading of her very song as she closed the distance between herself and Dode. She kissed Dode's cheek, despite the sharp tingling, and stepped back with a forced smile.

Tears glimmered in Dode's eyes, and the old woman, hands shaking, gripped Ra'ael's hands.

"Let us go!" The hunter's glee only reinforced the wrong.

But if, on some wind of chance, they could help, she would come back to Dode. And if they couldn't—or didn't—help, she would destroy the hunter's world, Gifts and all.

"The Justices have not arrived yet," Answer protested.

"This specimen comes of her own free will," the hunter said. "Oh, and I drop the charges against her. Therefore, she is free to go."

Answer narrowed her eyes. "The Justices have not released the prisoner to you."

"Leave him," the hunter said, his eyes flickering to the man from the Collective, cowering in the circle. "He can go."

Ra'ael squeezed Dode's hand. "See that he gets justice," she said, looking to both Dode and Answer. "Just punishment for the Collective's crimes, not to be hunted like an animal or to be forgotten."

And then Ra'ael followed the hunter and his colleague out of the Scouting Hall, once again leaving her friends behind with the tatters of everything else that had been ripped from her.

Ifreesian. Ifreesh. Frees. Fae-rees. Fae. The fae stole the embassy when it was abandoned. They stole the name as well, centuries later when the name was changed by time and forgotten in memory. The embassy was to their liking, the artwork strong in form and beauty. They liked the entrance through the eye.
—fragment safeguarded by the Monks of Annularei

"Master Pek, sir!"

The awe in the young guard's voice floated down the stairwell to Takiyah's ears. That and the name Pek tugged her from her tomb of bleak thoughts, and she huddled away from the discomfort, curling tight around her staff. Poisonous as they were, her anger and fear had become a familiar blanket against the uncertainty and risk of the world. The days had melded into one another while she had laid here, surrounded by stone. It comforted her, oddly enough, and the terrible memories that had seized her had gradually faded to the background. To the past, where they belonged.

A snort, all too familiar. She shouldn't have gotten close enough for such sounds to be familiar.

"Just Pek will do," the old Kamalti said. "I'm retired, remember? I came for the tall, red-haired one. The panic attack?"

"Here, she's just down here."

Takiyah hunched tighter into a ball under the lash of the voice. She was trapped again. She had been, this whole time. What had she been doing, forging relationships again? Friendships with Rothan, with Varen. With Pek. Being close to someone wasn't a defense—it was a vulnerability. If she hadn't been close to Kaemada, she wouldn't have gone under the mountain. If she hadn't been close with Taunos, she wouldn't have believed him that everything would be all right. If she hadn't been so close to Ra'ael, her words, her cold acceptance, would never have hurt so much.

And now here she was, dependent on someone else. Like she swore she'd never be again. Other people couldn't let her down if she refused to lean on them, but somehow, she kept leaning on people anyway, no matter how hard she tried to be alone.

"Why is she in the jail cells?" Pek's voice echoed on the stone walls, down the stairway.

Takiyah pressed into the wall, wariness filling her.

"She calmed down again once we got her underground. We left her staff with her because she got agitated again when we tried to take it."

Pek finally stepped down the last stair, into view. Humiliation boiled over in her. They'd called Pek on her, the same way adults in the kaetal had called her parents when she got to be too much: "Takiyah's arguing with the kaetal elders again," or "tell Takiyah she cannot just pick up rocks and smash them apart—she will not listen to me," or some such thing.

Except Pek was not her parents. They, too, had been betrayed, and no one had spoken a word on their behalf. She'd left her friends behind so they couldn't betray her again. So she wouldn't fall back on needing them.

And yet here she was, and here was Pek to get her out.

Pek plucked the keys from the guard's hands, ignoring the young man's cry of shame and alarm. He fit a key into the lock and turned it with a loud click, and then Pek pulled the door open.

Was it possible she could handle the betrayal that had to be coming? Takiyah could not be weak right now. She couldn't lean on anyone.

"Feeling better?" Pek asked. "Do you think you can avoid lashing out and screaming at people for a few days?"

"I wasn't trying..." She'd panicked. And everyone had seen it. Her humiliation.

Pek gave her a look, as if she were a foolish child. "Takiyah, no one's trying to hurt you."

"What are you planning to do with me?"

"Me? Nothing. I planned to drink. By myself. Instead, when I came back into the city, I got called here. Good thing I told the guard to get me if you were in any trouble. They didn't know what to do with you."

He'd expected her to need him, and she'd proved him right. A fire flared within her, more comfortable than the raw need crying out even deeper inside. "You shouldn't have done that. You cannot watch out for me all the time."

Pek shrugged and opened the door wider. "Coming?"

Takiyah took a deep breath, as if about to dive into treacherous waters, then put her head down and ran. Pushing herself off the wall, she raced past Pek, every fiber of her being tense. People bound each other to themselves, caught up in a web of connections that they thought made them safe. She had to get free, before that web snagged her too deeply in its mire.

She burst out into the sunlight. Dreading to hear shouts and cries to stop her, Takiyah sped up, sprinting across the courtyard and through the gates separating the guardhouse from the city.

Alone. She needed to be alone. Away from all these people. Away from the city.

Alone, she would be free. There were too many stares here.

Takiyah shook her head. She needed a plan. A direction. The maddening call tugging her eastward, seaward, never ended. She'd always loved the sea, but she'd never felt it quite so obsessively, like an itch she couldn't scratch. She headed for the docks, following the tug on her song like metal filings pulled by invisible forces.

The sea killed everyone. Everyone knew that. Why did it call to her so?

And yet, it was the best way out, the best way to be alone, to prove to herself that she was fully capable all by herself. She had to try the harbor again. Surely they'd have forgotten by now how she'd tried to argue her way onto a boat. The memory stung with a power all its own, Kamalti features frowning at her as if she were the foolish one. Sailors lining up and driving her from the docks.

Surely the tides weren't *that* bad, and someone would see reason. Someone would be able to teach her to sail. After all, everyone was a beginner at some point. Or maybe it would be like forging, and she would teach herself. Either way, she had to try again. More than ever, she needed a boat and to learn to sail.

Takiyah paused on the steps that led down to the cleverly designed docks. Peace washed over her as she watched the boats, the destructive strength of the sea. The ships fishing in the harbor navigated the glittering water with bright sails, ever wary of sharp rocks and unpredictable wave swells as they fished. They were why she came down to the harbor district most lunch times, not because she loved fish but for a chance to gaze out on the water. The urge to take a ship and sail beyond, absurd as that was, still gripped her. No one left the harbor, because no one who did so returned.

Yet, somehow, she could not ignore the call of the sea.

Wind gusted past, and the ships on the water either lowered their sails or turned to catch the wind more fully, sails full and billowing. Once she had a boat, she could go anywhere she wanted. She wouldn't be limited by her bum leg or the Angels or the desert—she'd only be limited by the wind.

Takiyah clattered down the steps until she got to the lower sections, where she had to push through the swarm of people along the docks. She held her staff in front of her to better plow through the crowd.

"What are you doing here? The fish markets are at the top of the stairs. Get out of the way." A burly Kamalti blocked her path, moving to loom in her face when she tried to go around him.

Her hands tightened into fists at her side, but she took a deep breath and looked past his shoulder. "I want work on a ship."

"And how many ships have you worked on before?"

"None." That was wrong. Not that it was a lie, but she should have worked on several ships by now. Except that the very idea was ludicrous, given that she'd only come to Tamarik a few moons ago.

The man laughed at her. "And your smart idea is to start while the sisters are dancing together overhead?"

"Surely the tides are less by now."

"Not enough, not until the sisters are much farther apart. Best time to learn's when the sisters are opposing, not together. Get back up the stairs where you belong and let us work."

"I cannot wait that long. Get out of my way." She barely got the words out through her gritted teeth. She would not be told what to do or where to go. Not anymore. She tried to shove past him, but he blocked her. Behind him, sailors from all around gathered, clenching their own fists and advancing on her with expressions that spoke of mortal seriousness.

"What's the problem here, Heprik?" one asked.

"This novice wants to sail. With no experience."

"Hey! That's the troublemaker from before."

"I just need a boat," she snapped. "Surely one's not being used."

"The ships are owned. They're ours. All of them, got it?" one of the sailors said.

"And no one's taking an ill-mannered brat out with them," Heprik said.

"Look, what will it take? Surely we can arrange something," Takiyah said.

"We don't do well with demands."

"You don't do well with rational thought either. What would it hurt? It's just me and a boat no one's using."

Heprik pointed a meaty finger toward the top of the docks. "Out. Get out, and don't let us see you again."

The crowd pressed forward, shoulder to shoulder against her, confirming his words, and Takiyah stepped back, letting the mob shove her up the stairs. She broke free at the top for one last glance back at the sea that stirred her song.

But it was lost to her now. There was no way they were going to let her back in the docks now, and from their expressions, they might press the issue even further than that. Rage contorted their features.

The whole city had turned on her. It wasn't safe.

It wasn't safe anywhere there were Kamalti.

Her hurried steps had already turned of their own accord toward her humble home. She smiled to herself, grateful at least part of her was thinking clearly. She'd come to the conclusion unconsciously before her stupid, sluggish thoughts could catch up.

She was leaving, and she would never return.

Takiyah was running by the time she reached her house. The awkward lock on the door delayed her. It always seemed to be stubborn or loose, whichever she didn't want at the time. This time, it was jammed, pure and simple. She slammed the butt of her hand against the frame until it jolted free and snatched up the go-bags she kept stashed next to her door. Turning her back on her former home, she left, not bothering to latch the rebellious door behind her.

The bags poked at her back and sides, jouncing with her uneven gait as she pushed her way through the streets. She should have done this long ago. Who needed this city with its sneering smugness and its pompous ways? Takiyah, do this. Takiyah, you'll have to work with Kamalti. Takiyah, you're being unreasonable.

She didn't need anyone. She was Fallen, after all.

The moment she stepped through the gates, the desert wind slapped her in the face, a harsh welcome for her out of the leash of civilization.

True freedom had no bounds. No other people to worry about—just the ferocity of nature. Takiyah bared her teeth at the thought, at the harsh wind, at the gritty dirt blown into her face, and at the sun that beat down on her. It was a small price to pay for freedom. A just price.

After all, what was one's story without struggles to prove one's self against?

Where had that thought come from? She had no answer, but it felt right and true. Somehow, she knew at her very core, that this was as it should be. Her against the elements, the ultimate test of survival.

Except there should be others with her.

No. That didn't make sense. She was going to be on her own. The whole point was that no one else would be with her.

So why did it feel like she was missing something important?

As if she could outrun the thought, Takiyah set off at a quick pace, locking her sights on the mountains in the distance. She would need shelter. She could probably find it there. That rang with rightness too, living under the shelter of a mountain. The comfort and truth of the notion was soured with fear and anger. Another thing the Kamalti had ruined for her.

She pushed it all out of her mind, stretching to ease the tightness in her shoulders and chest. Only the here and now mattered.

Takiyah threw her shoulders back. Free and proud and independent.

But her stubborn mentality could only last so long. She tried to ignore it, tried to pretend it wasn't happening, but before she was even out of sight of the gates, her limp had turned to a lurch in her gait. By the time the city was small enough to be blotted out by her hand, she was exhausted, even using her staff to take her weight. The mountains were still too distant.

She shook her head, grinding her teeth. If she pushed herself at this stage, her other leg would soon begin to ache from the work of taking her weight and the shock of the lurching. She sagged then crumpled to the sandy soil, staff across her lap. She wasn't going to be able to do it. Not walking, anyway. Not on her own.

There was no way she was going to lie down and admit defeat. What was the alternative? There had to be one.

But time, like everything, was against her. No viable solution came to her, not here. Not without more supplies. She turned, glaring at the city that even now ensnared her, whisking away the dream of freedom and mocking her with her limitations.

All the way back to the city, tears pricked at her eyes, but she refused to actually cry. She wasn't so weak.

The ache of her leg went bone deep as she staggered into her house, slamming the door behind her and sinking down to her mattress. The thick straw-and-feather-stuffed mattress rustled beneath her, a familiar sound, almost comforting if it weren't for the weight of her failure.

Her breath hitched, and she slammed her fist against the wall, bruising her knuckles.

No, she wasn't trapped. She'd never be trapped again. No laws held her, for she was Fallen. She could do whatever she wanted.

Like being found on the street having a panic attack. Like throwing a tantrum at the harbor.

If Pek hadn't come, how long would she have languished? Rothan or Varen might have seen her and helped, and would she really have lashed out at them?

Probably, and the admission turned her stomach.

If she was going to be on her own, needing no one, she'd have to be a lot more careful. She didn't have the backup to rely on which she'd trained for summers to expect. She'd left them behind. And because of that, she'd trapped herself in a city.

She turned onto her side to face the white dabbling of the poor paint job on the wall.

Being alone wasn't working. The only way she was going to be able to leave would be if she had someone's help. The thought drowned her in fear as thoroughly as the sea would.

Chapter Fifteen

The Tsaeyichape'itsan is secure. We will wait while he ripens, and at that time, he will still be accessible. To assure us of our access, we must continue to watch the protectors, to keep them aimed apart from one another, far from the Tsaeyichape'itsan, to prevent their meddling in affairs they know nothing of.
—part of a missive from "Sapol" in Life Valley

The enormous vaulted chamber rose around him, seemingly designed to make those on trial feel small. The two burly guards on either side of Taunos, each a head taller than he was, only cemented that feeling of insignificance. He stood in shackles on a round platform nine paces wide. Amanah stood, similarly bound and guarded, about a pace away from him, but the distance might as well be insurmountable. She stood there, sallow and bowed by grief and worry, and he couldn't comfort her. He wasn't even certain he could get them out of this mess if it went badly, which he was expecting it to.

Rows of benches rose to each side. The left was filled with the high priests and priestesses of each of the nine Dahuti deities, and the leaders of the nine most powerful city clans were arrayed on the right. Amanah and Emin's nomadic clan wasn't considered important enough to have seats on the council.

Taunos kept his breathing even, controlling that, controlling himself. Such an oversight—or blatant prejudice—did not bode well for the justice of this council.

Directly in front stood a raised platform with a large chair in the center, on which the queen of Far Dahutad sat with eighteen ministers seated on benches behind her. The room was round, encircled with guards positioned before the many arched windows, and the only sound was paper shuffling as scholars distributed the witness accounts they'd collected. There was one door, heavily guarded.

His thoughts turned back to the night before, and he shivered. They'd been chained in cells distant from one another, but he'd still heard Amanah weeping. The memory of her panic at finding Nasri missing tore at his heart. Dulara had been brought to tend to their wounds, but he ached from the cold, dank cell as much as from the burns and the stitches, freshly bandaged. But worse was knowing Amanah was charged with a crime, and she wouldn't even have been there if it weren't for him.

He hadn't tried to realmwalk out—he couldn't leave Amanah there. Not that he was sure he'd succeed anyway, given the wounds he still bore.

When the queen rose, Amanah looked up, her expression stern with fear and anger. Her normally intricate weaving of braids was askew, some of the locks falling about her face. Her eyes were red and swollen from weeping, and she trembled in her chains, creating a soft tinkling music to fill the vault. The sound was so at odds with the reason for it. He hated it, hated that he couldn't hold Amanah until she could steady herself once more.

The queen spoke, her voice filling the chamber. "You are charged in relation to the fire in our great library. Havi Amanah Teek, several witnesses told our scribes, individually, that a woman in a bimna uniform opened the door and let more bandits in—from my own personal gardens, no less. If that wasn't bad enough, you and your brother, Havi Emin Teek, brought an unauthorized person into the library.

"And you, Haari Taunos, besides being in my library without authorization, are a deserter from my army, it appears. It seems you vanished at the battle of Duma just before the Sea Peoples arrived. I find it extremely suspicious that once again, you appear, and so do the Sea Peoples, attacking my beacon of light and knowledge."

The attack was from Sea Peoples? Was that known or merely suspected? The speed with which they had appeared, struck, and disappeared was baffling. It was daylight, yet no one had seen where the group that had taken Nasri had gone.

Taunos shifted, aware of the guards behind him tensing as he did so. The deep gash in his thigh made walking difficult, and his broken wrist kept his right hand mostly useless. And yet they still deemed him a threat. He could use that. He just needed a plan that wouldn't get him and Amanah killed.

A minister cleared his throat, standing. "The mistress of the bamimri, Dulara, would like to speak."

The queen nodded, sitting down again, and Dulara was led forward to stand before the queen. She kept her head high and her eyes straight, not looking at either Amanah or Taunos as she passed. "Your Highness, I have worked with Bimna Amanah for many months and can attest to her loyalty. She is a hard worker and a gift to the bamimri. I am also missing a bimna from my bamimri—Guma Nasri Enarim."

"Thank you, Dulara. This was noted in your testimony," the queen said with a frown.

Dulara bowed. "I wanted it to come straight from my mouth as well."

"Thank you. Any other witnesses?"

The vault remained silent as Dulara was escorted out, and Taunos watched her go out of the corner of his eye. At least her speaking up was a pleasant surprise. And Dulara stressing Amanah's status as bimna instead of as havi... perhaps Dulara wasn't all harsh words and judgement, after all. Perhaps Amanah, at least, would make it out of this all right.

"There is still the fact that you, a havi, brought an unauthorized person into the library," the queen said. "One who may have coordinated with the Sea Peoples to burn it down. Several people were injured. Five died. Two stacks of books must be repaired and replaced. There must be amends made."

Tension radiated from Amanah, and Taunos clenched his fists. He couldn't hope to succeed in helping her, not in this room full of soldiers. That didn't mean he wouldn't try.

One of the priests leaped to his feet. "Sire, we demand this matter be closed, that Jattanu's justice come swiftly. Two havis bring an outsider into the library when they should have been grateful simply for access themselves? It bodes ill if not punished. And where is the brother, this havi guard?"

"Havi Emin Teek is hailed as a hero for his efforts driving off the bandits." The priestess who spoke waved her hand, as languid as her voice.

The priest scoffed. "A tactic to arouse sympathy, perhaps? Let us be done with this."

"Let them be dismissed from their posts and the deserter punished," a clan leader said from the other side. "Surely we have more important matters to attend to. What happened to the grain shipment from Imaha? It's two weeks late."

Some things were the same no matter what world one landed in. Taunos couldn't stand by and watch this sham. There was no grander plan here, no mission the Elders had sent him on. For once, his people's safety did not hang in the balance. There was just him and the injustice before him. To the right, the clan leaders were also rising, indicating they, too, considered the matter closed.

"This is not justice!" Taunos shouted.

One of the queen's ministers scoffed. "Such defiance. The standard punishment is a whipping—ten lashes. I suggest we double it and throw the others out of the city."

"No!" Amanah cried out, anguish in her voice. "He's already injured. He wouldn't survive twenty lashes!"

Taunos clenched his fists at his sides. He gave no reply—any argument he made wouldn't sway them. They'd already made up their minds. At least it wasn't his beloved facing the whip, again.

The queen shook her head, and the high guards stepped forward, their boots loud on the stone floor. Amanah's voice was abruptly silenced. Taunos controlled his breathing, keeping his expression still.

"Two lashes for the insolence?" a priestess suggested.

"Two sounds fair," a priest said. They sounded as if they were planning a time for a party, rather than setting a sentence.

Taunos's stomach turned, but he feared bringing more trouble on Amanah if he spoke again. Perhaps he could take her lashes, too.

Amanah clenched her jaw, head high.

One of the ministers behind the queen spoke up. "Do we investigate this matter further?"

A ripple of conversation ran through the two sides of the room, while the ministers merely looked to the queen. Then, on either side of the room, the clan leaders and the priests and priestesses made the sign of Jattanu. The sign of judgement.

"And again," the queen said.

As one, every member of the council, queen included, took small flasks from their sides and drank. Each of them again made the sign of Jattanu. Taunos frowned. A twist from the Dahuti tradition of considering important matters twice—once sober, once drunk—as they had during the meal at the market.

The queen nodded. "It is done. Amanah Teek and Emin Teek will be dismissed from their posts and shall leave the city. The whipping shall be done immediately, and then you will leave and never return."

Taunos didn't bother to shake off the hands that grabbed him. He just walked, his mind already churning with ways to escape along with Amanah. The dread in Amanah's eyes haunted him, muting his attempts to catalogue every possible escape route, scrambling his hastily laid potential plans.

The high guards were professional but unyielding as they hemmed them in and escorted them through the stone corridors. The sound of boot heels resounding off the passageways filled his ears, along with the tinkle of their chains. He watched, waiting for a moment of weakness, a time when he could strike, but with four guards and him injured, he'd only get one chance.

They came to a corridor that ended in a door built from an iron grid. Four sentries stood beside it, alert despite what must be boring duty, their stances too eager. Taunos kept his eyes fixed forward, intent on his peripheral vision. The high guards stood in a semi-circle around himself and Amanah with stances well-balanced and ready, hands near their swords.

"Prisoners sentenced to a whipping," one of the high guards said.

Amanah had her arms wrapped around herself, glaring at their captors.

The sentries saluted, and one of them turned to unlock the door between them. As he moved, his gaze paused on Taunos for just a moment.

Taunos recognized him as well. A soldier—he'd fought beside the man at Gahimbli during the war. Taunos watched him intently. Lately, his fame seemed to cast suspicion on him more often than it aided him.

One of the high guards took Taunos's arm in a firm grip just above the elbow. Had he detected that pause, that recognition, as well? Taunos let himself be dragged a step backward, keeping his expression blank.

"We'll escort them to the whipping posts this time."

The soldier smiled, his eyes cold. "No need. We can handle it."

"Then you can handle it while we supervise."

There was definite tension there, between the two groups, rife with suspicion of each other. Before Taunos could take advantage of the fact, the soldier stepped forward, and Taunos only just had time to tense and push outward with telekinesis as the man slammed his fist into Taunos's stomach. Might as well play up the injury, let them think him weakened.

He curled around the punch, dropping half to the ground, held up only by the guard holding his arm. A boot flashed by, and Taunos narrowly avoided it crashing into his face, catching it on his shoulder instead. He tumbled across the floor, torn from the guard's grasp.

"You thought I would go easy on the prisoners, High Guard Arar?" The soldier grabbed Taunos by his shirt, lifting him back to his feet.

Amanah's cry rang in his ears as he blinked and shook his head, playing up his shock. The suspicion was gone from the high guard's stance, replaced by boredom.

"The queen wants him whipped," the high guard said. "Don't kill him before then."

As the high guards stepped away and the three sentries surrounded Amanah, the soldier holding Taunos shook him. "I won't kill him. Just a little revenge."

Taunos focused on the fist holding his shirt, not too tight, and the way the guard used Taunos's jostling form as cover between him and the retreating high guards. A ploy then? A way to get free, if this was all an elaborate scheme to put the suspicions of the high guard at ease? It'd need to look good, of course. Taunos braced himself for the fist in his side, gritting his teeth as his stitches pulled and wetness spread across his back. He gasped, hearing in his memory Galod's insistence that he recover faster.

"Stop!" Amanah's shout was nearly drowned out by the shriek of the gate as it opened.

The high guards disappeared around the corner, and another punch slammed the breath out of him again. Taunos went limp and twisted, struggling for air as he attempted to roll free. More hands grabbed his shoulders, and his attacker lined up in front of him, drawing his arm back again.

"Not a rescue then, huh?" Taunos croaked as soon as he had breath. He spread his hands as much as the shackles would allow and lashed out with a telekinetic push toward the guards holding him. One stumbled back, but the other punched his splint, sending white-hot pain through his body. His knees buckled as agony roared through him.

The guard was staring at him when the world came back to him. "Do you really not even remember me?"

"We were in Gahimbli together. We fought together," Taunos grunted. His body trembled, barely able to push himself upright again. That didn't bode well for getting out of this.

"You caught me cheating at cards," the guard sneered. "But I needed that money. And then you saved my life the next day so that I couldn't even escape honorably. Do you know what the debt collectors do when they take everything you own and you still owe more?"

"I expect I'm about to find out?" Taunos eyed him, measuring the distance he'd need to cover to get inside the soldier's guard. It was unlikely he'd be able to move quickly enough to succeed, with the two guards holding him up and in place.

There was movement out of the corner of his eye, a familiar fighting form. Taunos kept his gaze on the man before him, granting him one of his most arrogant grins. The man glowered. His fist drew back.

"Do you have any creativity?" Taunos asked.

He hadn't really expected that the man's expression could get darker, but it did. Taunos leaned back, slipping one foot behind that of the guard holding him, and twisted as the first guard began beating on him in earnest.

A punch landed on his back and another on his side, lancing pain through his body.

But then the man holding him was off balance and falling, and Taunos was able to use him as a shield, while the third guard's shock allowed him to pull free of his hold. The three faced him together, but from the side, Amanah swept one of them off his feet and then stomped on his throat.

She'd taken out two while he'd taken a beating.

Taunos grinned at the remaining two. "You know you've lost, right?"

As the guards advanced, Taunos spun, his chains flinging out behind him, lashing out with a kick and then lunging forward to follow the momentum through with a punch to the first guard's nose. His injured leg buckled beneath him though, forcing him to follow through with telekinesis instead. Panting, he turned to deal with the second, but the man was already laid out by Amanah, who wore a face as fierce as he'd ever seen.

Thank the spirits for Amanah. Despite all of Galod's training, he wouldn't have made it out of that scrape alone. The high guards must have truly left them, for they hadn't come running with the commotion.

She immediately turned, making sure the guards were now all unconscious, and then snatched the keys. Her chains clanged to the floor at her feet moments later, and then she unlocked his.

Worry filled her voice. "Are you all right?"

He nodded. His body was ablaze with pain, and he put a hand to his aching stomach, but there was no time to pause. Taunos stumbled up the corridor to the intersection, his pace increasing once Amanah swept his arm across her shoulders and pulled him along.

Footsteps sounded around the corner ahead, and Taunos braced himself for another confrontation. Emin rounded the corner with a pack in his hand. Sagging with relief, Taunos leaned against the wall, catching his breath.

"What... already?" Emin asked.

"Late again." Amanah shook out her arm with a wince.

"Amanah did most of the work," Taunos said, gritting his teeth against the pain. "We're still not out of here."

Emin's gaze flickered across them as he fell in beside them. "And yet, you're the one bleeding. Come on, this way."

"I was the distraction," Taunos said. "Painful distraction, I might add."

They hurried after Emin toward the guardhouse.

"I cannot believe they didn't take you into custody as well," Taunos murmured.

"They tried to. Turns out Gurseh's not entirely useless." There was tension on Emin's face that spoke of pain. "And I don't think they were expecting my band to be loyal to me."

Taunos glanced out the window, wary of guards. "Thank you, Emin. You both deserve better."

"Couldn't let you have all the fun."

Amanah's voice was tight. "We should look for Nasri. No one's looking for her."

"We have to get out of the city first," Emin said. "They're not going to just let this go. Come on. My band's distraction won't last for long."

Movement out the large window just ahead of them caught Taunos's eye. He put out a hand, and Amanah and Emin pressed themselves against the wall. A guard passed by the window, and Taunos waited, barely breathing, until the guard had gone.

Gesturing to the others, he continued forward at a crouch.

Bunched tightly together, they made their way along the corridor to the guardhouse, where Emin's band was challenging the highest ranked war-band to a wrestling match. The commotion drew the attention of much of the guardhouse and clogged up the hallways, allowing Emin, Amanah, and Taunos to slip past.

As they exited the guardhouse and stepped into the city, Taunos's heart beat in his ears and his shoulders tensed, ready at every step for the shout that would single them out as escaped prisoners. He was never so thankful for the crowds of people of all sorts, enabling them to blend in, avoiding the red-vested pairs of guards on patrol who would be searching for them.

The enormous city of Arruk seemed to stretch endlessly, but they kept the gold-roofed temple and palace behind them.

Emin and Amanah dragged him forward, one on either side, while he kept up as best he could. When had he become the slow one, the one in need of saving? He liked it far better when he was the one saving others. Two men with nearly black skin jogged out of a side street, passing through with enormous logs of reddish wood carried on their shoulders, forcing them to the side of the street. Taunos glanced backward.

Red vests swam against the current.

"Guards." His voice was tight.

Without any other acknowledgement, Amanah turned them left, diving among the covered stalls of the market near the harbor. The damage the Sea Peoples had done was evident in the mound of broken stalls in the corner, but there was still a crowd of people, even if it was much smaller than it had been that night with Amanah and Emin and the band.

Shoppers shouted and haggled, and merchants called out, drawing customers to their stalls. The din made it hard to listen for danger.

Still, wary glances abounded in the crowd, many directed toward the harbor. That should help hide them, Taunos hoped. Just more tense people in a crowd of suspicion. Hopefully he just looked like he'd gotten into a street brawl or something.

Amanah and Emin waded through the crowd with loose movements on either side of him. They might have appeared unconcerned but for their quick pace and Taunos hanging between them. Emin even pointed out a carpenter with a shaved head fitting together complex dovetails such that the two pieces of wood formed an intricate pattern when combined.

On the far end of the market, however, a pair of red-vested guards pushed their way toward them past a group of musicians.

The road out of Arruk was full of guards—they'd never be able to make it that way, and even if they made it to the gates, no doubt the gate guards would be looking for them. Taunos's limbs felt heavy and slow. His body ached with the new bruises he'd gained just getting out of the palace, and he was becoming entirely too dependent on Emin and Amanah for movement. They'd have to head to the docks that jutted out into the harbor alongside the wide river that fed the people of Arruk with food as well as supplies by boat and barge. Hopefully the ever-present chaos and wider area there could hide them. An awful lot rode on hope.

"A little longer," Emin murmured. "I'll go ahead, see if I can cut down how long Amanah has to drag your dead weight around."

Taunos grunted, too tired to give a good response.

"Hurry. He needs rest." Amanah adjusted her hold on Taunos, pulling him closer.

The crowd at the docks was thick, with fishermen hauling in their catch and vessels of all sizes loading and unloading goods. They dodged past a dock master inspecting goods and then around a coil of ropes as thick as Taunos's wrist. Several paces in front of them, Emin's hands cut through the air in sharp gestures as he spoke to a captain, only to be turned down. The next ship in the docks pulled out just before Emin could get to them, red-haired sailors pulling on oars that flashed on the water.

"Wait!" Emin shouted.

The sailors didn't respond.

Emin grumbled under his breath. "There must be some ship that'll take us."

"There has to be another option," Amanah said.

"So far, Jattanu is not smiling on us." Emin glared at the other boats.

Shouts rang out from the market. Several red-vested guards pushed through the crowd toward them. Their way back was blocked.

Taunos scanned the docks, but most of the boats were occupied. At the end of the dock, a small single-masted boat lay on its side at the edge of the water. He pointed it out.

Emin shook his head. "Boats on the side aren't water-worthy."

"It seems we have little choice." Taunos limped to the edge of the dock to inspect the craft further.

Closer to the boat, it became evident how right Emin was. Several planks at the back end of the boat were shattered, as if it had hit a rock. Taunos shook his head, grabbing the canvas nearby and a pallet and tossing them in. He groaned as the movements tore open scabs. His aching muscles screamed at him for rest, but there would be no rest until they were safe. He shoved the boat toward the water.

"What are you doing? It'll just sink!" Amanah said.

Emin started laughing. "Are you fully accepting the role of sea-wizard, then?"

"I'm trying not to let us all get executed," Taunos grunted, shoulder pressed against the boat. He'd need all of his strength to keep the holes plugged and the splintered wood together long enough to get away.

The weight of the boat eased as Emin joined him. Taunos called out to Amanah, "Is there a bucket? We're still going to need to bail."

A small pail soared through the air toward his head. He caught it just as something struck it, punching a hole into the wood.

A crossbow bolt thrummed in the wooden side of the pail.

He spun around with renewed urgency.

"Time to stop dawdling!" Emin said, tossing his pack into the boat. With one more shove, the boat splashed into the water.

Taunos fell more than hopped in, dropping the pail in the bottom of the hull, which was already filling with water. He grabbed the canvas, spreading it over the leaking portion and then placed the pallet on top. Kneeling on the pallet, he pressed down with his telekinesis all around the hole.

All his pain, all his exhaustion, all his desperation, he channeled into his telekinesis. He was not going to let this be their end.

The canvas grew waterlogged, but the water coming in slowed.

"I'm gonna need this," Emin said, ripping a plank from the pallet. "Unless you can wizard us a paddle?"

"Little busy," Taunos said tightly, focusing hard on all the edges. "I only need enough planks for a makeshift patch."

The boat rocked as Amanah joined them, reaching past him to grab the pail while Emin ripped free another plank from the pallet.

In moments, they were moving, Amanah and Emin paddling with the rough planks between bailing the water that had made it into the boat.

Even so, their progress was far too slow.

In the back of the boat, Taunos had a clear view of the guards as they reached the edge of the dock and took aim with crossbows.

"Get down!" He flattened himself against the pallet as bolts whistled past. Cautiously, he peeked above the edge of the boat again, watching the guards cranking back the shafts to load more bolts. "Hurry."

"It'd help if you helped!" Emin said.

"I'm helping keep you from drowning!"

"Now is not the time!" Amanah pulled hard on the paddle, moving them further out into the current.

"I don't know. I think teasing Taunos to death is fitting," Emin argued.

"If you put half as much effort into paddling as you do in snarking off, we would— Down!" Taunos shouted.

The boat shivered as more bolts struck the hull, both inside and outside the boat. The holes they left leaked more water into the shallow bottom, and Taunos scrambled to plug the leaks. The boat lurched as Emin and Amanah paddled as fast as they could, working against each other in their haste.

"Pull in time with each other," Taunos said.

"One, two, one, two, Amanah, no!" Emin shouted. "Forward on one, backward on two!"

"You'd be in time if you weren't shouting at everyone," Amanah returned.

"On the beat." Taunos launched into the first song that came to mind, a Rinaryn song his mother used to sing to him, translated into Traveller's as he went. It fumbled the rhythm and rhyme of the song, but he was at least able to keep a steady beat with his voice.

"Life is what you make of it,
Challenges and beauty.
Though mountain peaks rise high above,
Still the winter flowers are blooming.
Experiences may hurt or bring joy,
But your story is yours to tell.
So weave your experiences into the story of your making
And put it to the tune of your song.
Life is what you make of it,

Challenges and beauty.
My love, meet challenges with head held high
And always be watching for the beauty.
The sun still shines. The grass still grows,
The roots still dig deep. The rivers still run to the sea."

The boat lurched forward, finally making good progress over the water.

Taunos crouched over the weakened floor of the boat, pressing down on the fabric and wood telekinetically to slow the leaks. Those in the sides of the boat, he had to plug with his hands, dividing his telekinetic attention. If he let up, the boat immediately began drooping in the water, slowing as water poured in.

It'd been some time since the last volley of crossbow bolts, and Taunos looked up. Another boat was racing toward them over the waves. Their little boat-of-holes joined the other riverboat traffic and scooted clumsily around a barge, and the other boat followed. The guard at the bow pointed at them, shouting something to his companions.

"Is the sail working?" Taunos shouted.

The boat wavered a bit as Amanah went to the single mast and pulled the sail to extend it. "It's moldy and moth-eaten, but it might at least give us some help."

"Warn me if you swing the boom around so I can duck, please," Taunos said.

"I don't know how to sail." Amanah hauled on a rope, and the boom swung, nearly cracking into his skull. "What's a boom?"

"That! Tie it there." Taunos pointed, taking up precious moments where more water flowed into the boat.

The hull lifted as the sail caught the wind, leaping forward. Water poured in at the forward portion of the cracks, and Taunos shifted his attention there, keeping the song going to help Emin and Amanah time their rowing for the swiftly accelerating boat. Their derelict little craft whispered along, lengthening the distance between them and the guards' boat. Taunos grinned. There was nothing quite like working in tandem with people you trusted, even if he'd prefer Amanah not be in danger.

Something punched into him, knocking him backward.

He tumbled into the bottom of the boat, smacking his head against the ribs of the vessel. Pain blazed in his chest from the crossbow bolt sticking out of him. He couldn't breathe.

Amanah and Emin moved around him, a flurry of motion he couldn't pay attention to. His mind went fuzzy, and cold soaked him, assuring him

that he had indeed lost his telekinetic hold on the bottom of the boat. Yet all he could do was struggle for air, the rest of his body refusing to respond to his demands to move.

"Taunos!"

"I think it hit his lung."

"No time to check."

Finally, he was able to draw in a shallow breath, enough to roll to his side. Emin was standing in the water—no, that was the prow of the boat, which was rapidly sinking. Amanah grabbed Taunos's arm and hauled him to his feet. He looped an arm around her waist, holding on as the woman he loved balanced him for a breath on the edge of the boat and then threw him into the river. She jumped in right after, with another splash heralding Emin leaping in.

Pain blinded him every time he moved his arms to swim, and blackness overtook him at the simplest motions, but he managed to make it to the surface.

Amanah. He had to make sure she was all right.

She surfaced next to him, looping an arm under his and holding him tight. He rolled over to float on his back, raggedly determined to breathe, while Amanah hauled him along.

An oncoming boat approached rapidly. He could barely move his arms, couldn't get the breath to kick, to help propel them along. They were dead. The guards would shoot them down. He hadn't saved them at all. For so long, he'd taken pride in the strength of his arms, and now it turned to weakness. The least he could do was shield Amanah from the crossbows.

A pale arm swung down, holding a rope, rather than a brown arm with a crossbow. Taunos gaped.

The man with red hair and a red beard peeked down at them. "Grab hold, but don't climb just yet."

And then the face was gone.

Taunos grabbed the rope, passing it on to Amanah. She held on to it as Emin swam over to them, trying to keep the pack he carried above the water. The current dragged at Taunos, numbing his fingers. What else was in the water with them? More importantly, where was the guards' boat?

But he didn't have enough strength for those questions. It was all he could do to keep his head above water. The others clustered tightly with him in the shadow of the boat. Breathing was agony, and it never felt like he got quite enough air.

He was thoroughly exhausted by the time the man peeked down at them again.

"All right," the man said. "Swing back a bit, and we'll bring you aboard. You don't need to hide against the hull anymore."

No one spoke. They just did what he said, sliding down the rope toward the stern until hands reached over the low side and pulled them into the boat.

The world spun as Taunos rolled down the sloping side, hitting a bag. Losing his bearings was only a minor terror against still not being able to breathe. Something clanked, and the splash of oars surrounded them.

Gradually, he was able to take stock of the tiny compartment they were squeezed together in. A canvas cover stretched tight over their heads, and barrels and crates of goods filled the available space of the boat.

"Good day!" The voice came from outside the cover.

Another voice spoke, distance muddying the voice to Taunos's exhausted ears.

Amanah hovered above him, pressing a hand to his chest near where the pain was centered. Taunos glanced down. The crossbow bolt was still sticking out of his chest, far too close to vital organs. He gritted his teeth, wavering in a half-conscious state, straining to hear what was happening outside, struggling to get enough air. His wrist was a counterpoint of pain, the broken bones unforgiving of the strain he'd put them through lately, and his various other injuries and burns joined the chorus.

"Ifreesians don't take passengers!" the voice outside the canvas shouted, and more voices raised in agreement nearby.

Another mumble.

"We are not beholden to Far Dahutad." A pause. "Skir, stop washing that rope and coil it up for the gods' sake!"

Another muttering, the tone tight.

"I suggest you look elsewhere. *The Flit* will not be docking at Arruk any longer while under my command."

The voice spoke again in supplication.

"No, I've made up my mind. Other captains can make up theirs as well, but I will tell them of this, you can be sure."

The conversation died, leaving only the sound of a rowing song with a strong beat in a strange language joined by the splashing of the waves against the hull.

The music wrapped around Taunos, carrying him away. Vaguely, he was aware of hands moving him, and then a sharp pain flared in his chest and through his back. Without the breath to scream, he bobbed in unconsciousness like a vast ocean.

And then he surfaced, back into the painful world around him. He drew in ragged breaths, grateful for the agony surrounding him, the proof that he was alive. With a groan, he lifted his head.

Emin was getting patched up by Amanah. More bandages wrapped Taunos's chest, along with a short plank tied to his side just beneath the bandages under his arm. He reached for it.

"Leave it there." Emin's voice was quiet and flat.

Taunos froze. It was rare that he'd seen Emin so scared he was serious. Humor was his weapon and his armor. Matching Emin's tone, Taunos whispered, "Is everyone all right?"

His chest ached with his breath, and the plank moved. He craned his head to look under his arm at the bandages.

"Emin and you took the worst hits," Amanah said.

"But I carried my weight, not falling asleep like some of us," Emin said.

Taunos mustered a grin.

Amanah shifted, taking the step needed to crouch by Taunos again. She leaned close, inspecting his face. So close, but the look on her face only heightened his worry. Then she nodded, withdrawing. "Good. Your color's better."

"My color?"

"Your lung collapsed. Don't lower that arm. I had to punch a hole between your ribs. There's a reed there under those bandages that's keeping you breathing. Leave it there and don't unwind those bandages holding it."

The canvas cover flipped back, its ropes loosening. A man with a braided beard hopped down the half deck, into the recessed portion of the hull where they lay among the goods. The deck was only raised up from the hold by half Taunos's height, but they were ringed in by fifteen tall, broad-shouldered men with pale skin and hair that ranged from reddish-blond to red to reddish-brown.

"Ifreesians." Amanah's voice was hushed and reverent.

The man standing before them crossed his arms. "We have a problem. Ifreesians don't take passengers. So what are these?"

Another of the men spoke up, the one who'd tossed them the rope and hauled them aboard. "Looks like cargo to me."

Taunos tensed. He wasn't about to be captive again.

But Amanah had a bandage on her arm, and Emin had bandages on his leg, waist, and shoulder. And they were completely outnumbered. Only three of them, against fifteen sailors.

The man before them grinned. "Cargo it is! Cargo doesn't speak though."

"Dunno, Captain. We do ferry all sorts of goods. Maybe we just never seen speaking cargo before." Their rescuer—Skir—deadpanned.

The captain of the boat dropped into a crouch.

Taunos tensed, but his muscles were sluggish.

The captain laughed. "All right, cargo. Don't be telling everyone. We only picked up your dead weight because you were abandoned goods floating in the river, lost bits from that boat that went down. Salvage, got it?"

"Why did you bring us on board?" Amanah asked.

Skir grinned. "Had to reward that show of bravery. Call it a weakness in me."

"You told them you'd never come back to Arruk," she said.

The captain waved that away. "They overcharged me anyway."

"Captain hates being overcharged."

The captain halfheartedly swatted at Skir, who ducked with a laugh.

"Now," the captain said. "We're heading down to the sea and along the coastline to the Hinanur Empire next. You being Dahuti maybe want off before that, but maybe not so close to Arruk. That right?"

Taunos glanced at the others. They should probably make a plan. And he himself needed to make a plan. Go back to his sister? Gather more knowledge to force the Elders to take her back? Weariness numbed his mind, and he let the odd impression of a forest breeze sweep the thoughts away, uncaring where it might have come from.

Stay with Amanah. Right here, that's where he should be.

The captain snorted. "Well, make up your minds. We aren't changing our speed or heading for cargo. It's just a matter of where the salvage happens to wash over the side. Fickle gods and their games of chance and all."

Emin tilted his head. "So, you went out of your way to rescue us, but now you're letting us rest here and carrying us as far as we want so long as it's not out of your way?"

The captain shrugged. "Up until we reach our Hinanuri destination. You get off there, regardless of whether you want to or not."

"How can we thank you?" Amanah asked.

"By not telling anyone," the captain said, the ease vanishing from his bearing. "Anyone. Ever."

Taunos's eyes flickered over the expressions of the people staring down at them. He understood that look, the emotion driving it. They, too, were keeping secrets from the world. Secrets no one could find out about.

"We understand. Thank you." Taunos grinned at Emin. "Besides, I'm sure Emin cannot wait to tell about the time he tried to sneak on board an Ifreesian boat and got dunked in the river for his efforts. Everyone knows the Ifreesians don't take passengers."

The captain's eyes bored into him for a moment, and then he grinned again, ease returning to his posture. "Exactly."

With a nod, the captain turned, hopping up onto the half deck. "All right, you laggards! Those on the second shift, get your sleep. The rest of you, what are you sitting around for? You're as bad as the cargo. Get the beat going. Oars out. We row 'till the sun sets the river on fire. Row!"

The boat filled with a flurry of activity. Eight Ifreesians left their rowing benches and joined them in the cargo hold while the other six began rowing.

Amanah smiled, her eyes alight as she took everything in. "We're on an Ifreesian ship. I never imagined anything this magical."

It was cramped in the hold, but with the wind in his hair and the woman he loved safe and by his side, it was tolerable. He was alive, even if he had a reed stuck through his side just below his armpit. He couldn't very well realmwalk until Amanah removed it anyway—none of his people would know what to do with such a thing.

He couldn't just leave Amanah. She had told him she didn't want to have to leave the bamimri, but now she and Emin had lost their home and jobs on account of him. They'd never be able to go back now. Just like he'd been cast out, along with his sister and her friends.

The Ifreesians were heading for the Hinanur Empire, and they had stories of sea-wizards, of multiple people appearing at once. The Darks attacked like that too, multiple people at once. He'd suspected the Darks might be a group of realmwalkers, like him. He had to confirm it, but he couldn't remember if he'd encountered a Dark with telekinesis in any of his skirmishes with them.

He was good at secrets—he would root them out.

And if the Hinanuri had sea-wizards, perhaps they knew a way to fix his sister. He could figure out how to bring a cure back later, if he found one. And hopefully, he'd find a way to fix the mess Amanah and Emin had dropped into with him while he was at it. He just had to figure out how.

Chapter Sixteen

*A troublesome line, both of them! But the mother is within reach. She is with
the elves of the First Stand. Sapol, you must press the elves to keep her there. The
elves are contrary by nature. They are uncouth and defiant, as were their rebellious
ancestors. Yet, what elf would dare to go against the full might of the fae?*
—part of a missive from "Mebril" in Stonefield

Training with Umril was somehow as different from training with
Galod as it was from those early training sessions with her mother. Galod's
training was full of challenges and stern, icy disapproval when she failed.
Her mother's had been full of warmth and games and teasing.

Kaemada missed that.

"Focus," Umril reminded, his voice a cold wind cutting through the
summer air.

Ducking her head, she reined her mind back to the task at hand. Her
eyes flickered closed before she remembered and opened them again, but
her telepathic casting-out wavered. She buried her hand in Nimae's fur,
while the wolf yawned and flopped onto her side, more interested in
sunning herself than what Kaemada was doing. So quickly, she'd come to
love the wolf, despite her remaining grief for Tannevar. She could never
replace him, but she could love both him and Nimae.

They'd spent several days alone together—except for the elves who
spied on them—to strengthen their bond before returning to the Stand.
After Umril took the thin circlet with the dangling charms back from her,
she'd spent several more days working under Umril with psionics,
breaking into his mind, past his many, many mental walls, and then
finding his mind among an increasing number of others'. And still, he
exhibited far more control than she'd ever have thought possible.

"Mind on your task." There was an impatient edge to his tone.

Across the garden, at the edge of the pond, two elves were walking
with a Rinaryn. This was not unusual—every newcomer was taken on a
tour, and most accepted healing right away upon seeing the Stand's peace
and calm. But Umril had told her to find out what was wrong with this
particular man without walking over there. It was too far for her psionics
to reach, and she was forbidden to dreamwalk until her bond with Nimae

strengthened.

So how to eavesdrop?

"Don't use that word. You'll only feel more guilty and—look, there you've done it. You've lost it." Umril's gaze remained fixed on the trio.

She pulled her shawl over her head, casting out again. Day after day, people from all over Rinara arrived in the Stand. Every time, the elves calmly discussed what was wrong and then went to work, setting bones, binding wounds, curing poisons and illnesses, soothing lesions, and calming mind-sicknesses. Every chance she had, she watched intently as they prepared their medicines and found the plants that would cure the given ailment, preparing it just so, and then treated the person, whoever it was. Healing was swifter than Kaemada had ever imagined, save for the Rinaryn healers, but the elves didn't seem to tire the way the healers did. They took turns tending to the needs of others or living their lives.

But this man was not receiving the normal treatment. Instead, when the elves had discovered the source of his sickness, they had become grave.

"Can you heal him?" she asked Umril. She'd used more psionics in the last several days than she had her whole life. Here, psionics were not strictly controlled. In fact, it was abundant, once she'd learned to look for it.

Umril stood next to her, hands clasped behind his back, tall and serene. "Of course we can heal him. We are Lanis in the forest. We are Lanis in the plains, but the plains are in winter and we are not Torkaema, coming just in time to save one so resourceful."

Rinaryn legend spoke of Lanis the Wild, a large woman whose skill in woodcraft and survival saved Torkaema and his companions on many occasions. Her knowledge had been preserved and passed down to the ancient Rinaryn—how to move silently in the forest, how to hunt and kill with little pain, how to use all parts of the hunted animal and not to waste. To live in harmony with the land and each other, so the wars of Torkaema's time would never happen again.

No wonder the elves chose her to represent themselves among Rinaryn legend.

Kaemada stared at the trio, at the calm waters of the pond, dark with shadow and distance. Everyone knew elves could heal nearly anything, unless the medicinal plants were not replaced and tended—that was why oath breakers were so devastating. She made the leap, guessing at the riddle. The most likely reason was that the elves didn't have the needed plant.

Umril scowled at her. "That was not the lesson."

She brushed off the fact that she hadn't spoken any of those thoughts aloud. "But it's true, isn't it?"

Oathbreakers were wrong to run, no matter how earnestly they argued. The elves were right. It was only fair, after all. She, too, needed to stay here for the summers asked of her or throw things wildly out of balance.

But that didn't make sense. Why couldn't the elves simply replace the plant? Why wouldn't they plant more when they knew they were running low? Any Rinaryn could teach them to never harvest too much of any one plant. That allowed the plants to continue to flourish as the community moved on so that when the kaetal came back there would be abundance. Her head hurt.

Something else was going on. The elves needed the Rinaryn for some reason, and it wasn't to tend plants.

"Light shine on us, we may have all our secrets found out," Umril said.

Her eyes narrowed further. His tone was kind, and all the words were true. But there was something about the way they were said. "Are you... insulting me?"

"Do not be offended." He waved a hand dismissively, and calm soothed over her.

He was too good at that, painting her emotions like colors on a brush. She clung to her indignation further, finding a new source of it in Nimae, who gathered her legs under her, attention sharply trained on the elf.

"What do you really gain from healing people? Is it workers, to do things for you? Like the Kamalti?" she demanded.

A heavy weight of calm pressed on her mind, burying her outrage, muting her frustration.

"You have seen for yourself the trouble that comes when someone takes and does not give back."

"That's not an answer. Though you do not lie, that does not mean you do not deceive. Kind words and smiles can hide insults."

"And you did not discover the man's ailment."

If he wanted to mince words, she could, too. "No, but not being able to be healed is part of what's wrong with him."

Umril laughed.

She glanced over at Cheros and the three Rinaryn he was hoeing a garden with. "It's true that you need resources to continue your work, but surely you do not need us for so long. You ask for much of our lives."

"The trees do not grow any more quickly depending on who tends them."

200

"I understand, but the sacrifice you ask is far more for Rinaryn than it is for elves."

"The timeframe is the same."

"But it isn't." She faced him, slicing a hand through the air between them. "Fifty summers for you is an inconvenience. For Rinaryn, it's the better part of our lives. That is why my people so fear to come here."

"Plenty of your people come."

"Because they feel they have no other choice."

"You know the agreement before you come. It is childish of you to protest after accepting help."

"I know." And yet, her point remained, buried beneath the frustration of being no match for his smooth words.

"You have spent your moons here arguing over and over with any who might listen to you. The agreement has been set down over a vast number of your generations. Who are you to try to change it?"

"Isn't there room to re-evaluate the fairness of it? Some of my people would like to go home and see their families."

"Ahh." Umril nodded to himself. "You are arguing for Cheros again."

Kaemada lifted her chin against his sure-to-come insinuation that she was again being childish.

"Your tenacity is commendable."

Was there a trick to the compliment? She narrowed her eyes.

He looked thoughtful for long moments and then shook his head. "No. It cannot be. The agreement must stand as it always has, and your race must pay the price required of any. Some of you require medicines. You must tend the plants for the next person who needs them. Some of you require rooms, housing. You must help tend the great trees to build rooms for the next who need lodging."

"These trees will stand long after I leave, and the room will remain after I have gone," Kaemada said. This was the way of nature, the seeding of the new, the recycling of the old. Not a strict transference, one to one, but a large-scale network of life and growth and death feeding life again.

"True, but the trees do not last forever. Death, disease, disaster—these afflict our great trees as well, and we must prepare for the future. What should happen if we did not require the tending of the trees? New trees would grow, yes, but not in the forms useful for lodging. We would have no space for the next psion who could not speak Traveller's."

Kaemada had no answer for that, just as she had been out-argued every time. Umril's smile spoke of triumph as he walked across the grass, leaving her alone.

She thought of Cheros with a heavy heart. There must be some way to satisfy both his desire to go home as well as the need to replace what was used to help him. She rubbed her head, for she was beginning to agree with the elves, and that felt like a betrayal of Cheros. He'd warned her not to trust them, but she found it difficult. She didn't completely mind the thought of staying here. Except that she was hiding, and that went against growth.

What nagged at her most was the worry of how much of her agreement with the elves' arguments came not from herself but from the elves. Time and again she found that their reasoning had crept into hers, like damp from the ground soaking up through a blanket.

Kaemada's fingers tightened on the corners of her shawl. She had to grow. She couldn't stagnate. After all, her story was not all bad. She worked as hard as any, and her body was strengthening again with the days of foraging and tending, sowing and weeding and harvesting. She had Nimae. The ability to speak Traveller's again, thanks to Umril. And her psionics should hopefully be steadying. Perhaps she could withstand the Collective if they ever found her again.

The Collective.

If she worked like the Collective did, she could reach across the vast distance even without dreamwalking.

Halfway across the grass, Umril stopped, his form stiff.

Kaemada ignored him and flung a telepathic questing out. Could she do it? She touched the mind of an elf, lightly, like a leaf floating on water, as Umril had taught her, and then tried to leap off to another.

But her strength fizzled, dispersing like smoke, leaving her panting on the grass.

"Again." Umril turned, his eyes fixed on her.

She winced, struggling back up. The elf whose mind she'd touched had turned to her with a stern glare.

"I'm sorry," she gasped.

"Do it again," Umril repeated, calm but implacable.

She threw herself out there again, toward the same elf, wrapped in her guilt and trespassing, but he caught her and she paused there in his mind. She needed more strength to make the next jump. How was she supposed to do that?

"Gather strength to you." Of course Umril was listening to her thoughts.

"Steal it?" She nearly recoiled but held on at the last moment, straining over the distance. Silence answered her, and she delved lower, to connect consciously with the elf.

But she couldn't do it. She couldn't just take from him.

It's not taking if it's a gift.

Kaemada stared at the far elf, just at the edge of her range. He nodded, just a subtle dip of his chin, and she gathered some of his strength to her, just enough to make the jump. From him to another elf and then to a third, before that elf resisted her.

She was nearly there!

Frustration mounted in her. She had almost made it—would make it, if only the elf would cooperate.

Her presence dissipated so suddenly the world shifted around her in a blink. Her stomach turned, and she heaved onto the grass, her limbs like liquid.

"The rebound will be sickening unless you go back the way you came," Umril said. "Retrace your steps exactly."

"I could have done it. I could have made him want to let me. I could have made him offer me his strength. Like you play with my emotions." Even the thought sickened her further, and she heaved again onto the grass.

"But you didn't." Umril sounded disappointed.

Kaemada lashed out against the weight of his disappointment when all she'd been trying to do was be polite. She refused to force someone against their will. She used Traveller's, both to practice the language she was regaining and to avoid sullying Rinaryn with her accusation. "That's how the elves reach so far, isn't it? How much of my emotions are real? How much of everyone's emotions are real? Do you pull people into the Stand? Do you make them want to come, when they wouldn't naturally?"

He turned away, as if she were a child throwing a tantrum. "Perhaps you're tired. You spend more time with elves than any of your people tend to. Always attempting to learn and converse. It's a shame you throw accusations against us."

A growl rose from Nimae, the wolf's anger rising in response to Kaemada's, feeding her own. They looped around and around in a growing cycle, and the anger boiled to rage, out of control, and Kaemada couldn't think, couldn't breathe.

Umril cut his hand across the air. "Enough of that."

Calm swept over her again, but this time Kaemada was thankful for it. She'd been out of control. What would have happened if that anger had continued?

"We are not fae, to play with others' minds as with toys," Umril said.

"You just did!" Kaemada panted.

"Not as a toy." His words were sharp as a knife. "Fae toy with everyone." His face wrinkled in distaste, contorting his beautiful features into a hideous mask for a brief, terrifying instant. "They are very secretive people and like to keep intact boundaries they perceive."

"Somewhat like elves," Kaemada observed.

"They come with war and death to those who oppose them." The terrible expression deepened like a looming thunderstorm. "We are nothing like them."

"You are a lot like them, actually. You even look alike—"

"Enough. We are done for today." Umril glided away, apparently deaf to voice or telepathy.

Kaemada grimaced and stumbled to join the others working in the garden. Her hands were healing, but her broken ribs slowed her work. As she entered the garden, though, the other Rinaryn glared at her and withdrew to other plots.

She pressed her lips together.

Their resentment of the elves had spread to resenting her, since she spent so much time with them. But that gave her time to talk to the elves as well, to help them see the situation from the Rinaryn point of view. It was exactly like her mother would have done, but instead of being honored for it, she was reviled.

How could she reach them, to let them know she was trying to intercede for them? She reached out with a tendril of thought almost reflexively, as natural as breathing, here among the elves.

An odd tune rang from the others, through their songs. It reminded her of Umril's.

She pulled back sharply to avoid impinging on their privacy further. It was bad enough for the elves to be influencing their emotions—perhaps even their thoughts—but for it to go so deep that their very songs rang of elf? She shivered.

"You spend too much time with the elves." Cheros stabbed the ground with his spade. "You should not be spending any time with them."

Kaemada blinked at him, her thoughts shattered. Without the elves, she put everyone at risk. "They're helping me."

"That's not the only reason you associate with them."

She bit back her frustration. "I'm talking with them. I'm trying to help them understand."

"You're falling to their wiles, just like they get all of us. Only you aren't even trying to fight them."

"We do not need to fight. I'm trying to figure out a way to—"

Cheros snorted. "You? You cannot figure anything out. Not even the blatant fact that the elves are playing with you."

She toyed with the edges of her shawl. "I know you're angry with them but cannot reach them, so you turn it on me."

"You see much and know little." Cheros stood, tossing his spade at her feet. The worn stone blade broke into three pieces as it hit a rock peeking out of the soil. "I will not be soothed by them or by you."

"It's hard to argue with those who know your arguments before you do," she said.

He paused. "Hold on to the truth of you. It's the only way to keep them from eroding your arguments away."

"And what's the truth of you?"

A smile flashed across his face, there and gone like lightning. "Anger."

~

Kaemada's mind was in turmoil, keeping her up at night and snatching her appetite during the day as she struggled to come to terms with what she'd learned. There were ways to boost a telepathic signal, even for a single telepath. There were ways to ask permission, just on the border of intrusion. The elves needed those who came for healing, to replace what was used. But how could that be all, when they asked for tens and tens of summers?

She owed them fifty summers, and yes, she was taking up much of their time. And yet, something was off with their arguments, and they were definitely hiding something. Her mind kept drifting away from something, and after every conversation with them, she left thinking she agreed with them.

All elves were psionic. They were much like the fae, though they apparently differed in creed. Elves were pacifists, but the split seemed deeper and more emotional than that. Elves could influence thoughts and emotions without the person ever realizing it.

The Storyteller had been plagued with bad dreams, so long ago when she was still a member of Torkae. Dreams influenced people—she'd seen enough to know that.

So if the dreams were sent by skilled psions…

Her skin went cold, and her chest squeezed tight. She pulled her shawl tighter across her shoulders.

Something was wrong with the Council of Elders.

They never should have declared them Fallen—at least, not Taunos, Ra'ael, and Takiyah. And they certainly never should have stampeded over the Great Mothers' protests or punished the Storyteller and Saimahkae. It was unheard of, like the taking of their names so no one would be able to speak for them. If the Council had been influenced—by fae or elves or anyone—Eian was not safe.

Who would gain by separating him from Taunos, Ra'ael, and Takiyah? Or was it separating the heroes of Torkae from Torkae?

Longing to talk it over with her friends, she pictured Takiyah's thoughtful gaze, Ra'ael's scoff, her brother's readiness. But they were far away.

She turned in the hammock, swaying gently in the breeze. Nimae shifted with her, head lying on Kaemada's stomach. Kaemada sifted through what she knew, thinking back to Umril's last lesson with her.

The elves influenced minds and never left the Stand. They read minds the same way she listened to birds. It would make sense that they gleaned the minds of those who came to the Stand for healing, gathering news about the land beyond. What they used the information for, she had no idea.

The only way to grow was to use her psionics more. Her powers still frightened her, even after all the training sessions. But now, with this new information... She'd told herself her son was safer away from her, but she couldn't really know that. She had to find out for sure.

Except she couldn't leave.

And she didn't need to.

Umril had told her not to dreamwalk yet, but she hadn't seen him for several days. Not since she'd accused him of being like a fae. Ever since then, the elves had been distant toward her. She'd worked with the other Rinaryn, taking on whatever jobs they left for her. But now...

Kaemada was going to find the truth, and not even the elves could stop her.

Fear built in her as she contemplated dreamwalking again. Last time, she'd barely found her way back to her body. She could die if it happened again. The fear rose between her and Nimae as they fed on each other's emotions. Kaemada sighed her breath out, pressing calm on the both of them.

"Shareil. Shareil. Nanovah," she whispered until she could breathe easily again.

Night blanketed the Stand. She stroked Nimae's fur until the last lines of tension left the wolf. Tension lay coiled within Kaemada though, right down to her bones. She rubbed the spot on Nimae's muzzle between her eyes until the wolf snorted and nudged her hard. She was stalling, of course.

With the warmth of fur covering her, she dreamwalked. She cast out and away, trailing behind her the gleaming lifeline that linked her to Nimae and consciousness, woven of the mixture of their songs and the will that bound them together.

She drifted away from the elves, searching the foreign landscape so different from reality. Colors muted, with features blurring together. No touch, no smell, existed here, and distance was warped and unreliable. Out and out she went, ever wider, as the calm detachment of the dreamscape seeped into her song.

And then, she felt a tug on her heart. She'd gone too far. Slowly, she drifted back along the tether. She had to find Eian. She had to.

The image of a hawk soaring crossed her mind, and she shared her gratitude with Nimae—of course. She should go up to search. Like Umril said, it was easier to find and to connect with minds familiar to her own, minds she'd shared with before. She'd already known that, but she could use that now, with Eian.

Drifting upward, Kaemada cast out for the familiar song of her son, the song she knew by heart. And there it was, the tune she loved more than anything. Too long she'd been without it, and her song twisted with mingled pain and joy.

Grabbing hold of it, she followed where it led, careful not to look around as she drew near. She wasn't sure she could trust herself not to become an oathbreaker if she knew where her son was. Keeping herself away from her brother and friends would prevent her from intruding on them, but oh how she ached to hold her son again! She glanced back, where the silvery tether that connected her to Nimae and her body spooled out, a long wavering line.

The Collective crashed down on her. She winced. She hadn't realized how close to the mountains she was. But she couldn't back down, and she couldn't let them stop her.

She leaned back into Nimae, trusting in the strength of her anchor in the wolf, and embraced the Collective. Their multitude of minds weighed her down, and she floundered, reaching for what she'd learned from the elves. Pain lashed her as the Collective bit at her with fear and anger.

The fear was new.

What is wrong? What scares you? Kaemada asked. She did as Cheros had advised and clung tight to herself, to her search for truth.

They hunt us. They're killing us all.

Kaemada had fought the Collective before. She understood them, and that understanding welled up sympathy in the core of her song. But she needed to check on Eian. *I have to make sure my son is safe. It's been too long. But then I will see if I can help you. Lend me your strength.*

They pounced on her, pummeling her, ripping her apart in wordless fear and pain. Just like Cheros, they couldn't reach the true target of their rage, so they took it out on her.

But she couldn't let them stop her. Eian was too important.

She seized them as they surrounded and crushed her, siphoning strength from them to go beyond the bounds she'd normally be able to reach, past where the tug on her heart should have stopped her. She fueled herself with the Collective's betrayal, despite how her stomach twisted at the bitterness therein. With Eian's song in her heart and Nimae's quiet strength steadying her, she propelled herself farther than she could go alone, until finally she drew up alongside her son.

There was her Eian.

His dark brown curls were still unruly as ever, dancing across his forehead, and he looked so peaceful in sleep. Such happiness filled her she could sing and, at the same time, such sorrow and loss she thought her heart might break in two. The notes of his song shifted, the harmonies whirling as if several songs were buried within, but the music was bright.

He seemed well. She smiled and reached out to touch his mind.

A blow hit her, like a boulder crashing down on her, and it seemed as if it was an angry strike, though she wasn't sure how. It had come from Eian but had nothing of him about it.

Kaemada tumbled away from him, lost and disoriented, propelled by the telepathic force that drove her from her son. Her mind whirled. She tensed for the tug of her tether reaching its end.

It hit, slicing her heart. She was still tumbling, the short, broken, silvery line fluttering behind her. Horror seized her.

Not again! No, no, not again! She tumbled forever, through life and death.

Her movement slowed, and she drifted. She had to get back. How far had she gone? Where was her body?

Kaemada searched frantically, for her body, for Eian, hoping to retrace her path. When that failed, she floated, lost, adrift. How much time was passing?

Once, long ago, she had dreamwalked without a tether to save Takiyah, and she had gone adrift then, too. Her brother and Eian had drawn her back. But she'd been away from Eian so long and couldn't hear Taunos anywhere. Had she been adrift now for longer than she had then? She didn't know. There was no way to compare.

Songs shimmered around her as people moved and dreamed and lived, but she couldn't tell waking from dreaming and the distance was so distorted as to be useless to orient her. Songs of all types, songs without time.

It happened, at some point, that a humming, complex tune drew near. She listened with vague interest. At what point had she grown so detached?

"There you are," someone said, relief edging his tune. "Follow me."

He turned and drifted away from her.

Curious, she did as asked, songs floating over her without touching her, just as emotions and even thoughts did. She had no other tasks. She glided after the strange song, past some songs, toward others. At some point, he stopped, and she did as well.

He disappeared.

She drifted along, not minding the passage of time. At some point, he sped toward her again, anger edging the sounds of his tune.

"Come with me, Kaemada." He sped away and then back toward her before she realized he meant her.

That name, Kaemada, applied to her. Blankly, yet compliant, she followed him again.

Umril's presence meant she was to follow him. It didn't matter why "Umril" applied to him or why "Kaemada" was attached to her. He stopped again, and she stopped too, looking over the dreamscape with docile interest. There were forms and shapes and muted tunes, along with one broken, silver line.

Did that mean something? Nothing. Nothing here related to her. Nowhere did. She only drifted.

The song known as Umril went quiet and then loud again, farther off. There was more anger there now. Why was that? He bade her follow again, and she did so, waiting for the mystery to be revealed to her.

"That is your body, Kaemada." The tune she followed dipped toward a cold, shadowy form with the remnants of a silver tether lying beside it.

"That is not mine." She would know her own body when she saw it. If she had one, that was. It seemed she had always been here.

More anger swirled through his song. "This is your body. You need it."

She couldn't imagine why. "I am content."

Interest faded from her, and she again began to follow the tugs and tides of others' passions and dreams and wills and desires. A wish for health here, for companionship there, and farther off, for recognition. The cold, shadowy form behind held nothing of interest to her. She had nothing to do with it.

"Kaemada!"

It took her some time to realize the song was following her again, speaking to her. Calling her by some name she did not know. Kaemada. The name did not belong to her. The song was clamoring at her now, overwhelmingly loud. It towed her back, away from the shimmers of interest of other songs.

"Enter the body."

She drifted down, but it did not feel right. Wouldn't her body feel like home, if she had one? She began to glide away again.

The song stopped her, gripping hers with the power of a waterfall.

"Enter the body."

Again, she had no desire to follow the command, and again she began to leave. One more time the song commanded, and she was thrust somewhere cold and lonely, full of sorrows and guilt and pain.

She did not like it here. She surged up and away. Life should not be cold.

"You will not leave. Stay in the body."

That song, pulsing with a vibrant beat, barred her path. She glided to the side, but there it was. She drifted in another direction, but again it blocked her.

It commanded her, demanded her obedience. "Stay."

She did.

Gasping and shivering, Kaemada woke up. How could it be so cold? Her teeth chattered, and she bit her tongue several times. Something lay over her, something soft. Nimae.

Her wolf lay still but for shallow breathing, unconcerned by her movement. Piles of blankets engulfed Kaemada. She moved slowly, having to remember how to do something so simple. There was light. Why hadn't she seen it before? Of course there was light. A blazing fire near her, cracking merrily. She was between a fire and Nimae, covered with blankets. Why was she so cold? Was Nimae all right? Had she harmed yet another companion?

Wait, hadn't she been in her hammock?

A face, brown as the bark of the trees, entered her field of vision. "You seem to be unusually adept at finding new forms of trouble to get into."

She blinked, then blinked again as she had to remember how to do that motion. It took her some time before recognition hit her. Umril.

The elf nodded. "Are you finished disturbing our rest now, young one?"

She stared at him. Why did she feel nothing? It was as if she were an empty vessel. His chiding should trigger some response, should it not? But what?

"I see not," Umril said.

She blinked again.

"Can you speak?"

Speaking. That required the movement of lips and tongue and mouth. She did so, then frowned. Oh yes. She had to breathe.

"Yes." Her voice sounded so strange to her ears. She winced, then wondered at that movement.

Umril nodded, sitting back. "Never before have we lost one of our charges in this manner. It would have been embarrassing, were you the first."

Her thoughts continued to flit away from her like butterflies. An odd fear welled up in her, but it washed away, as fleeting as her thoughts. Controlling either was as difficult as moving her noncompliant body. It felt strange, as if she did not belong there, as if it was not truly hers.

The elf sat her up, pulling on her arms so she was forced to bend.

A gasp escaped her as stiffness shot pain through her. Pain. That was an interesting sensation. Silently, dispassionately, Umril bent all of her joints several times, moving each of her limbs one by one, undaunted as she cried out and screamed. Finally, he stopped, once she could wiggle her toes on command.

She was still extremely stiff and cold, but she was her. This was her body after all.

Ennwhyn appeared, carrying a mug of something that steamed. "Here, this will do you good."

Shivers wracked her body, while fire pinpricked through her limbs as they came back to life. The shivering made it impossible to hold the mug, and Ennwhyn and Umril both had to help her before she could drink. Hot liquid slid down her throat like fire, a waterfall plummeting from the heights. Her stomach rebelled, and the hot liquid shot back up. Choking, she gasped for breath.

Humiliation burned within her, heating her cheeks as Ennwhyn and Umril cleared the vomit that had gone up her nose and cleaned up the rest of her mess. Without a word, they helped her drink again. She retched again but this time managed to keep the liquid down. They helped her with a few more sips, let her rest, and then demanded she drink a little more. As the mug emptied, the shivering faded away, and she merely felt weak and chilled rather than cold as death.

Nimae responded as well, stretching with a groan and opening her eyes. The wolf shook out her fur and stretched again, turning to groom herself. Relief filled Kaemada, and she stretched her hand toward the wolf. She hadn't lost another companion.

Ennwhyn helped her change and then lay back down while Umril took the mug away. She lay still under the blankets on the fire-warmed grass and stared at the stars until Umril came back in and sat down next to her.

"You lost your tether," he said.

She nodded.

"How?"

"Something shields my son. It..." She shuddered.

"It took us long to find you."

"Us?"

"Twenty dreamwalkers at a time searching in shifts. Many more days and you would not have survived."

"Days?" She jerked, trying to sit up, but her body refused to obey her.

Umril smiled. "I must say, I am glad to see spirit from you again. You were far gone."

She tightened her hands into fists, trying not to shiver with fear again. "How many days? Nimae?"

"Five. And Nimae is fine—better than you, really. And yes, you should recover, though there may have been damage to your mind."

She closed her eyes to shut out the horror.

His voice lowered, worry adding to the timbre. "You cannot do this again. Pushing so hard before made you bleed in your brain. Too much more and you will die. Next time, we might not be able to bring you back."

Swallowing hard, she nodded.

"No more dreamwalking for at least a moon. We'll figure out how bad the damage is after you've rested and build back up to it. You'll probably be weak and clumsy for a while, after an ordeal like that. And we'll need to repair your bond with Nimae, as well. Reinforce that tether."

She shifted uneasily as he left. It was almost as if she was no longer so tightly attached to her body. She could have died, so easily. But for the elves, she would have.

At least her son was well, for now. But what could possibly be protecting his mind that would so nearly kill her?

There is one called the Tsaeyichape'itsan, or he who comes again and again.
Look for his coming. He is the key to the ending of the cycles.
—part of a missive from "Nitil" in Dragonmoor

Onsívei's dreams were always full of exciting adventure. They were a plethora of people and scenes and situations, most of which he didn't understand upon waking but which rang of truth while he was asleep. He felt he should wake up exhausted, but instead he always felt refreshed.

This night, however, his dreams turned strange. A presence hovered near him. It was familiar to him, a person he remembered with love and with fear.

"Eian? Eian?" she called out gently.

He hid among the mists of dreams. He didn't know how he knew she was a she. It just seemed right. But she was calling to him, looking for him. His dreams never did that. They simply showed him things.

"Eian, do not hide, my little one. You are quite safe here. Where are you hiding?" He could sense a smile in her voice. He knew her. How did he know her?

"There you are," she said, and he knew she was still smiling. But he was confused and frightened. The strangeness of the dream only heightened his fear. He ran again.

Somehow, he knew she followed him gently and slowly as he hid again, yet at the same time, the next instant, she was there with him again. There in an instant, though she came slowly and gently. But it was a dream, and somehow that was acceptable.

"Who are you?" he asked, wishing his voice didn't tremble.

A voice cried out in his mind, new and somehow familiar, earthy and ancient. "Intruder! Get her out! Get her out! She should not be here!"

She did not seem to hear the voice. There was a touch of sadness to her. How did he know, when he could not see her? She was only a presence, without form. But then, she coalesced into a form, almost like the clouds making shapes in the sky. But she looked real and, to his mind's eye, beautiful, though still with that feeling of fear.

"Do you not remember?" she asked.

He shook his head.

"It has been a long time. I have missed you, acha'iyih."

He blinked at the name, and she smiled again, though sadness tinged it.

"Get out! Get out!" the voice repeated, and only Onsívei heard.

"You remember that."

He blinked again. How did she know? Her smile broadened. He liked her smile; it was summer berries and mock-fights in the snow.

Kaemada. The name sprang to his mind like he'd always known it.

Concern filled her voice. "It has been long, little one. Too long. I have missed you so greatly it's like I am only pieces of myself. Are you well, Eian? Are you safe? Are you happy? Are you loved?"

The questions tumbled forth from her like the breaking of a dam, like spring floods demolishing the bits of branches and mud that once barred the water's way. He blinked. There was earthiness, quiet, and seclusion in that image. Not the wide open spaces of Mountainhold. Somewhere else...

"Get out! Get out!"

He pushed away that voice to instead concentrate on Kaemada.

"Are you safe, Eian?" she asked again. There was patience in her voice but also tension. Realization pounced on him. She was reining herself in, trying not to overwhelm him.

He nodded. "The kaetalyn protect us from the raids."

"What raids?" She frowned.

"From the City of the Lost. They take food and supplies and children. We hid in a box today." He puffed up with pride.

But she sighed, vexation filling her voice. "Oh, Eian!" She shook her head, grief and rage in her expression, but moved on to her next question. "Are you well?"

He nodded.

"Get out. Get out," the voice murmured, and he pushed it down farther.

"Are you happy? Are you loved?"

He didn't know how to answer that. "Sometimes," he tried. "Yena loves me. I saved her today."

She smiled at that, a smile proud and pained all at once.

He went on, frowning. "Teryn takes care of me. He is Yena's father. He calls me his son, but he is not my father. I think I anger him much of the time, but I do not know why."

Her frown turned sharper than any knife he was allowed to have. "Teryn has you? The Elder?"

Onsívei nodded. "He says I need to stop talking nonsense."

"Oh, my son, you never speak nonsense. It's just that we do not always understand right away."

Clarity hit him, like the morning mist lifting. He was not her son. And yet, he was more loved by her, by the four vague figures in his memory, than by anyone else.

"I am not your son," he said, to see what she would do. Would she be like Teryn? A dream was a safe place to test, at least. Not like waking life.

"She should not be here!"

He suppressed the voice again.

That sad smile returned, but she nodded. "Not physically. And you do not belong to me. You are for us all. But my love for you is that of a mother for her beloved son. I love you, dear one. I called you once acha'iyih, and to me you are acha'iyih still."

He nodded. Slowly flooding over him, the love she had for him seeped out. It was a great love, a powerful love, a love that hurt like the deepest wound but also gave wings for her song to fly. It was a love that would drive her to do anything to save him. Anything.

And it all rushed back to him.

In the dreamworld, he fell back under the onslaught of memories, knocked flat by them, but at the same time, remained standing, his mouth open.

Recognition hushed his voice. "I called you Mahkae."

She nodded. "I was your mahkae."

"They took me from you." He frowned hard at her. "But you never came for me."

A terrible sadness came over her, pain flooding her face, but she nodded.

He shook his head at her. Hot tears of anger and pain spilled down his cheeks. "Why not? You loved me. I felt it. Why would you leave me?"

Her voice shook. "I thought you were safer without me. I thought being with me would only bring you harm."

"I was afraid, and you were not there to comfort me. You had always been there before!" he shouted.

The voice screaming in his mind broke loose from his grip, and she was gone, as if she'd never been.

The next moment, he was awake in the dark, lying on his mat. He curled into a ball under his blankets while hot tears rolled down his face.

"Onsívei?"

"She's gone," he wept. "She's gone, Teryn."

Teryn bundled him in his arms. It wasn't until he was moving, being carried out of the house, that he realized it wasn't for comfort.

"We must see the psions again, my son."

Onsívei peered out the doorway to where his father met with the other elders of the kaetal. Father gestured sharply toward the ruins of the homes burned in the last attack by the Fallen from the City of the Lost. Onsívei chanced a look toward the sparse woods outside the kaetal, filled more with brush than great trees—where did he know great trees from?

He felt like river currents were tearing him away. The feeling had been growing since his father had decided the only reasonable course of action was to surround the kaetal with walls to protect them from the bandits. The other elders were divided. Some stood with Father, but most opposed him, and they seemed angry. But why did the idea upset Eian so much? He wished he knew.

His gaze shifted between the elders and the woods. Faces occasionally flitted through his memory: a dark form he equated with safety and security, red hair that was associated with adventure, a man who made him laugh, and a warm presence connected with feeling utterly loved but also with terrible fear. He shuddered.

Coming up behind him, Yena placed a gentle hand on his shoulder. "Are you all right, Onsívei?"

He nodded mutely, keeping his eyes on the meeting outside.

She sighed, and her hand left his shoulder. "Why will they not leave us alone?"

Onsívei shook his head. He was supposed to be cutting vegetables for supper. Father had told him to. He blinked, the faces of other men coming to his mind's eye, all of them fathers, none of them his. A chill went through him. Father was not his father, either. Somehow, he was certain that this was not the first time he'd had this realization, and yet, he couldn't remember the other times.

His eyes drifted back to the knife as he raised it, setting it carefully on the yellow flesh of the vegetables. The blade was short and sharp so he wouldn't have to press hard to cut. Sunlight shone off it, and again a deluge of memories drowned him, none of them his. Other times cutting vegetables, other vegetables to cut, various ways to hold the knife, longer blades, thicker blades, double-edged blades, blades for cutting flesh and muscle, for biting into bone.

Bile rose in him, and he gagged, doubling over. His stomach hurt, and he longed for Mahkae, the woman who had come to his dreams. Yena said she was just his imagination and reminded him that Mother was dead.

But Mahkae was not dead, and Yena's mother was not his.

Another flash of memories, of various mothers who were not his. But the first one stood out in his mind, and he clung to her image like a life raft in the tossing sea—not that he knew how he knew of something like that, either. A small woman with eyes of blue and wild hair like his. She was not his mother either, but he knew in the depths of his spirit that she came when he called her, through fire and pain and fear and death.

If that wasn't a mother, he didn't know what was.

"Onsívei, are you all right? Onsívei!" Yena's voice rose in pitch, a sure sign she was distressed.

He blinked at her as she grabbed his hand. He'd cut it—the gash was filling with blood, spilling out onto his clothes. It coated the blade of the knife and sparked another drowning of memories of fights and blood and fear and pain.

He gagged again, but there was nothing in his stomach to throw up. He had forgotten to eat breakfast, he remembered. He'd been on his way and had seen a bird and…

And then he'd been at the edge of the kaetal and Teryn had been calling for him.

He had to remember to call Teryn "Father." He'd called him by his name once, and Teryn had been so afraid and angry. Onsívei never wanted to repeat that experience.

"Here, I found some cloths. We will get you all fixed up. But Onsívei, you must be more careful with knives! You have five summers now! You should be able to handle a knife."

He nodded, unable to respond. He couldn't even keep up with the swarm of memories of wound care that now deluged him. Various bandages and ways of wrapping them, various solutions to cleanse a wound. Stitches and other closures.

Yena made concerned noises as she bathed his hand in warm water, her touch always gentle. The others in the kaetal knew he was strange, knew he didn't belong. He could feel their eyes on him whenever he slipped up or had a moment. Whenever he did something they didn't do in this kaetal or spoke of things he should not know. But the words poured forth of their own accord, and often he wasn't even aware he was saying them until the reaction came.

The kaetal children didn't think much of him—they thought him soft in the head. He had very few memories of his story before living with them. Somehow, he felt he should have more. He had flashes of other places and people, flashes that seemed less personal but somehow more clear than those faint impressions of what should be his memories. The other children seemed to think it strange that he could tell them no stories of his past, and whenever Teryn heard them asking, he grew exceedingly angry. Onsívei shuddered again.

Onsívei. Even his name brought up a host of other names attached to other faces that he saw in his mind's eye. It meant "secretive one," but the other names had many other meanings. Why did he know them? One of those other names became clear like clouds unveiling the sun. He knew it. Ahtasí. The laughing man—he used to call him Ahtasí, little man. And Eian loved it when he called him Ahtasí.

Eian? Who was Eian?

"It's all right, Onsívei. Father and I know you, and we love you," Yena said. "You just need more practice, that's all."

He forced a tight little smile at her because she loved it when he smiled. She didn't smile back at him this time though.

Her brow remained knitted, her mouth drawn in a frown. "I do not think this will be enough. Come on, Onsívei, we have to go to the healer."

He nodded. Anaeah the healer always treated him gently, which surprised him, for she was consistently stern with his father. Sometimes, he caught her frowning at him as if she were sad, but she always turned away or smiled at him when she saw she'd been caught. Adults were strange. It seemed all the adults of the kaetal looked at him oddly.

Yena, of course, said it was nothing and he shouldn't worry about it. She never worried about anything, and she never needed to, for everyone loved her.

And Onsívei didn't mind. He loved her too, for her kindness and her gentleness and her willingness to help him at tasks that everyone knew he should have long since mastered.

"Oh, Onsívei!"

He blinked at the healer's voice, wondering when he'd gotten to her house. She'd unwrapped the cloths Yena had bound him with and was bent over his hand, clucking to herself. "Onsívei, this is a really bad cut. It might even scar. Yena, you were smart to bring him to me."

The healer cupped his hand in her own, and warmth bloomed through him. It itched and twinged, and some part of him screamed that he should be in pain, but he couldn't help but just watch with fascination until the warmth faded and the healer let him go. She smiled at him, and he smiled back, watching the lines of fatigue that appeared by her eyes. They called to him somehow and wouldn't let him go.

"Onsívei, wiggle your fingers."

He did so.

"Good, now make a fist. Now spread your fingers wide. Pinch? Pull apart? Tap one finger to mine. Good, now tap your thumb to each of your other fingers on that hand."

"What's wrong?" Yena asked.

"He should have been in much more pain. I thought there might be deep damage to the innermost parts of the hand, what carries the song through you, but if it was damaged, I repaired it, though I do not know how. I did not feel it."

"But he's fine now?"

"Yes, he's fine. But Onsívei." She knelt in front of him, looking up into his face, and he gazed down into hers, patiently. "Please, no more knives."

"I was cutting vegetables," he said.

"Did your father ask you to do this?"

He nodded.

Her expression darkened. "I will have words with hi—"

"Onsívei!"

The sound of his father's voice made him straighten. No, not his father; he didn't have a father. Although, a man with kind eyes and a deep laugh used to play seek-and-find with him. A smile spread across his lips.

Teryn ducked into the healer's hut and frowned. "Onsívei, this is not a game. You aren't hurting yourself on purpose, are you? You are trying to control the knife, right?"

He nodded.

Teryn's mouth formed a hard line, and then his expression shuttered closed as he turned to the healer, who folded her arms.

"Teryn, I told you," she said. "The boy has no business being around knives."

"Boys much younger than him are learning the control of tools. He must learn if he is to be a working adult."

"If you persist in this foolishness, that boy will cut off his fingers or worse."

"He will never fit in if he does not practice."

The healer shook her head. "If you continue down this path, it is only folly," she insisted. "If the boy was going to be able to control a knife, we would have seen it by now."

"He is not simple!" Teryn shouted.

"No, he is not."

"Then he will learn."

The healer glanced at Onsívei, frowning, before replying in a milder tone. "You know as well as I do that not everything has been…"

Teryn's expression darkened, and she trailed off.

She drew in a deep breath, as if to try a different tack. "Not every boy is built for swimming or for climbing or for learning the stories by heart like Storytellers do. You of all people should know this, Storyteller."

"What are you saying?"

"Find what he *is* good at and guide him to that."

"Spirits help me, I have tried! The boy broke his arm climbing a tree, and I will not have him breaking his neck. Instead of reciting the stories, he makes up fancies and insists they are truth. He nearly drowned in the pond with the other children this spring. If he cannot handle a knife, what am I to teach him? I will not send him out to watch the alanshorn. If the Fallen come, he would have to be alert to make it back to safety, and he often seems so…. addled."

"The laughing man could help against the Fallen," Onsívei offered.

"What laughing man, Onsívei?" his father asked. "The Fallen were everywhere, and no one was laughing."

"The laughing man. I knew him."

His father sighed, but he sounded angry. "Now, Onsívei, we have talked about this. You need to keep your daydreams to yourself. Better yet, you need to stop daydreaming and live your story."

Onsívei was about to protest that he was living, but the words died, drowned under images of stories lived, both dreamers and doers, story after story.

"There must be some gift he has," Anaeah insisted. "You have to find it. He is a bright boy with a good heart. Trouble cannot forever cloud the sun, for the light will eventually shine through."

Onsívei wondered at the riddle, turning it over and over in his mind as Teryn finally smiled at Anaeah and nodded to her, as if she had helped him with something. But he didn't understand. They did this sometimes— stopped speaking of things around him or changed to riddles—but he tried to collect them so that he could find the truth they were too afraid to speak around him. It had to be something interesting and perhaps a little dangerous, given their tight expressions when they changed to riddles.

Teryn hugged Yena close. "My daughter, it was smart thinking bringing your brother to the healer. Sprits bless him, he is lucky to have a sister like you."

Yena leaned forward to smile at Eian. "And I'm lucky to have him."

He remembered to return the smile, but his mind whirled and turned.

Teryn was not his father, something in him insisted, which meant Yena was not his sister. But he wanted her to be his sister because with her he felt safe and loved and valued, and that was what family meant. He sighed, wishing night would come soon and he could ask the woman in his dreams about it all. He wasn't sure exactly who she was, besides that his heart cried out "Mahkae" for her, but he remembered night after night how her love had washed over and surrounded him. He wasn't sure anyone had ever felt such a whole, unyielding, complete love for themselves, feeling the emotions of their mahkae for them.

Anaeah frowned at them. That sadness was back in her eyes, along with anger. "Please tell me this nonsense about a wall is a test, Storyteller Teryn."

"There were walls," Onsívei blurted. He couldn't help it—the images were overwhelming him, compelling him to speak them. "They were large and thick and grey. People huddled outside them, trapped outside. People huddled inside, hoping desperately they would be safe. And there were small things that bloomed like flowers into big things, and they broke the walls and brought death. And there were—"

"Enough, Onsívei," snapped Teryn. "I know the stories. There is no need to embellish them."

"I see it," Onsívei protested. "Small black spheres all of metal and—"

"You will keep your daydreams to yourself please, Onsívei. It is quite enough that they distract you from your tasks. You do not need to speak them and undermine my authority." Teryn's voice was sharper than any knife.

Yena shifted from foot to foot beside him, and Onsívei's eyes widened at all the fury in his father's face. He nodded.

Anaeah remained unaffected by Teryn's irritation. "It seems to me, Storyteller Teryn, that you are undermining your own authority more than this boy ever could, no matter what he says. You know the stories better than anyone. You should, as you are the Storyteller. You are the keeper of our history so that we do not repeat it. But now, I fear—and I am not alone —that you aim to have us repeat the same mistakes of our past. Walls, Storyteller?"

"A wall," Teryn corrected. "I am not only in charge of our history. I'm in charge of keeping our kaetal safe."

"You and the other elders," Anaeah corrected. "And our Great Mother."

"And I am in a unique position to help us do both—protect our people while avoiding the mistakes of the past. A wall does not have to be a bad thing. Why should we needlessly lose our children and our lives and our food to these bandits?"

"Some things are not meant to be toyed with, Storyteller," Anaeah replied, shaking her head. "Are we never to move the kaetal then with the seasons? Are we to throw away all the old teachings? The Great Mothers have not forgotten."

"Do not exaggerate. Your expertise is valued. You are not, however, an elder."

She smiled at him, her expression filled with pride and a hint of defiance. "No, I'm not. And you are not a king, Storyteller. Many of us women have spoken to the Great Mother. She may decide to choose a new Storyteller."

"Why are you, of all people, against me, Anaeah? You lost your children and your husband to those bandits."

"I will not have my people lose their way and descend into misery and madness. Not even on account of my family. Nor should you on account of yours, Storyteller. Yes, you lost Eisa. But you still have Yena and now Onsívei. They are depending on you."

"That is why I do what I must do," Teryn snapped. Fiercely, he turned, snatching up Onsívei's hand and gesturing Yena ahead, and left the hut. In silence, they walked back home.

ÌTAL-CHA'A
Chapter Seventeen

The City of Tamarik has existed for so long as an island, cut off from the rest of the land. The bounty of the sea and the crops we can grow sustain us, but knowing there is more out there, how can we not reach for it? This journey not only solves the "Takiyah problem" but also opens the gates for future possibilities. I stake my reputation on it, that even if it fails, we will be better for it. And I do not think it will fail.

—missive from Pek, former sparring trainer of Tamarik, retired

Pek was sitting outside Takiyah's house, his arms folded, when she walked out the next morning. She stopped, swallowing hard. Somehow, it felt like when Galod would scold her.

He stared resolutely across the street. "You need to leave the city."

"Don't you think I have tried?" Her hands curled into fists.

"I asked around. Varen said you told him about a city. He wants to go there to trade, and he's got a wagon. You're going to be his guide."

A sudden chill gripped her, though the sun was blazing hot. Varen, in the City of the Lost? "That's a terrible idea. The place is a prison full of bullies."

"He's got his heart set on it, and you know how he is."

She did. He was like a storm—unreasonable. "And if I say no?"

"I think he stands a chance of surviving if you go with him."

He had a better chance of surviving if she tied him up. But if she did this, if she went, she'd have a way to escape this city. It meant relying on Varen and Pek, but it also meant freedom. Depending on someone for less than a moon, in exchange for never having to depend on anyone else again? She'd have to risk it. After all, she would stay on guard, and once she was out of the desert, she'd be free.

"Why are you doing this, Pek?"

Finally, he looked at her. "You can't control yourself. You're angry, yes, but you're lashing out at the wrong people in the wrong ways. Do you know how many guards were deployed to the Docks to stop them from chasing you out?"

"So you're tossing me out."

"I hope you'll come back. But you don't have to."

~

The wagon bumped and clattered. Every rock the wheels hit caused Takiyah to lurch in her seat. Beside her, Varen chattered along about nothing, and Takiyah ignored him, glancing back at the crates and bags that filled the wagon. They were still secure, so she straightened with a sigh, staring at the world framed through the alansor's horns. The beast's long, shaggy hair had been shaved short, to help prevent her from overheating in the heat of the desert. It appeared to have helped, but alanshorn always looked silly when they were shaved. Ahead, the downward slope steepened; they were nearly at the bottom. They were nearly there, despite how part of her wished they were still days away.

She hadn't expected to enjoy herself on the trip, even if Varen talked too much. The noise actually helped keep her from thinking in circles, and Varen didn't stop her from cataloguing the Angels. In fact, he'd brought balls of wax that they used to plug their ears, muting the sound of the Angels' song. Now, Takiyah had a notebook filled with drawings of Angels, estimating their size and trying to capture if there was any difference between them. So far, they'd all been eerily similar in the metal sheet she used for reflection.

It was like the days living with Pek, learning how to survive in the desert, that sense of boundaries being lifted through knowledge. It was like hunting trips with Ra'ael and Kaemada, though it was just her and Varen and rather than evenly splitting tasks, she did most of the work that the alanshor couldn't, for Varen hated manual labor. The tasks were easy, like taking care of the alansor, though she couldn't fathom why he insisted on calling the cow Harry.

They rounded the bend, and the rock of the path they were following was swallowed up by grass.

There before them were the walls of the City of the Lost.

"By the Printak, it's real." Varen's awed whisper brought a smile to her face.

"If you thought I was making it up, why'd you come all this way?"

He glanced at her. "Pek can be persuasive."

She eyed him. Pek had insinuated it was Varen's idea.

"So," he said, far too brightly, "are you leaving me now?" She must have looked skeptical because he scoffed at her. "Come now. It's clear you don't like Tamarik. I doubt you're heading back with me."

"You're never getting this wagon into the city by yourself," Takiyah said. "I will help you get it to the market, and then I'm gone."

"Your generosity is astounding."

She pressed her lips together. She didn't want to remember the last time she was here, didn't want to worry about Varen. Didn't want to feel the hole in her heart where her friends should be, only she'd ripped her heart out and thrown her friends away, trying to rid herself of the pain.

In the fields before the city, people worked, watched over by guards. Two more bored-looking men guarded the hole in the wall, and everything she'd learned from the City of the Lost told her that bored guards meant trouble. Despite the fact that they had no reason to stop goods coming into the city—they hated anything leaving, but goods in shouldn't be a problem —that didn't mean they'd be reasonable. She bristled, surprising herself at the depth of her feelings. She was leaving after this, so it shouldn't matter. And yet, she climbed down from her seat, held tight to her staff, and walked the wagon along the wall past the guards.

She might try to shut out the pain and shove others away, but memories and loss still snapped at her, regardless. What was done was done. Now it was just a matter of what she would decide for the future.

The walls of the City of the Lost rose nearly three times her height, thick and straight. They were like a rundown version of the walls of Tamarik. But the gate was grand and forbidding, with arms of stone jutting outward to connect with the statues of the Angels, which towered even above the city walls. It echoed the way the mountains crowded around three of the city's sides, leaving only the plains free.

The statues were painted much like the Angels looked: winged men with bronze skin and enormous eyes in long, white garments like very simple dresses that left their shoulders bare. Their arms were crossed over their chests, muscles bulging as they stared at the ground between them. Their expressions were blank.

Takiyah shuddered. Those expressionless faces were far too like the real thing. Even when she and Pek had taken turns Angel-watching, she'd never seen an Angel's mouth move with the sound of its song.

She shook off the memories of Pek and the longing for that connection. She was free. She could do whatever she wanted, without any ties to anyone. But the loneliness ate at her, unconvinced by her feeble arguments.

Takiyah guided Harry the alanshor between the staring Angels and through the permanently open Angels' Gate. She glanced at Varen. "When you leave, go through the hole in the wall."

He didn't even look at her, staring around himself in awe and, once he stepped into the city and the smell of filth hit them, disgust.

"Why? There's a perfectly functioning gate here." He started to step backward, holding his nose.

Takiyah snagged his sleeve, yanking him into the city more fully. "The gate's always open, but it's never an exit. The statues burn right through anything that tries to leave."

Varen scoffed, and she scowled at him. But he hadn't witnessed the executions "King" Kunos had held like parties. She had, back when she'd lived in the city with Ra'ael, Taunos, and the shell of Kaemada. It'd given her nightmares for days. She grabbed the closest thing on hand—a small sack of grain—and tossed it through the gate. As it sailed between the statues, it erupted in a fireball, and by the time it landed, there was nothing left.

Face sallow, Varen smoothed his tunic obsessively, his mouth working but no sound coming out. He turned to her. "*Why?*"

It was as good a question as any, and hopefully now he'd take her warnings seriously. "It's a prison, Varen. I told you, over and over. You have to leave by the hole in the wall or not at all."

Trembling, he walked beside her as she guided the alanshor onto the rough road toward the market. Nothing had changed here, not really. The houses were still rough, with slapped-together barricades for doors, and the guards still patrolled in their armor and weapons, plowing right through anyone unlucky enough to get in their path.

By the time they reached the market, Varen was chattering away again, only a bit more subdued than his usual self. "You know, with this place being inland—you said there's no sea nearby, right?—we could sell fish for an amazing profit if we could only keep them cool—or maybe still in water!—on the way here."

Takiyah shook her head. It didn't matter if she engaged with him or not. Varen's thinking process was entirely external. She shoved the wagon into place without Varen's help and dusted off her hands. The other goods at the marketplace were pitiful next to theirs. Takiyah patted Varen on the shoulder, interrupting his stream of consciousness.

"You're not going to get what these are worth," she said.

"As long as I have things to bring back to Tamarik to sell, it'll be worth it."

Shaking her head, she walked away. She couldn't wait to get out of the city, even if she had no idea what she wanted to do next. The horrors of this place were bad enough, but now that she knew what a city could be, those nightmares were joined by disgust. The guards hadn't even built a gate for the hole in the wall where the psions had blasted their way through. All they'd done was a minimal job of patching up the edges.

Where was the Resistance now? Had they made their own kaetal? She shook her head, shoving those sorts of dangerous questions away. She might as well start worrying about her parents. She couldn't worry about such nebulous things. Things happened and not always for any good reason. The Elders had banished them on a whim, and that was that.

She was alone now, and it should be better that way. Less chance of someone hurting or disappointing her. But the knot of pain and worry inside her didn't lessen, no matter how hard she tried to convince herself.

Takiyah quickened her pace, eager to leave the city and the twisting of her heart behind, but as she approached the guards, her feet stopped. Varen and the wagon would never get past them. He'd be ripped apart if she left him here. She shouldn't have left him in the first place.

Well, that was his problem. He talked too much anyway—they might toss him out for being annoying.

She groaned. Even she didn't believe her argument.

If she left, Varen was trapped. She'd be dooming him.

Turning around, Takiyah stomped back toward the market. She'd meant to be free. Of course, Varen needed her, not the other way around, but she was still caught in a web of attachments. Still constrained by them.

Her sour mood grew as she approached the marketplace, and the last thing she wanted to do was be social. She lingered on the edge, watching the proceedings. A glimmer of admiration grew in her as she watched Varen field questions, haggle prices, keep track of what goods he'd bought and which he'd sold, and still protect the wagon from thieves, all at the same time. He was in his element, all beaming smiles and friendly tones.

Takiyah couldn't help but smile herself as she listened. Varen was letting goods go far cheaper and buying goods at higher prices in his dealings than he would in Tamarik. And these people with their threadbare clothing and handfuls of coins clutched in their fists needed it. A breath of hope. Ra'ael, Kaemada, and Taunos would have loved to see such hope. Her parents would approve, too.

The smile fell. Too bad hope was a weapon. Depending on it only made things hurt worse.

Most of the goods they'd brought were gone by late afternoon, when the guards arrived. They rode right into the market, their horses scattering the people before them, and began to unharness the alanshor.

"What are you doing with Harry?" Varen snapped. "Leave her be."

One of the guards stepped forward, and his casual punch knocked

Varen off the wagon. He tumbled across the cobblestones like a broken doll tossed in some child's tantrum.

Takiyah surged forward, reaching him just as Varen raised his head, sputtering at the guard.

"But she's my alanshor. I'll give you anything you like from the wagon instead."

"Quiet, Varen." Takiyah crouched over him, her wary gaze fixed on the guards.

"The king's supper should be tax enough, I think," one guard said.

"Maybe tax for the king, but I'll take my slice too." Another guard rummaged through the back, tossing bags aside like they were nothing. After the wagon was thoroughly ransacked, he turned and came over to Varen, his eyes lighting up with glee as he snatched Varen's purse.

Varen tensed, and Takiyah held on to him, shielding him from the guard's casual kick.

The third guard's eyes were fixed on her staff. "Where's your permit?"

Takiyah scowled. "What permit?"

The guard grinned, greedy eyes on her staff. "For having that weapon."

Her hand tightened around it. She'd made it with her own hands in her forge in Torkae, melting down blade after blade left behind from Dark attacks until she had enough material. It was the only possession she really cared about. "It doesn't matter. I'm leaving with it, so it doesn't matter to you."

"Wrong on both counts."

She stepped back, resisting the urge to burst into flames. "Must be quite challenging, beating up defenseless people."

"It has its advantages. The occasional trinket, for instance."

"No, no, please!" Varen shoved his way up from the ground between Takiyah and the guard. "Take Harry. But leave Takiyah alone."

Takiyah blinked. Varen loved that alanshor. He'd doted on the cow the whole way over. And yet, he just stood there while the guards sneered and led the shaggy animal away.

"Varen," she whispered.

He shook his head, lifting the shafts of the wagon himself. "Let's just go."

His face was turned away from her, but by the shaking of his shoulders, she knew he was crying. With firm movements, she stashed her staff in the wagon and jostled Varen aside. She took the cart shafts herself and silently followed him down the road toward the hole in the wall.

"You said this was a prison but... Those were really the guards? You weren't exaggerating? I thought a bribe..." Blood trickled from his split lip as he looked at Takiyah.

She shook her head. "Bribes just tell them you have more they can steal. But we're not out of trouble yet."

"You came back for me." Varen wiped the blood away and straightened his shirt. "Why?"

It rankled, even though she had told him she was leaving. The reminder of how shallow she'd been, how thoroughly she'd turned her back on any sense of loyalty, still slapped her in the face. She supposed that's what happened when a person was afraid to connect with others.

But when they reached the hole in the wall, the guards blocked their way. Varen wrung his hands, his face still wet with tears, unprepared for any further violence. Poor man. He came from a place where there was at least justice, even if she'd sometimes been too blind with fear and distrust to see it.

"No exit," the guard said.

Anger boiled over in her, and she stepped between Varen and the guard. "We don't live here. You'll all be better off if you let us leave and come back with more supplies."

"Where are all these supplies coming from anyway?"

"Another city, hidden in the desert. Maybe you should try finding it sometime," she suggested with a smile. "Of course, the dragons might eat you. Or you can let us go and we'll bring back more things to trade."

The other guard shifted. "We did see them come down the mountain. And it'll be a while before the fields can be harvested."

The guard narrowed his eyes. "Exit tax. Give me that staff."

Takiyah snarled at him, one hand on it possessively. "No."

"No staff, no exit."

"No, no," Varen said, turning back to the goods now scattered in the wagon. "Take anything else."

"You're not taking anything. You've already taken far more than enough," Takiyah snapped. The city only ever taught harsh lessons, but anger boiled over in her at how thoroughly they'd crushed Varen's idealistic expectations.

Of course they didn't listen to her.

Greedy stepped forward, and Takiyah spun, slamming the butt of her staff into his leg and then shoving the other end of the staff into the second guard's face. But when she completed her turn, Greedy had his sword pointed at Varen, who stood frozen but for the trembling that shook him from his worn shoes to the wispy tufts of his hair.

Takiyah extended her hands, loosening her grip on her staff. "All right. All right. Fine. Let us go, unharmed, and you can have my staff."

Greedy grinned toothily, beckoning. As she relinquished her staff, she snatched Varen, pulling him into her. Spinning him around, she hurled him into the back of the wagon and grabbed the shafts. She ran, with the laughter of the guards chasing her out of the city.

"Takiyah, thank goodness—" Varen's voice cut off as the wagon hit a bump, but she didn't dare stop. "Are you really going back to Tamarik?"

"I'm not going to go through all that and let bandits or dragons or whatnot have you," she grumbled.

"I'm sorry, Takiyah, about your staff." The words were quiet, broken.

The shattered pieces of Varen's optimism cut her deep.

She focused on running, hauling the wagon behind her. She had to get them far from the city before the Angels came. Varen had given up the alanshor for her staff, and she'd given up her staff for him. The loss hurt, but still it was the right thing to do. Seeing the City of the Lost again had shone a mirror on the path she'd been on if she continued to push everyone away and lash out in anger.

She'd betrayed everything she stood for, everything her parents stood for. She'd even realized it back with Pek, but instead of dealing with the issue, she'd run from it, leaving it to fester. Her reasons didn't matter. She'd used pain to embrace fear and lashed out at others over things they had no control over. She was no better than those guards in the City of the Lost.

Well. That ended now.

~

Takiyah cursed and threw herself against the wagon. "Pull, Varen!"

"I am pulling, what do you think I'm doing?" he shouted back.

"Not pulling hard enough." Her boots dug into the cracked, dusty ground as she leaned against the wagon, forcing it forward.

Varen detested manual labor and found ways around it whenever he could, unless the lure of money was large enough to tempt him despite the work involved. Even so, he'd helped haul the wagon forward, day after day, even in the rains. It'd been sixteen days, and Tamarik was finally in sight in the distance, tan stone among the scrubby landscape that bloomed with green.

But then the wheel had gotten stuck in a mud patch.

"It's stuck, Takiyah!"

"I know!" she roared. "I'm not blind. I can see it's stuck. I can feel it's stuck, the stupid wheels! Agh!"

They'd only needed it to last one, maybe two more days. Her leg ached, and their pace was slowed because of it, since Varen wasn't as strong as she was. And now they were stuck, and she just wanted to get Varen back to the city, to see him be him again. She had thrown away everyone else and didn't know how they were doing, if they were recovering, if they could smile again. She wanted to see Varen, at least, happy and safe again, and the mud-bound wheel was senselessly blocking her from that one small goal.

She pushed off from the wagon and kicked the wheel hard. It wobbled, and she shouted with frustration, slamming her booted foot at it again and again.

With a creak, the wheel fell off. The wagon tipped, sliding further into the mud.

Varen took a long step backward when she met his eyes. "Well," he said, swallowing hard. "This wagon's not getting to Tamarik now."

"Yes, it is." She'd been foolish, had lost control. She wouldn't let that ruin this, just like she wouldn't let a muddy hole keep the wagon of goods from the City of the Lost from making it to Tamarik. Because she had set herself a goal, and on her life, she was going to make it.

"It's not going anywhere without a wheel, muscle or no. We've lost. The desert beat us."

"I will not be beaten!"

Varen was going home safe, whether he believed it or not. The City of the Lost was not allowed to break everyone. She refused to let it.

Groaning, she took hold of the axle and lifted, shoving the rest of the broken wheel away. Her arms and legs strained, one boot slipping a little before finding sturdy rock. The wagon shifted.

She smiled, throwing herself into it. Something about this felt right. Lift with your legs and keep your balance centered, something within told her. She did so, and the wagon lifted just a little off the ground. The inner knowledge urged, and she responded, shifting her hand placements just so.

Then she staggered forward, one step at a time. Varen gaped.

"Pull, Varen!"

"I'm pulling! I'm pulling!" The man whirled around, hauling on the handles. Step by step, they walked forward.

"How long can you carry that for?" he asked after a few steps.

"I don't know," she hissed through gritted teeth.

One step at a time. One step, then another.

Her leg burned, but she kept her focus small. Small goals, something achievable.

Varen scrambled forward in front of her. The wagon lurched, nearly slipping out of her grip, but she didn't have the breath to yell at him. Her focus turned inward, so by the time the axle tore free of her numb, exhausted hands and the wagon crashed back down to the ground, surprised laughter burst from her at how far they'd come. There was still a long way to go, and her hands were raw, her shoulders and back and legs aching, but there was an exhilaration at the core of her, too.

She flopped down to rest in the shade of the wagon, rubbing her throbbing leg. Dust and sand sprayed her arm as Varen sat next to her, and she peeked over at him as he wiped his forehead.

"That was amazing," he said.

She grunted. "I need to be stronger."

"Truly, Takiyah, I do not think you realize what a treasure you are." Finally, some of his old optimism was peeking out. Perhaps people, once broken, could still be mended, after all.

Takiyah snorted at him. "It'd be easier if we could drag it, I think. Slide it across the ground." Knowledge struck her, blazing into her mind from nowhere, and she shook her head at herself. "No, that won't work. The weight of the goods would make it sink instead of slide. No, the ground needs to be harder, for the wheels."

"Well, we can't make it harder. This was a bad idea." He rubbed his eyes, resting his head against the wagon.

His surrender made her glare at him. He couldn't let the City of the Lost win. She made her tone as hard as she wished the ground was. "You give up too easy."

"Well, loaded carts work fine in the city, but the streets there are stone. We can't drag stone and pave the whole way to Tamarik."

Now, that would be a challenge, and her whole being brightened at the prospect. "Why not?"

"It's an enormous undertaking."

A scraping on the sandy ground reached her ears, drowned by the sound of his voice. "Stop talking, Varen."

"No, I'm telling you—"

"Shh!" She slapped her hand over his mouth, straining her ears. Yes, the sound of footsteps.

Black-clad figures surrounded them, fabric covering their faces, shielding them from wind and sun and Takiyah's gaze. She leaped to her feet, and one of the figures laughed. The others joined in, clearly taking their cue from the first, so Takiyah kept her gaze on the leader. She went to nudge Varen with her foot, but he was scuttling under the wagon.

She smiled.

"I do not want any trouble," Takiyah warned the bandits.

"Excellent. Give me your valuables, and you will have none."

Takiyah sighed. "Why does no one listen?"

"A woman and a man, out here in the desert, alone, with a broken wagon full of goods? You think anyone would listen to you?"

"It might do you some good."

The bandit stepped forward, and she reached for her staff, ready to let the flames from her hands cover the grey surface in heat and light.

But her staff wasn't there. She'd traded it for Varen's safety.

Raw loss coursed through her, and she gritted her teeth, channeling it into fury and flames. The bandit wavered, mouth dropping open, and she blasted him with a fountain of fire from her wrists then spun to scoop his legs out from under him.

"Roll in the dust to extinguish the flames," she told him, turning to the others.

Two more attacked, one from either side, and she whirled, catching one in the face with a kick and then using her momentum to punch the other. A third went for the wagon, and she shot fire at his back.

This would have been easier with Ra'ael and Kaemada fighting beside her.

She turned, sweeping a wide curve of flame from side to side, and the bandits scrambled back. One of them lunged for her when her back was turned, and she caught him with a punch on his chin.

They hesitated, but with half of them burned and her still uninjured, she'd clearly won. They ran, grabbing their singed comrades on the way. Takiyah shook her head as they disappeared among the rocks and scraggly bushes.

She missed the time when people believed her, believed she was capable, believed she was dangerous when she needed to be. Missing that brought back the pain of homesickness, so she grabbed the axle again and lifted. "Get out from under the wagon. They're gone."

With a squeal, Varen swept his legs out of the way of the wheels. He hurried to the front to pull the wagon forward again. "You didn't use your fire in the City of the Lost."

"Bad memories there."

Varen sighed. "I'm sorry again about your staff."

"Those weren't the bad memories I was talking about. But they're bullies. You cannot let them win."

Takiyah shoved the wagon forward, anything to put distance between herself and the pain. She had spent much of her time avoiding anything that reminded her of the past. Grimly, she thinned her lips and pushed thoughts of Ra'ael, Taunos, Kaemada, and home away, instead focusing on the walls of Tamarik before her.

"My muscle got me out," Varen said.

"What?" She gritted her teeth, lurching forward along with the pain in her leg.

"You saved me from the guards, just like right now, with those bandits. How do you handle bullies when you can't pay them off?"

"You beat them or burn them," Takiyah said.

"No, you bring your own protection."

"Ah, so they can beat and burn them."

"Exactly."

Takiyah shook her head, chuckling at his blooming confidence. She sobered though. "Be careful, if you do go back. Make sure you have good, steady guards." The thoughts came to her as she spoke them. "Pek can help with that. And more goods at once could reduce how many trips you need to do. Rothan could help with the wagons, maybe even banding the wheels to make them stronger. And you be yourself with the trades. You were excellent."

"What about the wheels getting stuck?"

"We need a road. I will handle that. And then your journeys will be faster." She smiled. The paranoia was still there, but it wasn't all encompassing anymore. Once again, her curiosity and imagination could light a way past it.

"What about the dragons? What about the Angels? We have been incredibly fortunate thus far. Only a few bandits."

"The Angels are focused on the City of the Lost. It diminishes the risk elsewhere." It didn't negate the risk, of course, but she'd take what she could get.

"Poor people. But you go building something like a road, and the dragons will come, mark my words."

"Why?"

"Why? This is their desert. They only suffer us to live because of legend. Everything outside of Tamarik is fair game."

"Tamarik has that fancy dragon barrier too. And besides, I'm changing the rules."

Varen snorted. "You can't just change rules. Can you imagine if people did that all the time?"

"I'm Fallen," she grinned. "Laws don't apply to me anymore."

"Tell that to a dragon when it blasts you into oblivion. I won't be there to watch. I'll be with all the other reasonable people, far, far away."

"Just pull, Varen."

"We'll never get to Tamarik before dark."

He was right, but they did get close enough to camp in the shadow of its walls. This close to Tamarik, bandits and Angels were less likely, and they could have a fire.

Takiyah watched Varen across the fire she'd built as he tallied costs and projected income, while in the distant foothills, the Angels sang their deadly tune. She dropped her gaze to her hands, so empty without her staff. But she'd gained an idea, one she wouldn't have thought of without Varen pushing her, just like she wouldn't have learned more of the forge without Rothan. She wouldn't even have found Tamarik, likely, if it hadn't been for Pek. And he'd had no reason to trust her, to help her. She hadn't given him any reason to afterward, either. And Varen... she wouldn't have made it through the desert with her leg without his help, despite his complaints.

"Why do you think people cram together all the time? It's not just Tamarik. The City of the Lost is like that, too." The words were out before she thought better of them, and she stared at the fire, pretending she hadn't spoken.

"The City of the Lost was a prison though, and no one could escape, you said," Varen replied.

"But that isn't true now. They could all leave. The guards cannot stop them all."

"The Angels hunt there."

"Maybe. But the Rinaryn cluster in kaetaln, and the Kamalti bunch together in cities underground."

"People like each other."

"Maybe." Takiyah stared at the walls. Would she be able to hold on to this growth when she was back in Tamarik, or would it melt away from her? She wasn't looking forward to facing those she'd scorned or antagonized, but she had to make up for the damage she'd done.

"Hey, you're not so hardhearted as you try to pretend. You saved me in that city, after all." He jabbed her in the shoulder.

She smiled at him. "Next time, remind me how much trouble you are."

Varen laughed. "No less trouble than you are."

They trudged through the gates of Tamarik in late morning, with the gatekeeper running to help them move the cart to the side of the road.

Takiyah groaned, massaging her blistered hands. "Varen, go get Rothan and a new wheel."

"I'm tired, too," he complained.

"You want to lift the wagon?"

His footsteps answered her as he fled down the street, far from menial labor. She leaned against the wagon. The sun was warm and her exhausted limbs were heavy, and soon enough her eyes fluttered shut.

When the wagon moved behind her, she woke with a start, flying to her feet.

Rothan laughed, struggling to lift the wagon. A new wheel lay behind him. "You carried this thing from the City of the Lost?"

"Not all the way. We were in sight of Tamarik when the wheel fell off."

Rothan stepped back, panting hard and rubbing his arms. "We'll have to unload it. Did you run into trouble?"

Takiyah sighed and rolled her eyes. Gripping the axle, she heaved, fatigued muscles straining to lift the wagon up once again. "No."

"It looks like it was damaged," Rothan said, shoving the new wheel on and attaching it quickly. "There, that'll at least hold 'till we get to the market. Where'd Varen go? I thought he'd be meeting me back here, not you."

"He probably went to grab a spot among the stalls." She sighed. He hadn't come back, and somehow that disappointed her.

"So what happened to the wheel? How was the journey? Tell me everything."

"The wheels got stuck where the ground was soft. We need a new solution."

"What's all this stuff in the wagon?"

Rothan's excitement was contagious, and she let it buoy her, igniting her enthusiasm.

"We need guards for protection," she said. "We should get a line of wagons to make the most of each trip. We'll need to shore up the soft parts of the path with stone. Varen and I pounded stakes into the ground to mark the path, but there are many dangers."

"The flow of goods will be welcome. Tamarik has been limited to only what we can grow and make and gather ourselves for a long, long time."

"So has the City of the Lost."

They wound their way through the streets to the market in Crafting Square, where sure enough, Varen was hollering to a huge crowd. The masses of people turned on her as soon as she and Rothan pulled the wagon into place, and she shrank from their attention.

"Look! Like I told you, Takiyah dragged the wagon all the way from the City of the Lost. And when the wheel fell off, she carried it. And when bandits attacked, she defended it."

Her face burned at all the attention, the faces looking at her with awe, respect, joy, and curiosity. It was too much. She broke free of the crowd, racing past several blocks, though Varen's voice carried as he discussed the goods and trade options.

Rothan caught up to her. "Are you all right?"

She nodded. "Just tired."

"Did you really do all that?"

"Varen makes it sound more spectacular than it was."

"What happened to your staff?"

She swallowed hard, the loss still raw, even if she'd gotten the better end of the deal—Varen home alive and well. "I traded it for something better."

Chapter Eighteen

The dragons are restless, making it difficult for me to get to the node. I've lingered in the mountains far longer than I've intended, but in exploring the set of caves, I discovered a signal. I am investigating, as it is clearly of technomage origin and getting stronger.

—journal entry

Step by step, Ra'ael walked. In the evenings, the Philosophers from Detr would "test" her with the Gifts of the Gods. She'd chosen this, but she hadn't truly understood the torment that lay ahead of her. The Gifts were not affected by her psionics, but she was intensely affected by them, even though many of them were so tiny she couldn't even see them.

"Detr understands how to deal with magic users. One must study them to fully root them out," the hunter said. He'd taken samples from her —her skin, hair, and blood. He'd captured her height, too, recording it as if it could tell him anything about her. "We will determine the seed of your witchery, to blight witches out from our number before they become apparent. As is meant to be."

The never-ending pompous talk was incredibly grating.

"I am Rinaryn," she bit out. "This is the seed of my 'witchery,' as you call it."

"You are more right than you know. The differences are not so great as they first appear, unfortunately. The offspring of those with the taint of Rinaryn in them are more likely to be witches. We cull them."

"How civilized of you." She shouldn't have engaged him, but somehow the words left her mouth anyway.

A fire lit in his eyes, and he pressed a piece of metal—a piece of a Gift of the Gods the size of her thumb—against her stomach, holding it there even while pain bit at her and she screamed and thrashed. His partner held her down. Still, perhaps this pain was worth it if through their sadistic experiments, they could cut out her psionics. Then, she could stay with Dode.

She didn't know what else to do. She had nowhere else to go.

Her limbs shook with every step for most of the next walk. The farther they travelled, the more the pressure grew, that sense of wrong she felt around them. She gritted her teeth, all too aware of the two of them behind her.

It was hard to keep track of the days in the tunnels without the dimming of the lights. Ra'ael had no idea how far they'd travelled either, for the hunters kept taking her off the main tunnel, down side passages. All she had was their lantern for light and the patterns they'd fallen into. Walk, "test" her, sleep. Then repeat it all again when they woke up.

Hushed tones behind her caught her attention. "The people of Codr and Hadr are nothing. Did you see their defenses?"

"We will soon have them under our domain again and teach them how they are meant to live. How a civilized person is meant to live."

So that was their true intent. Ra'ael scoffed, her hands curling into fists. "If they are so base, how then did they leave your domain in the first place? They broke away, however superior you claim you are."

One of them shoved her toward yet another side passage. The touch burned on her back. "We let them go because they do not matter. We were focused on things that do matter. But if your neighbor allows rodents into their home, those pests will spread to you. You must root them out. The same is true now. We remove the pestilence to prevent its spread, and then we will teach them the error of their ways."

Ra'ael snorted. How eerie that he nearly quoted the Rinaryn story of the boy and the rodent. And yet, the point he made was completely counter to the story's lesson. "If your neighbor has a rodent in their house, that shows they are more giving than you, and their excess goes to help the hungry. This is far more civilized, especially if they aren't calling their guests pests and plagues."

The hunters laughed. "I suppose an unclean thing such as you would know about unclean things such as rodents."

"Actually if you take care of them, they're quite clean. It's a metaphor. We're supposed to take care of each other."

They didn't answer her, and she spent the rest of the walk dwelling on the stories and the choices that had led her to this. They were supposed to take care of each other, but they hadn't. Taunos had tried, and she had rejected him. She'd become so obsessed with following the rules, with her own hurt, that she'd forgotten that main tenet of Rinaryn life, just as the Elders had dismissed it when they banished them without cause. She'd taken care of Dode, yes, but still she put her faith in the things others said she should do. She'd been so set on being Kamalti she'd been willing to sacrifice her very self, taking this wild leap into the hands of the hunters. She'd spent these moons chasing fleeting belonging after tossing away the belonging she'd already had.

Ra'ael challenged the hunters the next time they stopped. One held her with a metal pole looped through the chains that bound her, while the other secured small metal pieces to her skin. It burned, sharp and hot.

"How does this help me not react this way? If you're paying attention, this seems to be getting worse."

"It does indeed," said one, though not to her, of course. "Do you still think her increased sensitivity is due to her being Rinaryn?"

"No. The data makes it clear. The current is minimal. Most subjects only twitch a bit with the Gifts on low."

The pain increased until it lit every nerve, desperation charging through her veins, her hands clenching and extending of their own accord. Her stomach rebelled, and she threw up. Her mind buzzed, her scalp itched, and her skin crawled. Spirits above, she screamed, thrashing and bucking against the chains.

"Turn it higher." The voice floated, disembodied.

Fire flowed through her, her muscles spasming in turn, her song crying out. Was this how she died? The edges of her sight faded to black, and her pain-wracked mind refused to focus on anything in front of her, refused to comprehend anything she could see. Faces from memory filled her mind.

The desperation in Answer's voice as she argued for Ra'ael.

The anguish on Dode's face, there in the Hall of Scouts.

"If this keeps up, her heart will fail."

The anger and betrayal on Taunos's face when she told him they were leaving.

The way the last remaining flickers of light had drained from Kaemada's being when they came down the mountain and saw the bodies.

Takiyah's eyes, full of suffering, full of the torment the Kamalti had put her through when she and Taunos had shown up at Dode's door. Even with the desperate need to escape, still they'd come for Ra'ael first.

"Fine, turn it off."

The buzzing stopped. The Gifts tore free of her skin, bits of her going with them. Every muscle in her body sagged. The pole released her. She slumped to the ground. A foul taste twisted her mouth, and she spat. Red flecked the stone beneath her. Her stomach rebelled, and she vomited.

"Disgusting." The two Philosophers from Detr turned away, their steps receding several paces into the darkness.

Everything hurt. It consumed her thoughts, even though she was used to pain. She was Rinaryn, after all. But her very bones ached.

Why hadn't the blood rage taken over? Had that, too, abandoned her?

She should have entered blood rage long before now. She shuddered, seeing the connection. As long as the Gift was touching her, she had no control. No blood rage. No way out.

Ra'ael curled in a ball, her throat dry, her stomach in knots. She pushed at the shackles on her wrists, but they defied her telekinetic prying. This wasn't going to work. It didn't matter if they could break her reaction to the Gift—they would do it at the expense of her life. The man from the Collective had warned her of that. They killed psions. She needed to destroy the Gift, instead, even if it left her nowhere else to go.

She winced at the memory of how her psionics buzzed through her in response to the Gift. The forces that twisted her bones—that was her psionics, reacting to the metal, turning on herself. Another shudder wracked her.

Several paces away, the two Philosophers from Detr unrolled bedding. One of them glanced over at her, and she flinched involuntarily. She glowered at the smirk that spread across his face. Her reaction apparently had become even stronger. She didn't even have to see them to know where they were at all times—the prickling sensation acted like another sense, one she very much did not want.

"When will they be here?" one asked the other.

"We will either meet them on the road or in Detr."

"Hopefully the sensitivity is worthwhile to them. Perhaps we can ask for more counsel in return?"

The other scoffed in reply. "This one is already worth several crystals."

Desperately trying to find her peace, she hummed a tune to herself, one of her people's songs of strength in hardship. The spirits didn't change how you lived. They merely guided and kept you company, so the stories went. She had believed that, believed they gave counsel to those who would listen, though there was no guarantee it would keep you from trouble. After all, one's choices were one's own, and small changes could grow to big differences.

She couldn't control when her story would end, but she could control her song. That was always under her control and always had been, even when she'd neglected it. It didn't matter if she couldn't hear the song of the spirits. She could still sing, even if the darkness ate the tune.

For far too long, she'd allowed others to direct her, going along with what "wise men" said. She'd even tried to accept being Fallen.

But no more. This was wrong, and no more would she submit to it. Those who did wrong must be held to account—first these hunters and then the Elders.

She was no longer the leaf carried by the current. She was the current itself.

Ra'ael switched to a lullaby. It felt childish, but she needed the comfort right now. Images of Eian flashed through her mind. Was someone singing him a lullaby right now? She could only hope so.

The hunters came toward her again. No doubt she was annoying them. She smiled as they scowled and told her to be quiet, merely throwing herself into the song. She'd throw herself into the metaphorical song, too— those were the last measurements they'd get from her. One grabbed the large piece of the Gift which they used to "test" her.

She tensed as it sharpened the air around her, but she belted her song even louder.

He brought the hateful metal closer, and she narrowed her eyes, shoving at it with telekinetic force. It flew out of his hands, clattering across the stone. She pushed again, but it was too far now to reach. The hunter snatched it up and turned on her, fury contorting his face.

Another moment passing would be a moment too late.

Ra'ael rose, hands still shackled together but wholly dangerous as she embraced the blood rage.

Her body shook as if she were caught in the turmoil at the bottom of a waterfall. Ragged breaths wheezed in and out. She stumbled in a circle, staring about her. She'd never woken at the end of blood rage before, not without being knocked unconscious. The hunters lay in crumpled piles, staring sightlessly. The lantern lay on its side, flickering against the tunnel wall, and the bag of Gifts was shredded, with the metal fragments shattered into thousands of tiny shards.

Apparently, she'd emerged on her own once there was nothing left to destroy.

Blood streamed from numerous cuts and scrapes, mostly on her hands, which were still shackled. She righted the lantern then grabbed a knife from where it lay on the stone and worked at the lock with trembling hands. She couldn't stand it, not for a moment longer. Finally, with a click, she was free, and the metal cuffs fell to the ground.

There was peace, now, for the first time in a long time. No more humming of the Gift, prickling at her senses. No more sense of danger stealing her calm.

She sighed, her legs buckling under her, and lay on the hard ground, marveling at the stillness. All she had left was herself, and she embraced that.

Lying on her back, she sang in the dark.

A voice roused her from her stupor. "What have you done?"

She raised her head, blinking at the blurry forms in front of her. Two of them. She rubbed her eyes and lurched to her feet.

Fae.

"Why are you here?" she asked, her voice thick with sleep.

The fae glanced at the bodies. She blinked. The hunters had talked about meeting someone. Someone who traded counsel for crystals.

Her stomach turned. "What do you want with me?"

"You are very loud."

Ra'ael frowned. "That happens when you're being tortured."

"Mentally. You'll call down the dragons."

"Oh. I will try to be quieter, then. As I said, it helps no longer being tortured." Silence fell as Ra'ael eyed the fae, who watched her in return. The fae. Always meddling in things. "You told the people of Codr to shut down their machines, that the smoke would make the dragons come. Then you tell Detr to go to Codr and capture members of the Collective. And want to trade for me? What are you working toward?"

She didn't really expect a response.

The fae stepped forward in perfect sync, pausing when she flinched. She crouched, calculating her odds in a fight against the fae and finding them not in her favor. Could she even enter the blood rage again so soon? Normally she spent the next several days recovering. Except she had no way of knowing how long it'd been, it occurred to her.

The fae on the left extended a hand. From so close, she could see a mottling of grey wrapping around the brown fingers. She eyed the hand. They didn't really think she was going to trust them, did they?

"Come. We must leave here. That outburst of yours is bound to draw attention," the fae said.

Ra'ael backed up another step. "What kind of attention?"

"Such a battle between psionics and technomancy can surely be felt along both."

Her brow furrowed, and she shook her head. "Technomancy?"

A long-suffering look filled the fae's face. "The Gift of the Gods, as the Kamalti insist on calling it."

Could others with the Gift sense the battle? How long had it been? How far away were others with the Gift? Shudders overtook Ra'ael. She couldn't go through that again, and yet, what good had she done? She'd only destroyed a few pieces of it and killed two hunters. It wasn't nearly enough.

"Come, come. We're sorry we were unable to make it here sooner." The fae's voice was soothing, a bucket of water to wash away her tension and fear.

Ra'ael stared at them. She blinked.

There was something... some fear. Some desire not to go with them. And yet, she couldn't quite figure it out.

Her shoulders slumped as the strain flowed out of her, and she stepped forward. The fae fell in beside her, one on either side, their footsteps gliding while she stumbled over her feet. They turned toward Codr, and a moment of confusion passed over her before it eased. Of course. It was natural to go toward Codr. Detr must be too far away. That must be it.

Finally, after so long without it, peace descended on her. She no longer had to fight, no longer had to suffer. The song of the spirits echoed in her head for the first time in moons and moons, and she balked for a moment.

Something was off about it. No, no, it was just her exhaustion. It would all turn out all right, for she once again had the song she'd been missing so much.

"Ra'ael!"

The shout startled her from her stupor. Tjodlik and Answer were running down the tunnel toward them, light from Tjodlik's lantern throwing wild shadows on the walls. What were they doing away from the safety of the cities? Neither would be good in a fight—only the male Scouts were taught to fight, while the female Scouts kept and created systems. Somewhat similar to how Ra'ael had performed her priestess duties, she supposed, though she had the good sense to know how to fight.

Why was she thinking about fighting? The song vanished from her head, the peace dissipating like mist, and like mist, she couldn't hold on to it, no matter how hard she tried. The fae stood tall and straight on either side of her, staring at Answer and Tjodlik. What was she doing, following fae?

"Ra'ael, are you all right?" Tjodlik asked.

"I felt a great amount of turmoil in my Gift," Answer said.

Both of them glanced repeatedly at the fae, stopping a respectful distance away.

"It is all fine," one of the fae said. "We found her and thought we would escort her to safety."

Ra'ael winced as Answer stepped near, every nerve tingling. This was wrong. This was all wrong. She shouldn't be with the fae—she'd been suspicious of them. The Detr hunters were going to sell her to them.

"Be careful—step back," the fae said. "She has the psionic technophobia. She may be dangerous."

Curling her hands into fists, Ra'ael sprang toward Answer and Tjodlik. Answer stumbled back, arms flailing, but Tjodlik stood his ground, his expression becoming grim.

She grabbed his arm, as if she could hold on to a frame of mind so easily. "Something's wrong. Why was I with them? They're planning something."

Tjodlik steadied her, eyes hard as he looked past her.

"What are they planning?" Answer stayed out of reach, eyes darting from Ra'ael to the fae and back.

"I do not know. I…" A fog began to creep over her.

Answer stepped closer, and the tingles on her skin drove it away.

"I'm forgetting things!" she remembered in a panic.

Answer frowned at the fae. "You. Are you the same ones who warned of dragons attacking Codr?"

The fae smiled thinly. "Did you not heed the warning?"

Tjodlik's tone was severe. "What do you mean?"

"Dragons are very territorial," the fae said.

Ra'ael shook her head to clear it. It didn't work. She only knew that she was tired of darkness. Tired of being underground. She wanted to see Dode, but she needed to see the sky again.

A pulsing sensation beat against her, from Answer's direction as well as to the left. Farther on, there was an opening in the tunnel, a branch to the left. She embraced the pulsing as an edge against the calming that surrounded her when the fae had joined her. It sharpened her focus, but it set her nerves on fire. Her eyes locked on the tunnel entrance ahead as the pulsing of the Gift beat against her, coming closer. Was the one who bore it friendly? She shuddered.

The fae stood there, so calm, so serene. Everything she wanted to be. One extended a hand in a fluid motion, gesturing ahead. Did they not feel the pulsing? "We had invited Ra'ael to visit with us for a time, to soothe her hurts. If you would like to accompany her, we welcome you."

She blinked. They hadn't done any such thing. Oh, or had they? She was just tired, that was all. Stifling a yawn, she walked toward the fae, following them down the corridor, feeling altogether shabby.

But a few steps onward, Answer stepped close to her.

The prickling of Ra'ael's senses flared, and she stopped. What was she doing? She hadn't meant to go along with them again. The fae were doing something, and it surely wasn't going to be good.

"Tjodlik, Answer, get out of here!" Ra'ael cried.

Tjodlik looked at her, bemused. "Why? Come on."

She couldn't remember why, and her cheeks heated. She was acting foolishly. No wonder she was Fallen, would never be the Great Mother. No wonder no one would follow her. Instead, she followed, and the fae led, which was as it should be, after all.

The source of the irritation came closer, but Ra'ael ignored it. It was nicer just to relax and float along in the river. The waterfall would come, but what did she care for it? Rapids were beside her anyway, in the form of Answer. Answer paused now and then, but Ra'ael hardly noticed.

More and more, the irritation in the distance was closing. Something niggled at the back of her mind, but she couldn't identify it. Thoughts drifted past, out of reach.

She was missing something. She had to be aware.

Ra'ael drifted toward Answer until sharp clarity broke through the haze. They were in a tunnel, maybe another side tunnel. Where were they going? She concealed her awareness as best she could, remembering practice with Kaemada, training her mind against telepathic influences. If that was what this was, anyway.

She watched the others out of the corner of her eyes. Answer and Tjodlik glided along as primly as ever, but there was a vague distraction to their movements. The two fae, on the other hand, prowled like predators, graceful and lithe and powerful. The sound of their breathing echoed off the tunnel walls as they turned left at the side tunnel, sloping gently upward as the tunnel narrowed, becoming jagged. Large markers were carved into the walls, but Ra'ael couldn't risk the focus needed to decipher them. She drifted past them, waiting for some clear danger so she could make a decision on what to do and hoping it wouldn't be too late by then.

All the while, the sense of unease grew until she could hardly stand it, twitching, straying from Answer just to find some relief. It felt like sparks being thrown from a fire.

One of the fae paused with her, steadying her with one hand. She shook the hand off reflexively. Shivers took her, and she stopped, staring at the tunnel bend. She could count down the time to seeing the person who bore the Gift, the prickling fire was so strong. The others stopped, with the leading fae glancing back and then forward up the tunnel.

And then Galod strode into view.

His hard, grey eyes widened a fraction, pausing intently on her, scouring her song, and then the prickling went away. Ra'ael nearly fell over, gasping with relief. She stared at him and then the fae, wariness returning to her. Tjodlik and Answer stirred as if coming out of a reverie, and Answer narrowed her eyes on Galod.

"Outsider, I believe you are lost," she said.

He looked at her, disdain in his very being. "And I believe you have tech that does not belong to you."

"Excuse me?" Answer frowned.

Despite everything, Ra'ael smiled, relief washing over her. The ease with which Galod flustered others was a welcome breath of normality. His gaze flickered to Ra'ael again and then to the fae. A moment passed, and then he strode toward them.

"Galod, what are you doing here?" Ra'ael asked.

"Why do you have psionic technophobia?" he responded.

She wrinkled her nose. Of course he wouldn't be helpful.

Galod stared at the fae. "And why do you have my student?"

"It is none of your concern. Remember, you are a visitor in our lands," the fae responded.

Ra'ael edged to the tunnel wall, feeling the need for something solid at her back. What *was* Galod doing here? And how did he and the fae seem to know each other? Part of her hoped he'd come searching for her.

But he was familiar, even though he wasn't entirely safe, and her mind had felt fuzzy the whole time she'd been with the fae. Or had it been even longer? She edged toward him, gritting her teeth as the prickling increased, but at least it was a lot less than it had been when he'd rounded the corner. He must have turned something off, but she didn't see any metal on him. Ra'ael made eye contact with Tjodlik and Answer, trying to put weight into it, but neither moved.

And then a fae hand caught her shoulder, gripping her tightly. "Leave us to our business, Galod."

"I did not expect fae under the mountain."

"Nor the tech, I think." The fae's tone was level, and yet, there was an undercurrent of tension there.

"Let my protégé go."

Ra'ael twisted, bringing her arm back to jab into the fae's side. She halted mid-motion, unable to complete the move. The fingers like claws were entrenched in her shoulder. No matter how she tried, she couldn't continue her attack. A small prick of something sharp under her chin stilled her.

"You do not come into our domain and give us orders. We would rather not cause waste, but if an example must be made, so be it." Her attacker's voice was like music as the fae threatened her life.

There had to be something she could do. Ra'ael strained to look at Galod, who stood there like a statue, filling the tunnel. Tjodlik appeared paralyzed with fear, glancing back and forth between the fae and Galod, but Answer ran toward the fae.

Ra'ael nearly dismissed her until she realized Answer was attacking the fae who held her. Unfortunately, the woman had no combat training, and the fae that held Ra'ael used her as a shield.

Ra'ael put her arms up to defend herself as she was whipped from side to side, taking blows meant for the fae. The fae holding her lashed out with a small knife at Answer's wrist, but the blade slid right off her skin, leaving no wound. Wonder warred with aversion, and Ra'ael pressed backward into the fae, sending him stumbling off balance. He raised the knife, and she whirled away as it cut a shallow slice across her collarbone.

The fae raised a hand, and her feet stilled as if she were waist deep in thick mud.

"Enough. I will not ask again." Galod's voice boomed in the tunnel, and Ra'ael's stomach turned.

"Away with you, Galod. You are no longer welcome among the fae."

Apparently there was a lot she didn't know about her teacher, if he knew the fae and had been welcome among them.

"You're mistaken if you think I hold no power here." Galod made no move, but Ra'ael recoiled.

Aversion hit her, far stronger than when Answer had somehow avoided being cut. It hit her like a wave from Dead Man's Sea, and then the very air around her charged, as if a storm occupied their tiny tunnel.

The fae gasped, their knives dropping. Ra'ael stumbled. Now was her chance. Ra'ael couldn't compete with the power of Galod or the fae, but she could get Answer and Tjodlik out of danger. She grabbed them and shoved them toward the main tunnel, sprinting after.

Tjodlik swore as he ran. "Crystals and ships! What happened?"

At the intersection with the main tunnel, Ra'ael glanced back to where Galod and the two fae continued their standoff. The rock walls seemed to shrink in on themselves, crowding her, but the relief of being farther from whatever Galod was doing was greater.

The fae seemed to have grown larger, their shadows long and malicious in the light of Tjodlik's lantern. "You will regret that."

They needed more distance. Ra'ael hurried Tjodlik and Answer up the main tunnel as quickly as they could go.

"Who was that?" Answer asked.

Ra'ael bit her lip against the way her skin crawled whenever Answer got too close. "My teacher."

It was a good question. Who was he, really? What was he doing? She couldn't tell, but she was glad he was on their side.

Chapter Nineteen

Look to the sea and be watchful. Banded rectangular sails, bring out your goods. Purple triangular sails, bring out your weapons. Whatever your visitors, those who brave the wild waves are as rough as the seas. Take heed and take caution. For the wise and careful, the bounties of trade outweigh the dangers.
—Far Dahutad wisdom

Taunos leaned his hips against the side of the boat, hooking his good arm around a rope against the rocking of the waves. He grinned, watching as Emin sat losing—again—at a game of taj with one of the Ifreesians. Emin slouched on a crate with his brow furrowed, hunched over the strip of cloth they were using as a game board. His fingers wavered in the air over the different colored stone pieces. Surrounding them, sailors belted out a wild sea tune that Taunos tapped his fingers to.

Amanah's arm brushed Taunos's as she stepped to his side. "All right. New game. Which of the Ifreesians do you think are men, and which are actually another gender?"

"Trick question," said one of the Ifreesians, rewrapping a coil of rope. "On the sea, in the ports, we're all men. It confuses you less that way."

Amanah tilted her head. "Well, then, what about at home?"

The sailor paused for a breath to shoot a narrow-eyed look their way and then continued his work, pressing his lips together.

The Ifreesians were fascinating. Emin had tried rowing with them, but his shoulder wound was deep, impairing his strength. It didn't stop him from joining their songs, trading boasts with them, or learning to climb the rigging, to Amanah's consternation. Emin had made friends with the man he was playing taj with—Skir, a smaller Ifreesian with a leaner build, so that he could almost pass for Dahuti if his skin wasn't so light and hair so red.

But there was a cloak of secrecy over them which raised Taunos's wariness. Often, he caught them stopping mid-sentence or shifting the topic from Emin and Amanah's never-ending questions. He couldn't blame them—he wanted to know as much as he could about the sailors as well. Nor could he blame the Ifreesians—he, too, had kept secrets. So many secrets, for so very long. He enjoyed figuring out secrets, but he reined himself in. After all, these were their rescuers, even though it made their secrets vulnerable to their new passengers.

Taunos stifled a laugh as Amanah folded her arms, watching the sailor. The Ifreesians had been barricading against Emin and Amanah's curiosity with the patience of boulders the whole journey.

Nevertheless, she tried again. "All right, what port is your favorite?"

"The one where we drop you off," the one coiling the rope dead-panned.

Raising his eyebrows, Taunos leaned forward. "And what do you love so much about the Hinanuri port?"

"The peace and quiet."

Just across the boat from them, Emin wheezed with laughter. His mirth shifted to a scowl as another handful of his pieces fell to Skir. "Do you know many tales of sea-wizards? You being accomplished sailors and all?"

"Or Sea Peoples?" Amanah added.

The Ifreesians glanced at each other, but Skir was the one who spoke up. "Sea-wizards aren't Sea Peoples—not all of them. The Sea Peoples live on the waters. They live on their boats, on their rafts, on the islands. They aren't like you landers. For them, being on land is like you being on the water. Avoid them at all costs. They have no love for landers, only greed for secrets."

It was the most open the Ifreesians had been about anything that wasn't mundane, and Taunos hung on their words as if they were the last meal he'd get in a long time.

"So what are sea-wizards?" Emin asked.

Skir waved his hand. "Sea-wizards are nothing. Just stories."

"But they do magic," Emin protested.

"Anything you don't understand is magic. This is nothing new."

Emin narrowed his eyes. "Do you have magic? Is that why you know of sea-wizards? Turns out I've never seen you start the cooking fires. How do you keep serving us hot meals?"

Skir grinned, but the expression was anything but friendly. "If it bothers you, we can stop."

Taunos broke in, hoping to find a less prickly topic, though that was like finding secure footing on moss-covered rocks across a brisk stream. "Anything we should know about the Hinanuri? Anything at all would be helpful."

The broad-shouldered Ifreesian working with the rope—Igri, that was his name—frowned, his eyes going from one to another of them. Taunos kept his attention open, aware of the others around them, but no one seemed to be giving any signals, and he detected no undue tension.

"The Hinanuri celebrate their sea-wizards. They have for a few decades now. If you're looking for information on sea-wizards, I'd ask them. But be careful who you go asking. You ask a Sea People about sea-wizards, and you'll never get another chance to ask more questions. They'll haul you away to squeeze everything you know out of you, without ever giving you a scrap. So sail with care among the swells."

Amanah and her brother had both said the Hinanur Empire made the most sense as a destination, but while Amanah had been a battle-bimna in the war, healing instead of fighting, Emin had led his war-band against the Hinanuri.

Taunos searched Emin's face. "Emin, are you sure you're all right going there with us?"

He snorted. "I have no grudge with Hinanuri. Their army? Maybe some of them, but not the people. Our family traded with Hinanuri extensively all while we were growing up, after all. It's hard to hold a grudge against the same people you played with, people who were hauled to the river and scrubbed down by exasperated mothers same as you when you both fell in horse dung."

Taunos laughed, easily able to place Emin in the mental image.

Amanah leaned against Taunos, her shoulders shaking with mirth as she wrinkled her nose at her brother. "The smell though. You stunk up the tent for days."

Wrapping his arm around her, Taunos kissed her temple. No doubt the friendship between nomadic Dahuti clans and Hinanuri nomads had only deepened Dahuti prejudice against Amanah and her brother in the past summers.

The captain interrupted, swinging along the outside of the ship. "Frul, correct our heading. Is it storytime, or are we sailing?"

The steersman at the stern of the ship ducked his head, and the ship swung back ever so slightly to the right. As the captain passed, he grabbed the rope right by Taunos's head, and his sleeve slipped down. There, at the wrist was a slight swelling. A familiar swelling. He remembered Takiyah coming to him at Answer's home, her wrists red and swollen. Taunos glanced over the ship again, at the weather-roughened faces, the tattered hems of the sleeves.

All he could hear was Eian's little voice.

"The dwarves, the elves, and the gnomes."

"The Ifreesians, the Stormseekers, and the Kelm."

"Ifreesian dwarves," Taunos breathed.

Takiyah was an Ifreesian. And the Ifreesian dwarves had attacked the Kamalti in the mountain, according to Answer. And if they had, then they knew where Rinara was. What kept them away, then? Did these particular sailors know where Rinara was? The question died on his tongue, for they might not be friendly. He needed more information.

"What's that?" Amanah asked.

"Why are you called Ifreesian dwarves?" Taunos asked. Each of the sailors was taller than he was, built thick and tough. Most of them were even bulkier than Takiyah. "Aren't dwarves short?"

"Translation error," Igri growled. "How do you know that?"

Two could sidestep questions. "I heard it in passing once, long ago."

Igri hmphed and stood. "Captain, I think our cargo has developed ears."

"Well, that's unfortunate," the captain said, climbing back fully inside the boat.

"Every time, Captain, I tell you. Every time. Don't pick up strays," Igri said.

The captain folded his arms, staring at Taunos. Amanah tensed at his side.

What could he say? If he told them he knew one of them, they'd ask where. The Ifreesians had helped them, but danger lurked in the shadows of their secrets. Taunos couldn't give away the location of his island. Not to these people who were so intent on keeping their knowledge bound to them. Even for Takiyah, though?

New sympathy for how Amanah must have felt welled up in him, and he curled his arm more tightly over her shoulders. He felt torn apart, coming undone like the ragged ends of an overused rope, held together by the steadfastness of his love resting against him, yet ready to leap to defense. Why should she defend his secrets any longer? He would not put her in that position again.

"I know one of you. Though she doesn't know who she is. I cannot tell you where. But… she's got to be one of you." Taunos scowled inwardly.

That wasn't going to work. It was too weak. Why would they accept that?

The captain scoffed. "Not one of us. If she was one of us, she'd be here."

He scrambled for some other detail to give them. "She was found in the sea, in a little basket, as a baby."

A shake of that shaggy head answered him. "Not one of us."

But she had to be. If they could spout fire from their wrists like she could, it would explain why he never saw them start the cooking fires. The sailors regularly fished, cooking their catch in a metal container filled with coals, ringed round with another metal container full of sand. But he hadn't seen a single fire-maker on board, and the sailors got secretive when they lit the coals.

They might not accept her, but Takiyah was Ifreesian. He should have seen it earlier.

Except what did that information gain him? The attention of every sailor was on them, and Taunos could feel the danger increasing. Almost every Ifreesian was taller and broader even than Emin, standing beside him, with the captain and Igri being broadest of all. It was odd being one of the smallest in a company—among his people, his height alone had set him apart. Only Skir was of comparable size to Emin, and his height made him look lean, much like Takiyah.

"Purple sails!" The Ifreesian manning the rudder shouted, pointing out at the horizon.

The shout went up among the sailors, and in moments, the Ifreesians were scrambling, even those on the off-shift. Some ran for the oars, others for the sail.

The captain stood in the stern of the boat, eyes on the smudge on the horizon, and belted orders. "Frul, get that rudder hard to port. All the way, do you hear? No slacking! Igir, let out that sail. Skir, keep the tempo. Row, you laggards. Row!"

Tension flowed over Amanah and Emin, and Taunos's shoulders grew tight in response. Amanah took his hand, pulling him into the center of the boat as Emin joined them. The rest of the ship erupted in a flurry of activity, and the captain ran to the single mast of the boat, angling the boom just so.

"What's going on?" Taunos asked.

"Sea Peoples." Amanah's voice was quiet, but her eyes were fierce.

Taunos turned, taking everything in, as much as he could see. All fifteen Ifreesians worked with a quiet intensity to their actions that spoke of serious danger, while the ship fled, angling away from the distant shore. Behind them, a triangle of purple sat calmly on the water closer to land.

He'd spent the last several days watching constantly for Dahuti sails. He'd loved Far Dahutad, with its markets and mixture of peoples and love of learning. Too bad those in power hadn't continued that last trend.

But even when the Ifreesians were avoiding or outrunning Dahuti ships, they hadn't shown this level of focus. It was clear that he wasn't the only one to consider the Sea Peoples a major threat, powerful enough that they were best avoided, not confronted.

"Let me check if this reed is ready to come out," Amanah said, raising his arm above his head.

He peered around his arm at her incredulously. "Now?"

"Yes. If the Sea Peoples catch us, you want to be able to swim. Sit down here."

It was probably foolish in the extreme to be on a boat in the ocean with a hole punched in his ribcage, but there he was. The purple sail had turned toward them, and he kept his gaze on it as Amanah unwrapped his bandaging. Pain sliced through him as she removed the reed, her eyes watching him intently, full of sympathy. There she hovered, so close all he needed to do was lean forward to close the distance between them.

Taunos shifted his gaze back to the water, letting her work in peace. Their relationship had a chance again, but now was a time for preparing in case of battle, rather than for kissing. He was lucky she was willing to stay with him as he looked for more secrets to bring back to his Elders. The information about the Ifreesians belonged to Takiyah alone—he wouldn't trade that to the Elders. He had to look for more, no matter how much his heart screamed at him not to go back at all—to stay here with the woman he loved so much. Except his sister needed the Elders to change their minds. It may be futile, but he had to at least make the effort, and Amanah was right—she deserved the whole of him, undivided.

Her fingers spread salve over his wound and pressed a cloth there while she wrapped clean bandaging around him to hold it. They were fortunate Emin had gathered supplies in that pack before coming to their rescue.

"How's the breathing?" she asked.

He took a deep breath, pleased to discover he could. The last couple times she'd tried to remove the reed, his lung had re-collapsed.

She smiled, coating the bandages with a water-resistant sealant. "Just in case."

And then there was nothing else to do. The boat bobbed and dipped in the rougher currents of the sea, and Emin, Taunos, and Amanah sat among the cargo, as out of the way as they could be on the small ship. Amanah nestled next to him, and he put his arms around her, resting his cheek on her braids. With the warm breeze in his hair and his beloved in his arms, he could be content, if they weren't being chased by Sea Peoples.

Time stretched long while the Sea Peoples pursued them. The waves grew rough and choppy, and Skir moved around them, making sure all the cargo was tied down tightly, especially as some of the larger waves slapped over the low sides of the boat. He handed them safety lines, secured to the mast, and Taunos, Amanah, and Emin tied them on.

The shore disappeared on the horizon, but the Ifreesians never wavered.

Taunos watched them, a seed of wariness in his core souring his wonder. To sail so boldly without any landmarks, and to change course so quickly—it was amazing. And yet he couldn't help thinking how dangerous it would be for these people to find his land, and maybe they could. He'd never seen anyone sail so capably. Every landmark they pointed out, even days apart, appeared right where they said it would be, but he never saw any charts or maps. It was like they carried the charts in their heads. And if they did find his land, the city of Codr had stories of Ifreesians coming as conquerors. Would they do so again?

"I wish we could confront the Sea Peoples," Amanah said. "We have to search for Nasri. No one else will."

Emin scoffed. "I know you want to see the world, but—"

"Nasri is not a fighter. And no one else cares about her," Amanah snapped. She turned to Taunos. "What can you do to help?"

If only he could help that simply! But they didn't even know where to start. She was right, though, and he vowed to help her just as she was helping him. That meant knowing what he could—and could not—do.

"It's not really magic, Amanah. It's not like in your stories. I can push things with telekinesis. I can jump to other places, but without knowing where I'm going, it's extremely dangerous. And every time I realmwalk, there's a chance I could jump to a land that's not quite right—a near version, not quite the same—and never really know."

Amanah tilted her head, chewing on her lip. "Let's not dwell on that disturbing possibility for the moment."

"I wish we knew how the Sea Peoples took her," Taunos said. "No one saw them leave or come."

"Almost like they disappeared, sea-wizard?" Emin asked.

"Far too much like it, actually."

"There's nothing to do right now anyway," Amanah said. "We're not sailors. We'd only get in the way. Besides, Taunos needs to stay as still as possible, or his lung could collapse again."

"Slow as grass growing, you are. You don't have any fancy healing magic?" Emin asked.

Taunos shook his head, his mind on the puzzle of the Sea Peoples. They appeared out of nowhere, burned and killed, and disappeared. Eerily like the Darks. But this time, they'd taken someone, at least one person.

The Darks didn't do that.

Was he reaching for similarities, or could the Sea Peoples be the Darks?

Finding information on a people that could be from any land, from any world, was impossible enough a task, but the Darks were realmwalkers—they were known across too many lands for it to be otherwise—and if the Sea Peoples were realmwalkers too... His blood chilled in him. The task loomed large before him, but he wasn't going to back down. They had to make it to the Hinanuri and hope they had answers.

And the Hinanuri had the stories of the sea-wizards, stories that reminded him so much of his mother. Her story of going to the Darks to plead for peace was incomplete—she'd called herself an "ambassador," a word that had come from Galod. But how had she made it to the Darks in the first place? Had they taken her with them, like the Sea Peoples took Nasri?

A sudden chill went through him. Had his mother's demise somehow factored into the Elders' distrust of Galod? But then why would they allow Galod to continue to train Taunos?

Amanah tapped his shoulder. "Where do you go, so distant, so dark?"

He blinked. She watched him, so close, one hand on his. He squeezed her hand. "I'm sorry."

"That is not an answer."

"The story about Leen that Nasri read? It reminded me of my mother. I would like to know if she somehow came through that land. I was just wondering... There seems to be holes in what I know."

She nodded. "Parents don't always tell their children everything."

It was more than that. His mind shifted away from going home every time he thought of it, too. Almost as if something were affecting his thoughts.

The day wore long, darkening prematurely as storm clouds gathered above them. Amanah interlaced her fingers on the other side of him, pillowing her head on his chest, and he leaned his cheek against her hair. Though she appeared calm from the outside, her tears soaked into his shirt. He rubbed her arm, holding her close. She'd lost a dear friend, along with everything she'd worked so long and so hard for—she could cry as long as she needed.

The wind whipped past, and the waves tossed their boat. Skir went by again, tying the oiled canvas tightly over the hold area, providing some protection from the sea spray and the coming rain.

The captain shouted, and the drumbeat ended. "Get some rest, laggards. We'll head through the storm and out the other side, and let the storm gods have the Sea Peoples. Frul, keep us pointed head on to those waves, and let down the sea anchor."

A ragged cheer went up from the others, and the sailors stowed their oars, each of them double-checking the oars were secured. Most of them headed into the cargo hold where Taunos, Amanah, and Emin were. The hold was simply a sunken area in the ship, usually open to the sky, where the sailors slept, ate, lounged, and played when off-duty. No fishing or cooking was done this night. The sailors just passed out dried strips of fish from previous catches and made sure they were each tied securely to the safety lines. Some of them rolled themselves in blankets, lying among the crates and barrels of goods, while others sat and chewed their preserved fish, staring pensively out at the rising storm.

The captain tied down the sail and checked the boom was secured before camping out in the stern as the rain began to fall, directing Frul to get some rest. He hunched by the rudder, holding it steady, eyes on the horizon while water made rivers of his red beard.

The deck bucked, and Skir staggered for balance.

"Skir, tie yourself down, you fool!" the captain called.

The sea tossed the boat around like a child playing with a stick, but this stick bent and flexed sickeningly with the force of the waves. Skir headed toward the safety lines tied to the mast, and Igri went to meet him, carrying a spare line. A wash of water flooded across the deck, under the canvas, and the ship tipped. The safety lines went taut, but Skir toppled into the sea. A sickening thunk sounded as he disappeared, and the vibration of hitting something reverberated through the planks.

A knife gleamed, and Emin stood, his safety line falling behind him, sliced through. He ran to the side and jumped.

"Emin!" Amanah shouted.

"To oars!" Igri shouted. "Don't let them out yet—we don't want to hit him in the head."

The captain tossed a heavy rope overboard. Another wave crashed over the boat, drenching them and the supplies. The vessel rocked to such a pitch Taunos worried they might capsize. Still, he staggered to the edge, grabbing the lip on the hull to avoid crashing into the ocean which raged just below. Even when the sea was calm, the hull sat low, less than half his height above the water, which had let Skir so easily pull them inside back in Arruk. Now, it brought them face to face with the tall waves smashing into them. They all waited, tense, scanning the rough seas.

Amanah ran to the mast, cutting her safety line close to the knot.

"Where is he?" she asked, coming back over to Taunos and handing him the end of her line.

A flash of black hair. Emin bobbed to the surface with a gasp.

Taunos pointed. "There!"

Farther off, Skir slowly sank, red mingling with the water around him, more than just his hair. He appeared unconscious—or worse. Waves sloshed over Emin as he swam for Skir, submerging him and hiding him from view.

"I'm not letting him drown alone." In a breath, Amanah's shoes were off, and she was in the waves. The tossing boat nearly hit her head, and she went under. The line was too short—it only made her more likely to hit the ship. He couldn't help her from here.

Taunos was the better swimmer by far than either Emin or Amanah, but would he still be with his injuries? Yet he knew the dangers of swimming in rough seas—it was asking for death to leap off a boat in a storm. And there were Emin and Amanah, in the ocean. Taunos's heart pounded in his ears. He kicked off his boots, sliced through his line, and jumped in.

Water grabbed him, pulled him under. It burned, the salt finding every healing wound and searing him with pain. His arm screamed as waves battered it, but he fought his way back to the surface. He shouted with the agony, and a wave smashed into him, pulling him back down. He surfaced again, struggling to focus beyond the pain that lit his entire body.

Emin's face bobbed above the waves again as he shook the water out of his eyes. He pointed into the dark depths. "I can't reach him!"

"Head back," Taunos shouted over the wind, pointing to the rope the Ifreesians were dragging for them as the ocean swept them away. The waves dragged Emin under briefly before Amanah tugged him back to the surface, toward the ship.

The boat wasn't too far away, but it would be a challenge to get there with the waves so tumultuous. At least there were several sailors standing at the edge of their safety lines, ready to help if they could just get close enough. The summer storm roiled above them, turning day as dark as night. Time was running out.

Taunos turned to Skir, whose streams of red hair were quickly disappearing in the depths. With a gulp of air, he dove, kicking furiously to catch Skir, and grabbed the last snatches of hair in his fist.

The unconscious sailor's massive bulk dragged Taunos down, and every movement he made seemed to give the ocean more opportunity to find every wound. He kicked hard, hauling Skir upward as he fought through the waves. Pulses of telekinesis propelled him and the sailor back toward the surface. His lungs burned, and still there was a stretch of water between him and the surface.

The need for air became desperation.

Then Amanah reached him, grabbing his arm and pulling. Pain flashed through him, turning his vision white, and the next thing he knew, he was above the waves, coughing and drawing haggard breaths, water and mucus streaming from his nose. Before he got his breath back, another wave splashed him in the face, and he went under again. With Amanah helping to support the Ifreesian, Taunos was able to bob back to the surface.

"You all right?" she shouted.

Taunos nodded, choking and sputtering on the last of the saltwater.

Amanah turned on her back, just as she'd done before, supporting Skir so his head stayed above the water more often than not. Blood streamed from his temple, and the dragging rope streamed behind Amanah. She kicked toward the ship, and Taunos swam alongside as the Ifreesians towed her in. She'd tied her line to the heavy rope, making it long enough to reach.

Emin shouted encouragement as he climbed back aboard the ship. The waves dragged at Taunos, pummeling him. More sailors pulled on the oars, trying to keep the storm from separating them farther, beyond the length of the rope. He grabbed the rope behind Amanah through the hot throbbing pain of his arm, now surely re-injured, while the Ifreesians hauled them in.

Freed of worrying about the ship leaving them behind, Taunos did his best just to keep all three of their heads above the water. Skir was heavy, and Amanah's movements became slower and less graceful, marked by increasing exhaustion. They rose from the waves, and Taunos's grip on the rope slipped.

He gave Amanah and Skir one last telekinetic boost as Emin and the sailors pulled them onto the ship, though it drove him away and briefly underwater.

Pushing out with desperate strength, Taunos broke through the waves again, gasping for breath. Another rope splashed down near him, but he couldn't get a grip with his bad arm. He wrapped it around one leg to hold it as the waves fought him. His chest burned. His arm was agony. Blackness sparked in his vision. He pushed on the sea, pushed on the rope itself even.

Finally, he hung on, chest heaving, as the rope began to move, dragging him closer to the ship. He coughed, the sound rasping and hoarse to his ears, and shook his head to clear his face of water. Water droplets sprayed from his sodden hair.

Taunos tightened his grip with his legs and slid his hand upward to grab the rope higher up and pull himself farther from the ocean's grasp. Almost immediately, strong arms grabbed him and hauled him onto the deck.

He fell to the wooden planks as soon as they let him go, struggling to see, to breathe. He coughed, clearing the rest of the sea water from his throat, and lay on the deck gasping for breath while sea spray flew around him.

"Amanah? Emin?"

"Come on, under the tarp, little sea-wizard." A sailor dragged him to the lower half hold and laid him beside the others.

Everyone was breathing, at least, including Skir. Taunos laid his head back down with a thunk on the decking. Eyes half closed, he listened to the commotion as the sailors ran around the boat, presumably trying to make sure they didn't all sink.

Immobilized by exhaustion, with his arm in agony, along with his other wounds irritated by the saltwater, Taunos struggled to just breathe. It was far more difficult than it should have been, and Taunos focused on the exercises Galod had taught him, controlling his breathing. There still wasn't enough air.

When he woke, the seas had calmed. The boat wasn't rocking nearly as much, and the canvas had been rolled back. There was no sign of Sea Peoples, only the cloudy sky gently waving above him. He squinted up at it, raising his arm, which was in a new splint, freshly bandaged.

Amanah brushed his hair back from his face. She was disheveled but now merely damp instead of soaking wet.

"Are you alright?" he asked.

She gave him a tight smile and nodded. Emin watched nearby, huddled under a blanket.

"Did you rebandage my wrist?" he asked. Their scrutiny was too much. "You're going to run out of bandaging at this rate."

"So stop making me use it." Her voice wavered.

"I will try." Taunos groaned as he sat up. Everything ached as if he'd been pummeled by boulders.

"You're going to ruin your arm for good at this rate. And your lung collapsed again." Amanah's tone held deep currents of worry. "You were out all night. If you don't stop and let yourself heal, you're going to get an infection. With all that sea water, you might already have."

He took her trembling hands in his. "Thank you."

She threw her arms around him, burying her face in his neck.

Taunos held her, stroking her back, leaning his head against hers. "I'm here. And I'm alive, thanks to you, again."

"You jumped into an ocean for me and Emin."

"Of course I did."

"That salve only makes your bandages water resistant, you know. Not waterproof." She whispered into his shoulder, holding him as if she'd never let him go, and he hoped she never would. He kissed her ear, running his fingers through her damp, frizzy braids, his breathing matched with hers. Her words kept flowing like a jar unstoppered. "That big heart of yours? I love it. I love how you're always trying to help people. But it also terrifies me, because I don't want to see it get you killed."

Amanah pulled back and rested her forehead against his. "You don't always have to be the hero, you know."

He closed his eyes, their breaths mingling, her nearness more intoxicating than the fiercest firewater. What was he if he wasn't the hero? If he set that aside and the Elders and all of it, what use then were his gifts? Was he enough if he was just… him?

"Where are the Sea Peoples? We got away?" he asked.

"They're gone," Emin said.

"Sea Peoples are formidable sailors even in storms, but the force of the waves still makes them lose their bearings," Skir said. He sat nearby, his head bandaged. "It lets us slip past them."

"You're a sea-wizard," the captain said, stepping into the hold. "For real, not just joking."

Amanah pulled back, her stance ready next to Taunos. The other sailors crowded around, and the ship drifted, sail down, oars locked, and rudder tied in place. All eyes were on Taunos.

The captain dropped a blanket across his shoulders. "You three showed real mettle. We would have lost a great deal if our sailor had drowned."

"You didn't even try to save him. Why?" Amanah's tone bordered on accusation.

"Too risky, especially since you three were already in." The captain waved his hand as if to wave away her words.

"Why?" Taunos asked. "The Ifreesian I know would have jumped in just as quickly as we did to save a life. Why didn't you?"

The captain shifted, and then he sat down with them, his movement abrupt, as if too much hesitation would cause him to change his mind. He cleared his throat. "We don't normally share our secrets, but without you, we would have lost much potential." He took a deep breath. "All right. Here's what we do. The rules are simple. We take turns. You can either tell one secret truth, or you can arm wrestle for the chance to avoid it. If you win, it's the next person's turn. If you lose, you have to tell two secret truths."

"And if I do not play?" Taunos asked.

"You don't get to learn about Ifreesians." The captain smiled. "Come now. We would learn more about sea-wizards."

Taunos met him stare for stare. "I could ask someone else, if you're not in a sharing mood."

Beside him, Igri bellowed a laugh, and Taunos winced, rubbing his ear. The sailors ringed them in, shoulder to shoulder, a wall of will against his.

The captain shook his head. "Don't you know by now, after watching us all this time, so desperate for our secrets? We Ifreesians are a team. You can't go around me because we all stand together."

Taunos raked a hand through his hair, hating that he'd been seen through so obviously. "Who's to say someone doesn't lie?"

The captain's eyes glittered. "Liars get dunked in the sea."

Taunos hesitated.

"You can't possibly be serious," Amanah said. "You can barely stand up straight."

"Let me do it," Emin said.

His instincts roared within him, ready for the challenge, to prove himself, to not let this chance pass by. And yet, Amanah was right. The words lay heavy on his tongue.

She stooped, taking his shoulders in her hands as if she meant to shake sense into him. "Let us help you. Let us in."

He drew in a deep breath and passed his hand over his face. "Fine."

The captain grinned, shoving a crate between himself and Emin.

Amanah let out a breath, wrapping her arms around him. She leaned her head on his shoulder. "Thank you."

Taunos pushed aside the sense of loss that crept up on him. There was no reason not to accept their help in this game, and plenty of reason to allow them. Knowing more about the Ifreesians, more about Takiyah's people, that was a worthy prize, to be able to tell her what he learned. And Emin seemed eager for the contest, and he was more than capable.

Taunos closed his eyes, relishing Amanah's warmth, wishing he could stay forever, to never have to leave her side. If only he weren't torn in two.

It was odd, now that he looked for it. Normally by now, he'd be longing to return home. But now, that desire was entirely in his mind, and even then full of questions. How could he stay loyal to the Elders when they proved so faithless? A wash of a forest-scented breeze poured over him, washing away his cares as easily as the wave had washed Skir off the boat.

The captain slapped the crate with one meaty hand. "I go first. I'll tell one truth. What would you like to know?"

"You know I'm a sea-wizard," Taunos said. "What do you know of them?"

The captain laughed. "Nice try. I will tell you one thing." He considered him quietly for a while before continuing. "You're not just any sea-wizard. We don't remember you, but we do remember a name, Naransyn. Our memories aren't what they were."

"Naransyn? What does that mean?" Amanah asked.

"Collecting more names, Haari?" Emin teased.

"I don't know." Taunos stared at the captain. That would require more questions, clearly.

The captain grinned. "Your turn. Why do you keep asking about the Sea Peoples?"

"They stole away a friend of ours," Amanah said. "I want to rescue her."

The captain sat back. "That's a terrible idea. The Sea Peoples are dangerous quarry, even for a sea-wizard. And at this rate, this will be a boring game."

Emin leaned forward. "Tell us something else about sea-wizards."

"Purely for the sake of the game, I pass." With a daring light in his eyes, the captain set his elbow on the crate.

Emin gripped his meaty hand in his, staring with challenge at the larger man. Igri reached across to steady their hands and then let go with a flourish, and immediately the captain pressed against him. Taunos held Amanah's hand, watching the contest with tension as if he were the one wrestling. Emin strained, fighting with everything he had, but the captain soon slammed his arm down on the crate. With a wince, Emin shook out his hand.

"Not bad," the captain said. "Now, it's my turn, I believe. You know the term Naransyn. I saw it in your face. Now tell us."

"You don't know? You're the one who mentioned it," Taunos objected.

The captain shook his head. "I told you, we don't remember. It just flashed in my head and Igri's and even Frul's when we saw you using your sea-wizardry."

"Telekinesis."

"Sure. That."

"What do you mean, it flashed in your head?"

"Don't be cheating now. Talk, or your friend here goes swimming." The captain cleared his throat, the smug look on his face reminding Taunos that he'd shown how much Emin and Amanah meant to him when he'd leaped out of a perfectly good boat to help them.

Taunos hastened to answer. "Ah, Naransyn. I don't know, not really. But my people have an old legend of Naran, who took a group of people to scout new places to live. They all disappeared in the mountains without a trace."

"Naransyn," Amanah mused. "Naran's son?"

"But Naran didn't have children." Taunos shook his head.

Emin slapped the crate, perched on the edge of the crate. "My turn. Answer Taunos's question. What do you mean, it flashed in your head?"

"Well, being as I'm stronger than you, I pass." The captain set his elbow on the crate again, wiggling his fingers.

Emin clasped his hand with a glower. Igri steadied their hands and then let go again, and Emin threw himself into the contest. He leveraged his strength against the captain's, bracing himself against the crate and waiting for the captain to tire. The moment the Ifreesian's hand shifted, Emin threw himself forward, and the captain's hand hit the crate.

Flushed with exhilaration, Emin laughed, and Taunos cheered, caught up in the simplicity of the competition, the challenge of it, even if he wasn't directly involved. It'd been a long time since he'd had such a pure contest in front of him.

The captain accepted his loss with grace, laughing and clapping Emin on the back. "Genetic memory. My grandparents' memories passed to my parents and theirs pass to me, but we have to waken the memories through experience in order to remember them. That's why we couldn't risk ourselves to save Skir. This is my last voyage, mine and Igri's. We've woken all the memories we're likely to wake, while Skir has only just started."

Taunos gazed around at the ring of Ifreesians. The captain and Igri were the bulkiest of the Ifreesians, their broad shoulders almost cumbersome with their height, while Skir was lithe... much like Takiyah had been before their ordeal in Codr. Before she began remembering so many new things.

"So that's why you couldn't jump in the ocean," Amanah said. "You couldn't risk losing more memories?"

The captain nodded. "If the memories aren't wakened through experience, they don't get passed on accurately. But if you're dead before you have children, those memories don't get passed on at all."

Taunos stared at him. That must be what was going on with Takiyah, how she'd figured out the machines with the Kamalti, the way she built her own forge and worked metal, even though no Rinaryn knew such things. How different might her genetic memories be from these sailors', since she'd had such different experiences?

"You have something else to tell us," Emin prompted. "Since I won."

"Tell us something else about sea-wizards," Amanah said.

"Let's see... the next node of the nexus is in the Hinanur Empire."

Taunos blinked. "What?"

"The nexus." Frowning at him like he was stupid, the captain grabbed one of the nets and shook it.

Taunos shook his head, at a loss. There'd be a net in the Hinanur Empire? Why would that be important at all?

The captain blew out his breath. "You're a sea-wizard, and you don't know about the nexus. Well, there goes that theory."

"I'm here if you're planning to talk sensibly anytime."

Instead, the captain clapped him on the shoulder. "Take care, little sea-wizard. If you don't know about the nexus, for all the gods' sake, stay far away from the Sea Peoples."

"Are these answers supposed to make sense?" Taunos asked.

The captain grinned. "It makes perfect sense. And now, it's your turn. What do you want from the Hinanur Empire, if not the nexus?"

"Knowledge," Taunos said.

He tsked. "You have to do better than that."

"I heard a story, and the character sounded like my mother," Taunos said. "I need to know more. If she was there. And if so, why?"

The captain grinned. "The past does get messy, doesn't it?"

It did. It was as if he were caught in a web of secrets and lies, not just his own, but from his mother, from Galod, from the Elders. And all the while, he simply wanted to keep his people safe because most of them were good and decent people and he loved his land. He loved his sister, and his sister loved their land, too. And while the Sea Peoples were surely a danger, so might these Ifreesians be, with their sailing skills, that genetic memory... The Ifrreesians must have been close to Rinara before, since Takiyah had miraculously floated to safety, to be raised among them.

"What is the most dangerous sea you know?" Taunos asked. Perhaps he could gauge if they knew of Rinara, for he himself had never learned of a sea quite as impassible as that around his land.

The captain sat back. "The Mouth of the Grave."

Taunos raised his eyebrows. "You'll have to do better than that."

"To the south." The captain's gaze was intent on him. "Do you know the constellation of Malaliyne?"

He nodded.

"When you're near the Mouth, the moons pass through the circle of Malaliyne's arms one moon before the spring stars-falling."

Malaliyne was the Dahuti name for the pattern of stars the Rinaryn called Kalei after the legends surrounding that figure. He and Amanah had found those similarities before.

A shiver ran through him, and he suppressed it, squeezing Amanah's hand tightly. Rinara. The Mouth had to be near Rinara for that to be true. Perhaps the Mouth of the Grave was what they called Dead Man's Sea. And in that case, they could find his home, and with their skill, who knew? Perhaps they could actually navigate Dead Man's Sea.

The captain's eyes remained sharp, as if he saw through Taunos's layers of casual pretending. "And where are your people that you fear the Sea Peoples but don't know them?"

Taunos gritted his teeth. They were too near the truth, and he had no idea of their intentions. He'd said too much already—if the Ifreesians found his home, any damage they did would be because of him. He embraced the Ifreesians' slippery words. "Not here. Secret. Safe."

He waited, the wind whisking away his words. Had it been enough? It had probably been too much. Galod would surely be livid if he knew the risk he'd taken.

The captain reached out and clapped him on the shoulder. "I understand that. All Ifreesians do. The Sea Peoples and many others would love to find our dwarrows and raid them. We keep home safe by keeping it secret."

Taunos nodded.

"And now, I have a ship to run." With that, he got up and moved on, leaving Taunos reeling in his wake. Secrets for secrets, shared in the understanding that they now depended on each other. It was a rickety trust, and he wasn't sure he'd found out enough from it.

As the sailors dispersed to various tasks, Amanah took Taunos's good hand in both of hers. She grinned at him. "You did it. Not so hard, is it?"

Emin laughed. "More practice like that and you might one day be able to really work as a team instead of just in loose association with others."

267

It struck too near what Olorah had said. Taunos scowled. "I keep being told that I'm bad at working in teams."

"You are," Emin said.

He frowned.

Amanah snorted a laugh. "Why do you think Emin always gave you the scouting tasks?"

"Because I'm good at it."

She sighed. "And no one can work with you. Your presence on Emin's team helped lift him to celebrity status, it's true, and your skill gave the new recruits courage. Everyone wanted to work on the band you were on, but no one wanted to work with you."

"I work fine in teams," Taunos objected.

"That's why you looked like you were sitting on a chair made of daggers the whole time I was doing the contest for you, huh?" Emin asked.

Taunos bit back his response. It had been hard for him to let go, even though of all the people in the world, if he could trust anyone, it would be them. And still, he felt as if he were walking on a precipice after the Ifreesians' revelation.

He let out his breath. This paranoia, this distrust, was the result of so many summers being the hero, taking on the challenges, carrying the demands of his people on his own two shoulders. The priest in Codr had noticed, before the chapel fell and killed him. *Who put these burdens on you? Set them down.*

And yet he didn't know how to let it go—or even if he should.

"It'll be all right, Taunos." Amanah's eyes were intense as she gripped his hands in hers. "You don't have to do it all alone."

Chapter Twenty

Dragons are fiercely territorial, and the desert is theirs. The only shining beacon in the wasteland is the City of Tamarik, for all the rest of the inhabitants are bandits, hunted by dragons and Angels.

—*scrap of paper from the City of Tamarik*

The next morning, Takiyah woke up parched, sore, and hungry. Stepping out of her door, she shaded her eyes from the sun. There was no food in her house, but she had to go to the market anyway to check on the goods and get her share from Varen. Then she wanted to look at Rothan's new axle model he was working on, and finally begin planning a road.

It was difficult to go anywhere though, for she'd barely gone two blocks before strangers began to accost her, and it only grew worse, until she had a whole crowd of people around her asking questions.

"I heard you shot fire and scared away a whole band of bandits."

"Are you going back to the other city? Is it really real?"

"How did you escape the dragons?"

"What about the Angels?"

The questions, the people crowding her, all ratcheted up the tension until she could hardly breathe. She turned, trying to find a path forward, but all she saw were questioning faces and reaching hands. It was dizzying.

"Enough," she cried.

"How do you like being a hero, Takiyah?" Varen asked.

Latching onto his voice, she shoved her way to his side. "What did you do?"

He laughed, lounging against the empty wagon which still sat where she'd left it. "Nothing. This is all your doing. I finished the last of the trades just now. Here's your half."

She caught the large pouch he tossed her and scowled, not happy with counting her coins in front of a crowd such as this, but the need to make sure Varen hadn't made a mistake in his math won out. She quickly peered into the bag then tied it shut again.

"This is quite a bit." She narrowed her eyes at him.

"When are you going back to the city?" shouted someone in the crowd, and the question was taken up by others, roaring it at her, shouting out goods they wanted transported.

She waved her hands, taking advantage of her height to point at Varen. "Ask him—he has the ledgers. He'll take your information down and give you a price for carrying."

"What do you think, four wagons this time?" Varen asked. "Can we do that?"

Takiyah shrugged. "It's worth a try. I have things to do to prepare."

"One moon to the next transport," Varen shouted, and Takiyah sighed in relief as the crowd turned their focus on him instead of her.

She waded through the streets. Things had changed, and she wasn't sure how she felt about it. Fewer people grumbled at her in the streets. Some actually asked her questions about the City of the Lost or about the schedule for the wagons, though she always directed them to Varen. Who could have guessed that one trip to and from another city with trade goods could change the thinking of the people so much?

No, she couldn't keep lying to herself. She shook her head.

The people hadn't changed—she had. The City of the Lost had shown her a road, and now she was set on building a new one, literally and figuratively. She would work to help the city, to make up for the wrong she'd done them.

But there were still many issues to solve before the next trip to the City of the Lost. Not just the bandits—other Fallen, like her, so could she really call them bandits? And yet, that's how they acted, so bandits it was. Then there was the apparent threat of dragon attacks and the wheels getting stuck in the mud in the rainy season.

"You did a good thing for the people of Tamarik." Pek fell into step beside her.

She glanced at him. "How did you find me?"

"Oh, it wasn't hard. You're well on your way to becoming a hero. I'm so proud." He grinned, the grin he used when he was purposefully being excessive.

She shook her head. "Don't mock me. It didn't work anyway. It needs to be better."

"You got the wagon back home."

"I wasn't going to bring it most of the way and then let it sit just outside the gates."

"Exactly. That's why I'm proud of you. You could have let it sit. You finished the job anyway."

"I don't care if you're proud of me." The scathing tone she used should have blistered him. Should have covered the warming of her heart, betraying her words. How could he say that when she'd betrayed her parents, who she wanted most of all to make proud?

"Still so unwilling to open up just a little? I think it's a costume as if for a play. After all, your hard work benefits those you hate, as well as... do you love anyone?"

Her heart twisted at his words. And yet she couldn't ignore it, not in the face of the disappointed faces her parents would wear if they saw her. "I don't... hate. I was afraid, and I was wrong. I want to make it better."

She shook her head. Words weren't enough. She quickened her pace.

"Where are you going?" Pek asked.

"I have to make it better."

The mouth-watering scents of the grills a few blocks over filled her nose. She visited them first, ordering a few fish-on-a-sticks, then went to grab a pickaxe from Rothan and then back to her house for supplies. It was harder than ever to move through the crowd, so by the time she was ready, it was dusk and the nightbirds were singing their evening tunes. She slipped out of the gates as the guard began closing them.

"Hey!" he shouted.

She turned back.

"Don't you want to come back in? It's nighttime!"

"If I wanted to be inside, don't you think I would be inside?" she asked.

The guard frowned at her. "I'm closing up. You won't be able to get back in."

"Oh, well, in that case," she said, rolling her eyes. He hesitated, and Takiyah scowled. "Close the gate."

Shaking her head, she stomped away, across the moonlit sands. The air was chilly in the evening, and the salt air from the sea still called to her. She shouldered her pack, eyed the mountains in the distance, and headed around the city walls to the cliffs instead.

Rothan found her as the sun's heat began to really tell in the day. Still riding high on the elation of such focused exertion during the chill of the night, she dreaded the need to stop soon. But if she didn't, the heat would get to her, and her muscles were exhausted. Unfortunately, Rothan also had Tamarik guards with him, and they stopped to shake their heads and point at the stones she'd laid down in front of the gate for several paces.

One of the guards kicked at the stones.

"Should I kick your guardhouse?" With a scowl, she dumped the next stone into place and dusted off her hands. Stooping to catch a handful of sand, she let the grains stream down over and around it before blasting some fire over top of that. It didn't really do much, for her fire wasn't hot enough to melt the sand, but at least it made it goopy for a bit. She'd need to come up with a better way to put something between the stones. Something deep within her told her she was close, so deliciously close.

It was like water just out of reach of a dehydrated man, and a mirage was distracting her.

The guards folded their arms, except for one who stepped forward with his hand on his baton. "You can't be doing this."

"What is it?" Rothan asked.

Takiyah gave him a level look. "It's a road. Why can't I build a road?"

Baton-man's own idiocy apparently surprised him. "Because! You can't just... build a road!"

"What section of the law is that in?" a familiar voice asked, and Takiyah groaned. She didn't want to be saved by Pek yet again.

The guards straightened, and Baton-man opened his mouth again. "But surely, Pek, surely it's not allowed for people to just build roads."

"Has it ever been a problem before?" he asked.

"No, but..."

Takiyah tuned them out, hauling the next stone into place.

Pek continued. "It's her folly. She's not hurting anything, and anyway, the people of the city love her right now. If you annoy her, it'll annoy them."

"That doesn't—"

"Do you expect many people will join Takiyah here in working all alone at night to better the city?"

The knot of unease loosened as she worked. Building felt right. The shovel in her hands smoothing the sand for the stones felt right, and the way the pickaxe sat as she used it, hacking apart the rocks into manageable chunks. Finally, once again, she was making something, leaving the world better for her presence, but she wasn't doing it for praise.

"But where by the Printak would you even go? There's nothing out here worth building a road to."

"To the City of the Lost. You want more goods traded?" she asked. Yes, it was probably ridiculous, but she was going to do it anyway, partially because no one else would.

"Where did you steal these rocks from?" the guard asked.

She leaned against the pickaxe and stared at him. "Who says I stole them? Why do I have to have stolen them?"

"Where did they come from, though?" Rothan asked, still inspecting her road critically but with far too much awe in his voice.

"I cut them from the cliff and dragged them over." Takiyah set the stone with a grunt and scattered sand on it, spraying fire over it.

"You cut stone, dragged them here, and made a road two paces long all in the span of one night?" Baton-man asked. "Impossible. You must have had help."

Takiyah narrowed her eyes at him. Her leg was more capable now, even if it burned from the all-night exertion. That shouldn't count against her. Besides, she'd wanted to harvest stone from the mountains, but they were too distant.

"Takiyah is very determined." Pek grinned at her. "And it keeps her out of trouble."

"I need to come up with a more efficient way to haul the stone," Takiyah said, dusting her hands off and looking for the next piece. It wasn't there. She was done for now. She frowned. Well, now what?

"What you need is to come inside and get a drink, some food, and some sleep," Rothan said.

What she needed was not to be told what to do. "Shouldn't you be at the smithy?"

"What, you get to break the bounds of social expectations and I can't?" he asked.

She shook her head at him, a smile coming to her despite herself.

"We should think about getting you more help, too," Pek said. "We can't expect you to build an entire road by yourself."

"You're really going all the way to the City of the Lost?" Rothan asked.

Takiyah nodded. "The wagons won't break down as much if they're on a road, and the travel will be faster, which means less risk."

"Or more, since the bandits will know where to strike," a guard muttered.

Takiyah bit her tongue against a scathing retort. "The caravan will have to have guards anyway, and most of the desert has clear views for large spans. We should be able to see them before they're on us."

"We're forgetting something," Baton-man said.

Pek nodded. "Dragons."

Takiyah shrugged. "What about them?"

"The road will call them. They'll destroy it."

"Well, whatever is left will still help." Except the dragons were *not* going to destroy her road. She refused to let them.

"Why are you so insistent on doing this?" Rothan asked.

"Because I can. Because it's beautiful. Because it's useful, and I made it."

"You could build something else."

"If I wanted to build something else, I would." Takiyah shook her head, gathering her supplies. She looked at her road, something fierce burning in her. Even knowing it might be destroyed, she couldn't stop. She couldn't stop until it was done.

"Get some sleep, and I'll see about getting you help," Pek said.

Takiyah rounded on him, fists clenching. This was her gift to Tamarik, her way of making up for targeting them with her rage and pain. If others helped, it lessened the strength of her penance. "I don't want help, old man."

"You're getting it anyway. Can't have you getting all the glory. Just most of it."

When Takiyah woke up hours later, Pek was at her house with a freshly baked meat pie and two flagons of beer. She shook her head as she let him in and stepped away to splash water on her face and brush her short hair back into some semblance of order. "What are you doing, old man?"

"You need to keep your strength up. Working at night is smart."

"Oh yes, and I needed you to tell me that."

"You know, you could just accept the compliment for a change of pace."

She blinked at him then turned to the meat pie and dug in.

He pulled out the chair across the table and sat. "You need more men, or you'll never get to the City of the Lost."

"Men, huh?"

"The guards suggested prisoners. They can work off their debt, make something of themselves. Maybe learn something."

No. No, no, no. She refused to let that happen again. Not to her, not to anyone.

"No," she snapped. "No one works against their will."

He sat back. "And what if they volunteer to lessen their sentence?"

"No coercion," she snarled.

Pek watched her with those eyes that saw too much, and he nodded.

"They won't be mistreated. No chains, no branding, no whips. They get enough to eat, plenty to drink, rest when needed. They sleep on soft beds at night, no floors. No other work. No work when the sun is high, either, so they don't suffer from the heat. And nothing happens to them if they don't volunteer. Of their own free will." She was standing, panting. When had that happened?

Leaning back in his chair, Pek smiled faintly. "More and more, the people will esteem you, Takiyah."

"I don't care about that." She dropped back into her seat.

"Even more how you're changing. Thinking of others."

"Give it a rest, Pek. I wasn't a monster."

"No, you were hurt. And now I think I see how."

"You don't know anything," she grunted, slumping. "I just want to eat in peace."

"Thank you, Pek, for bringing me supper when I slept the whole day," he mocked her.

She shook her head, rising to his gentle jesting. "As you yourself said, I'm working for the betterment of the city. Bringing me food's the least you can do."

"Careful now, girlie." His eyes sparked as she threw his words back at him, but his mouth quivered with a suppressed smile.

She snickered, quieting it by stuffing more food in her mouth. It was good, she had to admit. Perfectly seasoned, cooked to perfection. Still hot, too, which kind of annoyed her. How did he guess how long she'd sleep?

Pek tilted his head. "Why does it bother you so much when I point out how much you're changing?"

"Why do you point it out so much?"

"Because it bothers you, of course," he said, eyes twinkling.

She snorted. She should have seen that one coming. "Now all I have to do to prove I'm reformed is save a wayward Kamalti child from a runaway cart or something."

Pek waved her words away. "That sort of thing is only in stories. Bad ones, at that."

Takiyah slurped down the last of the juices of the meat pie and handed the plate back to Pek. "I need to see about a better way to transport the stone."

"You never answered my question."

"Because I should have done it before, all right?" She grabbed her water pouch to refill on her way and her pack of supplies and then paused at the door. Looking back, she opened her mouth then grinned, shook her head, and left without actually properly thanking him.

His laughter followed her out.

It surprised her, how light her heart was. For the first time in a long, long time, she was almost… happy. No one had held her back, only herself.

She'd chosen fear when she could have chosen wonder. Her good mood continued as a woman pressed a wrapped bundle of bread and cheese into her hands when she stopped at the tavern to refill her water pouch.

She paused as a gust of wind swept past her, teasing her hair and filling her nose with the smell of the sea. The sea and its never-ending call... If the waves weren't so treacherous, she could go anywhere, bring blocks of stone easily from place to place.

Or, maybe she could harness the power of the wind like the sails of a boat.

Takiyah turned back toward the Crafting District. The sound of the forges comforted her, and she smiled at Rothan as he raised a hand in greeting. She kept going, past the forges, past the masons, until she found the craftspeople sewing great strips of cloth for sails.

She wandered into one such shop, frowning at the thick material. Sails were large and needed to be strong to withstand the winds, but she didn't want it to be too heavy or it'd be cumbersome. She needed a tiny "ship" to "sail" on, too, but first she wanted the sail to be right.

"What's the lightest, strongest cloth you have?" she asked.

By the time she reached home again, she was humming. The realization amused her, but she kept it up as she sewed the cloth around the light metal pole she'd found. She'd bought a few different metals, and she tested each, trying to bend them, until she was left with two good candidates. She sewed a length of cloth around each, fashioning herself two sails.

She needed somewhere to carry cargo, of course—that was the whole reason for this. The ground was too rocky for the sledges the kaetaln used when going to Feasts. A small wagon made more sense. Finally, she bundled everything securely and set it in the corner. If she could glide with the wind, she'd be able to bring rocks back and forth much more easily and quickly.

She'd need a cross pole like ships had so she wouldn't need to hold the rope to keep the sail taut. And she'd need something to help hold the pole up so the wind wouldn't pull it out of her grasp.

Clearly, she needed a forge.

Eagerness filled her with giddy energy such that she feared she wouldn't be able to sleep, though she laid down anyway. But when she opened her eyes, it was morning. Time to pay a visit to Rothan.

"Rothan!" Takiyah called as she strode into the entryway. She waited there while he finished beating on a piece of metal and thrust it back into the fire.

"Bellows," he said.

She didn't work here anymore, but she couldn't help but grin as she piled her bundle in the corner. She pulled the lever slow and steady, watching him for cues as to what he needed, while he reached in with tongs and turned the piece in the fires. She'd missed this, the forge work. Maybe even the company, honestly.

"What do you need?" Rothan pulled the metal from the fires and picked up his hammer.

Between rings of the hammer on the metal, she told him of her plan. The rhythm of the forge tempered her enthusiasm, creating a longer, stronger burn, just as tempering metal created a stronger tool. He grinned at her over his shoulder as they worked, turning a lump of metal into a shovel topped with a decorative curl.

"I missed this," he said, as he let the metal cool and wandered over to the water barrel for a drink. He offered her the ladle.

"Yeah?" she asked, slurping down a mouthful.

"You and your ideas, you and me working the forge together. Didn't think you'd be back."

"Me either."

"Did you miss it?"

Takiyah rubbed her forehead. "Has anyone told you that you are very needy?"

Rothan grinned. "That shovel you just helped me make? It's for a Kamalti customer."

She shrugged. She'd trapped herself when she'd embraced the betrayal and fear. It had been her the whole time. "Good."

The pride on his face dimmed a bit with wariness. "Takiyah, if I give you access to the forge again, you need to be all right with my customers, whatever they look like."

"Fine," she said.

"Even if they're Kamalti."

"Rothan, sands alive, man, what do you want from me? I said fine!"

"After the way you left—"

"I just want to try my idea. This could be an amazing opportunity. Can you imagine flying across the sands like the boats across the water? I want... I need to make things right, and that means making things better."

He grinned. "Good. Rent is this: one piece of work for a Kamalti customer per week while you are here."

She narrowed her eyes. "Any piece?"

"For any customer with clear Kamalti heritage, yes."

It was more than fair, especially for the secrets she was unlocking from the sand and the wind. A new way to travel.

Takiyah nodded. "Done. Can I show you now?"

"Are you sure?"

"If you make me repeat myself one more time, I'm going to beat your head with your own hammer until it can actually hold some brains."

Rothan laughed and walked over to her. "I believe you."

"You sure?" she shot back at him.

He grinned. "Sure. All right, let's look at this."

Over the next few days, Takiyah refined her design little by little, hauling stone and working on her road at night. She borrowed Rothan's forge daily, adjusting the height of the wheels to keep the cart low, yet able to glide over the rocks and grass that grew in patches on the hard ground. Soon enough, she had a small, light sled on top of wide wheels.

She took Rothan with her on the last trial, once she was pretty sure it would work. It was hard to celebrate when you were the only one in the world that knew of your own brilliance. So she and Rothan set out carrying the contraption, climbing the hill outside the city gates of Tamarik.

She slotted the pole into the attachment on the sled, turned the pins to anchor it securely, and then stepped one foot on board. Grinning, she waved at Rothan.

"You're out of your mind," he shouted, laughing.

"Watch this," she shouted back.

Takiyah hauled open the sail, stepped onto the board, and flew.

The board bucked, and she wobbled, but crouching low, she skimmed across the dusty ground, zooming down the hill so fast tears blurred her vision. Whooping and hollering and laughing, she stayed low as the board continued on uphill, cresting another hill. The land evened out, but the wind still had the sail, and though the wheels slowed significantly, she was still sailing. She looked back, laughing and waving at Rothan, who despite running after her, was being left behind.

Memory wakened in her, and she hauled the lines, cautiously at first, then more confidently as her sled turned.

This was the way to travel. Wind in her face, skimming across the sand, even though she couldn't let herself go too far yet. She didn't want to be stranded, especially with the toll the walk would put on her leg. And of course, it only worked while there was wind, but there was most days.

And what a feeling! She pulled on the rope, angling the sail, and slowed to a crawl as she turned back toward the city. She tried tacking, like she'd seen the boats do in the harbor, but they also had oars, which she lacked. Soon enough, the craft upturned, and she sat on the sandy dirt laughing. It was close to what she expected from the memories buried deep inside her.

Almost. She was still laughing as she dusted herself off and checked the sail and rigging for breakages. Rothan jogged up to her as she was untangling the lines.

"You," he gasped breathlessly, "are fearless. How did you make that? You were sailing like a ship, only the dirt was your sea."

That was exactly it, she realized, the tug of the sea calling to her again.

She was meant to be on the sea, doing things like this. Building roads was part of it, too. Just building. There was more, but it was hazy, still beyond her reach.

"It's like, the more things I try, the more I learn about myself, about who I am. It's like all these things are locked away inside of me and all I have to do is remember them." She laughed. "Wasn't it amazing?"

"Needs work, but yes. Yes, it was. When's my turn?"

"When you make your own." She grinned at the expression on his face and fell over, laughing giddily. Soon enough, he joined her, a huge smile splitting his face.

Once they'd sobered, he nudged her board. "Is this what you're planning to use to bring the blocks over? You said there had to be a better way."

She nodded. "I might need a bigger sail. And a bigger plank of wood or metal."

Rothan shook his head. "I still don't understand how you come up with these things."

"It just makes sense." She shrugged and slid the board closer to him. "Try it."

He grinned at her in return and stepped onto the little platform, while she showed him how to work the lines that ran the sail. And then, he was off, down the hill, before he lost his balance halfway down and tipped the whole rig over.

Laughing, she jogged down to him.

"Here, you get on, too," he said. "This is meant to haul stone, right? It should be able to hold two people then."

"I need to make it better before I can haul stone with it," she argued. "And besides, you're terrible at this."

"What, it was my first time. And you fell, too."

"All right, but I work the sail. I think it will work better if we stay as close to the mast as possible."

"A mast—just like in a ship?" Rothan asked.

Takiyah shrugged again. It was just what had popped out of her mouth. "That's what it is, isn't it?"

"You have a point."

They made it four hills before falling over and six on the way back. In between, they tested the craft on the packed dry ground that most of the desert was made of, for it had to work there or it would do no good. Only a small section of the desert had hills, except near the mountains.

"I need a much bigger sail," Takiyah decided when they got back to the beginnings of her road. She slowed the craft to a stop, frowning at the line of people that stood on her road in the late afternoon sun. "Who are all these people?"

Pek grinned at her, stepping out from the crowd. "Mostly prisoners, with some guards to make sure no one runs or fights. They're here to help you out."

"Already? You only just told me this idea."

"And then I put it together."

She groaned. "I could just do it myself."

"Takiyah, it's an enormous project. You're talking about going all the way to the City of the Lost. Why can't you just accept help now and then?"

"I do."

"Name one instance."

"I got a free sandwich."

"Kind of help but more a gift. And you deserve more than that."

"Why? I haven't exactly been wonderful to be around."

"You don't really have an option."

"I know." She pressed her fist to her forehead. Couldn't he see that was the worst part? This was something she had started on her own, and now it had been co-opted right out from under her and she had no say in the matter at all. The simplicity was gone, and it was no longer just her giving back.

With the extra help, the road lengthened at an astounding pace. Already they had had to set up tents for the prisoners and guards, a moveable camp that continued along with the road, supplied with materials by wagons from Varen. It was amazing to see it come along, despite how it rankled that she didn't get to do all the work anymore.

She hadn't trusted prisoners not to be mistreated with mining, but

Varen had rounded up craftsmen and paid them to mine at the quarry—another new word that sent thrills up her when it had popped into her head. Rothan helped with hauling the rocks to the road using her sand-carts when he could, as did some of the miners. That left Takiyah overseeing the whole process, but rarely able to work in one place for long. Most of her time alone, she spent setting the boundaries for the next section of the road, for no one else instinctively knew the precise direction in which the City of the Lost lay. No one else could keep her road running arrow straight without the markers aiding them, and even then, they tended to fail to account for its width, making the road wiggle.

The work in tandem with the various people—mining, driving the carts, or building the road—eased some of the knot in her. It may not be just her project anymore, but maybe this was even bigger, letting go of the project to allow more people to work on it. It certainly hurt like a sacrifice, but watching how the people went to work cheerfully and how careful Pek's guards were to make sure everyone was well-rested and not over-heating warmed her heart.

The prisoners had mostly proven to be good workers, and they'd gotten a system worked out now, she thought. They got a chit a day when she said they'd done satisfactory work, and each chit reduced their sentence. If they ran instead, well, living as a bandit in the harsh desert was considered a fitting punishment. Those who worked got several rest periods throughout the day and plenty of fresh water. It meant the only time Takiyah was working alone was at night, and she was too tired most of the time to work for long on her own.

The piece of her that gave her knowledge glowed with the rightness of it, pricking at her. Once this was done, she needed to go back to the others—Rinaryn weren't meant to be alone either, and she was meant to be working with her friends.

As the days went on, the begrudging attitudes of the workers had shifted to respect. She taught them how to build the road and how to keep it running straight and level. Level was important, and though she could have curved the road to chase the shadows of the mountains, the straight line running through the sandy ground brought her thrills of joy. It also meant the shortest distance, which meant fewer trips to the quarry. Several of the men had picked up the techniques and worked at it with levels of dedication that rivaled her own, though all of them relied on her markers to keep the road from wavering. None of them simply *knew* where anything was.

The workers had no fire, but they spread the sand over the course of the road as they placed the stones. She'd coat it with her fire when she had a moment. It was a rhythm. She spread her fire until she tired, made sure the road was straight, checked on the next batch of materials, and then returned to spray more fire.

How to seal the road better?

The answer felt like it was *right there*. She just needed more time to find it.

While the others unloaded a cart, Takiyah picked up a stone and slotted it into place, tapping it until the surface was level. She spread the sand over it and then blasted it.

"Dragon!" one of the workers shouted.

Takiyah shaded her eyes, looking up. The shape in the sky was definitely a dragon, wheeling and coming straight for them. For her road. She hadn't even finished it yet! And the prisoners were in the path, in danger.

Fury rose in her. It wasn't smart, but she couldn't help herself, possessed by wrath.

"Get to cover!" the guards shouted, running.

The dragon blasted fire, burning the ground and coming straight toward her. She gritted her teeth and thrust out her hands, streaming fire right back at him.

Amazingly, the dragon banked sharply, his fire guttering. The ground smoked and smoldered only paces away.

Takiyah glanced behind her, where the workers and guards raced toward the city, most of the guards huddling under cover. She narrowed her eyes at them, marking the guards' faces well. She would not allow them back on her work site, no matter how loud she had to be to make that happen. Anyone cowardly enough to run when they should be protecting others deserved to lose their jobs.

A thump on the ground nearly shook her from her feet. She straightened, her breath catching in her throat.

The dragon had landed several paces from her, but that was still too close. He loomed, casting a shadow that stretched all the way to her, with his huge wedge-shaped head pointed at her.

Gritting her teeth, she refused to let her body tremble and walked toward the dragon a few more paces. She stopped where she could still look at him without craning her neck too far and crossed her arms. "What do you want?'

The dragon lowered his head, revealing a rider straddling his neck about halfway up, between two spikes. The rider shouted down at her,

"You are Ifreesian."

The word thrummed through her, and she blinked rapidly as memory loosened inside of her, stirred and roused and made ready to drown her. Impressions of sailing, of mining, of building roads and walls and other great structures. It stopped short of memories, settling back down to slumber.

But it was answer enough.

Her body moved of its own accord, taking the stance of the statue in Codr that she'd seen outside of the Justice chambers, the one of the man with fire, the woman with the wild hair, and the child-sized tinkerer. Feet spread, hand raised in front of her, level with her chest, palm upward, just as it appeared on the man. She smiled, accepting the nudge of memory inside of her and letting a flame dance on her hand.

Ifreesian. That's what Eian had said, looking at the statues.

"I am Ifreesian." And then, one more time, because it felt so good and it was so *right*. "*I am Ifreesian!*"

"You didn't know?" The rider chuckled. "How crippled your mind is! And it stinks of fae."

The dragon reeled his head back, snorting. Takiyah narrowed her eyes at them, lowering her hand. Was the rider speaking for the dragon?

"I haven't had any dealings with the fae," she said, uncertainty creeping into her voice.

"Your people keep returning to the island," the dragon's rider shouted. Or maybe it was the dragon, speaking through the rider? It didn't really matter. "The fae won't let you have it."

She spat. "I don't care what the fae want."

Something deep and powerful built up inside of her, similar to the feeling she got when she thought of Hardy and Mettle and what they had done to her.

The dragon's rider laughed. "I can't kill the fae in your mind without killing your mind, little wayward Ifreesian."

"I don't care," she spat again. "Don't ruin my road. And certainly don't hurt the workers. They are not at fault!"

"You force others to your folly?" the dragon's rider asked. For some reason, she was becoming increasingly convinced the dragon was speaking through the rider.

"My folly inspired others to, in their folly, force the folly of others."

The rider laughed. "We don't allow roads in the desert."

"You find something beautiful, something delicate. Now, you have a choice. Do you add to it or destroy it? What you decide says something, I think," she said. Tamarik had taught her much. The dragons couldn't destroy Tamarik, and she wasn't going to let them destroy her road, either. "Besides, it's not yours."

"The desert is ours. Did the people from the city on the sea not teach you this?"

"You're not using it," Takiyah argued. Maybe she should have listened. But she wasn't going to accept this without a fight.

"Does that matter? We claim this territory. Why should we care if you see us use it or approve of our use?" The dragon's neck arched.

"I'll build it again," Takiyah said, unable to back down with the stubbornness rising in her to a swell. "The City of the Lost and Tamarik need to be able to trade with each other."

"And that justifies this?"

"No?" she asked, uncertain. But she shrugged. "But it's my reason for doing it."

"If you will not stop, I can just eat you." Yes, the rider was definitely talking for the dragon. Otherwise that was somehow even more creepy.

"You're a dragon. I suspect you'll do what you want to do." She paused. "But tell me something. You know of Ifreesians. You say the fae won't let my people have this land back. We came from here?"

The rider laughed. "It's not my place to tell you your past."

Her eyes narrowed. "Then what exactly is your place, you overgrown lizard?"

The dragon lunged forward, and Takiyah held her ground, presenting her hands ready to funnel fire. It was folly, but she couldn't let it go. The road was a solid start, and it was straight and beautiful and hers.

"There's no reason to die here. You won't save anyone. I can eat you and all the rest."

"Maybe, but I'll at least have tried to stop you." That was another thing that felt right and true. Standing strong in the face of fear. Being the shield for others against the rain. Against... Against who, exactly?

She frowned. "You smelled fae in my mind? Why? How?"

The dragon rider chuckled. "You really know so little. The fae influence is everywhere, like a pestilence, in the minds of these people."

These people. The Rinaryn and the Kamalti. People like her parents. Rage boiled up in her. "I won't let them continue."

"Oh really? Little you against the entire might of the fae? You don't even know how they've had you dancing from strings."

"It ends now. And if I won't let you, a dragon, push me around, do you really think I'll be quelled by going up against the fae?"

"Hmm, probably not. But your presence here will anger the fae, and your short-lived battle against them will be amusing, and that is more than payment enough. We will let you build your road and watch for that sport. Only this road, however. No others."

Takiyah nodded. "Thank you."

Great gratitude welled in her.

"And little Ifreesian, find out who you are."

Chapter Twenty-one

Are the protectors secured? I cannot find the hero, so I assume the sending-
suggestion is still working. The dwarf is still in the desert. The mother remains
with the elves. The berserker will be in our grasp soon. Then, we may turn our
attention to the Tsaeyichape'itsan and let him ripen further before claiming him.
The cycles will end, and the gods will return.
                              —part of a missive from "Mebril" in Stonefield

Nearly a moon after their escape from Far Dahutad, several days after
their flight from the Sea Peoples and the storm had driven them off course,
they arrived at the Hinanur Empire. The captain had told them he was
going to drop them off before they reached the port, for there was
something they needed to see and the port could prove dangerous for the
Dahuti.

The coastline dipped inland, while at either end of the small shelter,
outcroppings stretched forward like open arms. The ship glided into the
cove, swapping sails for oars, and the Ifreesians ran the vessel almost right
up onto the land. The beach ran a handful of paces wide before giving way
to sparse grass stubbornly rising from the sandy ground.

Emin embraced Skir, taking his leave of the sailors he'd enjoyed the
company of so much. Taunos stood at the prow, thankful for the warm
wind and for Amanah next to him, fingers entwined in his. He had to
figure out what the Ifreesians had meant, how this "Naransyn" connected
to his people, if it did at all.

The captain approached, pointing to where the land rose ahead of
them. "If you head to the top of that hill, you'll find a node in the nexus."

"Thank you. For everything." Taunos clasped the captain's arm.

"Your secrets are as safe with us as ours are with you." It was both
promise and threat, and Taunos inclined his head, accepting it.

They jumped down to the sand with the tide washing at their feet, and
Frul handed them two bags packed with smoked fish, water pouches, and
bandages. "Be wary of the Sea Peoples."

"And of the dragons!" Igri shouted. With that, the ship pulled away
from shore.

Amanah picked up one pack, giving Emin the other, and looped her arm through Taunos's good arm.

"While we walk, we should prepare," Emin said. "We're in Hinanuri land, so it's important to know some things. More than you know, so shut that mouth, Taunos."

There was a serious tone underlying his teasing words—Emin was in war-band leader mode. Taunos gave him a nod and his attention, just as when he'd served under Emin.

"The Hinanuri are matriarchal. Their Empress may be at war with the Dahuti queen, but their nomadic tribes are still friendly with ours. We need to capitalize on that. So while we're here, no flaunting, no showing off. We stay only as long as we absolutely must, and it's imperative we do not offend anyone, especially any woman."

Amanah nodded, and Taunos quickly assented. His gaze on Emin lingered. "Are you all right with being here?"

"I'm interested in answers just like you are," Emin said. "But I also intend we leave with our heads still on our shoulders."

The three of them staggered to the top of the hill, and Emin and Amanah stared around them at the grassland that went on and on, as far as the eye could see. Taunos barely saw it or the tents circled off to their right. On top of a small mound, a white tree grew, its silver leaves glistening in the wind.

Another Seeker Tree.

Taunos fell to his knees, gaping. The tree was impossible. It dominated his attention, demanded all his focus.

It couldn't be here, too. Two Seeker Trees was impossible enough. And yet, there it was. How many more might there be?

A sharp intake of breath told him when Amanah saw it, too. "How can this be? The Gods' Tree is the only one of its kind."

"Not the only one," Taunos said, barely aware of the words coming from his mouth. "My people have one, too."

"Only one?" Amanah asked. "Why would there be only one in each place? That can't be. The species would never survive."

"If you head to the top of that hill, you'll find a node in the nexus," the Ifreesian captain had said.

The tree was part of some sort of net? That didn't make sense. And Amanah was right—they'd never be able to propagate so far from each other. And why not just call them trees?

"We have trouble coming," Emin said.

The words came from a distance, drowned out by the mystery before him. Taunos couldn't tear his eyes from the tree, even as Emin hoisted him to his feet and shoved him forward. His mind was caught in a whirlpool of questions without answer.

"Taunos, snap out of it!" The whipcrack of Emin's voice grabbed him from the current and dragged him back to the present. "Didn't you hear me? The Hinanuri are coming."

Several riders galloped toward them, presumably from the tent circle. Amanah and Emin spun to face them. Ah, yes, they would be used to fighting techniques against horses, as their family had a large herd of the beasts.

Keeping his thoughts firmly rooted to the present problem, Taunos fell into a half crouch. Amanah and Emin flowed like water, each grabbing a rider and hauling themselves astride behind. In a breath, while he dodged hooves, they each incapacitated the riders and tossed them to the ground, grabbing the reins to turn their mounts.

But they were still outnumbered.

As one of the horses charged straight at him, Taunos turned in a complicated dance, avoiding stamping hooves and nipping teeth. His side pulled, his leg ached, and he feared his lung would collapse again. The oncoming horse kept coming, though, and Taunos stretched out his hand, shoving hard at it telekinetically.

It reared, and a flash of pain hit him as a hand grabbed his wrist and hauled him over a cloth saddle. He twisted, but a blow to his splinted wrist sent darkness dousing his vision with agony.

He bellowed out the pain, slamming his elbow into the rider's stomach.

The rider spun the horse in a tight circle, flinging him off. Wind whistled past Taunos, and then he hit the ground hard, rolling to a stop. Hooves danced by his head, and he leaped back to his feet, stumbling as the world rocked around him.

"Taunos!" Amanah shouted.

He turned just in time to see another horse bearing down on him. He shoved at it with his telekinesis, and it balked, snorting and stamping. The riders boiled away into a ring surrounding them, while Emin pulled his horse to a halt on one side of him.

Breathing heavily, Taunos turned, staring down their attackers.

Amanah danced with her horse's movement, bringing it in close on his other side. "Taunos, are you all right?"

He nodded, regretting it as the world wobbled. He pushed aside the unsteadiness and forced himself straight. Nagging worry itched at him—

this might be a danger he'd constantly have to be aware of from now on, between his lungs and his wrist. All his story, he'd depended on the strength of his arms, on his own wits and skill to keep him and others safe, and now that was failing him.

Several stern faces frowned down at them, with arrows nocked in bows and bowstrings taut. The riders looked very similar to Dahuti people, with their brown skin, oval faces, and dark hair. The clothing was different, of course, the Hinanuri clothes thicker and stiffer than the flowing styles the Dahuti preferred, but otherwise Emin and Amanah could easily pass for one of them.

A woman with a crooked nose and sharp eyes, such that she resembled a hawk, moved her horse forward. "What are you doing here, strangers? This is the Hinanur Empire's lands, not the lands of Far Dahutad."

"We're looking for shelter," Taunos said. "We do not need to fight."

Amanah leaned over, reaching toward him, but several of the Hinanuri shifted the aim of their bows to her. Taunos held up his hands, and Amanah eased back, raising her hands as well. The horse snorted and flicked its tail.

Taunos held the gaze of the leader, watching the others out of the corner of his eyes.

The two riders who'd been unhorsed circled them, but as one grabbed for Amanah's mount's bridle, Amanah shifted, and her horse tossed its head and stepped backward. The rider scowled and snatched at the bridle again, and again Amanah caused her horse to avoid her. Taunos clamped down on the smile that threatened to grow, but pride in his beloved's skills warmed his heart.

"Dismount, strangers," the leader said. "It is a great dishonor to steal a rider's horse."

"So is it a dishonor to give up such a beautiful mount so easily." Amanah lowered one hand, stroking the horse's neck.

Taunos spread his arms to bring the leader's attention back to him, away from Amanah. "We were, ah… directed to the tree over there." He indicated it with his head. "Any ideas why?"

"Or what a Naransyn is?" Emin asked.

He bit back a scowl. He'd been hoping Emin would forget that, at least until Taunos knew what it meant or could evaluate the potential harm to his people.

The unhorsed rider stepped forward again, but the leader snapped. "Patha, step back."

Keeping her glare on Amanah, the rider tucked her hands behind her back and retreated one pace, to stand with her back straight and head high.

The leader continued. "We'll take you to Dinweyi, but be aware you will be under guard at all times. Any false moves, any harm done to our people, and you die."

Wonderful. Taunos gave a slow nod.

Once again, Amanah leaned toward him, her eyes warily on the ring of archers, and offered him her hand. This time, he took it and swung up behind her. As they followed the lead rider, ringed in by archers, his gaze again went to the Seeker Tree on its lonely hill, impossible though it was.

"The Promise Tree is not for the eyes of the likes of you." One of the archers moved into his line of sight, her fingers tapping her bow.

Taunos tightened his lips against a response and his arms around his beloved. He was sore, exhausted, and tired of trouble, but it wouldn't do to show it. So he set his chin on Amanah's shoulder, as if they were merely out for an afternoon ride. She leaned into him a fraction, and he wished they had time to just be together.

Riding horses was not among his favorite pastimes. Every move of the animal shot bolts of pain through his side, leg, and occasionally his wrist when he held Amanah wrong. Each jolt reminded him of how poorly he would currently do in a fight.

Events seemed to be conspiring to force him to lean on others, when his strength all his story had been working alone.

As they approached the circle of tents, more details became apparent. The tents were decorated with swirls of color, and ribbons flew from their tops. An adolescent girl pressed her lips to a piece of colorful cloth and then raised it to the ever-present wind. The scrap of fabric fluttered and spun as the wind carried it away. Turning, the girl startled, staring at them, and ran away, her long vest whipping around her legs.

They stopped outside the tents, Taunos making an effort to look as relaxed as possible. Amanah leaned lightly against him, but her fingers fidgeted on the reins, belying her inner tension. Emin kept his horse close to theirs, his eyes scanning their surroundings.

Ahead of them, people moved about the circle of tents on their own business, wary eyes repeatedly going to them. Taunos watched the archers idly, eager to get off the horse. Leather armor covered lighter clothes beneath, and their boots were made of cloth as well. Most of them were women, and they, like Amanah, rode as if one with their mounts.

From the circle of tents, movement attracted his attention. A middle-aged woman approached them, a long, embroidered vest over a long robe swishing with her movements. She walked up to the leader of the archers and inclined her head toward them. "Who are these?"

"Dahuti near the Promise Tree. The one there, behind the woman, may be a sea-wizard," the leader said.

Taunos fought not to stiffen at that, but he felt Amanah tense in his arms. Was that the real reason they'd brought them here?

The middle-aged woman folded her arms, her gaze stern on them. "Tell me your names and why you are here."

"I'm Kanhu Amanah Teek."

"Kanhu Emin Teek. I'm the brains."

Taunos snorted, and Emin gave him a wide grin. So much for not boasting.

"Nomads? We welcome those of the Kanhu clan as our siblings," the leader of the archers said, her posture relaxing a fraction.

The matriarch stared at Taunos, and he gave her one of his more disarming smiles. "I'm Taunos. I came to learn of sea-wizards."

"And are you a sea-wizard?" The question came with no change in expression from that level gaze.

"That depends what you call a sea-wizard," Taunos deflected. Who knew if their definitions were really the same?

Emin scoffed. "He's a sea-wizard."

Taunos contained his grimace. Emin really needed to learn to keep his mouth shut.

The archer inclined her head toward the matriarch, though her eyes stayed on Taunos. "Did you hear the name?"

"I did. Send up the hawks for hunting. Set free the prayers to the spirits. And sound the meeting horn."

"Yes, Dinweyi." The archer hurried away, with one last backward glance at them.

The hair on the back of his neck prickled. All this commotion, based on his name? He needed more information immediately. "Dinweyi. Is that your name or title?"

"I am Dinweyi. That is all I am. I will take you to the Puwileh."

He glanced at Emin, who shrugged, and back at Dinweyi. "And who is the Puwileh?"

She smiled. "You may know her when you see her."

One of the archers spoke up, eyeing them nervously. "Dinweyi, I'm uneasy with them riding free on Hinanuri horses."

Dinweyi's eyes flickered from the archer to the horses and back to the three of them. Her gaze landed on his splinted wrist, and Taunos stiffened, angling his body to shield the injury from view.

"We will not chain them, just in case this one is who he says he is," Dinweyi said. "And the nomads are our family. They are wounded; they can ride with the livestock." A small grunt of dismay escaped Emin, and Dinweyi glanced sharply at him. "Do not toss the gifts of the wind to the soil."

The circle of tents had quickly become a flurry of activity, and a horn rang out across the grasslands with three long blasts.

Dinweyi gestured to the archers. "Show them where they will ride, and three of you will remain to keep them comfortable and stationary." Her eyes flicked back to Taunos, Amanah, and Emin. "Do not wander."

As she strode away, three of the archers, including Patha, the woman who apparently owned Amanah's horse, surrounded them, leading them around the circle of tents to a contraption in the grass. A set of wooden rods formed a platform attached to four pairs of wheels, and the whole thing was wrapped with grasses. Wooden posts attached to beams overhead, where more grasses were woven to form a canopy. It was like an enormous open-sided wagon, with just the floor and ceiling being solid. Rope wound around the edges as a kind of flimsy fence.

Where did they get all the wood for this? No trees dotted the landscape, aside from the one that looked like the Seeker Tree. And for that one to not be cut down for wood, it must be enormously important to these people.

Wicker cages filled with birds were hooked to the upper canopy of the wagon, swinging freely, and young goats and sheep were led onto the platform and tethered to the posts through the grass. The adult livestock milled around the outside, bleating. The only young livestock that were not brought on board the wagon were horses—apparently they could move fast enough to keep up. Emin, Amanah, and Taunos dismounted and were bundled into the wagon along with a few lambs, one of which was plopped right into Emin's arms.

Taunos grinned. "You wanted a herd, hmm, Emin?"

Emin set the lamb down, tethering it as the others were. "Of my own, I said."

Their guards kept a watchful eye on them, especially Patha, who obsessively stroked her horse's neck and glared at Amanah every chance she got.

Leaning close to her, Taunos murmured, "Why didn't you give up the horse right away? Emin said not to draw attention. And yet, he labeled me sea-wizard."

Amanah smiled, her breath warm on his cheek and ear as she

whispered her reply. "If I gave the horse up too quickly, that would have been an insult. I also didn't want to. But Emin likely wanted to avoid accusations of deception. The Hinanuri prize the truth, much like many nomadic clans do."

Taunos nodded, resting his forehead against hers. He would have to be careful. All his tricks, all his skills, seemed only to be liabilities now. At least he had Emin and Amanah to guide him.

They were underway in impressive time, the entire village of tents dismantled and the people mounted in long lines, ready to ride.

Dinweyi paused beside Patha, who still lingered by their platform, and her hand flicked in the air. "Patha, you lost your horse and, with it, your honor. You will walk to the City of the Promise and take care of the horses. If you can keep up, you will regain your honor."

"Yes, Dinweyi." Patha lowered her head but dismounted at once.

The travel was mostly idle, with flat grasslands in every direction and them confined, however politely, to the wagon. Young children clambered onto the wagon to rest at intervals before leaping off the platform to run alongside the horses again. As the day wore on, more and more horses carried children, riding with their parents or with the adults jogging alongside. Only Patha and the woman Emin had taken his horse from ran the whole time, and the only ones who never gave up their mounts were elders.

Taunos inclined his head to a father riding nearby with an infant before him, cradled in his arms, and nudged Amanah. "Born riding, like you? No wonder they're all such good riders."

Her chuckle rewarded him. "Keep practicing and you'll get better, too."

Taunos made the Dahuti sign to ward off evil, sending Emin and Amanah into fits of laughter.

By early evening, the platform was packed with children curling up to sleep while the company maintained a steady pace. He passed the time telling stories to entertain the children resting on the wagon and singing, since he had no pipe. It was nice to be able to sing again without fearing he'd re-injure his lung.

"Why are you always singing and telling stories?" Amanah asked.

"Because he's bored," Emin said. "He needs to be shot again."

Taunos scoffed at him, but answered his beloved truthfully. "My people are steeped in stories and songs. They're woven into the fabric of everyday life. It feels wrong to go for long without."

She smiled, nestling against him. "Well, I like it, so feel free to continue."

He chuckled. "Well, if I have your blessing..."

He scanned the faces of the children waiting for the next tale, and launched into the beginnings of yet another legend he picked up on his travels.

Several times as they rode, the horns blasted three long, low blasts, and hawks returned to handlers with rodents and small prey clutched in talons. Such food was skinned while riding, and Taunos idly wondered if these people would even sleep while riding.

It was not so. They stopped at sundown, fixing dung fires to roast the meat caught during the day and to cook the grains held in large sacks. The four of them were allowed to leave the wagon to eat, their muscles stiff from riding in the cramped space. Their guards followed them closely, eyeing every movement with suspicion. As the night wore on, the Hinanuri simply rolled themselves up in wool blankets and fell asleep on the grass.

Taunos smiled. It was close enough to home to make him homesick.

Chapter Twenty-two

She appeared out of the air itself, her hair like sunlight and eyes like the sky, sent by the wind itself. She reminded us with questions asked of the promises we made to the wind spirits. The dragons in those days were on the move, with many sightings, but she calmed them before she left us. Whisper to the wind and let it hear your prayers. Let it take your wishes and your cares, lest your heart become a dragon's.

—portion of a Hinanuri tale

Two full days of travel brought them to a city of airy wooden buildings draped in dyed cloth. The walls of most buildings were wool woven with the same designs he'd seen on the outside of the tents. Sometimes the cloth hung down, ropes stretching them taut, while in other buildings they were swept to the side like curtains, leaving the building open to the air.

Patha and the other rider had kept up the whole way to the city, and though they appeared exhausted and footsore, they did not complain. While the other rider kept her distance from them, Patha still glared at Amanah with every breath. Taunos tried to ignore the rider, intent on enjoying his first look at a Hinanuri city with his beloved and his best friend, all of them gawking unabashedly.

"The wind spirits are free to go where they will in the City of the Promise," Patha said. "Even the Empress in the City of Wind has many buildings open to the wind spirits."

"What is the Promise?" Taunos asked.

Patha sniffed. "The Puwileh will tell you, if she deigns to."

He leaned close to Amanah. "Will she try for revenge against you?"

Amanah shook her head, murmuring. "No, not unless Dinweyi tells her to, or she'll lose even more honor."

Unease sat heavy in the pit of his stomach as Dinweyi approached and beckoned them out of the wagon.

"Follow me." With a curt gesture, Dinweyi walked up the stone street into the city.

Three archers encircled them, their demeanors politely distant, but Taunos didn't want to chance another fight. He walked with Emin and Amanah into the city, craning his neck to see as much as possible.

The sky stretched vast and blue above, but Taunos kept seeing a cavern ceiling instead. The professional demeanors of the Hinanuri archers became the haughtiness of the Kamalti guards who had been there the last time he'd been marched into a city. The fluttering cloth walls became impassive stone in precise cubes, and even though it was Emin and Amanah with him, he couldn't help but look over and expect to see Kaemada, Takiyah, and Ra'ael.

The Kamalti had thrown his sister into a chasm, and he hadn't been able to stop them.

"Are you coming?" Dinweyi paused and turned back, eyes narrowed at him.

Amanah brushed her arm against his, concern in her dark eyes.

He clenched his hands, lengthening his stride against the slowing of his feet. He had to stay present. This wasn't the same situation. This time he was going to get information. And Eian was safe, wherever he was. The Council may have thrown them out, but they wouldn't endanger a child.

Still, fear weighed heavy on his shoulders, despite his gratitude for the presence of those who had proven themselves true friends. Especially with him so wounded and all his strengths turned to weaknesses.

While Dinweyi pointed out occasional points of interest, Taunos pushed down his rising anxiety, gathering up his control. He loosened his shoulders, breathed as easily as he could with his still-healing wounds, and held his head high. Amanah's face was alive with wonder, and he tried to ignore how much that wonder reminded him of Takiyah before the Kamalti had gotten to her. The memory stabbed him in the heart, and every step was a struggle to pretend.

The city folk went about their days with only occasional glances sent their way. Several called out greetings to Dinweyi by name. Taunos forced a smile to his face, wishing the knot in his stomach would loosen.

As they crossed an intersection, an old man hurtled toward them. His face was caked with moons'-worth of dirt, as were the ragged clothes he wore. His eyes gleamed with feverish light, and he screeched pure gibberish. Taunos dodged, but before the man got to them, one of the archers grabbed him by his rags, spinning him around and casting him back out to the crowd.

Dinweyi sniffed, sparing a glare at the man. "Filthy dragon monks can't simply leave people in peace."

Taunos snapped his focus to her, the worries of the past falling away to this dangling thread of knowledge to discover. "You have dragon monks?"

She waved her hand to the southwest. "Dragons infest the mountains, and sometimes the dragon monks come to the cities. Every one of them is without honor, but what are we to do with them? Allowing them to stay doesn't damage our honor at all. Come, this way."

No further questions yielded answers from the tight-lipped woman, but Amanah smiled at him with excitement sparkling in her eyes.

Taunos's thoughts spun. The dragon monks were named so similar, he couldn't help but make a connection to the Monks of Annularei, which collected knowledge of dragons and cared for those left behind when their dragons died. He glanced back, wondering how far the similarities went, for he hadn't encountered dragons—not up-close, anyway—on his travels besides in Rinara.

His thoughts faded as they stepped into the center of the city.

It opened into a large courtyard all paved in stone. Steps led upward on all sides of a raised square. Panels of cloth, painted with designs, rippled in the wind. At intervals, string stretched from panel to panel over their heads, hung with small triangles of cloth covered in indecipherable, artistic writing.

Despite the burden of remembered trauma, a small kernel of curiosity dared unfurl. Amanah took his hand, and he twined his fingers with hers, pretend calm coming more easily from her presence. He wasn't alone.

At the top of the steps stood a building, cloth walls fluttering in the wind, wooden frame stained dark in contrast to the colored panels. Dinweyi entered without a word or pause, and they followed with the archers at their backs. Inside, their feet met mats of rushes, and then farther on, carpets laid down along a corridor between more cloth panels. The archers paused on the mats to place their bows on a rack and then removed their shoes and shed their outer vests.

Dinweyi gestured to them. "Take off your boots and outer layers. The inner walls of the Puwileh are meant only for those willing to come unarmored and weaponless."

Taunos raised his eyebrows at Emin, and Emin shrugged. Trusting in his friend's assessment, he pulled off his boots. In moments, their dirty footwear was arranged against the wall in an orderly fashion, their packs laid next to them. None of them had outer layers, having raced from Far Dahutad too quickly to gear up appropriately for a journey.

A middle-aged man walked down the carpeted corridor toward them with a broad smile. Upon seeing him, Dinweyi bowed her head, but neither spoke until they were within arm's reach of each other. Then, the man bowed his forehead to touch Dinweyi's, and they held that position for a moment before stepping back, releasing one another.

His bright eyes went to Taunos, Amanah, and Emin. His voice when he spoke was barely above a whisper, and Taunos became aware of just how quiet the inside of this building was.

"Dinweyi, who do you bring with you?" the man asked.

"A sea-wizard. The Puwileh will want to speak with them, I think. These are Emin, Amanah, and Taunos."

The man's eyes sparkled with surprised humor, and another grin split his face. Taunos stood very still. There didn't seem to be any danger, and yet, the man didn't even look at the others. He only stood there, staring into Taunos's eyes, before nodding to himself, turning, and beckoning them to follow.

The back of Taunos's neck prickled.

Dinweyi waved them after her, following the man around silent bends lit at intervals with lanterns on posts. Finally, the man swept aside a curtain, paused to signal them to halt, and disappeared within.

Taunos shifted his weight, wiping his hands on his pants. He glanced up and down the hallway, but no one was in sight besides the three unarmed archers. His gaze went to the fabric walls. Armed foes could be lurking behind them, out of sight but near. But surely the fabric would tangle them up if they were to attack through the walls. No, it would make more sense to roll through from underneath.

He tensed when the man swept the curtain back and gestured them in, still silent. Taunos longed for some sound, some music, some conversation, anything but this stillness.

Dinweyi led them inside, where more carpets cushioned the floor while lanterns burned on small, circular tables set at the edges of the room a pace away from the fabric walls. In the middle of the other end of the room, a young woman sat cross-legged on a backless chair covered in furs. Her black hair was loose around her shoulders, and a strip of yellow ribbon was tied around her temples.

She tilted her head at them as they entered, and Taunos felt the weight of her gaze, heavy on him as he followed Dinweyi and the man to the middle of the room, where they knelt.

The man spoke, his conversational tone the loudest sound Taunos had yet heard in this building. "Puwileh, I present to you Dinweyi and her three visitors. These are Amanah, Emin, and I think you can guess who Taunos is."

Taunos's skin crawled at the focus on him. Why did they pretend to know him? He tensed, ready to fight, ready to flee. Emin and Amanah had paused as well, their gazes flickering between their hosts.

The Puwileh rose, walking toward them. Though Taunos didn't move, Dinweyi stepped between him and the Puwileh, as if he were a danger to her.

Staring steadily at Taunos, the Puwileh waved Dinweyi away. "Taunos will not harm me. Not if he is all his mother said he was."

"My mother?" The words choked out of him.

"I am the Puwileh, Leen. Named after your mother, the sea-wizard. And this is my father, Tānos."

Taunos gaped at them. The man was about the same age his parents would have been, had they lived, but Leen was much younger even than Kaemada. It didn't make sense. The Great Attack had been fourteen summers ago, and then his mother had gone to speak with the Darks, to make peace. But she'd been here?

He shook his head. There was no way he was named for this man. The spelling of his own name was not Rinaryn, but he'd already been born when his mother apparently came here looking to treat with the Darks. The timeline didn't make sense. Nothing about this made sense.

"Are you Darks?" He stepped back from them. Had he seen any black-clad warriors on the walk through the city? No, surely he'd have noticed. Besides, Hinanuri death teams also wore black, and he'd note the danger immediately if he saw one of them. The Hinanuri had metal, at least, so that fit, but many peoples had metal. Had he missed something so obvious, so crucial?

The Puwileh laughed. "No, we are not. But we were happy to host Leen the sea-wizard for some time before she went on to find such a people."

"How can that be?" His tone and pitch were both rising, but his control was slipping and he couldn't regain it. He was standing on a steep slope during a landslide, and at the bottom, the drop off into madness. "She cannot have realmwalked here. She did not have telekinesis. She went to find the Darks, to bring peace."

Their faces blended together, except for Dinweyi staring at him, stony-eyed. His mind raced, too fast to take in what he was seeing.

The man who had escorted them, the man with his name, approached slowly, hands out, as if he were a wild animal. "Leen the sea-wizard came here through the Promise Tree from the Secret Land. She would never tell us where it was, nor much about it. She came once, with a man, and then a second time many, many years later, alone. But she spoke of you, that second time she visited us. She was proud of you and loved her family greatly. She and I traded many stories on both occasions. She was brave, and we miss her. To see you, there is not much of her in your face, but there is much of her in your expressions."

"Twice? Once is laughable enough. She cannot have come twice." Taunos shook his head.

"Your name is Taunos. Spelled T-a-u-n-o-s, yes?" The man extended a triangle of cloth. There, embroidered on the fabric, was his name in Rinaryn script.

Taunos tightened his muscles, suppressing the shivers that wanted to break free.

The man smiled, extending another similar cloth. "And I changed my spelling. T-ā-n-o-s."

The way his name should be spelled, in proper Rinaryn. His fingers shook as he traced the embroidered letters. Rinaryn letters here, so far from home.

It was impossible, and yet here it was.

The Puwileh clasped her hands together. "It was such a delight when Leen returned to visit after so long. Dinweyi knows the stories of my father and his friend the sea-wizard. She was wise to bring you to me. She watches the Promise Tree in hopes that Leen comes again."

"The Promise Tree." Taunos clung to that idea, the one thing that made sense in this whole mess. It was like the Gods' Tree, like the Seeker Tree. "How can you have one? How are there more?"

"The Ifreesians call it a nexus. Leen said you have one very similar to ours?" Old Man Tānos asked.

Reflexively, Taunos shrugged off the question. "Similar enough, anyway. The Promise Tree. Promise to what?"

The man laughed. "How like your mother you are! The tree reminds us of the promise of the spirits to protect us. The wind spirits drive away evil spirits, and the Promise Tree reminds us of their function and our devotion."

Spirits. His people worshipped spirits, too.

No, that was likely a coincidence. He was grasping for something to make sense. He bent forward, shoving his hands through his hair and remaining folded that way for a bit. It was easier to handle surprises when they weren't secrets contradicting everything he knew.

If his mother had come here, surely the Elders knew that. He could confront them with that. Except if they hadn't sent her, they'd blamed Galod, and while Galod deserved plenty of blame for plenty of faults, this was not one of them.

"The Elders. Did my mother say if they knew she was here?" he asked, looking up.

Tānos shook his head. "She said they sent her to bring peace. No more attacks on your home."

He shoved aside the personal mysteries to snatch at a possible lead. "Did she describe the Darks to you? She went from you to them. We know she got to them because after they killed her, they came to my kaetal and slaughtered many in revenge for even asking for peace. My father tried to ask for her body, and they... they cut him down. They didn't..." Taunos shook his head, stilling his words, just breathing. He still had Kaemada, sort of. And Palon was safe with her dragon. There was that at least.

Suddenly rigid, Dinweyi stared at him, her jaw slack. "What did you say?"

What had he said that she would react to so strongly? A hand in his anchored him to the present. Amanah's fingers tapped his, the way they'd used to pass secret messages back and forth. *I'm here.*

He swallowed hard, holding tightly to Amanah's hand, her presence a shelter in the midst of the storm raging within him.

A storm raged without, as well. Fire burned in Dinweyi's eyes. "It is not so. It cannot be so. The sea-wizard Leen cannot be dead. We are waiting for her."

"Dinweyi, stand down." The Puwileh spoke with authority, and yet, Taunos met Dinweyi's torment-filled gaze for several breaths before the woman stepped back, her motions carefully controlled.

"Your honor is the honor of us all, as you are our hope," Dinweyi breathed, her eyes on the floor as she gave the Puwileh a nod.

The Puwileh's father broke the silence with his gentle voice. "It has been some fifteen years ago or so. I do remember that in our conversations, she began to ask repeatedly about the Sea Peoples. They are not a gentle people. They are not to be trifled with."

The Darks had murdered his family. They'd murdered his mother when she went to make peace. The Darks were not people to be trifled with either. Dread coiled in his gut. The Darks appeared, attacked, and disappeared, just as the Sea Peoples had at the library. "Far too many signs point to the Sea Peoples. I believe the Darks have an enemy, some threat they fight. I think they use my people to train their warriors. To get them used to killing."

"The Sea Peoples don't have any one enemy. They attack anyone and everyone. Even the Ifreesians won't go near them, and they're the most accomplished traders of any land," the Puwileh said.

What had the Sea Peoples called him when they attacked in the

Library? "Ungala. Do you know the term?"

The Puwileh shook her head. "It sounds Sea People, to me. But they hunt down sea-wizards, and those they find are never seen again. Do not seek them out."

"I might need to." He'd never been this close to answers. All those summers searching, and now that he was banished, thrown away like garbage, now he might be close to learning who the Darks were? It would have been laughable if it didn't hurt so much.

The Puwileh's tone grew stern. "Leen went to them and never returned. Let this madness go. Don't feed the Sea Peoples more blood. They're drowning in it already."

"I must prepare my people as best I can." Especially if the Ifreesians also knew where his land was. If he might have led them there with his questions.

Disapproval lurked in the harshness of Dinweyi's voice. "Then do so, but do not go to the Sea Peoples. I won't have you endangering my people by turning their eyes here."

He swallowed hard. His skin felt tight, his body heavy. Everything around him felt unreal but, at the same time, like he was drowning.

"Taunos." Amanah tightened her hold on his hand, iron coming into her voice. "You can't go after the Sea Peoples. They capture sea-wizards, and if they're also your 'Darks,' they killed your mother. Don't be rash. You are not indestructible."

Old Man Tānos nodded. "It's a bad idea, young man. Live your life. Find another way."

But what had he gained? The Sea Peoples might be the Darks, but he still didn't know their enemy. He still didn't know why they attacked but never looted—like the Sea Peoples at the library had. Surely there were easier ways to get whatever they were after. He rubbed his forehead.

"Taunos, are you all right?" Emin asked. "You look like you're going to vomit, and I want to make sure it's not on me."

Taunos stared at him. Emin stood a pace away at least, his face pinched in earnestness, and under Taunos's gaze, he withdrew a careful step farther.

Laughter broke out of Taunos and erupted into hysteria.

The Puwileh and her father had decided Taunos was tired from his journey and gave him, Emin, and Amanah a side room in which to rest. Dinweyi had left them there, her lip curled in disgust.

The room was cozy, with furs spread on the floor under colorful cushions, but Taunos still felt wound too tightly, like one of Takiyah's little toys twisted to breaking. Amanah sat next to him while Emin lounged near a small wooden tray of tea. With just the three of them, some of the hysterical tension had uncoiled, though he still floundered with what to think, what to do.

Taunos sipped his tea, his eyes on the fur he was sitting on, avoiding the looks the others might be giving him. He had to figure something out, but his mind kept circling back to the claim that his mother had visited here before and that he was named for the father of the Puwileh, while the Puwileh herself was named for his mother. And yet, there was the embroidered Rinaryn script, if the unusual spelling of his name and the strange choice of one of Kaemada's middle names being in Traveller's wasn't enough evidence. Lína had been thought untraditional. All of this made that a laughable understatement.

Emin jerked upright, leaning toward them with an intensity on his face that Taunos hadn't seen since he'd fought in Emin's war band. "I think the listeners are gone. I'm going to take a loop, make sure there's no trap about to snap shut around us. Remember to keep your heads down. The Puhwileh is under the Hinanuri Empress, and she may see us only as Dahuti, not havi."

"First time in my life I hope people think of me as havi instead of Dahuti," Amanah said with a snort.

Taunos placed his hand over hers, and she turned her hand to grip his.

Emin stood, going to the curtain that was loose from the floor. "Get your head on straight, Taunos. We're not safe here. Not with the way that Dinweyi looked at us."

"Keep your head down too," Amanah said. "Especially snooping."

Emin scoffed. "Me? The Hinanuri guards will only think I'm a lowly servant, sent out by you on some stupid errand."

With a flip of the curtain, he was gone.

Turning back to him, Amanah squeezed his hand again. "I'm so sorry about your mother. Would it help to explain your thoughts, what's troubling you?"

His thoughts crushed him once again in a flood. "My mother was a telepath—she could talk to someone, mind to mind. Realmwalking takes telekinesis. No one has both. No one but my sister."

"Do you not use the trees for your realmwalking? That's what Leen did, according to the stories," Amanah said.

Taunos shook his head. "Not usually."

Except for the most recent jump. And that was the easiest jump by far, and he'd ended up exactly where he'd aimed for. It was almost like it had pulled him, like a magnet pulling a shard of metal. Just like a magnet, it looked like magic.

"The Gods' Tree," he said. "I jumped there, accidentally, this last time. And it was the easiest jump I have ever made."

Amanah's grip tightened on his hand. "The Sea Peoples came in from the garden and left through it. Do you think... could they have realmwalked away with Nasri, using the tree?"

"I can't realmwalk with multiple people," Taunos said. "I have tried. Dragons do it somehow, but I have never been able to. Maybe using the tree... But if so, Nasri could be anywhere."

"So maybe it was possible for your mother too?"

He shook his head. "No. It's not."

"How can you be so sure?"

"It took me a long time to learn to realmwalk. My people weren't even sure it was possible. My mother would have told me if she had a way to help. I was the first to realmwalk."

"Then how did your mother find these Darks, to try for peace?" she asked.

He shook his head. "I assumed she went with the Darks, however they came and went. No one would answer my questions."

Amanah watched him a moment longer. "At least this explains why the most recent stories in the library at Arruk were Hinanuri."

Dragging his hand down his face, he stared at his cup of tea, willing everything to make sense. The only way it made sense was if he'd been lied to all his life.

"So either you're not the first realmwalker, or you're missing something," Amanah said as Emin reappeared.

"Or both. I mean, it is Taunos, let's give him some credit." Emin flopped down on the furs. "Overachiever."

A grin crept across Taunos's face despite himself. "All clear?"

Emin shoved his foot with his own. "Of course."

"Did anyone see you?" Amanah asked.

Emin waved her off, a grimace on his face like the prick at his ego had physically hurt him. "Of course not."

Amanah nudged Taunos. "Are you all right?"

How could he answer that? Everything he'd known had turned upside down. He sucked in a breath. "I will be."

The room fell silent for a moment. Taunos sipped his tea, still trying to make sense of things. His mother had been here. And the ruler of this area was named for her. It went against everything he knew.

If the Darks were the Sea Peoples, they might be using the Seeker Tree to attack. The Elders had shrouded his mother's mission to the Darks in secrecy, just as they had his own missions, and his family had suffered for it. His family continued to suffer for it.

He couldn't stay still. The agitation within needed some sort of outlet, so he leaped to his feet, pacing. "None of this matters."

Amanah raised her eyebrows. "Clearly it matters to you."

Taunos shoved his good hand through his hair. "No, I mean, it doesn't help my goal. I have to bring back something so powerful the Elders will have to take us back, or at least take my sister back. It's the only way. It's the only chance. And this isn't it."

Chewing lightly on her lip, she watched him. "You spoke of your island's secrecy being set up, but by who? Could it be all some design of the Elders?"

"No. They didn't know about other places, so why would they know to keep it secret? But if it was someone, who? Maybe it's all connected. It can't be the Kamalti—they were also isolated. Which means the dragons, the elves, or the fae. The dragons don't care about 'lesser people' generally, but the elves and fae sometimes meddle."

"Kamalti?" Amanah asked, just as Emin asked, "Elves? Fae?"

Taunos winced. He'd kept so many secrets for so long, and now... He hadn't even double-checked for listeners behind the walls. At least Amanah and Emin were safe, and at least Emin had walked a circuit. Taunos could trust him, even though habit itched at him to check for himself. He didn't want to leave them wondering though, didn't want to keep secrets from them. As he passed them, he paused and tapped their shoulders in the language they'd taught him. "People from home."

His steps took him across the furs, back and forth, back and forth. His mind went in circles as surely as his body did, the weight of his troubles burning inside him. What had he done, leaving his sister behind? How long had it been? Moons, at least. Why hadn't he thought more of her?

A breath of forest air, rich with life-giving soil. As it washed away, so too did his burdens and the urgency. He couldn't go back yet. There was more to do. Always more to do...

"You think these Darks might be the Sea Peoples. Your mother came here. There's more than one Gods' Tree. That's a lot to bring to these Elders, along with all the harm their years of secrecy has done," Amanah pointed out. "Perhaps the trees would help with your realmwalking. And even if the Sea Peoples aren't the Darks, they are the most dangerous force on the sea. Sooner or later, their ships will find your home, Taunos. It's better to be ready when they come."

She was right. How he'd missed her calm wisdom when he was away. His whirling thoughts slowed, calming. He nodded, pushing his shoulders back. He could handle this.

"They sent your mother to her death. Bring that to them." Emin slurped his tea. "We should leave the moment we can politely do so. Find answers elsewhere, where we're less likely to lose our heads."

"Taunos's mother seemed to be held in high regard here," Amanah said.

"Yes, but Taunos is not, and I don't like the way that guard Dinweyi looked at him at the end of that meeting," Emin said.

"She reacted badly to the news of my mother's death," Taunos said. "Far too strongly."

"Right, like she was personally affronted. And if we offend our hosts, we might not make it out alive," Emin said. "Which is why we need to stay calm, stay quiet, nothing flashy, no boasting, and most importantly, keep our visit short. If we can leave tomorrow or even tonight after supper, we should. If something happens, we work together like Ifreesians. Taunos, you stay with Amanah, and I'll provide distraction. We'll meet up outside the city—just head toward the sea."

Taunos shook his head. "Emin, we are not leaving you."

Amanah stood, resting a hand on his arm as he passed, stopping him. "You're always trying to save others. Who's saving you?"

"I'll tell you who," Emin said. "We are."

Entwining her fingers in Taunos's, Amanah nodded. "You can't carry all this alone. It's too much."

Taunos rested his forehead against hers, his heart bursting with worry and love. He needed her, her focus, her step-by-step approach to anchor his wild leaps. He'd figure out the answers and make the Elders account for their secrecy, but for now, he held his beloved, wrapping his arms around her and breathing her in.

Chapter Twenty-three

Gods in theory are fine. They can be controlled. It is much more dangerous when the gods come and walk among the people.

—Philosopher from Codr

Ra'ael hunched with her arms wrapped around her knees, staring back the way they'd come. They'd stopped for the night, for Tjodlik and Answer weren't able to go another step. Both lay nearby, groaning and rubbing their feet. She shook her head at them and then returned to her vigil. Either Galod or the fae would eventually come, and when they did, she'd be ready—with questions or combat.

The decision to go back to Codr was easy. The fae had spoken of dragons with the air of a threat. She had to check on Dode, especially as her arguing for Ra'ael surely did not make her any more popular. If anything had happened to her…

Her chest squeezed, too tight, and she concentrated on her breathing until the lightheadedness faded.

Footsteps scuffed lightly on the rock, and Ra'ael sprang into a fighting crouch. When Galod stepped out of the shadows into the light cast by Tjodlik's lantern, she sagged with relief. He glanced over her and the other two.

She narrowed her eyes, squinting through the dimness at him in return. Was he injured?

As he approached, something shimmered behind him. A fae floated in the air just a pace away, following him.

Ra'ael leaped forward. "Galod!"

He turned, but dismissed the fae with a wave of his hand, his casual response stunning her to a stumbling halt. She stared at the fae, her skin prickling. He wasn't moving. A sharp smell stung her nose, like a thunderstorm, like the sting of the Gifts of the Gods.

"What is it?" The words came out in a hoarse whisper.

"One of the fae left." His tone was sharp as ever, which she took for a good sign. "The other wouldn't let up, so I put him in a bubble."

"A… bubble."

Pointing at Answer, Galod continued, ignoring Ra'ael. "You.

307

Technomage female. Are you bleeding?"

Answer stammered a negative.

Galod turned to Ra'ael. "And you?"

"Only a little, from the knife. It's fine."

He nodded, and Ra'ael swore she saw relief in his stance. It tore her attention from the fae.

"I am not bleeding either," Tjodlik spoke up.

Galod gave him a flat look. He stepped closer, and his eyes flicked downward to Ra'ael's hands. "Blast, you said you weren't bleeding!"

She looked down at her bruised and scraped knuckles. "These are from before. I destroyed some Gifts of the Gods and the hunters who played with them."

His entire form bristled with tension. Galod reached for her, and she recoiled from the waves of *something* pulsing from him. Tjodlik dove between them as if to save her from Galod, as ridiculous as that was. She stared, stunned by the action that was so uncharacteristic of the nobleman.

With ease, Galod tossed him aside, and she willed herself not to retreat, not to run. After all, this was Galod.

"What are you doing?" she asked as he grabbed her elbows. His touch bit like metal. Why was he so worried about scrapes on her hands? Not worried—panicked. She extended her hands toward him.

"Hold still. No, don't touch me," he snapped.

She froze, terror rising in her. He released her, holding his hands above hers, scowling hard at them. Then he flicked his gaze to meet hers. "This is going to hurt. I'm sorry."

Never in twenty summers had she heard him apologize. It was like an integral part of who he was.

And then pain lit her ablaze from her boots to the tips of her hair, and she howled with it, trembling with the force of trying to remain still. When she spasmed toward him, Galod leaped back with a hiss, maintaining their distance. If she wasn't sure she was wrong, she'd have thought he was afraid of her. But she hardly had time or space to think through the pain, especially when invisible clamps grabbed on to her wrists and held her steady while she screamed her throat raw.

In the far, far distance, Answer shrieked, and Tjodlik threw himself at Galod, only to be tossed once again to the ground, dust covering his fine clothing.

And then, the pain ended and Galod stepped back, the invisible bindings releasing her. It was all too much, too fast, and she fell to her hands and knees, heaving and retching and choking as her body tried to breathe and vomit at the same time. Galod held his hands behind his back, but his sharp gaze was intent on her as the world returned.

"What was that? What did you do?" Tjodlik stood between them again, as if he could do anything against Galod. Galod had already proven that, so what did Tjodlik think he was doing?

Everything hurt, and she collapsed against the wall of the tunnel. Answer stepped toward her, and Ra'ael recoiled, her nerves on fire.

Answer spun, glaring at Galod. "What did you do to her?"

"I had to make sure there was no tech in you." Galod's voice was low, his gaze fixed on her. "You were lucky. It seems whatever you destroyed, the pieces were too large or inactive. I removed the inactive pieces."

"The hunters carried the delivery systems for the Gift of the Gods, which were themselves gifts," Answer murmured, glancing between them. "You destroyed them all?"

"It hurt. Why?" Ra'ael was exhausted, but she had to know. The Gifts hurt, just as Galod did, and from his reaction... She'd never seen him so worried, not even when they battled Darks, so whatever it was had to be even more dangerous.

"The pain, the reason you flinch from this one," he flicked a hand at Answer, "but can bring down Darks with no fear, that's the psionic technophobia. And if you think it's bad when the tech is near you, imagine what it would be like inside of you."

Answer folded her arms, glaring at him. "I am Lady Answer of the Scouts of the city of Codr, and this is Lord Tjodlik of the Philosophers of the city of Hadr. And who exactly are you?"

The old hermit did not answer, instead continuing to watch Ra'ael. It was not the predatory hunger of the Detr hunters, but more the concerned warmth of a vigil. Similar to how he sat and watched after the last Dark attack, making sure she and Kaemada were all right, always while keeping a distance.

"What is your plan?" Galod asked.

"We're going back to Codr," Ra'ael said. "A Kamalti city. We need to check on people there."

"Why do you have a fae floating behind you, apparently frozen? More importantly, how?" Answer's tone was as haughty as she'd ever sounded, but if she hoped to impress, she was doomed to failure.

Galod didn't even glance at her. "They have more of the tage tech there?"

Answer and Tjodlik exchanged puzzled looks.

Galod enunciated slowly. "The technology that allows you not to bleed when someone tries to stab you. Technomancy. Tage tech."

"The Gift of the Gods?" Answer asked.

"Yes, that."

"There are buildings of it," Ra'ael said. She was starting to feel better, now that the world had stopped pulsing.

His gaze flickered at her. "And you can't go in them anymore, can you. If you were ever able to."

For some reason, she felt affronted. "I used to be able to. Their gods have rejected me, just as the spirits have. Just as the Elders did."

He flicked a hand. "You don't need their approval."

"Galod, are you injured?" Ra'ael asked.

"No."

"What about the fae? How are you doing that?" Tjodlik asked.

"Will he get free of whatever that is?" Answer asked.

"Not unless I become very tired or very distracted," Galod said. "Therefore, I don't want to hold him forever. Haste would be appreciated."

"What are you planning?" Ra'ael asked, getting to her feet.

His mouth tightened a fraction. "I plan to teach the fae their errors, should they return or send more to this outrage. Don't worry. For him, no time is passing."

Together, Ra'ael, Tjodlik, and Answer led Galod down the tunnel toward Codr. They had chased after fae for her, had faced down Galod for her, needless as it was. And now Galod was with them, and he'd somehow managed to grow even more powerful. Warmth and wariness warred in her, now that the pain was only a memory. It wasn't simply a reaction to his Gift; Galod was endlessly testing them, and she endlessly wanted to succeed at those tests.

"How do you have Gift of the Gods?" Answer asked Galod as they walked.

"How do you have it?" he responded.

She drew herself up. "I am a Scout. I was deemed worthy."

Galod looked at Tjodlik. "And you?"

Tjodlik shrugged. "I haven't made the right people happy."

"Good for you." Approval colored Galod's tone.

Ra'ael scowled, suspicions rising in her. Galod was never so... friendly.

"And you?" Answer pressed.

"I got them the same way the originators of your Gifts did."

Tjodlik frowned, and he exchanged a glance with Answer.

After a blink, Answer gasped. "You are a god? A Takanis? Oh, Lady Dode will never let me live this down."

Ra'ael snickered. Trust Answer to think of her own position when faced with her own demi-god. What was Galod playing at, pretending to be such a thing? At least the pressure of his Gift had lessened; she was able to walk near him with only a vague itchiness.

Answer let out a sigh of relief when they reached the tunnel entrance to Codr. Remembering her first view of the underground civilization, Ra'ael flicked her gaze to Galod. Disappointingly, the hermit didn't gape or show much of any surprise at all. His eyes just flickered over the buildings and the Kamalti that moved about their business and then landed on the metal buildings and stuck. Nothing was odd about them—nothing more than usual, anyway—but her old teacher's gaze still hadn't moved on.

Tjodlik moved forward, and Galod's gaze finally broke from the buildings. The smoke in the air swirled around them, and Ra'ael coughed.

Galod frowned. "You're going to have a dragon problem."

"The fae also said the dragons would come because of the smoke," Tjodlik said.

"Only because they want to shut down our machines." Answer's features were set stubbornly.

"Dragons will come, but not because of the smoke," Galod said. "The fae lied to you. The dragons can smell all this tech. The smoke is only an extra draw."

Ra'ael shook her head. "Come on, I want to make sure Dode is all right."

"We cannot just walk through the city with a fae in a... in a bubble," Answer said.

"Where do you keep prisoners?" Galod asked.

Ra'ael glanced from Galod to the bubble where the frozen fae floated, expression caught in a snarl. "How long can you hold him?"

"I won't let him loose until we're outside the mountain." Galod started walking toward the metal buildings. "But there should be a holding pen in there. I can set him down and recharge for a bit."

Chewing on her lip, Ra'ael looked toward the column where Dode's house stood. She wasn't sure what his plans were or why he'd been so content to come along with them, but she found herself torn between her old teacher, who didn't know the city, and Dode, who had fought for her.

"This way," Answer said, stepping out in front as if going that direction had been her idea. "The Scouting Hall will have a place for the fae."

"The Scouts will not approve, surely," Tjodlik said.

Answer maintained her pace. "After what they have done, selling

Ra'ael to Detr? Let them face a Takanis, then."

A fierce smile curved Ra'ael's lips as she hurried along with them. Citizens stared as they hurried through the streets, and Galod barely gave them a glance, disappointing Ra'ael. Was it really so much to ask for a little awe? Instead, all she got was the increasing sense of wrong as they approached the buildings, rising even more when four uniformed Scouts stepped out to confront them.

"Lady Answer, what is the meaning of this?" one of them asked. "Where are you going with these Outsiders?"

"Look," one of the Scouts breathed, staring behind Galod. At the fae.

The wave of irritation, the power that pressed on her nerves and buzzed in her bones and smelled like a thunderstorm, crested higher as the Scouts spread out around them.

"What have you done?" the ranking Scout asked.

"He is a Takanis," Answer said. "Clearly."

"If Answer is admitting the gods exist, surely there is sufficient cause," Tjodlik said.

Galod still sounded bored. "And I'm quite displeased with the reaction my servant has to my powers. What have you done?"

Ra'ael squinted at Galod. His servant? Unlikely. But the Scouts could use their pride adjusted, so she said nothing.

"We do not tolerate those who pretend to be gods," the Scout said, stepping forward.

Galod watched the Scouts with a slightly raised eyebrow and a twitch at the corner of his mouth. He'd had the same expression when he'd learned of their plan to dunk Taunos in the pond—amusement at the edges of the hard planes of his face. Happier times, where mirth belonged. She'd seen that look when she was younger, too, and had attacked him in temper, always before he capably and permanently put down opposition.

"Stop," Galod ordered.

The sense of wrong roared out from him. It battered her like a boulder smashing down on her. She stumbled backward in her haste to get away, and Tjodlik caught her.

But then she was too near Answer, who was also wrong, and the Scouts were wrong, and she clamped her jaw shut on the urge to scream. She huddled in a ball, her gaze catching on the fae in the bubble, who was staring at her. He twitched and then froze again as the pressure from Galod sharpened abruptly.

"Stop it, all of you," Tjodlik shouted from somewhere very close to her. His hand fell to her shoulder, and she flinched. The hand immediately left, and she missed it, feeling very alone, the only one whose world was ending. Instead, she stared at the bubble, wary for any more hint of movement from the captured fae.

"Galod, the fae." Her voice was small to her ears.

Galod glanced at her. "It's fine."

The Scouts were kneeling as well, hands over their ears, shaking just as she was. And then, the wave of power receded, leaving her gasping with relief.

Whatever he'd done must have affected the Scouts greatly, for one of them swore as he straightened. "Crystals and ships!"

Galod's eyebrows edged upward. "More true than you know."

Stepping past them, he headed into the Hall of Scouts.

Tjodlik fell in beside Ra'ael. "Are you all right?"

She nodded. "They're just," she winced, "loud. The Gifts."

He gave her a tight smile. "I will check on Dode if you will keep an eye on… him."

That would be good. She gave him another nod, grateful, and he headed through the growing crowd.

Ahead of her, Galod stepped into the Hall as if he didn't hear, followed by nervous Scouts. The only one who looked back, guilt flashing across her face, was Answer.

Gritting her teeth, Ra'ael entered the Hall of Scouts with the others. The Gift pressed on her from all sides, screaming danger, drowning all her other senses with the metallic taste that filled her mouth and buzzed against her mind. All she wanted was to get as far away as possible, but she forced herself to take step after excruciating step.

And then, like the popping of a bubble, the pressure eased.

She blinked. No more sense of wrong was coming from Answer or three of the Scouts, and it was greatly reduced from Galod. They were standing in one of the metal corridors of the Hall, and Galod was pressing his hand into one of the occasional smooth black panels set into the walls.

"This way." The Scout's curt gesture rang of impatience.

"I told you to turn your Gifts off," Galod said absently.

"We did, not that we have reason to listen to you," the Scouts objected.

Ra'ael glared at the liar of the lot, the one whose Gift still pounded against her head. He carried his head high, as if he didn't see her accusing eyes, until Galod, without even looking, pointed at him.

"Shut it off, or I will intervene."

Surprise and then fear flashed over his face, and the pressure eased further. It still exuded from the very walls, but she could tolerate it, at least until they secured Galod's captive fae.

"How did you know?" the Scout asked.

Galod removed his hand from the wall and turned, walking past the Scouts through the corridor as if this were his house and the Scouts were the visitors. Behind him, the bubble of floating fae trailed.

"Ra'ael knew, too." His tone was distracted, almost leisurely.

The look the Scout gave her was full of malice, but she ignored it. Was this how Galod floated through life, untouchable and serene? Simply by focusing on the important pieces and always having those before him? Was he not so much distant but preoccupied?

Answer led them through the corridors to where they kept prisoners. Ra'ael wrinkled her nose at the memory of the time she'd spent in there with Takiyah and Taunos after Kaemada had fallen. Two of the Scouts left, while two more followed along, making excuses as to why Galod couldn't possibly be doing what he was doing.

Galod ignored them, occasionally stopping to tap one of the odd smooth panels in the wall, making symbols made of light appear and disappear on the panels, to the Scouts' increasing consternation. But Galod was Galod and they soon just followed. Apparently ignoring their worshippers was expected behavior for gods.

Given Kamalti attitudes, that actually made sense.

The pressure around her grew and changed, always spiking when he stopped by a panel, and then dropping sharply. Gradually, the building became more and more tolerable, pressing on her less and less. Was Galod doing that, for her? More questions to ask him later—questions he probably wouldn't answer.

Galod nodded when Answer indicated the holding room, and he passed his hand over the doorframe. The doors slid open soundlessly, and Ra'ael stopped outside. She wasn't about to give the Scouts a chance to lock them all inside, even though it appeared Galod somehow had control of their building. She stood there glaring at the Scouts until Galod came back out, this time without the bubbled fae.

"Now then. Control Center, hmm? Or, what do they call it... ah, the bridge," he said. "That'd be where the other two went, I expect."

He walked with purpose, and Ra'ael hurried to keep up. His expression was the most relaxed she'd ever seen from him. In fact, he seemed almost... happy?

She frowned. Happiness on the old hermit was just wrong. Sternness fit him or anger or impatience. Rarely, he seemed content. But she'd never seen him happy and never expected to in all her summers. But how had she not realized how sad that was until now?

How did he know where he was going? She didn't ask. The Scouts had finally stopped jabbering, and she didn't want them to start back up again. He led them to a set of closed doors engraved with curving geometric designs while the Scouts whispered and muttered to each other. Answer wrapped her arms around herself, her attitude forgotten. But there was no time for questions, as Galod passed his hand over the doorframe and the doors whispered open.

The room was filled with Scouts, chattering angrily. Glowing tables curved at the corners of the room in great arches, and one whole wall was filled with the smooth panels. Scouts bustled about at another edge of the room, some speaking to the odd rocks, which was the most foolish superstition she'd ever seen, while others sat in front of smaller panels of smooth black, tapping them occasionally. Stools sat before the curved tables, and one chair sat in the middle of the space. It was a very odd room.

"How did he know the way to the Crystal Room?" Answer whispered.

Ra'ael shook her head. "I have given up guessing what Galod can and cannot do or know."

"There is the imposter," shouted one of the Scouts who'd left them while Galod was securing the fae.

One of the Scouts, an older man, hurried toward them, jabbing his finger at them through the air. "Why did you bring them here? This is off-limits. It will be night duty for all of you."

"Lord Insight—" Answer began.

Ra'ael suppressed a snort. Who would choose Insight for his name? Either someone very pompous or very stupid.

"And Lady Answer, I would have thought you would be on your best behavior after the trouble with Detr. A good Scout does not miss her shift and then bring Outsiders to the very heart of the Hall of Scouts."

"This is a Takanis, Lord Insight," Answer said. "I found him in the tunnel to Detr and led him here."

Ra'ael kept her expression blank. If Answer wanted to claim credit, what did she care?

Lord Insight's mouth pinched in a frown as he walked around Galod. The hermit watched him, eyebrows raised.

Then Lord Insight snorted. "He bears a passing resemblance, yes, but he can hardly be a Takanis. Come now. Attend to the present, not to fancy."

Galod spoke, his tone stern as Ra'ael was used to. "Small minds should not tamper with what big minds have created. You have no idea what you're doing."

Scouts grabbed them, and Ra'ael shook them off.

Beside her, Galod reached out and rested his hand on the structure built out from the wall beside the doors that opened and closed by themselves. The metallic tang burst in her mind again, and she barely managed not to leap away from him, though she did step on someone's foot. The lights on the panels went out, and the room went quiet. A low hum started and then stopped moments later.

Ra'ael fell into a half crouch. Her heart pounded in her ears, her blood singing, ready for a fight. She had to get control of herself. She wasn't afraid of the dark. Why did she feel such fear?

"Ra'ael." Galod's murmur was like a lifeline, as well as an order to stay present.

She swung toward his voice, trying to orient, but all she could feel was the danger, the clogging thunderstorm in her mind, any time she got close to the walls or to Galod. Her stomach twisted until she feared she'd vomit all over.

Thin ribbons of light flickered on at about waist height.

"If you're ready to listen." A sense of menace exuded from Galod. "I'll turn the lights back on so you can see."

Not so "we" could see. Ra'ael barely had time for her thoughts to hiccup over that before the nausea took over her mind again.

"You cannot just capture fae, whoever you are," someone shouted.

Power was everything for Kamalti, and yet they showed only stubbornness in the face of Galod's power. She gritted her teeth on the bile that rose and tried to put bite into her voice, rather than trembling.

"You worked with Detr to kidnap and torture psions," she said. "You can listen to one of your own gods for a change."

"Or you can sit in the dark for a while until you see reason," Galod said.

"Scouts wouldn't know reason if it kicked them in the shin." It was all Ra'ael could do to force a casual tone to her voice against the waves of power and menace coming from him.

"All right. We are listening." Insight sounded defeated.

The lights sparked and brightened of their own accord, and Galod's thin smile sent a shiver down her spine. With a wince, she stepped away from the walls, repulsed by them as if they'd shoved her.

"How did you do that?" Answer asked, full of wonder.

Galod glanced at her. "To really know how a thing works—how to use it—you must know what it is. This is not a building."

Ra'ael's brow furrowed. "Of course it's a building."

The hermit's expression became expectant. "Come, now, Ra'ael. See the similarities. Jump across the distance of doubt to put two and two together and make five. Crystals and ships."

That couldn't be right. "It's a ship? But it wouldn't float."

Answer shook her head. "It is much too large. It has been here for generations, since the Takanis came."

"And how did the Takanis get here?" Galod asked. "Is there a size limit on ships? A mandate that they must always be where they're useful? Or that ships must sail through water?"

Ra'ael exchanged a glance with Answer. Galod wasn't making any kind of sense.

"You stole control of the Hall of Scouts," Lord Insight said. "Return it, immediately."

"If you make demands like children, I'll plunge you right back into the dark," Galod said. "Now tell me, what have you done to Ra'ael to make her so sensitive?"

A knock sounded at the door, and Ra'ael jumped. She stepped to the door as it opened, revealing Tjodlik and Dode. They stepped in slowly, taking in the room, and the door shut behind them again.

"Dode!" Ra'ael rushed to embrace her tightly, for as long as she could bear the stabbing pressure in her mind. "Are you all right?"

"Fine," Dode said. "But what about you?"

Antsy with the stares of the others and the prickling, nagging sense of wrong, Ra'ael just nodded. Dode squeezed her hands and then turned to Galod. The two stared at each other for a long time, as if taking the measure of each other.

"So. The Takanis have returned, then?" Dode asked.

Galod's tone matched hers. "And Ra'ael can barely stand to touch you, either, even though you clearly have a bond. Interesting."

"It's not interesting. It's awful. Make it stop, Galod." Ra'ael sounded like a child, but she couldn't help it.

"When did it start?" he asked. "When's the first time you had trouble?"

"I sensed something like this but less powerful before the chapel fell on us. On Taunos, Takiyah and me. We tried to stop it, tried to save the priest. And then there was the Running. And then when I came back here to live with Dode, it just kept growing."

"Such trauma, and then coming back while emotionally vulnerable, no doubt triggered the psionic technophobia," Galod said.

"How do we stop it?" Ra'ael asked. "The hunters from Detr would have killed me rather than stop it."

Dode grabbed Galod's hand, and the expression on the hermit's face was hilariously uncomfortable. Had Ra'ael ever seen such clear emotion from him, without being diminished and controlled by that iron will?

Dode either didn't see it or didn't care. "If you are a Takanis come again, you must help Ra'ael."

Ra'ael smiled. Only Dode would confront someone she considered a god. And only Answer would seek to use that god for her own gain. Ra'ael glanced at Tjodlik, who was watching the scene with his studying face on. Ah yes, Tjodlik would try to understand the nature of godhood.

"It may not be possible." Galod pulled away from Dode, who glared at him.

The fierce look on Dode's face resembled the one she wore to difficult meetings. "Detr will not have you again, Ra'ael. Mark my words."

Ra'ael forced a smile. "I'm just glad you're all right."

"What is this you were saying about the Hall?" Insight interrupted. "You called it a ship?"

"This is a technomage ship. Human in design. Low on power, too. But with your minimal understanding of technomancy, it's a feat you were able to link the ships with the power cables."

Dode shook her head. "By the stories, the Takanis did that before they left."

"Before they died, you mean," Galod said.

"The stories say they left." Dode frowned.

"They would have lived a long time but not forever. Perhaps they left to hide their demise, to let their legend live on among you. Or perhaps they were not aware of the dragons and what the atmosphere of this planet does to technomages."

Everything he'd said rolled together in Ra'ael's mind like the smoke that swirled in the air of the city. She gaped. "This 'ship' and the Takanis... they're from another world?"

Galod nodded.

She shook her head. "And the air... what does it do to... technomages?"

He looked at Answer. "You. Have you ever gone outside the mountain?"

Answer straightened and nodded.

"And how did it feel?"

The Scouts exchanged uneasy looks, but no one ventured information. Too much pride to admit whatever Galod was getting at, maybe.

"It felt like you were impotent. Your Gifts wouldn't work, would they." Galod pierced them each with his glare.

That didn't make sense. He was powerful even outside.

"But you can do things," Ra'ael said. "Your ripples—"

He cut her off. "I have my tricks. But you've never seen anything like what I can do down here, have you?"

She swallowed hard, thinking of the fae in the bubble, and shook her head.

Ra'ael stared at the room around her. This was all from another world? It was different talking to Taunos about other worlds because he was, well, Taunos. But this had been shaped by hands from another world. And Galod knew so much about it. Was he from another world too?

Was there a whole world full of dour Galods?

Drawing in a deep breath, she refocused on the bigger things. "So there's not much power left here? Does that mean we cannot use these... ships?"

Galod shook his head. "And the 'gift' won't last more than another couple generations, either."

"What is it?" Ra'ael asked.

"Tiny pieces of technomancy. Nanotech. Which is why you react to it, the ship, and to me, Ra'ael. It's all connected through the tech."

"Technomage... is that a race? A group?"

"Any race can become a technomage."

"Why did you not teach us any of this before?" Ra'ael asked.

"You didn't need to know before. Technomancy doesn't work on the surface."

"Come now," Dode said. "Has anyone given our guest anything to eat or drink? Where—"

The building—ship—rocked, and Ra'ael caught Dode as she stumbled. Other Scouts fell to the ground, looking very unhappy at their undignified positions.

"What was that?" snapped Insight.

Galod touched one of the shiny black panels. The entire wall of panels lit up with one huge picture, as if it were a window and they could see outside.

All chatter from the Scouts stopped.

Flame spouted downward from the top of the cavern, huge bursts of orange that stuck to the ceiling and the buildings, setting curtains ablaze as it flowed. As she watched, a sticky wad of orange fell from the ceiling, plummeting down to the streets, where it splashed apart, raining down on the market square. Another burst came from the vents in the ceiling, falling into the chasm.

Galod's expression went tight. "Dragons."

Few people were in sight, mostly Scouts, who ran to tend to the wounded and put out the fires that sprang up wherever the dragonfire hit something flammable. It wasn't like they could do anything else against dragons. Despite the fact that Kamalti built mainly with metal and stone, smoke was everywhere.

"I will call over the crystals to—" one of the Scouts began, opening a drawer, but Galod sprang over to him.

"And a dragon tooth?" He reached into the drawer and pocketed one of the crystals. "If they find out you have dragon teeth, they'll burn you down."

"Wha—"

Insight scowled. "Put that back! The fae— The fae warned of Outside influence."

"The way they influence you?" Ra'ael shot back. She waved at the wall that had become a window. "You're Scouts. You're supposed to protect your people. Get out there and protect them."

"What can we do about dragons?" Insight's voice went small.

Ra'ael kept her focus on the important things, just as Galod had when he'd steamrolled the Scouts earlier. "The dragonfire. Will this building withstand it? How do we get the dragons to go away? Not everyone can fit in these buildings."

"Dragons will do as they wish," Galod said. "Nothing can move them from their purpose. The only chance is to outlast them."

"The tunnels would shield people from the fire, but the smoke will be a problem," Tjodlik said.

"No." She shook her head. "The tunnels are too far with the fire raining down. These buildings are more centrally located, so a better option."

Galod's sharp eyes stabbed her. "The fae. We can rid ourselves of two problems at once."

Ra'ael blinked. "What about the fae?"

"Dragons and fae hate each other," he said. "The problem will solve itself."

It was a good idea. If they took Galod's fae out of the mountain and that drew the dragon away, the fire rain would stop. If anyone could face off against a dragon and stand a chance, it was a fae.

But Galod's power wouldn't work Outside. The Gift didn't work

Outside.

"Wait. Does that mean... Would I be better, then, Outside?" she asked.

"It's possible."

Tears sprang to her eyes, and she turned to Dode. "But then I wouldn't see you."

"Perhaps you could visit. Or I could visit you." Dode smiled and reached out to pat her hand before apparently rethinking that.

Ra'ael bit her lip against a scowl. Dode shouldn't have to rethink things like comfort. And she'd be leaving Galod behind too. There was no way he would go from controlling buildings with a thought to living without that again, even if his ripples were awe-inspiring.

She straightened her back. So be it. She would stumble onward the best she could. "All right, so you said the fae problem and the dragon problem could be solved together. And I need to get Outside. How do I get your bubbled fae Outside?"

Tjodlik's eyes widened in horror. "Not alone. You need help."

"I'm sure between Ra'ael and me, we can manage," Galod said. "We don't have much time. The dragons are angry. There's been too much technomancy here, not to mention the rippling of technomancy and psionics from whatever these hunters did to Ra'ael."

Too much technomancy, partly from Galod. But it was the "we" that grabbed her attention. She stared at him. "But..."

His face was expressionless. Masked again. "You thought I would stay with my power? Power leads to terrible consequences. It makes people think perhaps they could be gods. No, I cannot stay."

"Better go now then before anyone else gets hurt," Ra'ael said. She looked at Dode, loath to leave her, hating how she was also loath to hug her. Even so, she stepped forward and embraced the old woman. "Please be careful."

"Your beloved shroud. It is still at my house," Dode said.

She didn't need it, just as she didn't need the rules beyond what she knew to be truth. Ra'ael squeezed Dode's hands. "Keep it and remember me."

"Visit now and again," Dode said. "And I will visit you."

Tjodlik also stepped forward and hugged Dode. "Please do be careful. Tell my servant Vefng to keep my house as his own while I am gone. And I will be sure to catalogue all my adventures for you."

"Tjodlik?" Ra'ael stared at him.

"What?" he asked. "I am the only one you can touch right now. There is no guarantee you will not react to him on the Outside as well. You need someone not affected by this, someone you will not react to."

Warmth filled her heart. He was leaving his home behind to help her? It was too much. "You just want to find Tamarik."

Tjodlik laughed. "You will, too. I will make sure of it."

Ra'ael shifted her weight, torn, while Galod gathered up his bubbled fae. She fidgeted with impatience to leave, to get Outside where she would feel better and where they could hopefully save Codr again.

And yet, that meant leaving Dode, again, which tore at her heart.

Dode left briefly, and then returned, pressing Ra'ael's sword and dagger into her hands. Ra'ael gripped the familiar hilts, her throat too tight to speak, and Dode nodded, speechless herself.

The Scouts marched them out the door, with Tjodlik hurrying beside her. The last few times she'd left Codr had been nothing like this—first, with Kaemada, Taunos, and Takiyah, broken but foolishly hopeful, then with the hunters from Detr, running from pain, from herself. Now, Galod and Tjodlik accompanied her, and the Scouts were on their best behavior. Cloth was wound around each of their heads to combat the smoke, which nevertheless made her eyes water and lungs hurt.

Hope niggled at her, and she clamped down on it. If she got Outside and still couldn't handle being near Galod, at least she'd tried. She'd figure another way through it because she was not going to quit, and eventually, she'd be able to visit Dode again. She insisted on it.

But she wasn't going to abandon these people to dragonfire, and she wasn't going to leave Galod alone to confront the dragons and let the fae loose, psionic technophobia or no.

Another spout of flame rushed down, and they hurried up the steps, coughing. The fae moved a hand before stilling with a sharp scent of thunderstorm from Galod's direction.

Ra'ael winced, ducking away from him and the buzzing of her skin. She rebounded off the rock wall to race up the steps. They had to hurry. Galod was losing control of the fae, clearly—what little rest he'd gotten while the fae was in a holding cell was not enough. Tjodlik was fast on her heels, and the Scouts fell away behind them. Of course they did—it wasn't like they'd fight the fae for them if he did get loose.

Her lungs and legs burned as they reached the top of the stairs, and Tjodlik was puffing and gasping for breath, coughing in the thicker smoke. Ra'ael drew his arm across her shoulders, helping to support him while she struggled to breathe.

She pulled the door open until Galod waved a hand and the doors sprang apart. Ra'ael shook her head at him, shivering as she entered the strange little room between the doors, while Tjodlik followed, wide-eyed. Behind them, the door hissed as it sealed, the Scouts locking it from the cavern side against the release of a very angry fae.

The air inside was clear, and Ra'ael drew in lungfuls of clean air, while Tjodlik bent over, hands on his knees, breathing raggedly.

Ra'ael drew him upright. "Back straight. Lets you catch your breath better."

Galod looked around as the knee-height lines of light glowed on. "So that's what they did with the airlocks."

Ra'ael pointed at the door to Outside, just a few paces away. "That one sticks unless you're a Scout or they open it for us."

The fae in the bubble spasmed.

Ra'ael stepped between him and Tjodlik. "We need to hurry."

"As soon as we're out, run and find cover." Galod waved his hand, and the bubble swept past him, so it was between him and the door. The fae twitched again.

And then sharpness filled the air, and the door opened as Ra'ael winced. Galod sprang forward, the fae twitching in the bubble until it broke. Tjodlik stopped, covering his eyes from the blinding sun. After so long underground, Ra'ael squinted in the light as well. The ground was hot and smoking, and her stomach turned as a dragon, flying close by, banked and came around, heading right for them.

She grabbed Tjodlik's arm and hauled him in the other direction from where Galod and the fae had gone. The farther away they were from that clash of power, the better.

"Move! Come on, this way," she shouted, shoving him forward. They had to find cover.

They dove under the shelter of an enormous boulder just as the world exploded with fire. Galod crouched under another boulder many paces away, staring upward with a grim expression. She couldn't see any sign of the fae, and the hair on the back of her neck prickled. Tjodlik gripped her hand with a strength she hadn't been aware he had, and she gripped his just as tightly. Somehow, she didn't feel trapped in the close space, even pressed shoulder to shoulder with him. The claustrophobia only buzzed vaguely in the background. She certainly didn't want to be out there with the dragon.

"I'm sorry—" she started, but then dragonfire rained down again and the world was a roaring mess of heat and flames. She imagined the rock above her was melting, that the whole world was washed in flames, but

Tjodlik pressed against her—that felt solid. Felt real.

The fire paused, and Ra'ael's ears pricked. Was the dragon gone? Was Galod still alive? Was the fae? Some instinct roared at her that it wasn't safe yet, that they couldn't leave cover yet.

She turned her attention to Tjodlik. "I'm sorry. I almost got you killed —twice. And even after the first time, you still left home for me."

"I have never seen a dragon, much less the sky. Will we cook over a fire next? I should have brought a thicker cloak, I think."

It was ridiculous. Exhausted mentally and physically, in pain, Ra'ael crouched in a divot under a boulder with a Kamalti nobleman who wanted an adventure. Tjodlik was exquisitely himself, and there, hiding from a dragon on the surface of a mountain that hid a city she had saved—yet again—things snapped into focus for her.

Her relationships with others may have changed, and her role, even her ambitions. The trappings didn't matter, after all. She was more than that, more than what others said she was.

She'd lost faith in herself when she'd Fallen. Eloí and the spirits were part of her, part of everything. And because of that, no one could ever take her faith and who she was away from her.

And there, deep inside of her, was the song of the spirits, where it had always been.

Not in her head as with the fae's illusion but at the core of her, and it rang with truth and the steady existence throughout the turning of the cycles. It bloomed through her very being, twining around her own song. After so long without the song, so long worrying about who others said she was rather than just being herself, trusting in the guidance of her heart, she had it back. Purpose, direction. A story.

And so, while around them the world burned, Ra'ael laughed.

Chapter Twenty-four

The dragons are wind spirits weighed down and given form by their greed.
Give them a wide berth and shun those who associate with them. Choose honor and
do not close yourself away from the wind, lest you, too, become like a dragon.
—Hinanuri lore

The curtain rippled behind Amanah, and Taunos turned, spinning her behind him. It rippled again, and Emin stood, stance ready. The fabric wall was pulled to the side, revealing Dinweyi. Letting out his breath, Taunos tried to relax.

Dinweyi stepped in, letting the fabric fall. She flicked it, creating a ripple like they'd seen before she entered. "This asks for entrance. Like the knocks of the Dahuti, but fabric doesn't do well for knocking."

"Ah, I see," Amanah said.

"I came to tell you the Puwileh would like to see you for supper, if you can handle that." Dinweyi's tone was sharp with derision, her eyes locked on Taunos.

He drew himself up, despite the dread weighing him down. He'd shown weakness, a lot of it, and Dinweyi seemed the type to make him pay for it. He'd take whatever was coming, so long as Emin and Amanah were safe.

Amanah spoke up before he could. "That would be lovely. We're honored by such gracious hospitality from kind hosts."

Dinweyi's eyes flicked to Amanah and then back to Taunos. Behind Dinweyi, a woman's voice whispered, but Taunos could not make out the words.

Dinweyi nodded. "Keep watch. I would have words with this sea-wizard alone."

Emin shifted, falling into a ready stance just as Taunos did. Wariness pricked at the back of Taunos's neck.

Dinweyi snorted. "So prone to violence." She kicked the cushions on the floor. "So weak."

"You said you wanted to have words," Taunos said. "Were they all to be insults?"

"I will not allow our Puwileh's honor to be tarnished with lies. Did you speak the truth when you said you were the son of Leen?" The gleam in Dinweyi's eyes made Taunos's stomach roil.

Emin and Amanah had told him the Hinanuri despised lies. Taunos chose his words carefully. "I am Lína's son. I presume they are the same person."

"I brought you, in good faith, to the Puwileh. I waited faithfully for years to be the one to greet Leen when she returned. And all I find is you, pathetic. And you tell me all my waiting, all my faithfulness, was for naught?"

"Your insults are not welcome here," Amanah said.

Dinweyi's lip curled. "He flinched the whole way into the City of the Promise, cringing like a coward. He leaps to be ready to do violence at the merest breath, and yet he knows not where the danger is. And that display in front of the Puwileh... weak."

"I was surprised," Taunos said. Shocked, really, as if he'd been told up was really down and his teachers had always known it but kept it to themselves.

"You were hysterical. The son of Leen would not be so weak."

"You might be surprised how you'd feel to discover that much of what you knew was lies." He glanced at Amanah, a new wave of empathy for her welling in him.

"I will not let you tarnish the Puwileh's honor," Dinweyi spat. "You will show you have honor, like Leen, or I will not suffer you to live."

Patha poked her head in. "Dinweyi, hurry. The Puwileh's father is coming."

Dinweyi whirled to face her. "The Puwileh's honor is the honor of us all, and I will not let this coward destroy it." She sneered at him. "Here you sit, cowering with your friends instead of standing on your own."

Of all his faults, this was not one, and he refused to let her disparage his friends. They were the strongest people he knew, and standing with them was a strength and an honor. "I am no coward—"

"Prove it then. Realmwalk, and let me smell again the scent of realmwalking, the scent of a thunderstorm."

Taunos's brow furrowed. There was no smell to his realmwalking.

Emin leaned close. "Remember the plan."

"Prove to me you are someone we can say the Puwileh hosted with honor," Dinweyi said. "Prove you are Leen's blood."

"We have to work together to get out of here," Emin murmured.

"Have you no honor at all?" Dinweyi sneered. "Stand on your own, as a true warrior."

"Wars don't win with one soldier." Emin glared back at Dinweyi.

"You don't have to carry everything yourself," Amanah said. "Not your cares, not their suspicions."

"Your friends expose you for who you are. A gutless worm." Dinweyi shook her head.

Taunos's hands clenched. "I have never had truer friends."

"Choose now. Are you a hero, a man of legend fit for the Puwileh to host, or will you follow your friends into weakness and obscurity?" She waved a hand dismissively at him. "Perhaps your friends need to be taken out of the picture? You're so easily controlled by them."

With how highly the Hinanuri regarded their honor, what would happen to Emin and Amanah if he didn't play Dinweyi's game? If he did, it was a chance—possibly a better chance than Emin's plan. After all, Taunos could be the distraction, and Amanah and Emin were currently stronger than he was. They could run, and he could realmwalk to find them again.

Again he was asked to choose, but this time, he could hopefully save his friends some pain, maybe even gain them honor by association with a sea-wizard. They deserved all the honor they could get.

And this was something he could do, even despite his still-healing wrist. Every other wound was mostly healed, enough not to hinder him, but his song ached for the freedom of succeeding again without his wrist holding him back.

He set his mind on the Promise Tree, keeping Emin and Amanah in mind, too.

Nothing happened. He couldn't realmwalk, not with others, even as close as Emin and Amanah were, within arms' reach and held close in his heart. Yet again, he wasn't strong enough.

He looked at Amanah, letting his regret come through. "I can't."

"Taunos, no." Amanah's voice was full of worry.

He fixed Dinweyi with a stern glare. "If I realmwalk, I cannot usually make it back precisely."

"Taunos no!" Emin said. "You don't have to choose."

Emin lunged forward, but Taunos stepped in front of him. "This is one thing I can do for you."

He turned to Dinweyi. "Don't hurt them."

"Realmwalk, and they won't be harmed," Dinweyi snapped.

Taunos narrowed his focus to just himself and the Promise Tree.

Old Man Tānos's voice sounded beyond the curtain. "What is going on here? Explain."

Would he help or threaten them even more? He couldn't risk it. Taunos held in his mind every piece of himself and leaped for the Promise Tree across the Everything between realms.

Patha's tone was angry. "We will not let this man fool our Puwileh. You and she may simply assume he is who he says he is, but we will have proof. If the Puwileh is shown to be easily fooled, our whole region will suffer, for her honor is ours. Dinweyi is protecting—"

Her voice cut off. A crisp wind bit at him.

The Promise Tree stretched above him.

Taunos set his forehead against it, slumping. Again, he hadn't had to go through the waypoint first. Clearly, it was much easier to realmwalk to a tree. If only he could carry others with him. Immediately, he set his mind back on the room in the Puwileh's palace and realmwalked, once again ignoring the awful world he'd always used as a waypoint.

When he opened his eyes, he was standing in a small, dark room. Terror surged to drown his mind. He was trapped. The walls loomed too close.

Taunos scrambled for a door and tumbled through a curtain into a larger room with a bed, a side table, and walls made of fabric. He stood there, controlling his ragged breathing, pushing the claustrophobia back down. He must be in the city, then.

He brushed aside the curtain, wishing there were windows so he could see where he was. A corridor stretched before him, and he hurried down it. He had to get back to Amanah and Emin. If he tried realmwalking again, he was likely to end up farther away. He had to get back to the palace immediately. Anger and fear wrestled within him. If anything happened to them because he wasn't as precise as Dinweyi wanted, he'd never forgive himself. He'd failed to follow Emin's plan.

"What are you doing here?" A strident voice sounded behind him.

Taunos turned, hands raised. "My apologies."

A young woman confronted him, knife in hand. "Thief! Get out of my house. Do you know what happens to uninvited men in the City of Promise?"

Chased by the woman, he stumbled out onto the street, embarrassment heating his face. At least he had confirmation he was in the right city. He looked up and down the street. There was more traffic toward the left, so that was the direction he went. Hopefully that would lead to the main road and he could make his way back to the palace.

Once again, he was on his own. Olorah had said, back with the Resistance, that he was terrible at working as a team, and he seemed to continually proving her right, no matter how far away he was. He'd change that, just as soon as he got back to Amanah and Emin. Had they used his distraction to flee? He couldn't leave the city until he knew for sure.

Worry dogged his steps as he hurried through the streets, dodging people without really seeing them. He bumped into someone and stopped short, appalled at himself. What was he doing? He rarely bumped into anyone. He needed to pay more attention, to see the possible dangers before they arose.

An old man lay on the ground where he'd fallen, his nose wrinkled up and his eyes bright on Taunos.

Taunos knelt to help him up. "Please forgive me. I should have been watching where I was going."

The man rose to unsteady feet but didn't let go of Taunos's hand. "Realmwalker, are you?"

Taunos stared at him, unsure how to answer that.

The man gripped his hand more firmly. "I remember that feeling. I remember it. Tell me, do you fly?"

"Excuse me," Taunos said, stepping back and withdrawing his hand.

"No, no, don't go. Don't go!" The man clung to him, tears filling his eyes. "Remind me how it feels to fly, the dragon beneath you, the infinite worlds."

The truth struck Taunos, and he grabbed hold of the ragged man, both of them holding on to each other like a drowning man clinging to a log. "You're dragonbonded. They call you a dragon monk here? I saw you when we entered the city."

"Was," the man said, nodding. "Was. And you? You?" His face crumpled, confusion entering his eyes. "No dragon?"

Taunos shook his head. "Only telekinesis. But I realmwalk."

"Nothing like a dragon." The man grinned at him.

Taunos matched his grin. "Tell me, how do the dragons realmwalk with their bonded?"

A scoff answered him. "With their minds, of course."

"What are you doing?" another man interrupted, coming up on them. "Leave him alone."

Taunos was about to apologize, but the man swatted at the ragged man instead. "Useless beggar, accosting stand-up citizens. Please excuse him, sir. He's lost his mind."

"No, it's all right," Taunos said, stepping between the two. "This is just my uncle."

The man scoffed. "Your uncle? This madman is always on this street, drunk or otherwise."

"I've been out of town." Taunos put his arm around the ragged man's shoulders and steered him away.

"You're too tall to be bonded," the ragged man said. "Everyone's too tall here. Smaller's better. Take some weight off."

A laugh escaped him, and Taunos continued guiding the man toward the busier roads, hoping they would lead to the palace. "Come on. I have questions, and if you can answer them, I will get you a meal. I have to get back to somewhere first."

"I want to get back to somewhere too." The man's head came up, and a greedy glint came into his eyes. "A meal? A hot meal?"

Taunos nodded. "No less than you deserve."

"What do you want to know?"

"I need to know if there's a way for me to realmwalk while carrying others. Like the dragons do."

"Shhh," the man said. "Tell me telepathically. The others will think you're mad, too."

"I only have telekinesis."

The man stopped in his tracks, and Taunos turned, shielding him from the street traffic. The man trembled, his eyes shining. With one shaking finger, he poked Taunos hard in the chest. Taunos stepped back, scowling and rubbing at his chest. The beggar poked him hard again, and Taunos twisted to avoid the pressure.

"What are you doing?" he grumbled.

"Another Rinaryn?" The whisper was nearly inaudible. "Could it be?"

Time seemed to stop spinning. The hairs on the back of his neck prickled, and then Taunos seized the man by the back of the neck, bringing him forehead to dirty forehead with him. "You're Rinaryn?"

He released him, stepping back to take him in again. Short, light-boned underneath the bulky, dirty rags that covered him. Brown eyes and black hair could be Hinanuri, but that round face.

"You're Rinaryn!" It was barely a whisper from his lips.

Tears streamed down the ragged man's face. "My name is Upra, and I was from Dragonmoor. My old name," he sniffed, gulped, and sniffed again, "was Weros Ferei Tāta Upra Thulero, from Kirel."

"I am Taunos of Torkae, in Heartwood. And if you can teach me how, I will bring you home. The Monks of Annularei should welcome you."

Upra leaned against him, weeping and giggling all at once, clutching him for support. Wrapping his arms around the man's filth-ridden shoulders, Taunos half-carried him onward, up the street, regardless of the stench of the man and the looks passersby gave them. Impatience nipped at him, riding in the wake of his worry for Amanah and Emin. But he couldn't leave the man behind if there was a way to bring him home. There were dragonbonded other places than his home!

"I asked the Monks of Annularei about realmwalking long ago." Taunos kept his tone low, taking advantage of the wide berth others gave them as Upra collected himself. "They wouldn't talk to me."

"Ah, so I'm not the only one shunned, hmm?" Upra asked.

Taunos smiled at him. "You're not. I'm Fallen. That makes for a fairly complete shunning."

"A Fallen and a dragonbonded without his dragon. A fine pair we make."

"Can you help me? I've never been able to realmwalk with anyone. And it's always been difficult, except for the time I jumped to Far Dahutad. They have a Seeker Tree there, you see, and—"

"The nexus, of course."

They walked on, while Taunos waited for Upra to elaborate, but he was quiet. Taunos nudged him. "The nexus? The Ifreesians mentioned that, too. What is it?"

"The system of trees, you fool."

"And how does that help?"

Upra snorted. "We are Rinaryn. We are tied to this world, this one, right here." He stomped his feet as if to make his point.

Taunos shook his head. "I still don't understand."

The long-suffering sigh that Upra released was so emphatic that he nearly fell out of Taunos's grasp. "You may be tall, but goodness your mind is *tiny*! Look."

He shoved his hand in Taunos's face, and Taunos recoiled, blinking.

Upra wiggled his fingers. "Look, if you jump from finger to finger to finger, they're all connected, see? The system. The nexus. Much easier than jumping from one hand to the next or one person to the next."

Taunos frowned. "Are you saying that if I realmwalk from tree to tree I can bring someone with me?"

If he could do that… That changed everything.

Upra cackled. "Should work. Only one way to find out."

Taunos grinned. "I'm eager to try it. How can I know where other trees are?"

"The best way is on dragon back. By dragon memory."

"And if that's not an option?"

"Are you really going to take me home?" Tears welled up in the man's eyes, and he began weeping again.

Taunos held him close, his arm straining, trying not to bump his bad wrist. "What normally happens to you dragonbonded out here? Do you not have a Monks of Annularei?"

Upra shook his head, stumbling along beside him, shaking with some odd mixture of weeping and laughter. He still hadn't recovered by the time they made it back to the palace. Halfway up the stairs, a patrolling guard shouted for them to halt, racing forward to block their way.

"I was just here with Dinweyi. I met the Puwileh." Taunos stepped to the side, but the guard glowered and pushed him back. Unbalanced with Upra's weight, Taunos staggered down several steps before steadying them both once more.

The guard wrinkled her nose. "Right. You and the beggar man, I'm sure."

Taunos frowned. "Please, I need to get in."

"No admittance. The palace is not open for just anyone to wander through. Head back to your filth, or better yet, take a bath."

"All right, at least get Dinweyi. I need to speak with her."

The guard scoffed. "No."

"Did anyone come out? A man and a woman, from the Kanhu clan?"

"No one has left. Nor is anyone getting inside."

Taunos started to protest again, but she stepped forward, driving him farther down the stairs.

"Don't make me ask impolitely," the guard said. "Go home."

"I'm trying," Taunos grumbled. But he didn't want to go without Amanah, not if he didn't have to.

Upra shoved away from him. "You said you'd feed me. I have lost my dragon, but I am not a fool."

Taunos backed away from the menacing guard, reaching out for Upra, who swatted his hand, stumbling away. The guard watched impassively, and after glancing around for some other option, Taunos followed the beggar back down the stairs.

He had nothing. No money, no equipment, nothing to his name. And no idea what Dinweyi was doing with Emin and Amanah. They hadn't made it out—were they all right?

At the bottom of the stairs, Upra turned on him. "A fine joke, making as if you were my people, giving me hope, only to crush it. Dragonfire on you!"

"Upra, I'm sorry. I didn't mean any harm. I didn't expect a guard to stop us."

The man snorted. "You've never even been up there, admit it."

"I was just up there," Taunos protested. "Dinweyi wanted me to prove I could realmwalk. I wanted to save my friends."

"You should be careful who knows what you can do," Upra said. "People take advantage."

"I'm usually more careful." Taunos tilted his head. "You were dragonbonded. Can you do something with your telepathy?"

Upra snorted. "Not anymore. Once I could bond a dragon. Now I'm nothing."

"No, I'm not talking about bonding a dragon. I mean something small."

The scowl on Upra's face darkened. "No need to rub it in. I have no telepathy anymore, great or small. That is what happens when you bond a dragon and she dies."

"I'm sorry, Upra. I didn't know."

"And now you do."

"And I still intend to get you home. And a meal, if I have anything to say about it."

Upra jutted his chin toward the steps. "What's up there?"

"My friends, remember? I said?"

Shaking his head, Upra collapsed in on himself, rocking back and forth. The movement reminded Taunos of Kaemada, and guilt pricked him with its claws again. He had to get back to her, as well. He sighed, looking back up the stairs. He should take Upra back to the Promise Tree and see if he could take him home.

But he couldn't just leave Amanah. He should have followed Emin's advice. He shouldn't have separated from them. If Dinweyi hurt them…

He clenched his fists, narrowing his attention to his breathing until the swell of panic receded a bit. Guilt took its place, with cruel fangs. He couldn't protect anyone anymore. Not by himself.

Upra muttered to himself. Taunos crouched beside him, patting his bony shoulders while shame layered on him. Who was doing this for his sister while he was away? It'd been much longer than he'd intended, and he had avoided thinking of his duty for some time.

The smell of trees whispered through his mind, but this time, he seized the sensation and threw it out, holding on to what was important. Why did he think of trees whenever he thought of going back these past four moons? And why had it whisked his intentions of going home away like wind?

Upra's head jerked up, and he seized Taunos with hands curled like claws. The man sniffed, his nose wrinkling. "You stink like fae."

"What?"

The beggar blinked. "Your mind smelled of fae. It's gone now."

The forest. Before he'd realmwalked, he'd seen a fae face. He swallowed hard. Had they somehow influenced his mind?

Whatever was going on, he wasn't going to let it continue. First, he needed to make sure Amanah and Emin were safe. Then, to get out of the city along with Upra. And then, he had to check on his sister. It'd been far too long, and if he was going to bring the Elders to account, he should do it with his sister at his side, and Takiyah and Ra'ael.

"I'm going to get them. I will be back," he promised, tasting the ash of the broken promises of the past in his mouth.

And then he rose and headed up the broad, tall steps.

The same guard from before confronted him. "Last warning."

"Take me to the Puwileh. Dinweyi or Tānos would work as well."

Grabbing him by the back of his shirt, the guard forced him back down the stairs. "Prisoners don't get to make demands. I tried to be polite. Trespassers are not welcome."

His face burned, remembering his earlier unintentional trespass. But he needed to get to the others.

As the guard turned him parallel with the stairs, he spun free of her hold and charged up the steps. Her shout followed him, as did the sounds of her pursuit, but he raced into the palace, trying to remember the way to the room where he'd met the Puwileh. He wasn't sure where Amanah and the others would be by now, but surely the Puwileh would know.

His still bare feet were grateful for the carpets lining the floors in the palace, but his breath sounded loud in the ever-present silence. Before long, Old Man Tānos stepped out before him.

Taunos skidded to a stop. "Where's Dinweyi? Are my friends all right?"

Old Man Tānos lifted a hand to the guard coming up quickly behind him, and she paused just within arms-reach, gasping for breath. "Please, calm yourself. Running in this place? This lack of decorum is not—"

A murmur floated from the room next to him. Dinweyi. Taunos charged in, leaving behind Old Man Tānos's cry of dismay and shaking off the guard's hand when she tried to stop him.

"I did not wish—" The Puwileh paused, teacup half-raised, while Dinweyi leaped to her feet, spinning to meet him.

"There, are you satisfied?" Taunos asked. "Let my friends go."

"You have interrupted a meeting of women of high rank," the guard behind him growled. "Such things are forbidden."

"Do you see, Puwileh? He has nothing of Leen about him. No finesse, no strength. Yes, he disappeared before my eyes, but it was not the same as it was with Leen, and he left his friends to save himself. He is utterly without honor."

"I wasn't trying to save myself—" Taunos started.

The guard interrupted, leveling her knife at his throat. "And just now, he broke into the Puwileh's home."

"I do not want an enemy of you, but I need to know my friends are all right." Taunos glared at Dinweyi.

The Puwileh rose, her expression tight with disapproval. "Dinweyi's report is quite serious. Your companion skulking around, spying, and now this? Where did you go, and why? The only people who sneak around at night are thieves and assassins, cowards both of them. Which are you?"

"Dinweyi told me to realmwalk, to prove I was who I said I was."

"And you proved you're spineless," Dinweyi said.

"Dinweyi has faithfully served me all my life," the Puwileh said. "I will not have you sowing distrust."

Dinweyi's voice was calm, her eyes alight with a hint of triumph. "Regardless, he interrupted a meeting, Puwileh. The law is clear. We must be rid of him."

The Puwileh nodded, clenching her hands before her. "It is, unfortunately. Take him and the others and place them in the holding shaft."

The triumph disappeared, and Dinweyi's mouth twisted. "That is not what the law says."

"No, but it is what your Puwileh says."

"He could disappear again."

"Not, I think, if it leaves his friends behind. Look at what he's done so far for them."

Dinweyi scowled at him, and Taunos returned her expression.

"Dinweyi warned you they could not be trusted, Puwileh," one of the guards along the wall said.

Taunos forced himself to remain calm. "On the friendship my mother had with—"

"The memory of your mother only gets you so far," the Puwileh snapped. "I will hear no more of this. Do as I say. I will consider the matter overnight, and I will not be making a decision before morning. Is that clear, Dinweyi?"

Dinweyi glared at Taunos. "As clear as the wind spirits favor you, Puwileh."

Chapter Twenty-five

The worst thing about dealing with another psion mind to mind is the subtlety, especially if the other has been trained from birth. That talent to reach into your mind and feed you fears and dreams that come from the very deepest parts of you means it's hard to know that your thoughts are not entirely your own. I think it no accident that the elves are known for healing sicknesses of the mind. It's the purity of that healing that I question.

—notes from Kaemada Sierso, psion

Kaemada inspected the sapling in front of her. Its leaves were spotted, but it should recover. She reached into the bag of mulch next to her, patting it around the tree's trunk to feed the soil that gave so many rich gifts. The mulch fell between her fingers like life-giving rain. She had split the dead tree that made up the wood shavings and chopped it up with her own hands. The fungi had covered it, feeding on death, and had themselves fed others. She'd left parts of the fungi-covered log in the forest to continue their purpose.

Each part of the forest was connected, all with needs, all with gifts. Just as she'd been connected with Ra'ael and Takiyah and Taunos.

A rush of homesickness fell on her like a rotten limb from a dying tree, crushing her beneath it for a few breaths. Her newly healed ribs ached with remembered pain as her heart ached for her friends. They needed each other, as surely as the cha'awoods supported the rowoods that grew nearby.

What were her people as a whole in this system of connected needs? And what were the elves? She had watched as the elves took in travellers from all over, watched them heal. More subtly, she'd begun keeping her walls low around the elves, eavesdropping as they eavesdropped on everyone else. The chatter of the elves washed over her every time a newcomer came. She could learn some about the world through dreamwalking without leaving the Stand. The elves likely used dreamwalking as well as reading the memories of those who came. It gave them time and distance to avert threats.

The web of life fed on itself, sustaining itself. Each link in the chain was necessary, vital to the healthy function of the whole. Any imbalance created a sickness for the whole that would have to be corrected. And even those at the top still fed the others when they died.

Her stomach turned. Not that she was even contemplating killing the elves. Who knew if they were even at the top?

But the idea still stood. They were crushing Rinaryn who came to them, and while replenishing resources was necessary, there had to be a more fair way. The Rinaryn were not simply wells of power for the elves to use, as they had taught her. They were not simply memories to teach the elves what was going on in the world around them, with a reach as far as the distance people would travel for healing. They deserved to be treated with true dignity of their own, not falsehoods clad in smiles.

She'd said as much when Umril had told her to stay in the forest today. Balance. Roots entangled together, a network of connection. She'd pressed it on Umril like he had pressed calm on her before. They needed to give, too. A real gift, not a gain for themselves disguised as a gift.

It still hadn't swayed them.

"I should be so angry at you," Cheros said as he arrived, dumping his stone tools in a pile next to her. He moved around her, weeding the ground with vicious rips of his hands. "But they turn the psions first. No wonder you spend time with them."

She winced. "I have spoken to them, Cheros. It's true they need the resources they use to help us, but that shouldn't take so many summers of service. Instead, they rely on our strength. I'm going to continue to argue for you to be allowed to go home, but they will never let me go."

"A source of strength?"

"In me, they have... a psionic well, if you will. But it's all right. I promised."

"So did I," Cheros growled. "What would you do if you did leave? If you ran past the guardians they have on patrol?"

"The guardians..."

"You haven't felt that shiver of fear when the birds flutter past? Or the butterflies?"

She nodded, spreading more mulch. This simple task, she understood. How to help Cheros, not so much. She reached out to him mentally, brushing away the layers of calm the elves had placed on him.

He glared at her. "Do you have anyone you miss? Or do you care for no one?"

His anger, newly released, bit at her, and she wondered yet again if she was doing the right thing removing the elves' influence from him. But it wasn't right to bury someone else's emotions. It couldn't be right.

"I would see my son. I would hold him. I would make sure he was all right. I would make sure he knew I loved him."

Cheros nodded, and his expression softened. "See? It's not just us our work affects. It affects our loved ones, too."

"Friends and family. Kaetal." She swallowed back tears. She missed them desperately. They needed one another.

She'd made crude paper and simple dye, and she'd fashioned a brush from a stalk of grass fluffy with seed. She'd written down much of what she was learning about psionics, yes, but she'd also written to Taunos, Ra'ael, and Takiyah, explaining what she'd figured out about the Elders, wondering how they were. But she had no way of delivering the letters, no way to know where her friends and brother were.

"So why aren't you angrier?" Cheros asked. "Every time I see you, I get more angry."

"The elves... They suppress your anger. They do not get rid of it, but they mute it. I remove the muting."

His shoulders drooped, and he shook his head at her. "So you're helping me, and in return all I feel is more rage toward you."

She forced a brief smile. "I was afraid you would be angry, but I should have told you."

"I'm more angry at them," Cheros said.

Kaemada moved down the line, caring for the next plant in the row. It was important to give back for what she'd been given, and she was grateful for the psionics training, the space to heal, and the ability to speak Traveller's once again. While the elves served, they also benefited. But there was no balance here.

The thought disintegrated, floated away.

She shouldn't expect the elves to always put the Rinaryn first, she decided. The weight of the burden was less for her, with the freedom of dreamwalking, than it was for the others. It was too much for those confined here. More than they should bear.

Cheros stabbed his spade into the ground. "We need to rise up against them. They cannot take on all of us. There's as many of us as there are of them today, since they sent away the elf children."

Something in her shrank at the thought. "No, Cheros. It wouldn't work, anyway. They wouldn't fight, but they could keep us from fighting."

"Reason isn't working either."

"They let some go early."

"Have they? Or have they only made you think they did?"

She shook her head. The elves held such subtlety over their minds.

"No, perhaps they do not want people to know some were released early?"

Cheros scoffed. "Even if they did it, it's not enough."

"It might be a start, I think..." She shook her head. Why were her thoughts all cloudy? "No."

"I'm leaving. You should too." Cheros reached out for a moment and squeezed her hand. "If all you can do is keep my mind clear, well... That's something, anyway."

She nodded, though he was wrong. It wasn't nearly enough. And arguing wasn't working. But she needed to make that connection with the elves, the same as she did with Cheros. But building connections was far more difficult than she had at first assumed, for connections were impossible when the two sides didn't want to be linked, didn't want to understand. Words couldn't bridge the gap alone.

Maybe that was it. Elves were psionic and spoke mind to mind. She needed to use her psionics to convince them, not just words. Neither Traveller's nor Rinaryn swayed the elves, but psionics... That might be the way. She shivered, drawing in a deep breath, but resolve grew within her, blooming.

The elves at the edge of the plot stood serenely as they bent trees just so or tied branches together to fuse them.

Could she stop them, mind to mind?

She flinched, recoiling from the thought and knocking over the bag of mulch. The rich soil spilled out, flowing down the slope. Downhill, as was its purpose. When the hill became unstable, the heights flowed down to the depths. Nothing was meant to remain on high forever.

Reaching out with her mind, she took solace in Nimae's presence. The wolf was tracking a purisei and invited her to join, laughing when she declined. At least with Nimae, she had some small measure of balance again. How must her friends feel, at the whims of elves or fae who touched their minds or used their dreams? She didn't want to hurt them again, but fear kept a person stagnant.

She was getting better at dreamwalking, despite her still-limited range, but she hadn't found her friends yet. She had found elders in the kaetaln nearby with bad dreams and soothed them, but they kept reoccurring. At least she was certain the bad dreams didn't come from this Stand, for she sat and watched, but it was clear someone was affecting them. And she'd been trying to help the Collective in her dreamwalking sessions ever since they told her about the other Kamalti killing them, urging them to find safety rather than try for revenge.

If she found her brother, her friends, her son, she could serve the elves as required and at the same time comfort her friends if they needed it. But that left the kaetal elders caught in someone's web, and she couldn't let that stand. After all, they were all connected, just like the roots that tangled between the saplings she tended, sharing nutrients and holding the soil together. She needed to branch out like that, though she feared to get too close to Eian, for fear of his guardian.

Kaemada stifled a yawn. Even with Nimae as a buffer, dreamwalking every night took its toll. It still frightened her some, but the fear was fading. She had to practice as much as she could, here where she had the elves as backup.

But what of the others?

She had to leave, to join them.

Rising, she gathered her bag of mulch. She'd tended the last sapling assigned to her for the day, which meant it was time for a break and perhaps some lunch. But as she emerged from the grove, she spotted newcomers to the Stand unlike any who had come before. Fae.

She recognized them by their style of clothing: finely woven tunics and trousers with leather belts, as opposed to the elves' spider-silk robes and sashes. They looked exactly like elves, though their expressions seemed a bit more haughty. If the elves were all psionic, were the fae?

Kaemada quickly dropped her gaze to the soil before her, musing on the growing of trees and the spotted leaves of the sapling and the making of mulch. But beyond her thoughts, she listened, eyes open and feet walking, the way Umril had taught her.

She'd spent so long being mind-sick that it was easy to pretend. She relaxed into the emotionless state that had cocooned her after her accident dreamwalking and drifted into the Stand like a seed floating on the wind. The reputation still clung to her: she was a little slow, a little distant, a little unfocused, and everyone knew it. And she often followed the elves during the day, watching, learning, arguing, so it shouldn't raise suspicions for her to drift along in their wake today, too.

But all she got from the fae were demands. Their minds were filled with them. She brushed the mind of the nearest ever so lightly, only to be inundated with calculations she had no hope of figuring out, certainly not with so brief a glimpse. Eyes carefully unfocused, she continued her slow walk past the tree they were gathered in, thinking intently of herbs and not of the fae's gaze on her back.

She rounded the tree and ran right into Umril. "Ameyitum. I was—"

"—looking at the fae."

Kaemada frowned at him. "If you're going to finish my sentences, finish this one. You need to reduce the…"

Umril shook his head. "Why do you continue these arguments? The other Rinaryns don't even like you."

"It does not matter. They're right. You do not want to be compared to the fae? Do not be like them. Do not make people serve so long. It's not right."

She impressed on him her thoughts at the same time as she spoke. It was not right to force someone to think a certain way, to feel a certain way, to demand more than they could give. To serve. It was not right to treat someone without respect, not when every part of the system was necessary to the health of the whole.

Umril raised his hand, but she didn't let up, showing him the similarities between the elves and the fae, mind to mind. *Using others in this way, as a source of strength, it seems far more a fae thing than elven. You fell into using others, but you say you're not like fae. Prove it. Restore the balance.*

For a moment, his agreement and approval mingled with her lecture. *You are not wavering with psionic currents anymore. You are not bending in the elvish wind. Good.*

Will you do it? She narrowed her eyes, wary for the next attempt to distract her, but caught sight of a fae approaching from behind Umril. The fierce look on the fae's face set Kaemada's heart racing, and her chest tightened.

Umril's eyes widened with a hint of fear. He touched her forehead. "Sleep."

She woke in a large room. Her shawl blanketed her and Nimae, asleep on her chest. The sunlight streaming through the window was at the wrong angle. The room was filled with elves, and they were all talking, discussing something by the sounds of it, probably in elvish, since she did not understand any of it. The room was full of the hum of musical voices, raised in debate, she decided after listening to the tone of the speeches. She lay there and drifted, lest she be made to sleep again. Opening her awareness again, she let their thoughts wash over her. Thought to thought, language barriers were easily hurdled.

You will keep that psion here for her entire lifetime.

That is not our agreement with her.

We suffer you to live. Do not tempt our patience. You will not go against us in this.

Kaemada is free to go when her time is up. Our honor demands it.

What honor does an elf have? You live because we allow it. Do not forget who your betters are, elf.

You felt the brush of her mind because she is a child, that is all. She surely meant no harm in it.

I will not let a Rinaryn touch my thoughts and go free. We will take her then. For safekeeping.

She didn't like the sound of that.

The sleep was unnatural, and she didn't care for being a plaything of either fae or elves. But what could she do?

She slipped deep into Umril's mind. *Do you see the similarities?*

Now is not the time.

If not now, when?

Kaemada felt his discomfort as if it were hers. She tasted the truth of his words. *You're right. If we survive this, we will reduce the summers we ask for, in accordance with your lifespans.*

Her gratitude flooded her, and he dampened it. *Do not draw their attention.*

The fae. Their thoughts were tinged with violence, far greater than that of the Collective's thoughts. She let the arguments wash over her, drowning her own thoughts underneath them. Could she purposely set off another mind-burst? The last ones had been when she'd been trying to do something beyond her abilities. She wasn't sure she even wanted to know if she could do such a devastating thing. She was supposed to be healed, after all.

But the elves were influencing the thoughts and emotions of all in the Stand, and from the brush she'd had against the fae's minds, they would be even worse. She had to give the others a chance to leave, at least, and disrupt the fae's plans.

You have to dance to your own music. You cannot follow along in another's story. Her father's words had helped her hold against the Collective. She had to embrace the power she held, all of it. Growth and destruction. The psionic burst was her best option, if she could do it at will.

Kaemada drew in a slow, deep breath, willing herself to be uninteresting, looked over. And then she *roared*, pouring as much power into her psionics as she ever had before, aimed at the fae visitors. *You may be more powerful, but you are not better. Let the elves be, and let the Rinaryn people go.*

Her psionic effort lashed out. Nothing happened.

Umril's eyes widened. *You were by the Collective each time. A massive group of psions. It wasn't you who could release the mind-burst.*

The psionic burst didn't die after her shout. Umril added to it, harmonizing, and the other elves, each adding their power, while the fae lashed out to break it as she had against the Collective. She poured all of herself into it, all but for a message to Cheros.

Run, now. Take the others.

Sometimes, the more she learned about the use of psionics, the more it seemed to be a liability rather than a strength. Dreamwalking gave her no time to truly sleep and required a tether. That tether forced her to continue to depend on an animal bond. She would always need an animal companion. Psionics were strictly controlled under Rinaryn law, and because of that, she had exploded in the minds of nearby psions twice because of inadequate practice. And now, she was susceptible to an elf who manipulated her emotions and thoughts when it suited him.

But also because of all those things, because of her connection to an elf and her bond to Nimae and her barely controlled strength, she lashed out at the fae in a way the elves would never do.

A psionic burst exploded, made up of the minds of the elves of the First Stand twined with the minds of the fae. At the last moment, something blocked her, kicking her back into Nimae. Kaemada stared in awe and horror as the elves and fae collapsed.

She swallowed hard, trembling, separating her mind from the wolf's again. One figure remained sitting, and he turned to face her. Umril.

"You have done well. You and all the others are free to go. Run, before the fae wake up. Be far away from here by then. Up to now, all you have done is ignite fires and create chaos, but we believe you have the capacity to bind together and to put out fires. So, in your chaos, we will send you out to go forth and spread order… chaotically, if you must." Umril wobbled to her and kissed her forehead then pressed his head against hers. "Go. This Stand will be healing no one else."

He took in a deep breath, sighed it out, and slumped to the floor.

A cry escaped Kaemada, and she checked him for life. But he seemed to be only sleeping. Her hand trembled. Why did it feel as if something terrible had just happened? She stumbled out of the tree and into the sun. The last of the other Rinaryn raced into the forest, heads covered with the strange circlets of the elves. The elves who had been outside lay on the ground, as well. She turned in a slow circle, certain she was missing something. Some horrible thing.

She thought back to the way Umril had said goodbye to her, how permanent it seemed. And the fae… *You live because we allow it.* Her stomach turned. Umril and the elves had helped her create a mind-burst. The fae would not look kindly on such a thing.

Kaemada turned, running back to Umril and kneeling beside him. She delved into his mind, for after so many contacts between them, his mind would be the easiest to reach, the easiest to comprehend. She didn't have to search long for confirmation, for he had held it in his mind, hoping she would do exactly this.

The fae would come, with swords and murder in their eyes. But the elves were pacifists. Even if they had time to prepare, they wouldn't fight, and how long they had was unknowable. It all depended on if the fae had hidden an army nearby, predicting their disobedience, or not. Which is why the moment they saw the fae coming, they sent scouts to the other Stands, along with their children. Scouts to carry physical messages, and their children to keep them safe.

"Why? Why did you do this, then?" Kaemada cried aloud, weeping. It had been her idea, but she never would have been able to successfully do it herself.

That answer was there, too. It was like talking with him again, infuriating as he always was. The fae wanted to control her movements. And if the fae wanted her so badly, it was surely in the elves' and others' best interest for her to be free, especially since they could no longer shield her from fae mental manipulations.

Kaemada sniffed, sobs still wracking her body. Such an immense sacrifice to keep her from the fae. Surely no one was worth so much. She wouldn't allow it.

And so, one by one, she carried the elves out of the Stand. As many as she could save, she would.

"It's not for you exactly, not after all you have done to us. It's because this is who I am," she told Umril as she dragged him toward the river. "I'm the one who's not going to let you die. Especially when it was my mind-sick idea you decided to support."

Chapter Twenty-six

*The falling stars are not for mortals to enjoy. They are only to remind us of
how very small we are. So as the stars fall, reflect on your lives. Are you weighed
down with cares and grudges, or are you living your life to honor the gods?*
—fragment of a letter from a Dahuti priest

Taunos shivered in the damp. He, Emin, and Amanah were in a hole
several times his height with water up to their ankles. None of them were
shackled—there was no need for such restraints. The cell was like an
enormous well, pitch dark.

"Yes, this is so much better than running. Good thing we didn't follow
my plan," Emin said, again.

"I'm sorry," Taunos repeated. "I will make it right."

"You try, I'll give you that, but you keep mucking things up," Emin
said. "It's just like wrestling in the mud as a kid, all over again. You try to
clean it up, and it just coats more of the tent."

"The only way out of this is together. This is the dunk-them-in-the-
river-and-scrub part of the story," Amanah said.

"You are both right," Taunos said. "I admit it, I'm bad at working as a
team. But I'm trying."

"Failing a lot, too," Emin said. Taunos rubbed his face, and Emin
patted his shoulder. "Trying, though, yes."

Taunos paced the perimeter, splashing through the water, though the
rough rocks bit at his bare feet. The darkness and the water were
disorienting, and he couldn't be sure when he'd completed a full circuit.
He turned his back to the wall.

"Emin, stretch out your arms."

"Why?"

"So I can measure."

Emin blew out a long-suffering sigh, as if Taunos had just asked an
enormous task of him. Taunos traced the fingers of one hand on the wall
and stretched his arms out, beginning his walk again. Far sooner than
expected, his fingers hit Emin's arm.

"All right. Go out to my hand, then," Taunos said. "Amanah, I'm going
to try not to hit you."

"Don't worry. I'm avoiding you," Amanah said.

He grinned and then continued on. Several more paces, and nothing. He paused. Had he missed him, or was the space that wide?

"Keep going," Emin said.

Taunos splashed forward another couple steps.

"There, stop."

Taunos waved his arms slowly, testing if he was just missing Emin's hand. The very tips of their fingers brushed past each other. Taunos hm'ed, walking back toward Emin.

"It's wide." Taunos said.

"Here, get back to where you were." Emin grabbed his hand, and Taunos extended his arms as far as he could reach.

"I'm not sure it's a true circle." Emin started to walk, and after a breath, Taunos began to move as well, keeping their arms straight.

He was right. After a few paces, Taunos's hand brushed the wall.

Emin stopped. "Taunos?"

"I'm touching the wall."

"I have my palm flat on the wall," Emin said.

Taunos brushed his hand down the slick surface of the stone, trying to peer through the darkness. "It's a long way up."

"We'll freeze to death down here," Emin said. "Your hand may be warm, but Amanah and I are freezing."

Taunos agreed. "We have to try it. Back to back?"

Amanah tapped his shoulder. "I should climb with Emin. I'm as tall as you, Taunos, and uninjured."

Taunos hesitated, but her logic was sound. "I hope there's no one waiting at the top."

"We'll bring back rope." Amanah's voice was firm, though her teeth chattered.

The scrape of their boots on the stone was the only sound for a little while and then a splash as they fell.

"It's all right. I just slipped," Emin grumbled.

"The algae's thick," Amanah said. Water dripped from her clothes. It'd only make her colder.

"Careful," Taunos said. It was irritating, being helpless to do more.

"It's not easy being the one waiting, is it?" Amanah asked lightly.

He had no answer for that one. Shivering, he listened to their progress as they slowly, slowly ascended.

Even so, before too long, they came crashing back down into the water at the bottom. Neither moved, stunned by the impact, and Taunos scrambled to them, lifting them so they could breathe.

"Let me try," Taunos said.

"You're not recovered enough." Amanah's voice was tight with pain.

"I have telekinesis. And you're right. It's hard, waiting and worrying."

"I twisted my ankle anyway. You can take this turn. But be careful," Amanah said.

Taunos and Emin turned, back to back, and looped their elbows through each other's. Then, pressing their shoulders against each other, they walked, step by step, up the stones. Taunos pushed outward with his telekinesis each step, matching his movements to Emin's, while Amanah whispered encouragement from below.

The cold leeched through their sodden, filthy clothes, and they shivered uncontrollably, nearly losing their bracing against each other. But step by step they went, testing each step before committing their weights to it, urging each other on as if this challenge meant nothing, distracting each other from the severity of the situation.

Fatigue set in before the hole ran out. They were too far apart to even rest against each other, and their breaths were coming ragged. One step, then another. Taunos focused on just the next step, not the way his legs were shaking, the pain in his wounded muscles, the burning in his shoulders. They were too high now to stop. Too high to fail. If they fell now, they wouldn't have another chance, even if Amanah wasn't hit by their plummeting bodies.

Finally, Taunos's questing foot hit empty air. He paused. "Emin?"

"I think we're at the top." Emin's breath came in ragged wheezes.

"All right, on three, I will give you a boost. One, two, three." Taunos shoved hard at Emin, slamming himself into the wall on the other side of the hole.

His bad wrist screamed with pain, and white filled his vision, but he managed to grip the lip with his other hand. He needed to be more careful. If only life would let him be. If he kept injuring himself, his wrist would never heal.

Taunos pulled himself up and lay, gasping, at the top. Wherever they were, it was dark as a moonless night up here, as well. There could be danger. He should look for it, but exhaustion weighed him down. As soon as he could manage it, he rolled to the side, away from the well, though the world felt like it turned around him. Amanah needed to know they were alright. Emin had to have made it, right? He hadn't heard him fall. He dragged himself forward, testing the floor before committing to it. It was dirt, except for the stone around the hole.

"Emin?" he whispered.

"Here—" Emin's voice cut off sharply.

Moments later, Taunos's breath was cut off, something thin squeezing tightly around his neck. He gagged and gasped, but his muscles were too tired to respond the way he wanted them to. Instead, he rolled sharply toward the well.

The pressure on his neck tightened and then vanished, leaving him coughing and gasping, rubbing his neck. The stone scraped as his attacker fell down the hole, and then Amanah screamed.

"Taunos? Emin?"

"Here," he croaked, shuffling his way toward Emin.

His fingers brushed fabric, and he tugged sharply toward himself. A foot lashed out, and Taunos reached higher, still unsure if this was Emin or another attacker. But Emin had been silent too long. Taunos swung his hand at about the height that a kneeling opponent might be. Hitting flesh, he snatched at it. Someone drew in a haggard breath, and the air moved as someone rolled away near his knee.

"Cough once if you're alive, Emin," Taunos said.

Whoever he was holding lunged forward, while ragged coughing came from Emin. Taunos grappled with the stranger, using all his training to keep track in the dark.

"Who are y—" Taunos started, but fingers clawed for his throat.

He kicked away his opponent with limbs far too tired to do the work and shoved as hard as he could with telekinetic force. Wind moved and then all was still.

He fell onto his back, exhausted, unsure where the attacker was, and equally unsure he could fight him off a second time. A yelp of surprise sounded, and then a splash from the hole. Another gasped breath.

"Still not us," Taunos whisper-shouted down the well, one hand reaching out to pat Emin's back. "You all right?"

"Barely. Get me out before you toss anyone else in here," Amanah said, fear sharpening her tone.

Emin didn't respond, still doubled over, wheezing.

Taunos shoved his shoulder lightly. "Are you going to make it, or do you need a carrying chair?"

Emin's swat collided with the back of Taunos's hand, and he moved away. At least Emin was well enough to take offense. Taunos dragged himself to the edge of the room, stopping when his hand hit fabric. He lifted the bottom, but there was still no light, no sound other than his and Emin's pained breathing.

349

The air on his wet clothes was cold, and he shivered as he worked the cloth wall down. Then, he tore it into strips, knotting them together. How long would be enough? He wasn't sure but didn't want to do it again, either, so he took down another wall worth of fabric and tore it into strips as well, adding it to his rope. His fingers were shaking, and every limb was bone weary by the time he was done. There was no way he'd be able to hold it, so he tied one end around himself and cast the other into the well.

"Can you reach the rope?" he whispered.

Splashing answered him, and then the rope tugged at his waist.

"Testing it now," Amanah said.

"Wait!"

The tug that followed nearly pulled him into the hole, except he fell forward and hit Emin's side. Sprawling themselves on the ground, the two were able to provide enough resistance to not slide across the floor, while the rope wobbled.

It pinched painfully around Taunos's waist as he lay there, just trying to breathe. His muscles felt like water, every limb far too heavy, and his headache proclaimed he'd used far too much telekinesis. And they still had to finish their escape after this.

The air moved, and Taunos couldn't dodge. Even if he hadn't been holding the rope for Amanah, he'd likely have been too slow, exhausted as he was. More pressure around his neck, as if someone had tied a rope around his throat and was tugging on it. Emin was fumbling beside him, no doubt fighting their attacker. Gasping for air, Taunos grabbed for the enemy and tried to throw them off, but their attacker evaded him. Finally he grabbed hold of cloth but couldn't move his opponent. He didn't have enough air.

The weight on the rope around his waist abruptly eased. Cloth rope swept across his face. The pressure on his throat ended abruptly, and a foot hit Taunos's shoulder. Amanah grunted. There was a tug at Taunos's waist and then a scraping as someone fell down the well. Taunos tried to rise, but it was hard enough to just breathe. His muscles refused to obey him. Had Amanah taken out their third attacker using the cloth rope? He hoped so, hoped the scraping wasn't her falling.

A familiar touch caressed his face. Amanah crouched between him and Emin. "You all right?"

Taunos rubbed his burning throat, rolling to his back. "Amanah." He grinned, picturing the fight. "That banner dance was probably more useful than the showy one in Gahimbli."

"I thought it was you, you know. Both times. You terrified me." She untied the rope from him and tossed it into the hole then lingered, kissing his cheek.

"Sorry," he mumbled. "I was being choked. Emin got the worst of it."

"I'm just glad you're alive. Both of you."

"We need to move." Taunos's body didn't want to cooperate. He needed food and rest, desperately. But he wasn't going to get either if they waited around to be attacked again.

Amanah groaned, lifting her heavier brother to his feet, and then helped Taunos up. Leaning on her, they stumbled forward through the dark.

They encountered light and a patrolling guard at the same time. Blinded, with his muscles still watery, Taunos tried to dodge, but nothing wanted to move. Amanah dropped Taunos, stepped inside the guard's reach, and struck her hard in the chest before sweeping her feet out from under her. Her movements were so quick, Emin had barely grabbed the torch by the time the guard dropped, and as Amanah kicked the guard in the head, he grumbled to himself, his pride obviously stinging.

Amanah helped them dodge another guard and then took out a third before they stumbled into the open air. All three paused, shivering in the wind. Beside them, the wide stone steps ascended to the palace.

They were out. But they couldn't marvel for long. Upra was still waiting, he hoped, and no doubt guards would be set on them soon.

"We have to go around the steps," he rasped.

"Why? We should just get out of here." Amanah's objection sparked a nod from her brother.

"I left someone behind, and I don't plan to do it again." Taunos lurched forward.

Amanah huddled under his arm, shivering violently against him. They all needed to get warm, but first, Upra. He'd told Upra he'd be back, and he couldn't stomach breaking more promises.

"Can we head away from the palace a bit? We're exposed here, and we need to not get caught, after all," Amanah said.

That was smart. They angled further into the city, Taunos scanning the streets for the beggar. Relief sighed out of him when he finally spotted him, not much more than a pile of rags huddled beside the road.

"Upra!"

The man raised his head, blinking at them. Emin recoiled.

"Come on, Upra. Let's go home," Taunos said.

"Wait, who is this?" Emin demanded, his voice raw and scraping.

"I will tell you on the way."

"Found your friends, then? Whew, you stink," Upra complained.

Taunos couldn't help but laugh. "We make a good pair, then."

They were such a collection of misfits it was no wonder that people in the city seemed to mistake them for a group of drunks set to collapse in the road. The streets were fairly empty, but with every step the notion that soon, surely, guards would be on them weighed on his mind.

Amanah raised her head and pivoted on her heel, hauling Taunos and Emin across the street. Taunos looked around, trying to figure out what had caused the change in direction. The smell of horse dung hit him, and then the space opened up into a fenced area.

Canopies stretched between wooden posts, creating a ceiling for one corner of a pen in which milled several horses. Taunos groaned under his breath, but of course, it was a good plan. He was shivering hard, his muscles so tired he could hardly walk, and the others weren't much better.

While Emin leaned on the fence, Amanah hopped over, walking boldly among the horses, who raised their drowsing heads and snorted. A dog barked somewhere across the open space. Taunos and Emin worked with Upra to dismantle one of the sections of fencing, taking down the logs that ran horizontal. By the time the boy sleeping in the corner of the pen had stirred and woken, Amanah was astride one of the horses and most of the rest were walking toward the hole in the fence.

"Stop! Thief! Thief!" The boy's cries rang in the night with the dog's barking.

Amanah clucked her tongue, and the horse leaped the logs on the ground and pranced to a halt, while the rest of them scrambled to mount up. Emin and Upra each rode alone, but Amanah swung Taunos up behind her. He wrapped his arms around her waist and curved his body around hers as they galloped, streaming horses behind them.

The boy's alarm outran the horses, though, and soon enough bells were ringing. The edge of the city approached, but so did mounted archers. Amanah pushed the horse hard, and Taunos tried not to bounce, striving to match the horse's motions as Amanah had once taught him. He held tight, shielding her back as they galloped for safety. What were the archers waiting for?

He began to put his hand out to pulse a burst of telekinesis but thought better of it. He needed to work with Amanah, not on his own. He needed to stop mucking things up, as Emin had put it.

"How can I help?" he asked.

"How much more magic can you do?" she asked.

"A little more before the headache increases too much," he said.

"I need to grab a bow."

He tapped assent on her hand, and she swerved closer to an archer. The woman drew back an arrow, and Taunos pulsed a telekinetic burst at her arm. She shouted, her grip faltering, and Amanah snatched the bow from her fingers.

Another archer drew alongside them. Patha. She grimaced at them in the dark as she took aim. "I'll have my honor back from you."

"Don't hit the horses!" Dinweyi's voice snapped through the air like a whip from behind them.

Taunos lashed out sharply at Patha's horse. With a squeal, the horse tumbled, sending the shot wide.

But Dinweyi appeared on their other side, hatred in her eyes as she pushed her horse hard. "I won't let you steal our Puwileh's honor, thief. Either you come back with me for trial, or I'll kill you here, whether or not you're Leen's son."

"We have done nothing against the Puwileh," Taunos said.

"You take advantage of her hospitality and escape her justice."

"It sounds like you're more upset we bested you," Amanah said.

"Let us go, Dinweyi," Taunos said.

"And lose more honor? Never."

Amanah leaped at her, and they grappled, both barely clinging to Dinweyi's horse. While his broken wrist would be trouble if Dinweyi struck it, Amanah had no such limitations. But Taunos could support her, like the teamwork of the Ifreesians. He grabbed the reins, guiding his mount close to Dinweyi's. When Dinweyi and Amanah fell, Taunos turned his horse hard, letting Dinweyi's go by. He guided the horse next to the fight, kicking Dinweyi when she lashed out at Amanah and making her stumble. He put his hand down for Amanah, but it was Dinweyi who grabbed his arm and swung astride. A knife pricked his back, and he shoved hard behind him with his telekinesis.

As Dinweyi tumbled off, Amanah leaped astride, bow and Dinweyi's quiver in her hands. Her expression was fierce as she fired an arrow at Dinweyi, and Taunos urged their horse after Upra, who raced far ahead of them. Emin rode nearby, a bow and quiver in his hands as well, and together Emin and Amanah fired arrows rapidly, covering their escape. Taunos glanced back, but their pursuers were smudges in the darkness.

"I'm out of arrows," Emin said.

"Me too. They should have landed more shots than they did," Amanah said. "Good thing they were worried about hitting the horses."

"Even so, I lost two horses," Emin said. "Had to steal this one from an archer. And we're not away yet. We're days from the border, and I doubt they'll give up."

"We will head back to the Promise Tree," Taunos said. "If Upra's right, I should be able to realmwalk with people if I go from tree to tree."

"And you trust him?" Amanah asked.

Taunos nodded. "He's a Rinaryn dragonbonded. Dragons can jump with their dragonbonded, so it has to be possible."

As they caught up to Upra and continued toward the Promise Tree, Taunos explained how he'd met Upra and what he'd learned. When dawn broke, they paused to rest the horses and take stock of their wounds. Emin and Taunos had swollen, red lines across their throats, and all of them had various scrapes and bruises. Amanah and Emin each had cuts where arrows had narrowly missed them. Upra had a twisted ankle from falling off the horse.

"We'll have to be wary of infection," Amanah said. "We don't have any supplies."

"If we can get to the Promise Tree, I will take you to my tree, the Seeker Tree," Taunos said. "I would love to show you my home."

"Do they have a bamimri there?"

"No." He tried not to tense, swallowing hard. Would she decline in favor of finding somewhere more knowledgeable where she could practice her skills?

Amanah grinned at him, her eyes teasing. "A difficult decision. Stay here, where we're hunted, or go to Arruk, where we're vilified, or go with you to see this whole new land you're so secretive about."

"Really?"

She laughed. "These past moons with you, I've gotten to sail with Ifreesians and meet a Hinanuri Puhwileh. You open up possibilities I'd never have dreamed of before."

Taunos's face heated, but he wrapped his arms around her. "I want to show you everything. If this works, it opens up so many options. There'd be ways to send for help if we're attacked or send people to safety. And I need to confront the Elders. And..."

Curiosity glimmered in her eyes. "And?"

"And if this works, there's no reason to choose. If you want to come with me, I can do my duty and also share my story with the woman I love." His heart thundered in his ears. She had her own family, a land of her own that she loved, and what if she hated it in Rinara? If she came and hated his home and wanted to leave, could the memories of Rinara somehow be removed to keep everyone safe? Could he even do that to his beloved? No. This would be leaping off a cliff with no bottom, no way back, and he still wanted to do it anyway.

She pressed her forehead to his. "Haari Taunos, I would love to see your home and meet your people."

"Me too but not in the same way," Emin interrupted.

Taunos gave Emin a level look, but the broad grin he returned made him break out in snickers.

Upra rocked, his stick-thin arms wrapped around himself. "It's going home that draws a Rinaryn. Bound to this world. The dragons bring us out, and we pull them home. True, true, every time."

The draw of home... He'd noticed that, how during his journeys he would feel a longing for home. He'd also noticed its conspicuous absence this time. He shivered. Every time he'd thought of going home these past moons, he'd thought of the forest and found an excuse to stay—not that he'd needed much convincing. The possibility of the fae influencing him for so long was terrifying. And if they were influencing him, who knew what they were doing to his people or why.

The sky drew Taunos's gaze and held it, vast and blue. "It's close to the Feast of Starfall. My people will be gathered at the Seeker Tree."

"The starfall? The rain of the gods?" Emin asked. Dahuti people stayed inside during the starfalls, singing and drinking and trading stories to drown it out, for the priests said it was the fragments of a dying god. Bad luck was said to strike anyone who went out while the stars fell.

"It's a celebration for my people," Taunos said. "Joyful. Except that I'm Fallen, banished. Hopefully I can get them to see reason."

"And if not?" Amanah asked.

Upra clutched his hands together. "They'll kill you. They'll kill you, Fallen."

"I will jump out with you all before they stone me."

Amanah shivered, squeezing his hand. "Not quite the idyllic picture I was thinking of."

"Oh, my land is beautiful. You will see."

"Should we just wait until after the starfall?" Emin asked.

"I need to speak to the Elders right away. And they will all be gathered there, so they will not be able to keep any more secrets. Everything needs to be out in the open. The Sea Peoples might be the Darks, and the Elders kept my mother's work a secret, and there's more than one Seeker Tree. And... it's possible the fae have been influencing me, and if so, it's probable they're influencing the Elders."

"I'd tell you to be careful, but you're not going to listen anyway,"

Amanah said. "Are you sure this will work?"

Taunos shook his head, stroking his thumbs over her fingers. "No, but I have to try. And if the Sea Peoples are Darks—and even if they aren't, my people need to know that eventually they will be attacked from the sea. They have to know to prepare. Even if they don't listen, my sister and her friends were an amazing team. I can work with them, help them get the Elders to see reason or bring them to account."

Amanah smiled. "You learned something from the Ifreesians after all. You don't have to stand alone."

"And there's possibility for trade. We could get rich, never mind a herd of my own," Emin said.

Taunos snorted. "My people don't use money. And besides, Galod warned me not to bring tech back home, way back when I first started realmwalking. But I had hoped to find a solution the Elders and my people would accept."

Galod. The Elders had pointed suspicion at Galod, using Galod and the Darks as a reason to cast them out and make them Fallen. He should figure out what was going on there, too, if he could. In the meantime, he had friends worth as much as family, and he'd found hope that he could help them all.

It was early afternoon on the third day before the Promise Tree glimmered into view. Across the plains, horses and riders raced toward the tree from their left. Aching for a rest, he, Emin, Amanah, and Upra nevertheless pushed onward, pressing the horses for more speed.

By the time they stumbled to a dismount in the shade of the solitary tree, the other group of riders was close enough they could see their stern expressions. Amanah urged the horses on, away from the tree. Taunos closed his eyes, keeping Amanah, Emin, and Upra in mind, and bringing to mind the Seeker Tree. Nothing happened.

He opened his eyes, turning to Upra. "It's not working."

"Be a dragon," Upra shouted.

He couldn't just be a dragon! He was about to snap that to Upra when his mind turned it over, as if it were a stone and he could twist it to see it from another angle. Dragonbonded rode the dragons. They were in contact with their dragons. "Hold on to me."

Taunos winced as several hands slapped his shoulders, while the archers thundered ever nearer. Amanah, Emin, Upra. He fixed them in his mind, pictured the Seeker Tree, and realmwalked.

Jaetan-cha'a
Chapter Twenty-seven

It may be some time before I check in again. There are forces moving that I must understand. The balance has shifted abruptly, and with my students lost, it is even more imperative for me to study these changes. With the dragons so agitated, I may be cut off from the node for a while. Do not send any messenger.

-journal entry

Finally, no more dragonfire came, though the moments stretched long since the last blast. Ra'ael cautiously peeked out from the hole. The ground was uncomfortably hot to the touch but not to the point of serious burns, at least.

"Come on," she said. "I do not want to stay here in case that dragon decides to land and make sure we're finished off."

"Good idea," Tjodlik said. "Do you think the fae is gone?"

"I hope so. Galod?" The rock he had hidden behind was blackened on the one side, and there was no sign of him.

"Silence." Galod stood a little way down the slope on the other side of them, watching the vast blue sky. How had he gotten there? "We don't want the dragon coming back. Hurry."

He turned, his long-legged stride taking him quickly away down the mountain, and Ra'ael hurried after him, twisting to watch for any sign of the fae. Unease welled up deep within her that there was no sight or sound of him.

Beside her, Tjodlik stumbled and cringed, staring around himself rather than paying attention to where he was going.

"Crystals and ships!" He shuddered.

Ra'ael smiled. "Welcome to Outside."

"It is... so open."

A laugh snorted out her nose. "Well, it is outside."

After a while, Tjodlik fixed his gaze on the trail, though his shoulders still hitched, and then he kept up easily, his rugged Kamalti form perfect for mountain terrain, it seemed. Ra'ael watched the skies for dragons and the mountainside for fae. Where had they gone?

They walked in silence for some time. No dragon wings shadowed the ground, no fae appeared with malignant beauty. The breeze played with

357

her hair, and the sun shone warm on her shoulders. Even more, there was no sense of wrong, no revulsion bubbling up in her. She could breathe easily, and gradually, she relaxed for the first time in far too long.

Tjodlik began to trail behind, caught up in staring at the plants or the clouds or the height of the ridge of the mountain. Finally, he raised his browridge at her. "Do you often fight dragons?"

She snorted. "That was hardly a fight. More a run-and-hide."

"Still, we survived. If I am going to continue to associate with you, I may as well understand the risks." He grinned at her, and she couldn't help but grin back.

"The risks are that if you don't stop talking, the dragon will come back," Galod snapped.

Ra'ael narrowed her eyes at Galod, thinking back to the dragon attack. "The dragon seemed to focus its fire on your boulder."

"They hate the fae," he returned.

"You aren't fae."

Galod turned, fixing her with that stern expression that used to quell her instantly. She stared back, holding his gaze with a strength she'd never expected. In fact, he was the one who turned and broke the stare, continuing on his way.

"Where are we going?" she asked.

"Out of dragon territory."

"It would be easier to walk on the paths," she pointed out. "We do not want to be stuck in a trap."

"Oh." Tjodlik tilted his head. "I had known the Scouts check the traps, but I had never thought it would affect me."

"Why do they?"

"It is a very old arrangement. The fae encourage us to continue."

Back to the fae again.

"It's nearing the time when your people walk those paths," Galod said. "Do you not wish to give them space?"

Ra'ael's feet stopped. It was near the Feast of Starfalls again? It was far too easy to lose time under the mountains. But everyone would be gathered. She could check on the Saimahkae and Storyteller and see Eian. She could hardly breathe through the hope suddenly swelling in her. Her eyes stung with tears, and she blinked rapidly to banish them, taking a deep breath. "To the Seeker Tree, then."

Galod narrowed his eyes. "What are you planning? You are Fallen, remember? Your people will stone you if they see you."

Ra'ael shook her head. It didn't matter. And how did he know, anyway? "I want to check on them."

"They will stone her?" Tjodlik asked, aghast.

Galod barely spared him a glance, so Ra'ael explained. "We are no longer part of Rinaryn society. To prevent our influence from spreading, we were cut out, as a diseased plant. To prevent us from returning, the punishment is stoning."

"And they would actually do this? Your loved ones?"

Ra'ael shrugged uncomfortably. "There's something wrong with the Elders. Their 'justice' last Feast of Starfall was not justice at all, and the safety measures all broke down at once. I cannot simply accept that it was coincidence. Some sort of influence has twisted them, and I do not know how far it's spread. I do not know where it came from. But if the fae are using Kamalti, it's not a big jump to think they're influencing the Rinaryn too. My elders had nightmares, much as your nobles have had."

"That was from the Collective, we are certain," Tjodlik said.

Ra'ael shrugged. "Who's to say the fae wouldn't use a similar tactic against my people? Not in revenge, but in 'guidance'?"

"They are not your people anymore," Galod said. "Not your problem."

Anger rose up, and she took a deep breath to quell it, to find her peace. "The Elders twisted the law and got away with it. I mean to confront them —someone has to. What else has happened while we have been gone? And I have to at least try to see if the Storyteller, Saimahkae, and Eian are all right."

She was supposed to wait a summer, but the Elders had taken the proper way to appeal for mercy and twisted it, made it unusable. But she was not the same Ra'ael who blindly followed the rules others laid down for her as good. If no one else was holding the Elders accountable, she would. Someone had to.

Slowly, Galod nodded. He continued along with her, and she paused, eyeing him. "Why are you following?"

"Why not?"

"You have never shown interest in the Feasts before."

"I'm not interested in them. There are other concerns I value more highly."

Her brow furrowed and she turned to Tjodlik, who shrugged. "I came for the adventure. Where you go, I go."

Ra'ael swallowed her surprise and her worry behind a mask of confidence as she led her mentor and a Kamalti toward sacred ground. The Elders were worried about outsiders, just as the Kamalti were. And she was bringing two with her.

But as they reached the rim of the valley, Galod and Tjodlik both stopped. The smoke of the fires spiraled into the evening sky, and the sun painted the sky in hundreds of colors as it slowly sank toward the horizon. Soon, the stars would begin to fall, and the starsong would be sung. Tears pricked her eyes. This was the most festive of times for a Rinaryn, and she had no place in it.

A hum came from Tjodlik, who stared into the bowl of the valley, as rapt as if it had been a book.

"What are you doing?" she asked Tjodlik.

Tjodlik raised his browridge. "I am Outside, with no roof over my head, just an endless expanse of sky, with a rather frightening man and you. I have plenty of things to commit to memory until I can finally write them down like a civilized person."

She smiled, shaking her head. Her gaze went to Galod, who was watching her with eyebrows raised.

"What are you going to do?" he asked.

Her gaze returned to the valley, the people who had cast her out, and her resolve hardened. "I'm going to right some wrongs."

Galod smiled at her, but she shook her curiosity about that away. A smile looked odd on him. But at least she could be near him with only minimal discomfort—little more than the wariness of the next test. It was something she was both thankful for, and hated, because it confirmed that she had to stay Outside from now on.

"Do you really think that's wise?" Galod asked.

She scowled. "I think the time for wisdom has past. It's down to standing for right or allowing wrong to continue."

Baffling as it was, his smile broadened. "Take care. Remember your training."

She hesitated. "Are you coming?"

He stared at her, expression flat the way he did when she was missing the point of an exercise.

She nodded. "This is something I need to do. Alone."

Or rather, with Takiyah, Kaemada, and Taunos, as they should have been working together all these moons, but since they weren't here, she would do what she could on her own. She took a deep breath, turning back to the valley. "I will see you after. Write me a story about this, will you, Tjodlik?"

His smile calmed the flips of her stomach. "I will look forward to singing you the Ballad of Ra'ael when you come back."

Biting her lip, she squared her shoulders and started down the trail which wound down into the valley. The trail that would bring her inevitably to putting the Elders on trial, to taking a stand against the perversions of the law they had allowed.

The infant Zeroun and I found in the sea seems unharmed. It's hardly believable, but the truth doesn't always care about credibility. She almost appears as one of us, and yet, there are significant differences. I consulted with some acquaintances from a race calling themselves fae, but they did not know her origins either. This will be an interesting mystery to solve.

—journal entry

The dragon's words echoed in Takiyah's head. Find out who she was. But how much did some mystical people she didn't know and had never met matter? How much did that affect who she was?

She'd fallen a long way from who she had been. Her friends, her family, her choices. They made her who she was. And she'd tossed them away in fear and anger, let her family be torn from her, and made awful choices. All these amazing things she'd done—trading with the City of the Lost, the sailing sand-carts, this impossible road—but she'd left behind the ones she wanted to share them with.

"Excuse me. Are you still teaching forging classes tomorrow evening?" Fim, one of the men working on the road stood before her, twisting his fingers together. Just like Kaemada used to do, though his were pale instead of deep brown.

Takiyah nodded.

"Pek said if I asked you, if you said yes, I could receive special dispensation to return to the city and join in. If the wind cooperates, that is."

"You're near the end of your sentence now, aren't you?" Takiyah asked.

He nodded.

She smiled. "Fim, you're one of the hardest workers on this road. And you probably know more than anyone else about it, how to keep it level and strong."

"Other than you."

Takiyah brushed that aside. "I'm going to ask Pek if we can consider your sentence done. No more stealing, right?"

"No, Master Takiyah. No more stealing."

She snorted at the title. She was no sparring master like Pek, but the workers had decided to name her "Road Master," and she hadn't been able to stop them using it. It was better than "Dragon Master," she supposed.

Fim lingered before her, his huge, light grey eyes fixed on her. "Are you all right?"

It had been half a moon since her standoff with the dragon, and she'd only grown more popular. Dragons weren't known for stopping in for a chat, after all, and the workers had spread the news of how she'd stood to protect them, while their guards had run away.

The questions were never-ending:

"Can we travel and camp in the desert now?"

"Can you make them do something about the bandits?"

"I never even knew dragons could talk."

The work on the road was a good distraction, especially as she and the others had a good rhythm now, and her earlier prickliness about her project being stolen had faded.

Even now, one of her sand-carts rolled down the road toward them, its striped sail filled with wind, its wagon filled to the brim with fresh stone from the quarry. The work camp bustled with chores, and those that were on rest rotation took their ease. The road grew longer, stone by stone, such that the work camp had to be dismantled and moved every night to keep pace. And still, she couldn't get the dragon's words out of her head.

She was in the wrong place, and while she'd grown to enjoy the company of these people, they weren't the people she really missed. She longed to see Taunos, Ra'ael, and Kaemada again. To see her parents. To go home.

Takiyah forced a smile and clapped Fim on the shoulder. "Why don't you take over? Show the new workers how it's done."

"Really?"

"You can do it. I trust you. I need to speak to Pek."

She walked away, waving at the cart-driver as it passed, while Fim's voice carried on the wind, patiently explaining the process and why things must be done just so. She'd like to finish the road herself. She hated that it wasn't complete, that she would be leaving it unfinished.

But just like that, she'd decided. It was nearly the Feast of Starfall, and she was leaving. Takiyah swallowed hard, glancing at the arm of the mountains that towered above her. She may be Fallen, but she could at least catch a peek of her parents and make sure they were all right. It'd been too long.

A strong, favorable wind hurtled her back to Tamarik in a sand-cart that evening. After cleaning up and sleeping in, Takiyah found Pek at his favorite tavern around midday the next day. She slid into the seat opposite him, pushing his foot off as she did so.

He frowned at her. "That seat's taken."

"By me."

"By my foot, actually." He shifted and settled his foot on her knee. "Ah, that's more like it."

Takiyah debated the merits of pushing his foot onto the floor again.

Pek raised his browridge at her. "Aren't you done early?"

"I want Fim to be the head of the roadbuilding project."

"Really, now?"

"He knows the most, and the others respect him, and—"

"The prisoners. You never call them prisoners, but they're still in jail."

"Technically not *in* jail anymore. They do good work. You yourself said they could work off their time. They've more than proved the merits of—"

Pek laughed, cutting her off. She subsided, thinking back through what she'd said. None of it was funny. Raising a hand, Pek gestured for a moment. "Never mind. I just think it's adorable when you get all defensive of your team. You're right. And Fim's a good choice."

"He's near the end of his sentence by now, surely."

"You're here to ask for him to be set free?"

"Many of them are near the end of their sentence. And several would like to continue the project with full wages. They deserve it."

"And where do you fit in this picture? All I see is you cutting yourself out of it."

Takiyah looked down at the table.

"Ah. You're leaving."

"I can't stop thinking about what the dragon said."

"'Find out who you are.' Frankly, I'm surprised it took you this long."

"It's near the Feast of Starfall. I should be there. Taunos probably will be there to argue with the Elders. We should have a chance for mercy next starfall, but the Elders removed the normal way to ask, since no one can speak for us if our names are forgotten, and my parents—"

"Takiyah."

She'd been babbling. She never babbled. She shut her mouth.

Pek's foot slid to the ground, and he reached forward, taking her hand. "You don't have to justify yourself. This means a lot to you."

She nodded. "I'll just... miss you."

Pek waved her off. "Grumpy me? No, you won't."

"Remind Varen when he takes the sand-cart caravan to the City of the

Lost to leave the sails out of sight, or Theron will steal them. And remind him not to trust Theron or any of his guards. And make sure they have plenty of well-trained fighters to protect them."

"Of course. You know, people are grateful to you. No one believes your tough act."

"That's just it, Pek. I don't deserve their gratitude. I was hurt and angry and lost, and I took that out on everyone."

"And then you changed, giving free lessons to those who need it most, defending those workers from that dragon and even from me."

Takiyah glared at him. "It was a start."

Pek grinned. "I suppose it is, at that. Still troubled? Or can you rest now?"

She traced her finger through a line on the table, like the line her road made through the dry land. "I wanted to make a new beginning, but I should never have thrown away what I had in the first place. Even though I value all I've learned here. The people I've met."

Varen's pushing and Rothan's banter weren't Taunos's. And Rothan's door being always open to her, and Pek somehow always knowing what she needed, they weren't Kaemada. And none of them argued quite the way Ra'ael did, with the fierceness in her eyes and the full force of her passion. And none of them were her parents.

The trouble was, she missed them desperately.

It didn't help that something in her heart tugged her alternately toward the sea and toward the Seeker Tree, tearing her in two. No wonder she was grumpy, when nowhere was the right place to be. She'd made new friends but left old ones behind, and that didn't sit right with her. It itched like a bite she couldn't scratch.

"I can't rest yet. The dragon let my road stay because it would annoy the fae, because the fae wouldn't let my people come back. The Ifreesians. And he said my mind stinks of fae." She scowled. "All I know is, I have to find my friends because I have to find home. No, it doesn't make sense."

A grin broke like the dawn on his face, and he stood, wrapping his arms around her in a brief, fierce embrace. She froze for a breath then awkwardly hugged him back.

"Thank you," she whispered.

He grinned at her as she stepped back. "For being myself? Any time."

"No. For everything. For acceptance. You took a chance on me. I'm giving Rothan my stuff."

Pek snorted. "He's busy making these sand-carts for everyone. It's not like he wants for anything these days. Those sand-carts of yours will change Tamarik forever, you know. The desert has opened up with this faster route of travel and Varen's ear plugs."

She smiled. Varen never failed to find an opportunity to make money. "Take care of the road builders. I think they've paid off their debts."

The mirth faded from his face, replaced with seriousness, and he nodded. "I hope you find what you're searching for. And remember, I'm here if you need to talk."

Takiyah nodded and stood. There was one more class to give tonight, and then she'd go. She'd take the old prototype sand-cart. It worked the least well anyway. They'd been meaning to dismantle it, but it could take her across the sands one last time.

That night at class in Rothan's forge, she announced her departure, though her packed bags in the corner could have announced it all on their own. It made class awkward with goodbyes, and Fim hugged her hard, crying when she told him he'd be head of the road project.

Rothan embraced her last, once everyone was gone. "I'm going to miss you."

"And I'll miss you. I already told Pek, but you can have my stuff. Everything in my house."

"Wait, I have something for you."

Rothan turned and fished in a crate that he typically kept locked. He hid something behind his back when he turned around. "With all your work on the road and the sand-carts and everything... I made you these, but I was waiting for a good time to give them to you. Now's a good time, I suppose."

He extended his hands, holding a matched set of sawback knives each as long as her forearm. Takiyah tested the edges with her thumb, unsurprised to find them razor sharp. She grinned, her grin growing wider as he held out matching sheaths for the knives with orange flames stamped and painted on the leather. Attaching the sheaths to her belt and securing the knives, she felt... right. Something niggled at the back of her mind, an expectation for something slung behind her back—a shovel, maybe, or a pickaxe.

She shoved that away and hugged Rothan again. "Thank you so much."

"Thank you, for everything you've taught me," he said. "I'll keep the sand-carts going, and when you return you won't believe the improvements I'll have made to your design."

She laughed, shaking her head. Goodbyes were hard, so she took her moment then, stepping out of the forge for the last time with one final wave. She shouldered her pack and headed for the gate. The night breeze tousled her hair as she climbed onto the prototype sand-cart and sailed for the mountains to the west.

Neither city had to be self-sufficient anymore. And neither did she.

With the fantastic speed of the sand-cart and the smooth line of the road, even with the wind against her, it only took her four days to cross the desert—much better than the sixteen days it once had taken. She left the prototype at the edge of the sand where the road-building team would find it and then turned to find her way up the mountains, missing her staff but strangely comforted by the two large knives at her hips.

A dragon winged its way overhead, dominating the sky, and her mind turned back to what the dragon had said. She'd never really considered that the dragons and fae might have a grudge. She hadn't considered either of them much at all, really.

But to be manipulating the Rinaryn… was that what had happened with the Elders?

Maybe Kaemada could tell if the dragon was right, if there was fae influence on her mind. And Taunos wouldn't be far from his sister. The normal paths for appeal were closed to them, since the Elders declared that no one should even speak their names. It meant no one would speak for them, to introduce them for appeal.

Takiyah grinned. In that case, she'd just have to speak for the others, and they'd speak for her. If the Elders wanted to play with the law, she'd give as good as they did. She raised her chin. She couldn't forget her parents—they needed to right that wrong as well. She picked up her pace.

Once she reached the Valley of the Seeker Tree, though, she slowed, swallowing hard. There on the grass below her, the people went about their days, untouched by the turmoil of her past moons. Where were her parents? She wiped her hands on her pants, searching through the throng for the familiar smile of her mother, her ears straining to hear her father's voice as he spun a story.

She found them, and her breath stilled. A grey-haired woman stood, shaking her finger, in front of Takiyah's mother, whose back was bent under a large pack.

Takiyah released her breath in a hiss. Who would dare to scold her mother, to make her carry a load when her back already hurt whenever the storms rolled in? And her father was not telling stories, preparing the songs of the kaetal for the starsong, but instead laboring with much younger men to put up a tent, his cane on the ground a pace behind him.

The supports collapsed, falling onto her father, and Takiyah's hand went to her knife.

How had her parents fallen so far? Why did people allow this to go on? They were all complicit. Even the sight of some of the kaetalyn helping her father to his feet and away from the tent didn't soften her outrage, for her mother continued to be verbally berated and the kaetalyn nearby only gave her a wide berth instead of helping.

Takiyah prowled down the slope, holding her anger as tightly as the hilt of the knife in her hand. On she went, just as if she still belonged there —and really, who were they to say she didn't? She tuned out everything else, stalking toward the woman who still dared to lash out at her mother. Her mother, who looked so tired, so worn down. Her mother, whose eyes went to her and widened.

"Have some respect," Takiyah said, slamming her knife further into her sheath. This was not a task for it.

The woman turned, her eyes widening, but Takiyah's mother moved first. "Takiyah, my darling, you must leave, quickly. You cannot be here."

Even as she spoke, Maeren wrapped her arms around her. Takiyah removed the laden pack from her mother and then clung to her, though she stood head and shoulders taller than her. Had her mother shrunk in the past moons? She seemed so small, so frail, and Takiyah longed to never let her go, to shield her from the injustices of the world. She glared over her mother's head at the woman, a stranger. If she was among the kaetal of Torkae, Takiyah should know her. This was wrong.

"Who do you think you are, to force my mother to work when there are other ways she can contribute to the kaetal? Ways that do not further injure her back?" Takiyah snapped.

"I am the Great Mother of Torkae," the woman said. "And you are Fallen."

Chapter Twenty-nine

Those who are Fallen may bring their case before the Elders at a Summer of Mercy. They only need someone to speak for them and to come to the Feast of Starfall. There, they may present their grievances for the Elders and Great Mothers to review for fairness, but if they are found guilty once again, they must exit Talahn Valley. The Feasts of Starfall are not for Fallen.

—fragment of a scroll safeguarded by the Monks of Annularei

Music filled the air as two gasps rang out beside Taunos, along with Upra's cackled laughter. Mid-note, the music died. The breeze played with the silver leaves of the white-barked tree, but the landscape was changed. Gone were the wide open, flat steppes. Instead, white-capped mountains rose around them from every side of the bowl-shaped valley, spotted with hundreds of fires. Afternoon had been replaced by evening.

And facing Taunos, Emin, Amanah, and Upra were the astonished faces of his people, all gathered around the Seeker Tree in their finery. Eyes lit with fear and surprise then recognition then the realization that Taunos was Fallen. And he'd brought in non-Rinaryn. In some ways, his people were as close-minded as the Kamalti were.

It was true. He'd never had to choose. He'd torn himself apart between his land and his heart, never dreaming that he would one day stand as he did now, preparing to do the work to better his land with his beloved at his side.

"Taunos?"

The familiar warmth of Storyteller Zeroun's voice filled Taunos with a rush of longing and homesickness. For so many summers, he'd looked up to the Storyteller with his wisdom and calm, no matter the crisis. But the old Storyteller had been stripped of his status. He could not help Taunos now.

"Everyone keep hold of Taunos," Emin warned.

The knot in Taunos's belly tightened as he looked out at all those familiar faces. There they were, the masses of people he thought of as family and friends, who he had fought for and put his own wants to the side for, for so many summers. And they'd cast him out the last time he'd come to the valley. They'd turned their backs to him, as if it had all meant nothing.

Well, this time, he was coming for an account from the Elders. This time, the story would be different.

This time, the Elders were the ones on trial.

"Storyteller Teryn!" he bellowed. "Storytellers of the Council of Elders and Saimahkaen of the Council of Great Mothers! We have need of words."

"Who are these people? How did they come with you?" Storyteller Sarik, one of the Heartwood Council, approached. He'd sent Taunos on missions and had refused to let him explain why he was gone so much.

Searching his face for any remorse, Taunos found only deep lines of worry. He turned away, scanning the crowd as the Elders approached. Sarik held no authority over Taunos anymore.

Teryn pushed his way forward. "What is the meaning of this? Fallen and non-Rinaryn in our sacred valley? You go too far."

"You went too far," Taunos growled. Yes, it was daunting to be under the eye of all his people, confronting those who had cast him out, but he had friends and family at his back. He was not alone. "Last time, you hid away your shame. This time, let it be known by all. We speak under the sky this time, in the light of Eloí."

There was some scuffling in the back of the crowd, but Taunos was more worried about the people gathering, surrounding him, Amanah, Emin, and Upra.

Amanah grabbed his hand, drawing his attention back to her. "Are they going to stone us?"

He swept his thumb across her knuckles. "I will not let them stone you. I will get you out."

Her lips twisted. "I'm not asking to be rescued. I want you to share your life with me, even the ugly parts. I'm not leaving until you do."

Taunos forced a smile. "Hopefully there'll be plenty left to share."

He'd brought them here, and his heart hammered at his ribs that they might die. But no, if he needed to realmwalk them all out, he could. The thought struck him. Could he send members of the crowd elsewhere? How many? The strategic repercussions astounded him for a moment, and he had to pull himself back to the present.

He squeezed Amanah's hand and lifted his voice. "I come to warn you. I may have discovered who the Darks are. Regardless of whether I'm right or wrong, they could attack from the sea. And our Seeker Tree? It is not the only one of its kind. I've found at least two others, one of which the Elders of Heartwood know about."

"You dare try to sow fear on a sacred Feast?" One of the Elders shook his head. "Everyone knows the seas are impassable, just as the Seeker Tree is the only one. You stir up trouble only because you seek revenge for your just punishment, Fallen."

Taunos searched the faces of the crowd. "In all your time, Rinaryn people, kaetalyn all, have you ever witnessed a judgement closed off from the sight of Eloí? Elders, search your memories. When has this ever before occurred?"

A moment, a breath, filled with murmurs from the people crowded around.

He started again, before Teryn could break in. "When in all our stories have a Saimahkae and Storyteller been stripped of their positions? When in all our summers have our laws been held higher than what our songs know is true and right?"

"Nonsense," Teryn interrupted. "No Rinaryn will listen to a Fallen. You are all to be stoned on sight."

"A clever trick," said a voice from the other end of the crowd.

Taunos's heart quickened, recognizing the voice as Ra'ael, and he scanned the faces of his gathered people. Against all odds, hope lifted his heart. Had Ra'ael, Takiyah, and Kaemada come back together? Had his sister been cared for while he'd been so long away? They should have worked together to form a plan for this, long before now, but now would do.

The crowd parted to form a path through which Ra'ael walked, her head high, black hair gleaming as it swished behind her, every aspect of her attire in perfect position to make a statement.

She spoke as she sauntered forward, seeming perfectly at her ease, playing to the crowd as she always did so well. "A clever trick, I say, because it is a trick. Tear away our names so that no one can speak for us. Stone us on sight, so that we cannot tell of the evil you have done. Well, I am done letting the evil people do bind me. I am Mírah Tirith Shonae Ra'ael Tsrian of Torkae of Heartwood, and I speak for Taunos of Torkae, Takiyah of Torkae, and Kaemada of Torkae."

Ra'ael's dark eyes flicked to Amanah, Emin, and Upra. She faltered, the first crack showing in her demeanor, though she regained her composure before her next foot hit the ground. "And whoever Taunos brought with him."

Taunos grinned, taking the opening she left for him. "And I speak for Ra'ael of Torkae."

"That is not possible," Teryn objected.

Taunos turned his grin on him. "I'm not beholden to your laws anymore, Storyteller Teryn. We're here to talk about your crimes."

Ra'ael's voice echoed across the valley. "Come for judgement, Storytellers and Saimahkaen. You refused to listen to our stories. Your songs were turned to fear instead of wisdom. You took our names to steal away our chance for mercy, and we call you to account for that."

"You installed tyrants not even from the kaetal of Torkae to take over for my parents." Takiyah's voice rang out. The turbulence among the crowd increased until she burst into view, hauling an older woman by the arm as if she were an unruly child.

No longer lean, Takiyah was formidable, her short, red hair like a fire on her head, her towering height accentuated by the breadth of her shoulders, half again as broad at the woman she was pulling along. Taunos stared in wonder at the evidence of his guess from the Ifreesians. Takiyah must have learned much from her genetic memories, though she still had a way to go before matching the Ifreesian captain of *The Flit*.

Takiyah looked around in fury. "Who is this woman who says she is Saimahkae and sees fit to abuse my mother? Who are these strangers who put my father in danger, setting him tasks better suited to younger people?"

Ra'ael's nostrils flared, her eyes widening with fury as she rounded on the Elders. "How dare you? You would spit on our way of life and endanger people for your own petty pride, all while pointing fingers at us? Who's to say this will not happen elsewhere?"

Murmurs filled the crowd, and a growing number of Elders and Great Mothers exchanged looks, guilt pinching their expressions.

Spit flew from the corners of Ra'ael's mouth, she was so incensed. "If your Storyteller and Saimahkae refuse to support a lie, will they also be replaced by someone deemed 'unspoiled'? Someone who will follow the Elders' will? How many times has this already happened?"

"It's not just pride," Taunos said. "It's fear of their deeds being known. You Heartwood Elders sent me out into the world, outside of our laws, with immunity, again and again. And then, when your own skins were in danger, you threw me out! I have come for account. Facts do not match up. My mother realmwalked *twice*, and the Elders knew and kept it secret."

"Even more concerning, someone has been influencing our minds, our memories." The voice was quiet, but in the pause before the next response, quite clear, and unmistakably Kaemada.

Kaemada, speaking in Traveller's, just as if she'd never lost that ability.

Taunos twisted, scanning the crowd for his sister as his blood rushed in his ears. But all he saw were kaetalyn shifting their weight, eyes going back and forth between them and the Elders. Takiyah and Ra'ael were looking around too, so at least it wasn't just him.

"Lies," Teryn said. "Of course you would return to stir up trouble."

A cloaked woman behind him stepped past the Elder, drawing back her hood to reveal a torrent of brown curls bound with a circlet with wooden charms. A wolf padded at her heels, but no one seemed to notice until the woman spoke, shaking her head slowly at Teryn. "Then why does your song reflect undercurrents of fae? Why do so many of you bear the marks of fae influence, including almost every psion?"

Teryn leaped away from her.

Taunos swallowed hard, rushing forward. He scooped his little sister up, squeezing her hard as he spun her around. "Cha'atanahn! Please forgive me."

Kaemada laughed, embracing him. "For what, brother? Acting as a Rinaryn should and caring for me when I was in need? The fools filling this valley could learn a thing or two about hospitality, about hope, about not throwing people away when they become inconvenient to your story."

He let her down, and she fell into the arms of Ra'ael and Takiyah, all three of them weeping and hugging each other. Taunos took Amanah's hand again and kissed it, even as he spoke to the crowd. "We cut ourselves off. We stopped looking for what was good and right and true and started looking only for what was comfortable and safe."

"That sort of path leads away from the spirits," Ra'ael said, arms still around Kaemada and Takiyah. "Storytellers and Great Mothers are to lead the people, one by looking to connections and the other by looking to the past to guide the future. You failed to do this. You broke connections instead. You sentenced the people of the City of the Lost to continue their untold horrors because you could not be bothered to spare a thought for them. Rather than helping them to find a way to live, teaching them to be Rinaryn, you condemned them and, in doing so, condemned yourselves."

Takiyah prodded Ra'ael, giving a significant glance to her parents. Ra'ael nodded. "And when two spoke out against your folly, rather than listen to their wisdom, you stripped their status and cast them out. Is that the story of our people? To ignore wisdom and spread fear of speaking up against injustice? No. You have wronged the people of Torkae."

Taunos suppressed a grin. Ra'ael's voice carried—she always had been good at bringing people to task, and with Takiyah standing beside her with a formidable expression, large knives at each hip, they drew everyone's eye, while Kaemada so deftly proving her ability to slip right past them without drawing their notice had those in power shifting uneasily.

He indicated the Great Mothers. "The Council of Great Mothers was meant to balance the Council of Elders in case of corruption. What happened? Why did you fail your duties?"

Silence answered him, cut only by the whistle of wind and the anonymous murmurs among the crowd.

And then Maeren stepped forward. "The Elders threatened the Great Mothers. By keeping secret 'Storyteller business' from the Great Mothers, by giving us only dire warnings and fear, the Great Mothers could not gauge the threat for ourselves. We caved to that threat. Most of the Great Mothers and Storytellers alike had had nightmares daily for many moons, but still, when the time came to stand, we stooped instead, and that shame lies on us."

It was just what he had done for all those summers. He had kept secrets, keeping Amanah from holding him and driving away anyone else who could have lent him aid.

Taunos shook his head. "How easily we fall to cowardice, leaving those few who are brave to be cast down and trampled. How easily our secrets cause harm to those we love, those we should protect. Thank you, Saimahkae Maeren, for being everything a Great Mother should be."

Taunos turned to Kaemada. "Can you remove the fae influence? Especially from the Elders?"

Kaemada gave him a flat look. "That's over one hundred minds. I'm only one person, brother."

He grinned. "One powerful psion."

She wrinkled her nose at him and waved him away. "I will do what I can. But look for Eian for me."

"I will."

She sank onto the grass with her wolf, just behind where Taunos, Ra'ael, and Takiyah faced the Elders. It was a daunting task, to counter mental poison placed there in dreams for over a summer. But hope filled him. The lesson had come at great cost, but so too he prized it, squeezing Amanah's hand as she held his. Working together, they had a chance, a far-sight better one than letting themselves be scattered to the winds by who knew what.

By the fae. He'd realized it before, when Upra said he smelled like fae. But fae influence or not, he'd left his sister alone and vulnerable, while she'd just now covered for him in sight of his people.

He turned back to his sister, trembling under the weight of his guilt and remorse.

Kaemada grinned. "They have no more sway over you."

"I'm sorry." His whisper was hoarse and choked.

She shook her head. "Nanovah, brother."

"I should have done more," he said. "I should have been there."

"No one person can be everything to another. You needed help, and I needed to be alone to grow, too."

Amanah's fingers tapped a pattern on his hand. *One thing, then the next.*

The world shifted back into balance a bit with Amanah's familiar saying. He nodded to his sister and returned his focus to Ra'ael's tongue-lashing of the Elders, leaning his shoulder lightly against Amanah's.

Ra'ael's voice filled the valley. "The Elders laid the fault at Galod's feet for the crime of being other. Do you know who else has trouble with those they do not understand? Many of the Kamalti do. Taunos, Takiyah, Kaemada, and I went underground confident of our superiority and now I see that it was all falsehoods. Our leaders can be just as close-minded as theirs."

Taunos turned back to the crowd and raised his voice. "You accused us of being Dark-touched, of falling to the influence of Galod. All of this while you yourselves were under the influence of the fae."

Murmurs ran through the crowd. Teryn shook his head. "What proof do you have of these stories?"

Kaemada stared at them. "I studied long with the elves. I do not believe they did this, but the fae… not only could they and would they, but it appears some among you would welcome their involvement. Do we play at being fae?"

Ra'ael cut off Teryn's response. "Do we fail to do good to avoid being accused of consequences beyond our control? Do we turn a blind eye to those in need because something somewhere might go wrong? Is this the Rinara you are leading us to?"

Ra'ael ticked off the points on her fingers. "You accused us of being Dark-touched because we were not perfect in defending our kaetal. Which of you has defended your kaetal without loss? You banished us because Kaemada showed mercy to one who tormented her. Is mercy now a crime? You banished us for freeing those trapped in the City of the Lost—people who were born there, people who freed themselves at their first opportunity, when you never gave them such a chance. You declared us Fallen for talking to the Kamalti, while you of the Heartwood Council sent Taunos off on dangerous missions and turned your back on him when he needed you most. Dishonor on you all. This shame is smeared on us all because of your cowardice. And Eian. You tacked that on at the end, the peril Eian was in. Meanwhile, according to the law, we should have left him to die. We should have left him to the horrors of the City of the Lost. We rescued him instead, as was *right*."

"Answer for the wrongs you have done us, done to my parents," Takiyah said. "This is your only chance to regain your tattered honor."

"And where is my son now?" Kaemada asked. "I have not seen him."

"You will be silent," Storyteller Teryn snapped. "You cannot fight all of us."

Taunos shook his head. "We don't have to."

"Listen to you, with your poisonous, divisive words," Teryn said. "This is why Fallen are not allowed among us."

Taunos's hands clenched into fists. "I don't divide my people."

The murmurs of the crowd grew like a roiling thunderstorm, and angry, fearful people were hard to predict. They might turn on them simply because they were outnumbered. Many of his people watched their leaders with sharp gazes, unsure what to believe. Others shouted against their leaders, while still more shouted in support of the Storytellers and Saimahkaen. The charges Taunos and the others had brought were serious, and their people reacted with affront and anger, though not always in the direction he'd prefer.

And the Heartwood Council stood divided, Storytellers and Great Mothers arguing. Many of them glared at him, and he matched them expression for expression. If Kaemada's task was succeeding, there was not nearly as much effect as he'd hoped. Emin stood beside him, arms folded, glaring at everyone. But Upra was just staring at the mountain peaks.

Taunos glanced at Amanah, who was watching him. His beloved, witness to his people bickering. "I'm sorry. I wish it had all gone better."

She squeezed his hand. "Minds are difficult to change. It's not a failing on you that someone else doesn't listen to your arguments, doesn't wish to be persuaded."

Ra'ael and Takiyah were still shouting back and forth with the Elders, and kaetalyn argued with kaetalyn. No solution was coming. They could probably go to the Resistance, at least. They could finish catching each other up on the last few moons and offer a place for any who wanted to live free of the poison the Elders were influenced by. They could form a plan for protection if the Sea Peoples—or Ifreesians—came by sea.

But there was one face he never saw, and it caused him to shiver, glancing at Kaemada's friends. "Do either of you see Eian?"

Ra'ael and Takiyah looked at each other, but both shook their heads.

"No," Kaemada roared, her wolf snarling. "You're not taking my son!"

"Kaemada, where is he?" Ra'ael asked.

She pointed through the darkness to where blue lights floated on the slopes. "Fae."

The protectors have returned, escaping the snares we set for them. We must secure the Tsaeyichape'itsan now, before it becomes too difficult to gain access to him. When he ripens, we will have him already.

—part of a missive from "Nitil" in Dragonmoor

Kaemada raced after Nimae up the slope of the mountain, leaving behind the Saimahkae and Storyteller, the people she longed to reconnect with. But not all of them. Ra'ael and Takiyah were close on her heels, along with her brother and the strangers who stuck close to him. Their reunion hadn't been long enough, but once Eian was safe, they would have time for stories, for laughter, and for tears.

"Fae." The man Taunos had brought with him, the one whose mind smelled of dragon, bristled.

Nimae growled.

"Upra, you seem more angry than fearful," Taunos observed.

"Hate them. Dragons hate fae!" Upra wrinkled his nose and hissed.

A glimmer of light shone for a moment, blue against the greys and browns of the desolate landscape. Off the path, once again, but fear no longer held her back. They ran, following the twists and turns of a narrow wild-trail while the mountains rose high around them. The blue light flickered ahead, sometimes obscured by rocks, other times revealed for a moment, a glimpse of brightness guiding their path.

Clearing the Elders' minds of fae influence had been exhausting, and it had attracted the attention of the Collective. Kaemada gritted her teeth, depending on Nimae to guide her body while she closed her mental walls against the Collective's demands. While they were not so angry with her anymore, still they asked more of her than she could give: safety, aid against the Kamalti, and an end to their fear and pain. She promised them she would do what she could to help them, but she needed to get her son safe first.

Turning a corner, Upra halted and Kaemada nearly ran into him.

"Hurry," a little girl whispered. She was several paces ahead of them on the trail, running hand in hand with a little boy. "Hurry, or we will lose it!"

It was dangerous in the mountains, as Kaemada and her friends knew all too well. Two small forms sped behind a jutting boulder, chasing the blue light out of sight. Skin prickling, heart pounding, Kaemada sprinted to catch up.

A voice oozed from the darkness. "Children."

The children gasped, and Kaemada drew in a sharp breath as well, pushing herself for more speed. With such melodious tones, that voice had to be fae. She raced around the protruding rock. There stood a fae holding a lantern glowing blue, confronting two children clutching hands. The girl had perhaps eight summers, the boy maybe five.

"Come away, little children," sang the fae. "Come away and play."

The girl shuddered. "Onsívei, we should get back."

The boy nodded mutely, and the girl pulled him backward. Kaemada stared, her stomach twisting. He might have been called Onsívei, but she would know her son anywhere. But another shape emerged from the darkness between her and the children, cutting off their retreat. Another fae. The girl held tightly to the boy.

"Stop," Kaemada shouted, stepping into the blue lantern light.

Both fae hissed at her.

The girl's expression only became more terrified. "Onsívei, I'm so sorry. I'm so sorry. I never should have made you come out here! Fae and Fallen!"

Eian watched them, his face calm except for his tight grip on the girl's hand. There was no light of recognition in his eyes. That fact alone stabbed through Kaemada's heart. He looked at her as if she were no one to him, but she was his mahkae, the one who kissed away his hurts and held him when the nights caused him to fear. She was his mahkae, who had faced down the Kamalti, the Collective, and the City of the Lost for him.

Her voice broke. "Acha'iyih, do you not remember me?"

What kept taking his memories of her? It hadn't been so long since they were Fallen, though those six moons also felt like an eternity.

Taunos stepped up beside her, eyes on the fae. "Leave these children alone."

The near fae smiled. "You cannot stop us."

"Too bad the dragon did not get you," Ra'ael said, joining them with Takiyah next to her. "You failed to grab me, so you thought you'd take children? Go be bothersome elsewhere."

With a cry of pain, the girl crumpled, grabbing her head.

"Yena!" Eian crouched beside her with one arm over her, as if to guard her. He turned to the fae. "Stop! Stop hurting her!"

Ra'ael sprang forward, lashing out to kick the nearest fae in the face. He dodged away, but she whirled, slashing with her sword.

Behind her, Eian sobbed. "She just wanted to see if the legends were true. If the lights were the fae walking around on the grass."

"Onsívei, run!" the girl—Yena—shouted. "Run!"

Crippling psionic pain struck Kaemada. She crashed to her knees. This was worse than the attacks of the Collective, and she crumpled, battered beneath it as surely as if the whole mountain had fallen on her.

"Take Eian and run," she shouted to her friends. Her eyes welled with tears. "I love you, little one, more than all the spirits above can ever know. Never forget that."

But Eian only shivered and shook his head, standing his ground. More fae emerged from the shadows, all holding lanterns. Each was tall and beautiful, in a terrifying sort of way. Terrifyingly beautiful, every last one of them.

"Leave these children alone. They are ours," Ra'ael said.

"Rinaryns are no threat to fae. We may take as we please."

Around and over the fae, Eian spoke, just as he had done under the mountain. "We want the boy, He Who Comes Again and Again. Your puny efforts to stop us will not succeed. You must remember your place—far, far beneath the fae."

Again with that unnecessary translation, speaking the undercurrents everyone knew were there, the words that lived between those spoken. Bittersweet love pounded with her heart as Kaemada pushed back against the mental attacks on her. Except, what had he called himself?

The mental pressure vanished, and Kaemada sagged to the rocks.

The fae stood still as statues, staring at Eian. Eian stared back.

"He is awake." As one, the fae spoke in a whisper that made the hair on the back of her neck stand up. "The Tsaeyichape'itsan. The Tsaeyichape'itsan."

Another breath and then the fae turned inward, as if the rest of them weren't there. Their murmurs to each other held a sinister tone. "This is unexpected."

"We did not anticipate this."

"We must reconvene."

"The Tsaeyichape'itsan is awake."

"It is too soon."

"He should not ripen for years yet."

"He is not ready."

"There is no other path forward."

Rocks tumbled down the slope to Kaemada's left, and Tjodlik slid to a stop in a cloud of gravel and dust, staring at the fae with horror on his face. Where had he come from?

"Tjodlik," Ra'ael cried.

As one, the many shadowy fae swarmed toward them. Tjodlik yelped and retreated. With the Collective's mental pressure mounting, Kaemada braced herself to defend, while Takiyah, Ra'ael, Taunos, and his friends ran to meet the fae with attacks of their own.

"Tell me, why did a dragon tell me my mind stinks of fae?" Takiyah asked, fire flowing down long knives she held in either hand.

All of Kaemada's friends had had fae influence in their minds, and she'd relished dismantling it. Now, she focused on defending her friends against the psionic attacks the fae threw at them, lifting mental pain before it could become debilitating from one after another.

Off to the side, Upra hissed at the fae, who, strangely enough, recoiled from him. Upra hissed again, and the fae echoed the sound.

A bright light flashed over them, and two of the fae howled, crashing to the ground.

Galod's ripples.

Kaemada smiled. She'd know them anywhere.

Just before her fought Taunos, Takiyah, and Ra'ael, along with the tall man and woman Taunos was with, all working together, giving her time to deal with the telepathic attacks. Their coordination was beautiful, and Kaemada wished she had a moment to appreciate it. But against the might of the fae boiling forward, they were barely holding, and it wouldn't stand for long. Anchored in Nimae, Kaemada shielded their minds from psionic blows as much as she could. She struggled to keep track of Eian, now curled with the little girl between two boulders off to her right.

Ra'ael's fighting form shifted to the ferocity of the battle rage, while Taunos, Takiyah, and the others protected her sides and back.

As one, the fae stretched out their hands. The weight of their telepathic attack crushed Kaemada's defenses like reeds in a tempest. Ra'ael stumbled, and Upra sank to his knees with his hands to his head, howling. Taunos's knees buckled all at once, but the woman beside him threw a rock, hitting one of the fae in the temple. Taunos quickly regained his feet as the woman hefted another stone.

A moment later, she and the strange man crumpled, too, hands to their heads. Taunos lunged at their attackers, side by side with Takiyah, who struck with knife and fire, hard and fast at the fae that surrounded them.

Kaemada shook her head. She was not losing Eian again. Especially not to the fae. She couldn't fight the fae and the Collective both, but perhaps she could fight the fae *with* the Collective. She turned to the Collective still battering at her for attention.

Just as she had done the night she found Eian, she seized them.

I know your arguments, and I know your pain. I understand your anger, and I have taken your punishments. I have tried to help you, but now, my son is in danger, and I will not let your vengeance leave him to spirits-alone-know what fate at the hands of the fae. I would rather fight alongside you, instead of against you.

The Tsaeyichape'itsan. The Collective roiled.

What is this word? she demanded.

We do not wish the fae to succeed in this. But if we help you, you will find us a home where we will not be hunted.

As I promised, I will do everything I can to do so.

A great weight eased off her crumbling mental walls and hurled itself at the fae's might. Kaemada flew after them, attacking with everything the Collective and the elves had taught her about psionic battles. The struggle roiled with psionic turbulence like the waters of Dead Man's Sea.

Around her, grunts of effort and the scream of metal on metal sounded —the others were still fighting. When she pulled from her psionic battle for a moment at a time, she could see flashes: Taunos and the woman fighting side-by-side, covering each other's movements as they defended the ragged Upra, who lay crumpled on the ground; Ra'ael, lost to blood rage, throwing herself into the fray while the strange man threw more rocks when fae tried to flank her; fire streaming down long knives as Takiyah parried a strike and took advantage of the opening; Galod's ripples tossing two opponents backward; Eian and the little girl, still tucked away between two rocks, while Nimae bit an approaching fae.

Kaemada ached, her mind battered and bruised as surely as her body in a battle. Exhaustion gripped her, but this mental battle was no less vital than a physical one. She gritted her teeth and kept going, shielding her friends and boosting the Collective against the fae whenever she could.

Even ten fae could not hold for long against the Collective.

The fae drew back their mental attack, their bodies swaying, as if indecisive. "You may have him, for now. It is too soon anyway."

And then, they melted into the darkness.

Takiyah's shout chased them. "If you ever come back, I have questions for you!"

Kaemada collapsed, her head pounding. Ra'ael turned toward Takiyah.

Oh no, the blood rage.

Taunos gathered himself to help, but he was going to be too slow.

Through the pain, Kaemada reached out to Ra'ael. So long had they trained together, lived together, fought and laughed together, her friend's mind was easy to access. As easy as Umril had entered her own. Rather than imposing her will, she knew what Ra'ael would want and gave her that, touching Ra'ael's exhausted mind. *Sleep.*

Ra'ael crumpled.

Taunos ran forward to kneel beside Ra'ael.

The strange woman crouched beside him and pressed her fingers to Ra'ael's neck, checking her over. "She's just unconscious, I think."

Taunos glanced at Kaemada, and she gave a wobbly smile, sagging back against Nimae. She had helped save her son, and she hadn't lost control of her psionics to do so.

"Eian," she slurred.

"They will return," Eian said, his expression blank, his curly hair a mess. "But they're afraid of you. All four of you."

The girl with him still held his hand, clutching him tightly as they crept out of their hiding spot.

"How did we win?" Taunos's eyes widened on Kaemada. "You, little sister?"

"The Collective," she said, sending gratitude their way.

Help us. You must help us.

I promised, and I will, once I have tended to my son.

Ra'ael groaned, stirring. She looked around, bafflement on her face as she got to her feet, and Kaemada smiled. Rarely did Ra'ael emerge from blood rage without needing the healers' care for days on end. Upra uncoiled, too, staggering as the strange man Taunos had brought with him helped him stand. They were all right. Wounded, yes, but nothing serious she could see.

"Tjodlik?" Ra'ael asked.

Oh, that's right. She'd seen him earlier, at the beginning of the fight. Clothes rumpled and dusty, Tjodlik eased toward them from around a boulder, looking distinctly embarrassed. "I apologize. I am not a fighter."

"Hiding was smart," Ra'ael said. "It's over now."

Kaemada's body was heavy, her mind aching, but there was still one more thing she had to do.

"Acha'iyih," she breathed as she reached out to him. "What have they done to you?"

As gently as she could, just as she had with the others, she swept away the traces of fae influence, brushing away too the crumbling walls the psions had made around his memories. They wouldn't have held much longer anyway, in the face of whatever power protected her son's mind. She was grateful for that because her strength was fading.

Eian straightened with a gasp. Finally, recognition lit in his eyes, along with fear and pain and betrayal. His hands curled into fists. "You never came for me. I needed you, and you did not come. You said you would always come."

"I'm so sorry it took me so long." Her voice cracked. Nimae hunched, ears flattened, and whined.

"Eian," Taunos started.

But the boy swung around at him. "No! Leave me alone."

Kaemada bit her lip. "It seems that Rinaryn psions were repeatedly blocking off his memories of the time before Storyteller Teryn took him. But the force that protects his mind kept dismantling them. I'm sorry for the shock, acha'iyih."

Takiyah shook her head. "The past doesn't stop being just because you don't want to think about it."

With a sob, Eian flung himself into Kaemada's arms, and she nearly fell backward with the force of their reunion. She rubbed his back and stroked his hair, and tears fell from both of them to water the ground.

Kaemada wiped the tears from Eian's eyes. "I named you Eian. My wish for you. An absence of danger. But if danger finds you, so will I, no matter what I have to do to get to you or how long it takes. Always."

"You cannot take him," wailed the little girl who had been with him.

"This is Yena," Eian said. "Her father is Teryn. He said he was my father too, but he isn't. He isn't, right?"

The confusion in her son's voice tore at her heart, fueling her anger toward the Storyteller.

"He isn't," Ra'ael said, smoothing his hair. "That was a lie."

"Lies," hissed Upra. "So many lies."

Kaemada reached out to Yena mentally, clumsy in her exhaustion. She'd only meant to assure the girl of their good intentions, as speaking seemed far too much effort, but once again, she hit walls, walls that had the distinct feel of Rinaryn psions. Yena gasped.

Kaemada shook her head, trembling with exhaustion and rage. "How far does this memory manipulation go? What is Storyteller Teryn doing?"

Eian's eyes welled up, and he wrapped his arms around her tightly. "Do not leave me again. I do not want to go."

She kissed his head, holding him tightly. "Then you will stay, I promise."

"Me too," Ra'ael said.

"No one will take you away again," Takiyah said. "They'd have to go through me first."

Taunos knelt beside them, his familiar smile crinkling the corners of his eyes. "Welcome back home, ahtasí. Now, we make things right."

Kaemada spoke into Eian's hair, unwilling to let him go. "We need to get everyone safe and Yena back to her family before they leave."

"You think they will?" Ra'ael asked.

"I think anyone who would alter a little boy's memory to avoid questions is not going to stand and face the consequences of their actions," Kaemada said.

~

Taunos let out his breath. They'd found Eian, and he was safe. Kaemada was safe too, and even speaking Traveller's, and everyone was here: Ra'ael, Takiyah, even Tjodlik from under the mountain. Even, unexpectedly, Galod.

"Technomage!" Upra hurtled past Taunos, scratching and biting and hissing at Galod.

Galod's mouth thinned to an even more severe line, and he put out his hands.

Oh no. The beggar was already so frail.

Amanah grabbed Upra, spinning him out of the way of the ripple, which just barely missed her.

Taunos gritted his teeth, clenching his fists at his old teacher. "Don't you ever do that again. You really need to stop blasting everyone you disagree with. Amanah, are you all right?"

Shooting a scathing glare at Galod, Amanah nodded.

"Keep the dragonbonded away from me, or I will defend myself." Galod's voice sliced through the air.

"Stop, everyone, please." Kaemada scowled at them all. "We have only just reunited and we're fighting again? We need to work together. Especially after just fighting the fae. They do not forgive easily."

"Come on." Taunos gestured toward the valley. "This whole tangled mess leads past the Elders, but we need to finish what we started regardless. Let's go."

Taunos scooped up his wobbling sister, carrying her back toward Talahn Valley with Eian scurrying along nearly underfoot. They'd confronted the Elders, though justice still needed to be done, and he worried that leaving the valley so soon might have weakened their place in the eyes of others. But any who would sacrifice a child for their own comfort, he didn't care what they thought.

He kissed the top of Kaemada's head, shifting her so her slight weight didn't press on his bad wrist. She slumped against him, exhausted, but it didn't dampen the joy in his heart. He had so many questions for all of them. Just as she had been before their banishment, here she was, barely coming up to his shoulder but no less vibrant for her short stature. He hated that he'd ever let her go in the first place, marveling at the change in her.

Lucid. Whole again. He could hardly believe it.

Emin's heavy footsteps followed him, along with Ra'ael and Takiyah ushering the little girl along and Upra thrashing his way through bushes. Tjodlik stumbled along with them, staring with huge eyes at the landscape. And right next to him, shoulder brushing his, walked his beloved, staring at the peaks high above with wonder in her eyes. Emotion clogged his throat. He no longer had to choose between his beloved and his land—and in fact, he never had—a dream he'd never thought could ever come true.

Galod's disapproval shattered his good mood. "Taunos. It appears we all have introductions—and explanations—to make."

No. After disappearing for six moons while Taunos struggled to keep everything together, Galod did not get to show up and judge him. Nothing was ever enough for the hermit. No matter how well he did, there was always something to point at as a fault, but not this. Everyone had abandoned him, and he'd tried to help Kaemada alone. That was far more than Galod or even Takiyah or Ra'ael had done.

He ignored the hermit, unwilling to submit to a rant when this should be a celebratory moment.

"What exactly do you think is accomplished by bringing them here?" Galod didn't stab his finger toward Amanah, Emin, and Upra, but if he'd been anyone else, he would have. He loomed over Taunos with his height.

Taunos glared at him. "Did you know I could realmwalk with others if I used the trees? The nexus? Surely you realize how many possibilities this opens up."

"That doesn't mean you get to endanger everyone. You're still a selfish boy."

"Selfish? I have been out there day after day for summers, risking my life to keep my people safe. I sacrificed every friend I had—"

"What is your plan then?" Galod interrupted. "Do you think it wise to bring just anyone here? Have you tossed reason out with my teachings?"

Emin and Amanah weren't just anyone, and Taunos bristled at the implication. During every tense meeting after a mission, Galod would question everything he did, every mistake. Always pushing, constantly demanding more of him, never letting anything be enough.

It was time Galod felt that himself.

"Where were you, Galod?" Taunos asked. "I spent my story roaming other lands more than I was at home, endured every side-eye and muttering about my perceived deficiencies, and for what? When the Heartwood Council sacrificed me, sacrificed everyone, where were you?"

Galod drew himself up. "You knew the risks when you started."

Would he never get a straight answer from the hermit? Did he really think so little of Taunos? "As did you. There are questions that have been suppressed. How in all the worlds did my mother realmwalk? It never should have been possible."

"Our mother could not have realmwalked," Kaemada objected. "She had only telepathy."

Ra'ael stomped alongside, watching Taunos and Galod with a critical eye. Takiyah had her eyebrows raised, green eyes curious as ever.

"Exactly," Taunos said. "So how did she go to the Darks, and why would no one answer these questions? What are you hiding?"

Galod cleared his throat, his gaze fixed on the far peaks. "I helped her. Lína. I can realmwalk, though not like you, Taunos. Different way of walking, different limitations. I never intended..." His throat bobbed. "But that does not excuse you bringing people here. Of all the things I warned you about. You know the risks—"

"Don't change the subject." Taunos's finger trembled in the air between them with the force of his rage.

Training with Galod all his life, learning to read the tiny hints of expressions of the man, were all that allowed him to see the pain, guilt, and even fear that lurked curtained behind the wrath in Galod's eyes. The man had closed himself off, the way he always did when Taunos got too close to the truth. There was a sense of retreat, even though the man didn't move away.

"We were declared *Fallen*, Galod. It destroyed Kaemada," Taunos shouted. His sister's mostly limp weight in his arms reminded him vividly of those moons where she was a shadow of herself. "They threw us out because of your influence. What did you do?"

"I do not think it was Galod. I think it was the fae... why the Elders banished us." Kaemada's words were slurred, her head lolling against his shoulder, but she roused herself enough to speak. "Oh, and brother, I am far from destroyed."

"And I'm glad to see it." Taunos rested his cheek against the top of her head tightening his arms around her. He looked at Amanah—perhaps his beloved could help his sister regain her strength.

"Let's deal with the remnants of our people first and then figure out what to do about the rest of this," Ra'ael said.

"We left a mess behind with the Elders," Takiyah said.

He nodded, the storm inside him easing a little, especially with Amanah and Emin's closeness, their quiet support. They were all together again. Surely not even the corruption of the Elders could stand in their way.

Soon Taunos was entering Talahn Valley once again. No longer the solitary hero but one hero among several, finally working together as a team. And they would need to, with the fae as an enemy.

The Valley of the Seeker Tree was filled with far more tumult than he'd ever seen before. The chaos they'd started when they confronted the Elders hadn't yet died out. As the grass overtook dirt and stone, Galod separated from their group, skirting along the edge. After a wordless exchange with Ra'ael, Tjodlik followed him. Upra hissed at Galod's back, taking a step forward, but Emin caught his shoulder, tugging him back. Taunos gave Emin a nod of gratitude.

They crossed the grass to the Seeker Tree through those who called them Fallen and those who shouted questions. Hardly had Elder Teryn's enraged face come into view than Yena gasped and ran to him.

"Father!"

"Storyteller Teryn," Taunos called, settling his exhausted sister on the grass. "Your daughter, Yena."

"Why were psions altering her mind and the mind of my son?" Kaemada accused, gathering Eian into her arms.

Taunos suppressed a grin. After the way the Council of Elders had chastised her last time when she was no longer able to speak Traveller's, now her voice was clear, if breathy with fatigue.

Ra'ael was there to give her voice strength. "Rinaryn psions are forbidden from altering memories, and to do this on children? Multiple times? On your own daughter? Shame, Storyteller Teryn. You do not deserve that title."

Shock and anger murmured through the crowd. Some kaetalyn called the accusation ludicrous, while others turned on Teryn with demands and questions. Teryn sent Yena deeper in the crowd, away from the tumult, with an older woman presumably from his kaetal.

"I warned you of this folly," the Great Mother of Teryn's kaetal said.

The Great Mothers who stood nearby withdrew, buzzing with fury, and more of Teryn's kaetalyn turned on him with appalled rage.

"Is this true, Teryn?" Maeren asked.

"Who would you believe?" Teryn asked. "Fallen?"

"Your own Great Mother charges you," Maeren said.

"You have no voice here, Maeren. You are not Great Mother anymore." Teryn drew himself up, but the kaetalyn only grew louder.

"You will find the Great Mothers will not bow to your will a second time," Zeroun said, stepping up beside his wife.

Shouting broke out, the people dividing into sides. Some demanded answers from Teryn, some defended him, and others turned narrowed eyes on psions—including Kaemada. Taunos shifted to shield his sister from those gazes, grateful when Amanah stood at his side. He glanced at Upra, afraid the commotion would spark a flare of temper in the man, but Upra was once again staring at the mountain peaks with fervent intensity.

"Now you have the start of a riot," Emin said.

Taunos winced. "I didn't mean for the psions to be targeted—except perhaps those who had played with Eian's memories specifically."

"Sea-wizards seem set apart in many lands," Amanah said. "It's easier to blame those already set apart. And some will blame anyone to avoid facing their own guilt."

Before them, Storytellers argued with Storytellers and Great Mothers with Great Mothers and kaetalyn with kaetalyn. He'd sparked a wildfire, but Wildling was there. She might be able to make them listen where he wasn't.

Taunos leaned toward Ra'ael. "The Elders might not listen to reason. It might be too much too fast."

She turned on him, her eyes glittering with fury. "Then they can leave."

Taunos blinked. "Wait... They?"

"Yes. If they aren't going to act Rinaryn, they do not get Talahn Valley."

"That's going to make a lot of people unhappy," he said.

"Good, they deserve it."

"Fine," Taunos said, raising his free hand. He glanced at Ra'ael, and she nodded. He gazed out into the deepening dusk, the faces gathered in the light of the fires, and raised his voice to reach them all. "If we cannot come to an agreement, you can leave."

Silence filled the valley.

Teryn spoke first, his voice tight with outrage. "What?"

"You heard him," Ra'ael said. "If you do not wish to live by Rinaryn law, Rinaryn ideals, why should you stay here, in Talahn Valley? You are a disgrace to everything we stand for."

Taunos spoke loud but slow, to help his words carry. "If you want to stay, to right the wrongs and heal the wounds caused by the Elders as they followed the poison in their minds, you are welcome to. But if you want to follow the Elders into darkness, well, the darkness is that way."

"It's already nearly night," argued one of the Elders.

"So you *can* see," Takiyah said. "Interesting. Now we just need to check that you can hear."

"You would throw us out to the Angels?" another Elder said.

"You did not care about the Angels when you threw us out," Ra'ael said. "But stay on the edges of the valley this night. You will be safe there and have time to think, to process. You make your decision in the morning —stay and be Rinaryn or follow this folly."

"What about everyone else?" someone from the crowd shouted.

Taunos stared at the Storytellers in turn as he answered. "We can talk tomorrow to plan a way forward—Great Mothers and Storytellers together, as it should be. Anyone who wants to live according to Rinaryn ideals is welcome to stay. We will not turn anyone away."

"You cannot banish us," Teryn said. "You have no authority. We will not go, and we outnumber you, Fallen."

"We should be watching the starfall," Ra'ael said, folding her arms. "Instead, we're watching the Elders fall."

Taunos stepped toward Teryn and the other Storytellers. "I fought for you. I bled for you. I killed for you. And now you think I will not use those skills on you after you betrayed us and all of our people?"

"All arguments are to end with the day's light," objected one of the Great Mothers.

"In that case, argument over. Leave," Takiyah said.

"It's not like you have not broken the law before," Ra'ael spat. "Do not pretend to love it only when it suits you."

Takiyah drew her knives and spun them, fire flowing down their tips and arcing toward the ground. Taunos fanned out with her, with Amanah at his side and Emin taking up a position on the other side. Kaemada's wolf stalked forward, head low.

"I will not forget this," Teryn threatened.

"Fear," Kaemada growled, where she hunched with Eian.

Gasps in the crowd. Terror on many of the faces, most of them the Storytellers who had confronted them or those who had supported those

Elders. Teryn broke first, scrambling to his kaetal, and many of the camps hurried to move toward the edges of the valley, opening the space around the Seeker Tree even farther.

Taunos stood, watching the Elders run as if their own guilt were nipping at their heels.

As the last rays of the sun died and the starfall sang as it shrieked across the sky, Taunos stood shoulder to shoulder with Amanah against the puppets of fear and hate. Takiyah fell into her parents' arms, who came to join them with tearful embraces, though many other kaetalyn kept their distance at first. Even though the valley was fraught with tension and they had more questions than they had answers, there were possibilities now.

They had Eian, and they had each other.

Ra'ael's voice rose, leading those kaetalyn who were left in the starsong, and Taunos joined his voice to that of the priestess, Kaemada and Eian joining soon after. There was Takiyah's voice, along with her parents, and voice by voice, those who remained in the valley added their songs to the greater song of all. Taunos leaned his head against Amanah's, feeling more at peace than he had in a very long time.

With time, perhaps they could come to agreement once again with the leaders of the Rinaryn, but right now, it was clear: the Council was Fallen, and the fae were an enemy to reckon with.

Thank you for reading! Not ready to leave the characters? Sign up for my newsletter to get a free short story from Amanah's point of view! Find out what she's thinking as Fallen ends and Memories begin!

If you have a spare moment, please leave an honest review. Reviews are the best way to help other readers find books they'll enjoy, and they make an enormous difference for independent authors especially! If you want to help support your favorite authors, telling others about them and asking your local library to stock their books are among the best ways to do so. Thank you so much!

Don't forget to stay in touch to get more exclusive content, including bonus short stories not available anywhere else: Simply go to skaeth.com and subscribe to the newsletter!

A Reference of Terms and People

I am updating this guide with further information. Why, I am not certain, as it's quite possible Lenatis and the others will never see this. Perhaps it is the habit of years of study and record keeping. Perhaps it is merely the whims of a hermit.

The People

Kaemada Sierso - a psion who has access to powers of both telepathy and telekinesis. This allows her to bond tightly to animals, as well as to dreamwalk. She is one of my pupils. Taunos calls her "cha'atanahn".

Ra'ael Tsrian - has the blood rage, causing her to go on a rampage during battles, and telekinesis. She is also one of my pupils. Taunos calls her "Wildling".

Takiyah Tiros - the adopted daughter of the former leaders of Torkae. She is of Ifreesian descent and is another of my pupils. Taunos calls her "Tinker".

Taunos Sierso - Hero of Torkae, and my star pupil, as well as Kaemada's brother. He is powerful in telekinesis and can realmwalk. Also called "Haari Taunos" by the Dahuti—apparently this means "Wanderer" and is something of a title.

Amanah - a human "bimna" (doctor) from Far Dahutad, and Taunos's beloved.

Emin - a human soldier from Far Dahutad, and Taunos's best friend.

Dode - an elderly noble Kamalti from the city of Codr, of the Philosophers.

Tjodlik - a young noble Kamalti from the city of Hadr, of the Philosophers. Nephew to Dode.

Answer - a young noble Kamalti from the city of Codr, of the Scouts.

Elisabei - a healer from the City of the Lost and part of a rebellion

Reinan - an explosives expert from the City of the Lost and part of a rebellion

393

Pek - former sparring trainer for the city of Tamarik

Rothan - a smith in the city of Tamarik

Umril - an elf and psionics master among the Rinaran elves (yes, they spell Rinaran with an a instead of the y the Rinaryn people use).

Terms

Rinaryn - a native people of the land of Rinara. The Rinaryns themselves are less than extraordinary. They are bipeds, a little smaller on average than humans, and a great deal lighter in build (I expect they have hollow bones). They have round faces and brown skin and their hair tends to be black or brown, although children can have golden-blond hair which often darkens as they age. Their eyes are typically brown but can also be blue or grey.

Kamalti - a native people of Rinara who live only in the Holy Mountains. The Kamalti are said to live under the Holy Mountains, and at first I thought they were probably dwarves. However, the mountain range is also infested with dragons, making the existence of a dwarven kingdom unlikely (and making it difficult to properly investigate the matter). I find it most likely that the Kamalti grew as an idea from the fact that the journey is treacherous and rife with dangers, as a sort of childhood monster to keep their young in line.

Darks - an ancient enemy of the Rinaryns. These people send their young raiders to the Rinaryns, possibly through the use of realmwalking, for I have not detected the presence of technomancy (though of course the limitations of the atmosphere mean I cannot rule that possibility out.) They bear iron weapons and leather armor, painted black, and tend to wear black, as they attack at night almost exclusively. They never take land, or seem to want any resources, really. I suspect the raiders are sent to give them a taste for battle, a taste for blood. (Yes, as you've reminded me, I have not intervened.)

Far Dahutad - a human country on this world with a dual governmental system. From Taunos's own words: *Far Dahutad is led by the member of the royal family who is elected by the officials from the religious and secular branches of the government. The three High Priests and Priestesses who are most highly ranked for each of their nine deities serve on the religious council, and the three most powerful representatives from each of the nine "central" clans make up the secular council. At the end of the royal's lifespan, a new member of the royal line is elected by these two councils to reign and serve as a balance for the two hands of the government.*

Tamarik - a city in the desert region between the mountains in Rinara. Apparently it has an interesting mechanism to repel dragons, which I very much want to learn more about.

Sea Peoples - a raiding force that seems comprised of a vast union of pirates, terrorizing the coastlines of much of the world and claiming the islands around the equator as their own.

Ifreesians - a people who are able to shoot fire from their wrists through the combination of explosive biochemicals and have genetic memory. They are tall, over six feet in height, and broad-shouldered with reddish hair. Sea-faring merchants, they nevertheless are very secretive about their homeland and lifestyle.

Torkae - a small kaetal in the region of Heartwood, in the north-eastern quadrant of the island nation of Rinara.

Heartwood - a region in the northeast of Rinara

Life Valley - a heavily forested region in the center of Rinara

The Angels - a creature who hunts by song, stunning their prey so they can feed. These interest me a great deal and I hope to learn more of their function soon.

The City of the Lost - an ancient city where the Rinaryns send their banished people, "Fallen". This is the last remaining city in Rinara. It is said the gate is guarded by great statues which annihilate any large creature moving outward from the city, effectively making it a prison. I have not been able to confirm, as no Rinaryn will answer me as to the location of the city, and my explorations have thus far been fruitless.

Codr - a Kamalti city

Hadr - a Kamalti city

Anathel and Tharahel - the Rinaryn names for the two moons of the planet. The moons are of similar size, in a co-orbital configuration around the planet. This creates extremely dangerous tidal effects, which no doubt contributes to the Rinaryns not being a seafaring people.

kaetal - the semi-permanent villages the Rinaryns live in. They will abandon the kaetaln (plural of "kaetal") for each Feast of Starfall, as well as during harsh winters, and then come back together for spring or after the Feasts. When they leave the kaetal for the twice-yearly Feasts, they will dismantle each hut and refashion them into sledges or use them as firewood for the journey. Whenever the kaetal is broken apart, the Great Mother is responsible for keeping the flame of the central fires alight until all the people return.

ehreideikae - Lit: "one who watches/knows" - The Rinaryns call them "priestesses" and "priests" but they are in fact more akin to what we would consider therapists and counselors. While they do lead religious ceremonies for the kaetal, they spend most of their time soothing social fractures and tending to the mental health of the kaetalyn. Religious duties do not occur with the regularity we've noted elsewhere, for each Rinaryn is responsible for practicing their faith alone in the best way they see fit.

Saimahkae - lit: Great Mother. The highest ranking woman of a Rinaryn kaetal. Her responsibility is to keep the kaetal functioning day to day, attending to social matters and helping to ease any disputes.

yah - the coming of age ritual of the Rinaryn people. At around puberty, when the family of a youngster and the elders of his kaetal (including the Storyteller and Saimahkae) have judged them able to succeed, the young Rinaryn will set off on their own to live alone off the land with no help for one month. Typically youngsters are sent out several at a time, so the kaetal can celebrate success all together (or mourn, If disaster strikes). A Rinaryn is not considered an adult until they pass their yah.

aeneshenon - winged Rinaryns. Very rarely, some Rinaryns are born with wings, creating six limbs instead of four. These are given much honor, and amazingly enough the wings are functional, allowing brief bursts of flight. According to their legends, when the Rinaryns were created, all had wings.

tailosae - a Rinaryn primate well known in the forests of Heartwood and Life Valley. Large eyes, prehensile tails, and a fruit-based diet are the main characteristics of this social primate species.

tserwora - a large, venomous lizard in Rinara. They dig large dens which they are extremely territorial of. The venom in a tserwora bite can kill a Rinaryn, and there is also the risk of infection.

zeriy - a large canine in Rinara who prefers the grasslands. They have long legs and are known for speed. Sometimes tamed as pets.

toelfa - a large feline in Rinara who lives in the forests. They have a curled ruff around their necks and a long tail with a venomous barb at the end. The venom is enough to kill small animals, but will merely wound and sicken a Rinaryn.

tsífíorse - Rinaryn for "thank you"

ameyitum - Rinaryn for "forgive me"

shareil - lit: "peace"

acha'iyih - a term of endearment. Lit: "dear little one"

cha'atanahn - Taunos's pet name for his sister, literally meaning "abundance of heart/life"

nanovah - a Rinaryn word basically meaning "Forget about it"

Betah teimelei - a polite Rinaryn greeting, often shortened to simply "Betah"

Acknowledgements

I never would have gotten this story as polished as it is, saying all the things I want to say, without the help of my community. I'm forever grateful for the support and encouragement from my writing community, family, and friends. You make me not only a better writer, but a better human.

To my family, thank you for always being supportive of my writing efforts, including the time I carve out to write, and edit, and edit some more. You're wonderful alpha readers and your critiques made this story far better than it was before you saw it.

To my incredible critique partners, whew! All the effort and time you put into this project of mine, helping me to hone it—I simply can't thank you enough. The four of you are amazing and I'm honored to have you as CPs. R. Lee Fryar, thank you for reading this whole beast of a story twice, helping me to really look at plot lines critically to see if they were what I wanted to say. Thank you for never failing to encourage me to dig deeper! To Ariana Townsend, for your enthusiastic critiques, seeing straight to the hearts of my characters and their arcs and helping me to make them shine! Especially when I forgot what things would look like from other characters' points of view! To KJ Harrowick, your insight into tension and plot and realism were absolutely necessary and helped me to make sure not to forget to mention things like time, while also not straining unbelievability to a breaking point! And to 🚀, for looking at interactions with a keen eye and helping me to show the diversity I wanted to without falling back on "norms".

I'm lucky enough to have a fantastic team of hand-picked betas, as well, and I'm so thankful to each and every one of you: to Jerusha René for reading some sections multiple times to hone in on the balance I wanted, and for your insightful remarks; to Thuy, for your insightful critiques and suggestions; and to Paulette, for your sharp eyes on the plot and arcs, thank you all!

Thanks to my writing groups for your support and critiques, both in writing and in industry: the Parliament of Pens, Quillhaven, WriteHive, the Writer In Motion group, and the Indie Authors Discord, thank you for providing such community and encouragement. I have my tribe and I'm so thankful for it! You're all amazing. Thanks especially to Justine Manzano, Whitney Hill, Ben Gartner, Kota Rayne, and Tyler Zeoli for all the support. Thank you also to Ysabelle Suarez for government and religion ideas. Thanks to Teacup Dragon, as well, for being so supportive and inspiring.

To my editor, Jeni Chappelle, thank you for your attention to detail and your finesse with the line edits, putting on that last bit of polish so that my words could flow! And not just that, but also for your heaps of editing advice given so generously over the years not just to me but to any who need it. You're a phenomenal person, and I'm glad to know you.

Thank you to my phenomenal cover artist, Dave Brasgalla. You gave my character a face yet again, and the attention to detail and your work over these months astounds me. Even going back and forth a couple times on details, you have always been patient, understanding, and supremely talented. I'm wonderfully lucky to work with someone so skilled!

And to you, dear reader, thank you for taking this journey with me, and I hope we continue to travel together into the future!

About the Author

Ever since a college professor told S. Kaeth she'd have to eventually focus on just one thing, she's been dead set on proving him wrong.

From charging through the wilderness, wrangling alligators and snapping turtles, trapping and counting moles, or supervising prairie burns for college credits to doing research and training frogs, lizards, and a lungfish, she treats life as an adventure. She traded hikes, natural history interpretation boating tours, and creature encounters for the slightly-less-exotic-but-no-less-fun mammal training about the same time she began to get serious about her writing craft.

You can find her teaching herself languages and lesser-known fiber crafts, hiking, or playing Capoeira when she's not practicing the fine art of weaving a tale.

Stay in touch: Sign up for the newsletter at skaeth.com !

Other books by S. Kaeth

Windward

When dragons fight, mountains weep.

Dragonbonded Palon and her partner, the dragon Windward, are renowned for their flying skill among the dragons and dragonbondeds who make up their family. Palon's days are filled with everything she loves, especially riding the wind. Even being tasked with teaching their way of life to Tebah, a newly bonded teenager, can't bring her down too much.

But when treasures from the dragons' hordes are found in Palon's collection, her idyllic life comes crashing down. Framed, she battles to find the truth, to prove her innocence, while her every move is cast as further evidence against her. As if that wasn't enough, her teenage charge's increasingly dangerous behavior puts them both at risk. Tebah's suspicion, homesickness, and defiance would be frustrating enough even if Palon wasn't in the spotlight, with a rival smearing her name at every turn. Dragon tempers shorten, and challenges and disputes shake the ground.

Windward and Palon must find a way to clear her name while also keeping a teenager who hates her and everything about dragon life safe, before their community turns completely against them or vigilante justice succeeds.

Children of the Nexus series

Between Starfalls (Book One of Children of the Nexus)

Never leave the path.

It's sacred law, punishable by exile.

When her son goes missing in the perilous mountains, Kaemada defies the law to search for him. She enlists the help of her hero brother, a priestess berserker, and a fire-wielding friend.

But the law exists for a reason.

When the search party is captured by the mythical Kamalti, they learn that Kaemada's son was sent to an ancient prison city. As they battle for freedom, they discover a horrible truth that will change the future of both races forever.

With their world in upheaval, Kaemada must find a way to peace if she's to save her son—but tensions between the two races are leading to war.

Let Loose The Fallen (Book Two of Children of the Nexus)

The priestess searches for her faith.

The fire-wielder wrestles with her past.

The psion dreams of peace.

And the hero is torn between his heart and his duty.

While grief scatters the four protectors to the winds, outside forces write history according to their own whims. The fate of the Rinaryns lies twined with that of the boy, Eian, caught in a tug of war the heroes are unaware of.

But the evidence lies waiting for Taunos and the others to see, if only they can move past their betrayal.

Beneath the Gods' Tree

Amanah knows all-too-well the dangers of catching the attention of the upper class of Arruk. Using her position as a guard to steal secrets of healing and help other lower class people means she must remain unnoticed, working from the shadows.

Fellow guard Taunos is boisterous, laughing, larger than life-and always around. He attracts attention as easily as breathing, which makes being associated with him dangerous. Better to stay far away, regardless of her attraction to him and his easy calm.

But when Amanah inadvertently insults a magistrate, she must flee the city to avoid his vengeance. She takes a last-minute job escorting a pair of noblemen to another town-a job Taunos is also hired for.

As she spends more time with Taunos, his confident charm draws her in, especially when he uncovers her dream of becoming a healer and offers to help make it a reality. Taunos sees her as no one else has, even when she's doing her best to be invisible. But opening herself to romance might be as dangerous as the wildlife and bandits they face in the wilderness.

Yet as the end of her mission looms, she's not sure she can resist the draw of Taunos and of pursuing her dreams, even if it means drawing the ire of those in power.

(This book takes place about three years before Between Starfalls, a little after Prelude Cycle)

www.ingramcontent.com/pod-product-compliance
Lightning Source LLC
Chambersburg PA
CBHW020415030726
47495CB00006B/1517